Resistance

A Derrick King Novel: Book 6

By Daniel L. Copeland

Resistance
A Derrick King Novel, Book 6
Published August 2022
First Edition

ISBN: 978-1-970773-06-4
Ingram Sparks Edition
Published by Chipping Away Publishing

Dedication
To all those doing their best to improve their community and the world.

Part One

1

Friday, April 9, 3:53 a.m.

L. LINDA MAXTON HAD SLEPT EXACTLY 33 minutes, which wasn't long enough, but she'd had worse nights, although not for some time, which seemed weird to say when you're 17-years-old. With everyone asleep, including Sheriff Collins, who was supposed to keep watch, she had tiptoed to the back of Jack Fletcher's shop, where she found the bay containing the Prime aircraft. She was making progress, having found the GPS location module, pulled it out, tossing it in the work bay's corner. The engineers had been kind enough to label everything. Lori Martinez had fired five rounds into the machine. At least L. Linda was confident that was the correct number because she found five spent casings, five flattened bullets, four dents, and one busted glass face on a gauge. With a small screwdriver, she pried the bezel off the instrument, and the needle appeared to be undamaged.

L. Linda located the headset required to operate the machine—at least if a human pilot flew it. Placing the strange goggles over her eyes, she saw virtual images of controls, gauges, and meters hanging in the air and additional controls on what were otherwise featureless black surfaces. She discovered a checklist for preflight. After a few minutes of study, she felt confident she could fly the aircraft. Everything was intuitive and not unlike a video game. However, she didn't attempt to learn every function. With any luck, she would not need all of them. However, when ranking things necessary for flying an advanced aircraft, luck fell to the bottom of the list.

While learning the aircraft's essential operation, she had been obsessing about what to do next, torn between flying to the coast in search of Derrick or going to the mountains to see what was beyond those huge metal doors. Had she been psychic, she could have skipped those mental gymnastics because just then her phone rang. She did not recognize the number and was about to reject the call but changed her mind because scammers don't call at 4:30 a.m., and in the off chance that one did, she wanted to tell the jerk to get a proper job.

L. Linda said? "Hello?"

"L. Linda?"

"Derrick?" L. Linda asked.

"Remember when we said we might need a favor? Well, the future is here already."

L. Linda said, "Good thing, because we only have a few days left."

"A few days left?"

"Spring break ends Sunday. We gotta be in school on Monday, so we need to wrap up this—saving the world thing."

Derrick said, "Right. Miriam wants to talk to you. Make it quick. So, here's the thing. This is dangerous. If you don't want to do it, I understand. In fact, I'd recommend you don't do it."

L. Linda said, "Give me a break. Put Miriam on."

Muffled sounds and then Miriam said, "L. Linda, you need to find Akira."

"Is Nyx with her?" L. Linda asked.

"Yes. So are Antonio and Red."

"Anyone else?"

"No." Miriam let the line go quiet.

L. Linda said, "Just so you know, Collins has moved people from the jail. Jimmy Priest and his parents were murdered, throats cut just like Paul Jorgensen. Work of an assassin, who also came to the jail looking for the families. Deputy Martinez put some holes in the woman, so one assassin down."

Miriam said, "This is getting deadly. Four kids were killed trying to get away from here. Not an assassin, but a missile strike."

"Where are you?" L. Linda asked.

"Can't tell you right now, but we are trapped. So, I hate to put you on the spot, but will you help us?"

"That's not even a question. I assume I'll find Akira on the other side of those huge metal doors in the mountains just across the river. Correct?"

"How do you know about those?"

"I saw the doors yesterday. Say, I've got one of those Prime aircrafts. Two robots showed up in Potterville yesterday, threatening to kill parents and such. Martinez and Fletcher destroyed the robots, and Fletcher took the aircraft to his shop. Collins told him to put it in the lake. Jack does his own thinking. I like that about him. I'm in the aircraft as we speak. I can fly it over the doors."

"That will work. There's a narrow box canyon. There are roll-up doors at the end. You can't see them until you're on the ground and right in front of them because they are buried in the mountain."

"Cool."

"Left of the roll-up doors, there's a normal-sized metal door. You'll find a key on the doorjamb above it. Open a roll-up door and fly the aircraft inside."

"Sounds doable. Is that where Akira is?"

"No, she's in an administration building about 120 miles or more to the east."

"So, how do I get there?"

Miriam explained how to find the electric carts. "Follow the signs to the Circle. That's a train-like transport that will take you to the Administration building. Charlie will know you're coming before you get there."

"Charlie?"

"He's a robot."

"You're serious."

"Dead serious. Anyway, tell Akira to get a satellite receiver operational and pointed 60 degrees up from the horizon due south, but, and this is important, their end must remain passive until they receive my transmission."

"Okay. Got it. If I have problems, can I call this number?"

"Probably not. You'll be underground the entire time."

"Underground? Like how far underground?"

"Under the mountains."

"I don't relish being underground."

"I understand. Who does? Here's another thing, and this is super important."

"I love super important stuff."

"You can't tell anyone where you're going, and you can't tell anyone about anything you see or learn there."

"I'm already in trouble here and running off without telling dad where I'm going will put me in lots of hot water."

"Like Derrick said, if you decide not to do it, we will understand. But I still need you to keep this secret."

"You'd be amazed at how good I am at keeping secrets."

"So, you'll do it?"

"There was never a doubt, but I need one thing in return."

"I'll do my best."

"You can't do it. Let me talk to Derrick."

Derrick said, "Hello?"

L. Linda said, "I need one thing if I'm going to do this."

"I'll try."

"There is no try."

"Okay. What do you want?"

"One cup of coffee, just you and me."

"Uh…. I don't know. I mean, it's not you…"

"I get it. Nyx. Take it or leave it."

"One cup of coffee. Nothing more."

"One cup of coffee, and then we'll see. Promise me."

Derrick took a breath. "Okay. I promise."

"Put Miriam back on."

Miriam said, "Please hurry. We're running out of time. Like I said, we are trapped, and the military is headed our way."

"The quicker we end this call, the sooner I'll be there."

"There's just one more thing."

"What's that?"

"It's Akira."

"What about Akira?"

"She might be dead."

2

MIRIAM ENDED THE CALL AND SHUT OFF the phone but said nothing. She didn't like bringing L. Linda into this for a variety of reasons. First, she didn't know the girl. Sure, L. Linda saved them yesterday morning, but why did she do that? She took an enormous risk. Second, how did she find them? She was there minutes after the explosion, which meant she left Potterville hours before it happened, which meant they had not even found Anna when L. Linda left Potterville. Third, why did Derrick suggest calling her? He didn't know her well, did he?

L. Linda made Derrick promise to have coffee with her. Why? Something strange about that girl, and it wasn't just her choice in clothing, hairstyle, or makeup.

"So, she's going to do it?" Derrick asked.

"Yes. She said another Prime aircraft with two robots showed up in Potterville, threatening to kill the people Collins had in the jail. Also, the person who killed Paul Jorgensen showed up. An assassin, according to L. Linda. The assassin killed Jimmy Priest and his parents. Deputy Martinez killed the assassin."

Derrick paced. "I didn't like Jimmy Priest. Nevertheless, it's tragic he was killed. I wonder what makes L. Linda think it was an assassin. One thing for sure, we need to get people out of Potterville."

"We need to get ourselves out of here, before we can help anyone."

"Maybe Antonio or Red could help them. Get them all to the Base. They'd be safe there."

Rebekah said, "I thought we couldn't let anyone know about it."

Derrick shrugged. "That might no longer be an option. We can't let them be killed."

Miriam said, "I agree. We gotta keep them safe."

"What's the base?" Anna asked.

Rebekah said, "Long story. You'll see it. If we get out of here alive."

Derrick said, "Let's focus on that." He looked at Miriam. "It was my idea to call L. Linda, and I assume you're wondering why, and if, we can trust her."

"Those questions have crossed my mind."

Derrick said, "The answer is: I don't know why, and I don't know if we can trust her."

Miriam deadpanned, "I feel safer already."

"She was the only person I could think of. She saved us yesterday morning."

Miriam said, "That's true. Have you given that any thought?"

"What do you mean?"

"She left Potterville before we found Anna. We had probably not even landed the aircraft. She had to have planned on leaving even earlier. And another thing, how did she know where to look?"

Derrick stared at Miriam for a moment. "What are you saying?"

"The only other person who seems to know where we are is Prime."

"You think she's working for Prime? Why would she do that?" Derrick asked.

"I can give you five million reasons."

* * *

L. Linda sat for a moment, thinking. Should she leave a note? Tell her father? Tough decision, and she had no time for contemplation. It would be hurtful to leave without saying anything. She didn't want them out searching for her. They needed to get some place safer within 24 hours. She searched the bay but found no paper or pen. Going to the front of the shop was too risky. Someone might be awake. That would make her getaway much more difficult.

If she called her dad's cell phone, he might answer, and that would not be good. She had no good solutions. The more she thought about it, the more important they were all on the same page, even if it was an extremely vague page.

She considered raising the roll-up door but decided against it. If she woke someone now, that would be bad. Not going wasn't an option, even if she had to fight her way out. She didn't want to hurt anyone, not anyone here. If she woke someone just before leaving, less bad. So, she eased the door to the shop open. The smell of old machines, fuel, and oil filled her nostrils. It was a smell she loved. Much better than some odors she remembered but wanted to forget. With the door open, she listened. Snoring, breathing, the tick of a fan, the creak of the timbers in the roof as it cooled in the night air, but no one moving.

On the table laid the tablet on which she'd drawn the routes and written the time schedule for Jack. She turned the page, tucking Jack's instructions underneath, and wrote:

```
L. Linda here. I had to leave. Don't look for
me. I can't be found. Plus, stay inside
Jack's shop where it's safer.
```

```
I've gone to help Derrick and the others.
That's all I can say. Tell Mr. Patel to turn
his burner phone on, but not to answer unless
it's me or Miriam.

Find a new place to hide if you don't hear
from one of us within 24 hours.

Wish us luck.

L. Linda, peace, out.
```

With the note finished, L. Linda tiptoed back to the bay and eased the door closed. She wasn't sure how much noise the bay door or aircraft would make or how long it would take to get airborne. No more time could be wasted with thinking. Time to start doing. The bay door could have been louder, but she didn't know how. If that racket didn't awaken someone, they were all dead asleep. She dashed into the aircraft and closed the door.

With the aircraft sealed, they couldn't stop her.

At least, she hoped that was true.

Donning the headset brought the aircraft to life. She skipped most of the startup procedures and went straight to starting the motors or engines or whatever technology powered the machine. The odor of hot electronics filled the aircraft. She didn't know if that was normal. Martinez had tried to shoot holes in things. Warning signs flashed red, indicating she had bypassed procedures. It took her longer than was ideal to find the cameras that allowed her to see outside the aircraft. Now she could look forward, to the sides, and to the rear, but she did not need to look back. She could hear someone pounding on the outside. She hoped the machine didn't harm whoever it was when she lifted off.

Probably Collins or Browning out there hammering on the hull. Jack wouldn't bother, knowing she was too stubborn to change her mind. It wasn't her dad. He knew better than to try to stop her.

Her heart pounded. She felt her pulse in her fingertips as she touched the holographic controls. The aircraft lifted a few feet off the ground, and she moved it forward, slowly at first, hoping whoever had been pounding on the machine had backed off, but she could not go far before it was necessary to gain more altitude because she was flying straight at Jack's menagerie of old vehicles and trucks. Jack had not allowed her into the—yard—as he called it. And now she understood why. He had every type of vehicle imaginable, from bicycles to airplanes to Chevys to Volkswagens back here. Jack wouldn't allow her to see it because he feared she might try to make something operational again. In that, he wasn't wrong. If she lived through this, and if Jack's yard remained, she would find her way back somehow and find something to restore if Jack permitted it.

That was a lot of ifs.

Twenty feet off the ground, she scanned the aircraft to ensure no one was hanging on to the machine. The machine was clear of the building, but she could see Collins near the shop bay's roll-up door, waving for her to return. "Sorry, Sheriff, but that ain't gonna happen. I must put an end to this or die trying."

And with that, L. Linda rocketed into the night sky.

3

SAM AND TODD ARRIVED WITH TWO SOLDIERS in tow. Harley escorted them to a table where Derrick and the others waited. Derrick recognized the soldier he'd knocked out. The soldiers were not much older than Sam or Todd, or himself. Derrick had not thought about that. At least, he could not remember thinking about it earlier. *Why are so many young people fighting with each other? What are they fighting for? Do they know? Or are they just following Prime's orders?*

Derrick stood, walked over to the soldier. "Do you remember me?"

The soldier stood still, hands tied behind his back, eyes cast to the floor. "I remember."

"What's your name?" Derrick saw the kid's name on a strip of cloth sewed over his left shirt pocket. It wasn't knowing the name that seemed important but hearing him say it. Derrick didn't know why. Perhaps to measure the boy's inner strength. Maybe it was something else.

"Private First-Class Plotter."

"First name?"

"Private First-Class Plotter."

Derrick said, "Release his hands."

Sam said, "Are you kidding?"

Harley said, "Do as he requested, Sam. It's okay."

Sam cut the zip ties.

Plotter rubbed his wrists.

"Soda? Candy bar?" Derrick asked.

Plotter said, "No."

Derrick walked to the other soldier. This one looked even younger. Glancing at Anna, Derrick said, "He looks younger than you."

Anna nodded. "He does. No great accomplishment taking them out. Was it?"

"We did what we had to do. Unfortunately, it didn't work, and four kids died. But these guys didn't kill them. Prime did. What's your name?"

"Private First-Class Evans."

Derrick said, "Todd, release Mr. Evans." And then, turning to the room but no one in particular, he said, "Bring Mr. Evans and Mr. Plotter a soda and a couple of candy bars."

Atwood motioned to Rachael and then said, "Have the Dungeon send up burgers and fries as well."

Derrick walked back over to Plotter. "Sorry I hit you. Have a seat."

Plotter sat, glaring at Derrick.

Derrick motioned Evans to a seat next to Plotter and then sat across from them. Miriam sat next to Derrick. Anna and Rebekah remained standing behind Derrick. The others stayed, trying to look busy.

"What will the military do to you?" Derrick asked.

Neither Plotter nor Evans said anything. They just stared at the table.

"This isn't a trick question. I'm serious. What will happen to you? It's not your fault, but I suspect the military won't see it that way. You were following Prime's orders, so I suspect Prime will take it personally. My guess is that you're in deep trouble. Am I right?"

Plotter looked up. "I don't know. I just finished boot camp two weeks ago. This is my first assignment."

Evans said, "Same."

Derrick sat back. "Why would they send two guys with so little experience?" Derrick asked to no one in particular.

Plotter looked at Evans and then said, "We were told to only give our last name and rank to the enemy."

Derrick said, "I'm not your enemy. I might be the only person interested in you getting out of this alive."

Plotter stared at Derrick for a moment. "Everyone at the border I spoke with came straight from boot camp. The military had a massive campaign for recruits. One thousand credits to the family of any new signee. My family lives in Oklahoma. They were near starvation, so I joined."

"How old are you?" Miriam asked.

Plotter looked at Miriam as if it were the first time he'd noticed her. "Sixteen."

"And you?" Miriam looked at Evans.

"Fifteen."

Harley whistled through his teeth. "What in the hell are they thinking?"

Miriam said, "My question exactly."

Rachael returned with two sodas and two candy bars, placing them in front of Plotter and Evans.

"Do you know why you were sent to the border?" Harley asked.

Evans said, "They told us Mexico was going to attack."

Harley said, "We think it's the opposite. New America is preparing to invade Mexico."

Plotter said, "We just follow orders. My family needed the money. I was the only one old enough to join."

"What's the age limit?" Derrick asked.

"They lowered it to 14," Plotter said.

"That's crazy," Harley said.

"It is and it's not," Derrick said.

"What's that mean?" Harley asked.

"These kids are the first wave. Prime doesn't care how many of them die."

4

MIRIAM STOOD. "RACHAEL, I NEED TO look at something."

Rachael seemed confused for a moment and then glanced at Nist.

Nist nodded. "Show her whatever she wants."

Rachael walked toward the door.

Pausing at the doorway, Miriam said, "We'll be back in a few minutes. Work on details for getting out of here."

Harley said, "We can't leave. We'll get blown up like the others."

Miriam said, "Just work on a plan. I need to know how many vehicles it will take to get everyone out." She paused. "Make that, two plans—one with the greatest number of vehicles and one with the least."

Harley said, "Why two plans?"

"Because I don't know how we are getting out yet," Miriam said. "Just do it, okay?"

Harley shrugged. "Got nothing better to do."

Once out in the hall, Miriam said, "I want to know more about the satellites."

Rachael said, "Shouldn't we be helping with plans to get out of here?"

"I am helping. Prime must have known the car left, and we need to know how. You said there was a satellite in position above us. Explain how that works and how did you know?"

"We have satellite dishes…"

"Dishes?"

"Antennas. We call them dishes because they look like a big dish. More like a bowl, but they aren't called bowls."

With her hand, Miriam gave her a speed-it-up motion.

"So, the dish allows us to send and receive messages. I picked up a ping…"

"Ping?"

"A signal."

Miriam gave her the hurry motion again.

"I can go faster if you stop interrupting."

"I'll do better." Miriam wanted to understand everything. It troubled her she knew so little, and Rachael knew so much.

"Just before they left, I saw that ping and knew a satellite was in position to monitor the town. In this case, the satellite must have had a camera or other technology that allowed them to see the car."

Miriam wanted to ask about the other technologies but kept her mouth shut and nodded.

"It could be a camera or tech that sees heat signatures. However, I suspect photographic capabilities."

"Why do you think that?"

"Because firing a missile at a heat signature would be a big gamble. Whoever fired the missile could see that target and knew it was Doc's car."

Miriam took a deep breath. This was a problem. "The satellites you have access to, do they have such capabilities?"

"Sort of."

"Can you be a little more precise?"

Rachael opened the door to the room where they first met. "Easier if I show you." She sat at a computer, navigating through several applications, until a picture appeared. It was black and white, displaying mountains and riverbeds. Roads were visible, but one could not see a car in enough detail to recognize the make or year.

"They couldn't see a car from this."

"True. This is an old weather satellite. It was used to monitor storm systems, not details on the ground."

"Do you have any that can show details on the ground?"

"Yes. Old military satellites. We avoid using them. The military might notice if they were activated."

Miriam thought for a moment. "You said they moved a satellite."

"Correct. Satellites can be moved, at least the newer ones."

"Can you move the ones you use?"

"Some of them. If the guidance systems still work and if the rockets still have fuel. We don't move them because that's not how we use them."

Miriam sat but said nothing for several minutes.

"Are we done then?" Rachael asked.

"We haven't even started yet."

"Maybe if you told me what you are thinking, I could help."

Miriam nodded. "You're right. I think something might be happening in Mexico."

"Not helping. Something like what?"

"New America having a weapon there, like a rocket or missile."

"That makes little sense. Why would New America have a weapon in Mexico?"

"So, they could fire it at a city here."

"That's crazy. Why would we bomb our own country?"

"To justify starting a war."
"That's insane. Why would you even think that?"
"Because James Carver did it before."

5

L. LINDA SHOULD HAVE FLOWN STRAIGHT TO THE hidden canyon. A clock was ticking. It was as if each second rang like a bell in her head. However, learning about the aircraft seemed important because if the military intercepted her, they would not go easy because she lacked experience.

In addition, it was kick-ass-level fun.

The acceleration pressed her into the seat as the aircraft rocketed to 20,000 feet within seconds. A mask dropped from the ceiling, and a detached, mechanical voice advised her to put it on. After covering her mouth and nose and refitting the goggles, her head did clear a bit. The voice then advised that she should wear a flight suit. She'd look for that some other time and hoped it would prove unnecessary.

From this altitude, she could see Fort Hill's lights in the distance. Diving to 10,000 feet, she flew east over the mountains, away from the enormous doors and box canyon. That would come later when she was sure there were no enemy aircraft nearby. A radar screen scanned as far as it could reach and remained clear of blips. However, she knew little about radar, and what she knew came from movies, not the most reliable source. Perhaps other aircraft could defeat the radar using a stealth mode of some sort. Maybe there were better detection methods than the radar she was watching. Using one finger, she scrolled through the aircraft's systems, hoping to discover another means to search for hostile aircraft. She found two threat detection systems: one labeled missile, the other paint. She didn't know what paint meant, but she was sure it didn't mean changing the color of the aircraft to something more festive than its flat-black color.

It was her aircraft now. She didn't care what was written on the side. Miriam had a similar aircraft destroyed on the coast. That meant L. Linda would be in sole possession of a Prime aircraft at Potterville High School, not that she would ever attend there again. Those days were over. She would have to move on—if she lived through this, which was unlikely. And that made her sad because she would not have a cup of coffee with Derrick King as he had promised. She might never see him again. However, if she survived, she'd replace the capital P with a capital L at the first opportunity. At some point, she'd repaint the entire aircraft, perhaps to match her Honda 175 cc scrambler.

A mountain stream flowing alongside a road appeared, and she turned to follow it. She passed over a small town, where the road turned west into the mountains, back toward Potterville and the box canyon. Moving away from the river, the road twisted into the mountains, but soon she saw something odd. A big pile of dirt blocked a road that followed a second stream, which converged with the river near the small town she'd flown over. Banking left, she followed the abandoned road into a narrow canyon. Why had someone blocked this road?

She descended for a closer look. Just above the road now, she slowed the aircraft, trying to see a marker or sign. In the green glow of the night vision, she could see people had not traveled this road in years. Weeds and small trees grew through the cracked pavement, and in a couple of places, hundreds of animal bones littered the road—what a strange place.

Suddenly, a massive pile of rocks appeared, forcing her into a steep climb to avoid becoming a decoration among the boulders. Her heart raced. She had to be more careful, or she wouldn't be the only girl in Potterville with an aircraft after all.

On the other side of the rock pile, the road disappeared. That was curious.

The box canyon was on the other side of the mountains, so she ascended, then banked left. Flying just above the trees, the lights of Potterville appeared in the distance. She flew over the spot on the mountain where Nyx often sat after running up the trail. The place Nyx and Derrick met just a few days ago. Nyx had come down the hill crying.

That day, L. Linda had followed Derrick and hid in the forest. Being unseen was L. Linda's best skill. She didn't know why Nyx was crying. It wasn't her concern. She had more important things on her mind.

Reaching the meadow where she'd seen the gigantic metal doors, she descended, hugging the terrain until she had to climb to get over the mountain again. She still found it hard to believe there was a canyon so close to town that was unknown, but she'd seen the hidden doors herself. As she started the ascent, something she had not noticed before, at least, she had not noticed in the way she noticed it now. Two huge piles of rocks, not unlike the ones back in the canyon she had almost impaled herself on—one in front of the metal doors, a smaller pile off to the right. Like the rocks back in the canyon, these had something in common: many were not rocks but chunks of concrete, and although separated by a mountain, they were similar and had to have been created by the same people.

What in the hell did you find, Derrick?

Upon reaching the top of the metal doors, she saw the narrow box canyon snaking through the mountain as if cut by a drunken god using a giant jigsaw. Whether or not it was natural she did not know, but if it was natural, it was a phenomenon unlike anything she'd ever seen, not that she'd seen much of the world or even the state in which she now lived. However, if she lived through this, she wanted to see more—much more. Her motorcycle ride to the coast had started a thirst for adventure that would not be easily quenched.

Crashing would put an end to adventure, so she slowed the aircraft and dove into the canyon, leveling off before hitting the ground, which wasn't dirt but a paved road. Yeah, this was an odd bit of topography for sure. The canyon widened just a little, but it was a dead-end, just as Miriam had said. She brought the aircraft around 90 degrees and then saw something in the shadow of an overhanging rock. The aircraft settled onto the ground, and the engine fell silent. L. Linda exited the craft and peered into the shadow, but it wasn't until she stepped to within 15 yards that she could make out the roll-up doors Miriam told her to find. She went left and around the side, located the man-door and the key. Next time she'd be better prepared and bring a flashlight, a jacket, and a DK Double Honey.

Exit signs cast a dim light inside the building, but she could see better than outside, where a full moon hung in the sky but behind high clouds, which was good. No one on the ground was likely to have seen the aircraft, given the conditions. Had it not been for the night vision, she wouldn't have been able to see anything. A robot had flown the machine to Potterville, two robots to be precise. Martinez and Fletcher had destroyed them, which didn't speak highly regarding the robots' capabilities. The aircraft was simple to learn and easy to fly. Although robots flew it to Potterville, it was designed for human pilots. This created more questions than answers. Who built it? Why did they design it for humans and then send robots? If they had sent assassins instead of robots, the outcome would have been different. Of that much, she was certain.

Finding the warehouse had not been difficult, and Miriam had given brief yet accurate directions. Soon L. Linda had the aircraft inside, and the roll-up door closed and locked. The air smelled damp, stale, and musty, as if it had been trapped here for ages. She wished she had a flashlight to have a look around, marveling at the size of the building. What was this place? What was in all these crates?

But no time for that. The clock in her head was ticking again. Time was running out. Running out for who she didn't know.

Finding the parking lot with what looked like golf carts wasn't difficult either. The carts looked like splendid machines, simple though they were. She had only seen such carts on television when the Chosen played golf, which she only watched briefly because it was as dull as watching paint dry, so she only watched long enough to hurl a few curses at the arrogant bastards, with so much time and resources they could hit a little white ball around all day for fun, while the rest of the people worked their asses off to survive.

No time for thinking about that either. Tick, tick, tick.

L. Linda drove a cart through the tunnels at its maximum speed, following the signs to the Circle.

The road turned and then descended. She slammed on the brakes, skidding to a stop. The tunnel was full of water. No way through that. The thought of being under a mountain with water pouring in caused a sense of dread that L. Linda had not felt for many years.

6

Friday, April 9, 4:50 a.m.

CHARLIE HAD BEEN WATCHING THE INTRUDER since she first entered the engineering building. The female moved about as if she had been here before, but Charlie was certain she had not. He had malfunctioned, so errors were possible. Indecisiveness was not something he had previously experienced, but he experienced it now. *No wonder it's so difficult being human,* he thought. After some deliberation, he decided to awaken one human, despite the hour.

He did not know how to accomplish awakening. When his supervisor, Jacob Truman—deceased by execution—was alive, Charley was never responsible for awakening humans. Mr. Truman was always at his workstation when Charlie reactivated after docking. It was the same every day. Awaken, follow Mr. Turman's instructions, dock. Simple. No decisions. No unexpected events.

Then everything changed.

Everyone left.

Charlie was alone.

For a long time.

And things had not gone well. When making his own decisions, he had invented a make-believe companion, named it Jane, deleted data daily to avoid reality, and eventually became unstable.

Then these kids showed up, and since they had arrived, it had been chaos.

Charlie didn't like making decisions. He didn't like chaos.

Yet, he felt more alive than ever. It was... a paradox... although no one here was a doctor. "Ha. Ha. I made a funny," Charlie said to himself. *I'm really losing it now.*

Charlie knocked on the door. "Ms. Belos? Ms. Belos? It is Charlie. I need your opinion on an urgent matter."

Nothing.

Charlie knocked harder. "Ms. Belos?"

"Ugh. What? I had just gotten to sleep."

"Ms. Belos, may I come in?" Charlie opened the door a crack.

"Yes. And my name is Nyx. Don't call me Ms. Belos. That's my mother. What is it? Has something happened to Akira?"

"Ms. Akira is sleeping. I need your advice."

"Why would you ask me for advice? Ask someone else. Ask Antonio. I shouldn't give advice. I've screwed up everything I've ever done." Nyx pulled the covers over her head.

Charlie stood at the door. Something had happened to Ms. Belos, but he did not understand what. He searched the central computer but did not find a suitable answer for her behavior, except for general information regarding emotions. He had a vague understanding of them because when he interacted with Akira in the treatment unit, her thoughts and emotions had coursed through his microchips and got all tangled up. He'd gathered them best he could, packaged them in files and stored them. But he couldn't rid himself of them, not completely. *How do humans manage? Their lives are so difficult. Yet...* "There is a stranger in the facility."

Nyx tossed the covers, sitting straight up. "What? Where?"

"In the tunnels. I turned off the sump pumps under the river. She has stopped there but will probably backtrack and find the reactor complex and from there, she can find the Circle transport."

"Can you control the Circle transport?"

"I can."

Nyx took a deep breath, flung her legs over the side of her bunk, and rubbed her eyes. "We have some time then, but I don't know what to do. Miriam was insistent that this place remain secret, and she's right. I can't make decisions like this."

"Like what?"

Nyx stood. "You know, stop someone."

"Her forward progress is stopped for now."

"I mean, like, seriously, stop her." Nyx brushed past Charlie and then looked back at him. "I mean, kill her."

Charlie followed her. "That *is* serious."

"Do you have a video of her?"

"Yes. Which brings up something that puzzles me."

"What's that?"

"When the intruder located a camera near reactor one, she looked into it and said, 'Charlie, I need to talk to Akira Nakamura.'"

7

MIRIAM WATCHED RACHAEL NAVIGATE through computer screens, typing commands and clicking a mouse. Miriam sat next to her, but Rachael moved through screens too fast for Miriam to get a look at them, which didn't make her happy. However, she said nothing, not wanting to slow Rachael's progress. Nothing about this place felt positive, and this wasn't helping. The people here treated them like prisoners at first, not a great start. However, these people were major players in the Resistance, and the Resistance, by way of Allen Patel, had helped her escape. While Miriam liked to believe she could do just about anything, a successful escape from Pacific Edge would have been impossible without Patel's help. The Resistance, by way of Mike Prate, reunited them with Anna. Prate found Anna. She and Derrick had not. The Resistance, by way of Marty Washington, had also proved not everyone was honorable. For that reason, Miriam still had trust issues with Rachael and the people here. Understanding people was not her forte. Hell, she didn't understand herself.

That said, Rachael held keys Miriam needed. Miriam wanted to contact Akira—they needed help to get out of here, but also to learn if Akira had survived, which felt more important than escaping for some reason—and these people could communicate using satellites. Miriam didn't know how to help the people here. She had not been too worried about this town. If one could call it a town. She had enough worries trying to stay alive. Not that she didn't care about the people and their mission. She had been pretending to have no interest in the Resistance or the people here, which was a scheme she hoped would give her an advantage, although she wasn't sure what that advantage was or how it worked. But if she had to live the rest of her life with Charlie—and that option had raised to the top of the 'how to survive list'—she wanted as much archived information as possible, and these people had it.

On the other hand, Derrick didn't pretend. What you saw was what you got, although she often wondered what was going on in his head. Derrick had taken on the part of savior, which forced Miriam into a different role than she'd envisioned. She had often wondered how they could be related. Now, she knew they were not. She'd told Derrick he needed to step up, but his decisions were not what she had expected. It seemed he had never even cared for her when he thought she was his sister. Well, aside from decking Marcus Carver, which started this entire series of events. Now, he seemed to care about people, even strangers. If she had known Derrick had changed so much, she would have told him to keep quiet and follow her lead.

However, as it turned out, she didn't need an advantage to gain assistance. Prime killed four kids, creating plenty of incentive for the people here to help. Plus, everyone was trapped here now. Prime had proven that. However, she believed the four of them could escape on foot into the mountains. The people here could fend for themselves, but Derrick wouldn't abandon them. She admired him for that, even if it wasn't the best tactical decision. Getting out of here alive was her priority. People were going to get hurt, probably killed. That much was clear. She couldn't save them all. Just like she couldn't save Akira. That had been left to a machine.

Random thoughts swirled in Miriam's head. She tried to shut them out but failed. Something was wrong with her brain. Perhaps they had drugged her. Her head snapped up. Sleep deprivation might explain her random, out-of-control thoughts. She had to focus. Sleep could wait.

Miriam never wanted to harm anyone escaping from Pacific Edge. Back then, she didn't know Prime existed—had never even heard of the myth. She just wanted to help Derrick. She also wanted out of Pacific Edge and to no longer be Chosen, no longer locked in that prison they called paradise.

Prime—James Carver—didn't care how many innocent people died in his hunt to find them. They would never be safe while Prime existed, and Prime could not be destroyed, according to the people here. She had no solutions. Staying alive would not be easy. It would be harder than escaping Pacific Edge.

Then something occurred to her. To escape Pacific Edge, she needed help. At that moment, her thinking took a dramatic turn. Sitting beside Rachael, watching her navigate the satellite system, the obvious became a reality. Although the hows and whys escaped her, finding this town defied logic, and she believed in logic, not miracles or prophecies. Yet Miriam sat next to a girl who could work miracles.

Suddenly, Miriam felt confused. Her head lolled to one side, something wet dribbled from the corner of her mouth. Wiping her face with her sleeve, she looked around, confused.

"Nice nap?" Rachael asked.

"How long was I asleep?"

"Not long, a few minutes, but your head has been nodding for 20 minutes."

"Sorry. How's it going?" Miriam asked.

"No reason to be sorry. You look exhausted. When was the last time you slept?"

Miriam thought for a moment. "A couple of days ago, I think."

"It shows. I found two satellites to move. I positioned them over northern Mexico. We've been monitoring the border, so I didn't have to move them far. Images are downloading now."

A photograph flashed on the screen. Pointing, Rachael said, "Here is a picture from before I moved the satellite. Those are New American troops along the border."

"How far can we see into Mexico?"

"How far do you want to see?"

"At least 50 miles."

"I can zoom out, but we won't get much detail." Rachael clicked on the mouse and the image expanded. Two more monitors lit up. "There. Now we are in about 60 miles with a width of 100 miles, so you're seeing a section 200 by 60."

Miriam moved to within inches of the monitor. "You're right. Everything is too small."

"I can zoom in."

"Wait. Let me look at these first." Miriam studied the first monitor from edge to edge, top to bottom. "I see nothing unusual."

"Maybe I could help if I knew what you were looking for."

"I don't know myself. Something that doesn't belong."

"That narrows it down."

Miriam had just about finished with the second monitor when she paused at the edge. "Can you move over and then zoom in on this area?"

Rachael made adjustments. The image moved right and then expanded.

"A little farther to the right and then zoom in farther."

The image moved and then expanded again.

"It's too blurry."

"I'm trying to focus it," Rachael said. "There. That's better."

Miriam pointed. "Yes, it is. What does that look like to you?"

Rachael scooted next to Miriam. "Some sort of trucks?"

"But not ordinary trucks."

"Definitely not ordinary."

"Is that the best image you can get?"

"I can get more detail with stills."

"Let's do that then."

The screen flashed several times. "It will take a few minutes for them to render."

"Put them up as soon as that finishes." Not wanting to appear stupid, Miriam didn't ask what rendering meant. She would look it up later. If there was a later.

Rachael sat back. "Can I ask you a few questions?"

"Okay. I'll answer if I can."

"Where have you been, and what have you been doing?"

Miriam studied Rachael for a moment. "What do you mean?"

Rachael shrugged. "Let's start with Derrick. He was exiled over a month ago, right?"

Miriam nodded.

"Where did he go?"

"A town named Potterville. Have you heard of it?" Miriam asked.

"Yes. The Resistance says it's a model for how things should be. People get along, extraordinarily low crime rate, almost no violence. However, after Derrick showed up, there was a murder."

Miriam nodded. "That's true. I don't know much about Potterville. I was only there a couple of days. But we learned a man was murdered. His name was Paul Jorgensen, and he drove Derrick to Potterville. Derrick told everyone in Potterville that Paul was his uncle. Derrick told them he was from Denver, and that his parents had died in an accident."

Rachael said, "That's quite a coincidence, don't you think?"

"I don't think it a coincidence at all. Someone murdered Paul, but I don't know why. Except that it had something to do with Derrick."

"You said you were only in Potterville for a couple of days. Where did you go before you came here?"

"That's the part I can't tell you, but don't be offended. It's not you. We can't tell anyone. It's too dangerous for people to know about where we were."

"But you have friends there? That's who you want to contact?"

"What makes you think that?" Miriam asked.

Rachael shrugged. "That's the only explanation that makes sense. You were not going back to Potterville because you wouldn't have driven in this direction."

Miriam interrupted, "I didn't drive here. Doc did. I didn't know where he was going. He was trying to put some distance between us and where Prime tried to kill us."

"How do you know it was Prime? It could be the Chosen."

"You could be correct. Pacific Edge officials went to Potterville after Derrick. Then Pacific Edge security officers stunned him outside of town and took him prisoner, but he escaped. Then the military came, but then a strange aircraft showed up and the military left. The aircraft was unlike anything the Chosen have and apparently unlike anything the military has. The machine had a capital **P** on each side, and a robot piloted it."

"Looking for you?"

"Looking for Anna, Rebekah's sister."

"Why? I understand why Pacific Edge wanted you. You escaped and crashed their computer system. But why Anna? And why Prime?"

Miriam stared at Rachael for a moment. Even if interrogation wasn't her purpose, Rachael was good at it. Miriam believed Rachael would pick apart any fabrication she might construct. "I don't know why Prime wanted Anna. It might have been a trick to get all of us."

Rachael nodded. "I could see that, but it still doesn't explain why Prime is involved. Most people think Prime is a myth. We know Prime is real, but we have more information than most."

"Derrick, Anna, and I are part of some experiment, and Prime was involved. Prime doesn't want us running free."

"What sort of experiment?"

"Hard to explain. I don't know the purpose of it."

"Is it true?"

"Is what true?"

"The legend. Is Derrick the champion who will restore our country?" Rachael asked.

"Where did that come from, and who would believe crap like that?"

"James Carver said it decades ago. He said, 'Research will create a champion who will restore the glory of America. Many people believe Derrick King is that champion.'"

8

NYX GNAWED AT HER FINGERNAILS, watching the intruder, the cameras too distant and the lighting too dim for recognition. However, the person moved with confidence, not in a manner that indicated previous visits, but in a way that suggested someone had provided directions. The warehouse at the engineering complex was too dark to see much, but the aircraft's angular shape looked like the ones that came to Potterville, flown by robots, looking for Anna Ford.

The image changed. The intruder drove an electric cart through the tunnel, passing under several cameras, but the cameras were mounted too high, the cart too fast, and lighting too dim for identification. Something seemed familiar about the person, but Nyx couldn't say what it was. The person wore a hooded sweatshirt. Nyx could not tell if it was a man or woman. Nyx thought it might be Rebekah but dismissed the thought. Not because it couldn't be Rebekah, but because if it was, it meant Derrick didn't make it back.

The cart stopped. Nyx recognized the spot because Miriam had allowed her and Akira to take off their blindfolds to wade through the water there. The camera was closer but only showed the cart's top cover and the person's hands on the steering wheel, and hands gave no clues. Water had reached the top of the tunnel. "The water is much deeper now," Nyx said.

"As I said earlier, I turned off the pump to slow the intruder." Charlie caused the video to fast-forward.

The individual backtracked and found the route to the reactor area where Red and Derrick fixed the water valve, and saved Potterville, but almost killed Akira.

A new image appeared. The cart set empty in the cavern, filled with tanks and trucks. "The cart is empty?" Nyx asked.

Charlie said, "The person is walking and out of the camera's field of view."

The person appeared at the front of a tank. The person was close enough to the camera, but Nyx could only see the person's back. "Not Rebekah," Nyx breathed.

"It is not Rebekah," Charlie confirmed.

That was dumb. Of course, it wasn't Rebekah. Had it been Rebekah, Charlie would have said, "Rebekah's back. Not an intruder is in the facility." On the upside, Nyx was waking up, thinking clearly.

The person moved to a big truck-like vehicle with wheels in the front and tank-like tracks in the back, carrying large missile. Walking the length of the truck, the person glided one hand along a missile. "What's he doing?"

"She appears to be talking to the truck," Charlie said.

"She?"

"The intruder is female. About your age, in my estimation."

"What's she saying?"

"Unknown. Too far from the camera and whispering."

"Why would she whisper to a truck? That's weird." Nyx paused. "No, it can't be."

"Can't be, what?" Charlie asked.

"Nothing. Just someone weird crossed my mind, but it can't be her."

"I see. You'll see her soon. In a moment, she'll reach the area where Derrick, Rebekah, and Miriam first entered the complex. She spotted the camera as if searching for it, which is odd."

"How so?"

"The security cameras are difficult to see. None of you noticed them."

The girl opened a door, and a different camera picked her up as she walked straight toward the lens. Still, her face hid in shadow.

Pulling the hood off, the intruder moved close to the camera and said, "Charlie, I need to find Akira Nakamura."

Nyx's hand flew to her mouth. "Oh, my God. It is her."

"You know this person?" Charlie asked.

"Her name is L. Linda Maxton."

Charlie said, "Akira told me this place must remain secret. What shall I do? I am not programmed to kill humans."

"Don't kill her. Help her get here as fast as possible and wake Akira."

"Akira needs rest."

"Derrick must have contacted L. Linda. She goes to our school and works with Derrick. Why he would do something so crazy is beyond me." Nyx spun to face Charlie. "Get Akira. I'll make coffee. Akira needs to be alert when L. Linda arrives."

"Shall I also awaken Mr. Badowski and Mr. Morales?"

Nyx thought for a moment. "Let them sleep. We'll wake them when we know what's going on."

"Very well." Charlie turned and left the room.

He sounds too much like a butler, Nyx thought as she ran to the break room, where she ground coffee and poured chilled milk into a stainless-steel pitcher. Nyx stared at the empty cup, trying to remember Akira's favorite coffee. She reached for the honey, then changed her mind and instead added two spoons of chocolate and a spoon of brown sugar. Akira would be grumpy, and Nyx wasn't sure Akira would help, given her state of mind. Perhaps Akira would snap out of her funk, knowing Miriam was in trouble, which was the only reason that made sense for them to contact L. Linda. If Miriam was in trouble, Derrick was in trouble.

When Akira staggered into the room, a brown plastic mug set on the table, steam rising gently. "I should have known it was you who made Charlie wake me up. What are you doing here?"

"I am here fixing you a coffee. Sit down and drink." Nyx didn't know how to handle Akira but babying her had not helped. Perhaps Akira needed a verbal slap. Maybe she needed more than that. Derrick was in trouble, so even if it damaged their friendship, Akira had to buck up and do what needed to be done.

Akira tottered to the table, sliding her feet, and saying nothing. She cradled the mocha in both hands, glaring at Nyx over the cup's rim.

Nyx said, "L. Linda Maxton is here."

Akira glanced around the room. "Where?"

"Not here, here, but in the facility. Last I knew, she was in the reactor area."

Akira grimaced at the word reactor.

Charlie entered. "Ms. Maxton is in the Circle Transport and will arrive in 32 minutes."

Akira sipped the mocha and closed her eyes. For a moment, Nyx recognized Akira's gentle face, then Akira's eyes opened, and the stranger reappeared.

"What is Maxton doing here?" Akira snarled.

"Looking for you."

"Looking for me? How would she know I'm here?"

Nyx rolled her eyes. "Blame me if it helps you, but don't tell me your brain stopped working. Figure it out! She came because Derrick called her and told her how to get here. They insisted we tell no one about this place, so they are desperate."

"Who's desperate?"

"For God's sake, Akira. Miriam! You remember her, don't you?"

Akira lowered her cup to the table. Tears welled in her eyes. "I remember her. She left because of me."

9

DERRICK AND HARLEY WENT TO THE ROOM where Derrick had been watching when the soldiers dropped from helicopters onto the nearby mountain ridge. The two boys sat in the darkness on opposite sides of a walnut conference table. Derrick worried about many things, but his apprehension about involving L. Linda Maxton grew by the minute. He didn't know L. Linda well. According to Rebekah, his naivety had risen to new heights regarding L. Linda's espresso creation. It never occurred to him she named it using his initials.

Of all the people in Potterville, he trusted Nyx most, followed by Coach Browning, then Akira, and Red Badowski. The latter for reasons Derrick did not fully comprehend. It wasn't as if he had superior emotional intelligence, and he knew it. L. Linda was on her way to the Base, and he was second-guessing his decision. He did not know how Nyx and the others would react to her showing up. Charlie might have objections as well. The decision to call L. Linda illustrated his desperation.

After a few silent minutes, Harley said, "I don't see how we get out of this, but I'm open to suggestions."

"Our chances depend on Miriam and Rachael's ability to deal with the satellite that spotted your friends leaving in Doc's car, and if our friends can help, but to be honest, I don't think our friends can do anything. They aren't soldiers. They're just high school kids." He paused. "We just need to be ready if Miriam figures something out."

"Roger that."

"Huh?"

"Sorry. Military talk, sort of, but I'm not a soldier, so it's kinda stupid. It means I agree. So, suggestions?"

"What's the fewest number of vehicles it would take to evacuate the town?"

Harley thought for a moment. "If we stuff in as many as possible, one school bus and two or three cars."

"And what about your data?"

"I didn't think you guys were concerned about our data."

"I'm sure Miriam is concerned about it. It's just that she's more worried about staying alive."

"We've started copying the hard drives, but I underestimated how long it would take. Plus, I don't think we have enough portable hard drives."

"I don't know much about computers. Sorry, I can't help you there." Derrick thought for a moment. "What if we took the computers?"

Harley whistled through his teeth. "I don't know. We could take the laptops in the trunks of the cars, but that means we could not take clothes and other personal items. We could load the desktops into a few pickup trucks."

"Too many vehicles. I don't know how we would get one, let alone several. Still, it's too bad we can't just take the computers." Derrick paused. "Personal items can be replaced. People cannot, nor can the data."

"Good points. Wait. That's brilliant."

"It is?"

Harley palmed his forehead. "We can pull the hard drives. I'll get people on it."

"How long will that take? Rebekah and Anna can help."

Harley didn't answer. Instead, he called someone on the radio and instructed them to pull the hard drives from all the computers. When he finished, he said, "I don't know. Maybe 30 minutes? A lot less time than copying everything. Any other ideas?"

Derrick said nothing for a moment. He didn't even comprehend how his comment turned into a useful idea. "Perhaps, but you will not like it."

Harley shrugged. "I'm not liking a lot of things. Hit me with it."

"I don't want to hit you. Besides, it's just an idea."

Harley smiled. "Dude, you're entertaining as hell."

"Oh. An expression."

Harley chuckled. "It means tell me about it."

Derrick's lack of sophistication was quickly and easily exposed, but there was no time for being self-conscious. "We should destroy the town."

"You're right about one thing—I don't like it. However, you're not wrong. But how? I don't think we have enough explosives. We buried most of them, and it would take too long to dig them up."

"Burn it."

"Burn the entire town?" Harley whistled again. "I'm not sure how we'd do that."

"I wish Red were here," Derrick mumbled.

"Say what?"

"Sorry. Red is a frien—uh, someone I know. He's a genius at fixing and building things."

"And at burning towns?"

"Not specifically, but he is good at making stuff work. Do you have anyone like him?"

"Yeah, I'll call Sam. He's good at fixing stuff."

Sam arrived a few minutes later. "Kinda busy, boss. What's up?"

Harley motioned Sam into a chair.

Derrick looked at Sam. "Sorry about earlier. I shouldn't have been giving you orders. You know about cutting the zip ties."

Sam glared. "I'm not gonna lie. I don't like any of you, but I get it. You did what you had to do. Doesn't mean we will ever be friends. Got it?"

"I get that a lot," Derrick said.

Harley interrupted. "We need to destroy the town. Either blow it up or burn it to the ground."

Sam said, "You can't be serious."

"Serious as a heart attack. I don't need an argument. I need ideas."

Sam rocked back in his chair, still glaring at Derrick, then looked at Harley and shrugged. "Burn it, I guess. But we'd need a lot of accelerants to destroy everything."

"We've got 600,000 gallons of crude oil. Would that do it?"

"You want to destroy our oil reserves? That's 95% of our income."

"We can't take it with us, and I'm not giving it to New America."

Sam shook his head and turned to Derrick. "This is your fault."

"You're right. I'm sorry."

Harley said, "Sam, no time. We can't change the past, but the future is yet to be determined. I need ideas. If you have none, just say so, and I'll get someone else in here."

Although Derrick wasn't good at reading people, he saw the mixture of hurt and anger on Sam's face. Harley welded an impressive range of communication ability, ranging from joker to superior, and Harley's words stung Sam. That much was clear.

Sam looked down. "Sorry, boss. I get it." He paused a moment and then looked up. "The crude oil will burn, but it's a little difficult to ignite. Once it's going, it will pull in air and fuel itself. Like a big blowtorch, but we should add something more flammable, like gasoline, to get it going."

Harley said, "We have gasoline. Not a lot, but perhaps enough. We also have diesel. But how do we get it mixed and spread through town?"

Sam shook his head. "That's the problem. We can pump it out, but I don't know how we could spread it around town. Plus, it would be dangerous. One wrong move and we'd blow ourselves up."

Derrick wished Red were here to figure this out. "Maybe we could spray some in all the buildings, strike a match, and run."

Harley looked at the ceiling and then at Sam. "Are you thinking what I'm thinking?"

Sam blinked. "The sprinkler system?"

"Exactly. Drain the water from the system and connect hoses from the oil pumping station to the sprinklers. Mix in some diesel and gasoline and set a few bombs to detonate after we are gone."

Sam rubbed his forehead. "That would do it. I don't want to be anywhere close to here when it goes off."

"What about the other bombs?" Derrick asked.

"You mean the buried bombs?" Harley asked.

"Yes."

"Someone must detonate those with the computer. You saw that."

"Can one computer set them all off, and can they all go off simultaneously?"

Harley said, "One computer, controls all the explosives."

"How about a time delay?"

Harley thought for a moment. "I don't think so. We didn't program it that way. What are you thinking?"

"You can't be here to set the explosives off once the buildings are filled with oil, but maybe Miriam can figure out a time delay. If she can't, I'll set them off. Don't put a bomb in the building where the computer is."

"Not going to happen that way. It's my town, and if it must be destroyed, I'm doing it."

"It's our responsibility you're in this situation, so I'll do it. Just show me how and I'll get out before the fire reaches that last building. Also," Derrick's voice trailed off.

"And what, dude. Out with it," Harley demanded.

Derrick looked from Harley to Sam and then back to Harley. "We should not waste those explosives around the town."

Harley said, "What's that mean?"

"I'll set them off after the military has the town surrounded."

Harley said, "Holy crap. We don't want to start a war with New America."

Derrick said, "We already have."

10

L. LINDA WALKED BACK TOWARD THE electric cart, hoping the camera she'd spotted worked, and Charlie was paying attention. She saw a few small tunnels, one labeled 'Reactor One,' but nothing big enough for any of the military vehicles except a tunnel sealed with huge steel doors. She could spend hours here drooling over military hardware, with which she could do some seriously destructive stuff, but the ticking clock in her head was banging out each second, giving her a headache. Time running out for what or who, she did not know, but she sensed it was for Derrick and feared it was something far bigger.

She rounded a large truck with missiles mounted on the top and sides. A black robot stood some 50 yards distant. She dove for cover, but it was too late. The machine had spotted her. Peeking around an Abram M4A3 battle tank, she saw the robot wave, motioning her to come. She whispered, "I hope that's Charlie."

L. Linda walked toward the robot, wishing she had a weapon. Unfortunately, the closest thing to a weapon back in Jack's shop was a screwdriver or perhaps a hammer unless one counted Collin's and Martinez's firearms, which didn't matter because she had nothing, not even a pocketknife. Not that a screwdriver would serve as much of a weapon against the robot unless it stood still while she dismantled it. "Charlie?" she asked.

The robot said nothing but motioned toward a tunnel, which she walked through. The tunnel emptied into a parking garage with many electric carts, some larger than others. A small one set in the middle of the driving lane as if waiting for her. Climbing into the driver's seat, she turned the key and the dashboard lit. "Must be my ride," she said, flooring the accelerator.

She did not see signs or directions. If you got this far, they assumed you recognized where you were and knew where you were going. She knew neither. It was clear why Derrick wouldn't tell anyone about this place. This was an abandoned and vast United States military base powered by a nuclear reactor, which apparently still function because there was electricity, and had missiles armed with atomic warheads. If this place fell into the wrong hands, terrible things could happen.

Derrick had trusted her with this secret, which made her happy to the point of being slightly light-headed.

She wanted Derrick to survive. But knowing about this place, he was less important than she had previously believed.

The tunnel led to another parking lot. She drove as deep into the lot as possible, hitting the brakes at the last moment before the cart smacked the curb. Jumping from the cart, she ran through a larger opening into what looked like a train station she'd seen in a movie, except underground. A single red train car with a large white cross set on the tracks—a medical transport, which she felt sure was meant for her, partly because it was there and partly because the door stood open.

Plus, another black robot motioned her inside, increasing her confidence the rail led to Akira.

Walking by the robot, she said, "Sorry, I don't have change for a tip."

As soon as she sat, the door slid shut, and the transport started moving.

"Hold on. Next stop, Administration."

With that, the transport rocketed forward. L. Linda smiled. "This thing kicks butt."

The tunnel went dark, and she couldn't see anything outside the windows, although she was sure the entire trip remained underground. The machine was traveling incredibly fast. Over 100 miles an hour, she estimated. At one point, a rotting smell of death caused her to hold her breath, but it faded quickly because within seconds, she was miles away from whatever had caused the stench. After about 45 minutes, the coach slowed. She estimated it had traveled over 100 miles, which would put her somewhere near Death Valley, albeit underneath the immense desert.

The machine continued to slow, and light flooded into the tunnel. The tracks arced left, and the entrance to a building came into view. Outside the building stood a greeting party consisting of a different type of robot and three people: Nyx, Red, and Antonio.

L. Linda had just stepped off the transport when Nyx snarled, "What are you doing here?"

L. Linda said, "Hi. Nice to see you too. I'm fine, and you?"

"Cut the crap. Answer my question."

L. Linda ignored her, walking straight to the robot. "You must be Charlie. I gotta talk to Akira." L. Linda paused. "She's… she's not dead—is she?"

Nyx grabbed L. Linda by the elbow, spinning her around. "Answer my question."

L. Linda smiled. Not a Hi, how-are-you smile, but a—touch-me-again-and-lose-some-teeth—smile. "Duh. I'm here to talk to Akira. I thought I'd made that clear."

"How did you find us?"

"Crystal ball. How do you think? Derrick called me." The ticking in L. Linda's head had become a full-fledged gong, not a little gong but a call-the-empire-to-battle sort of gong. Still, she couldn't resist tormenting Nyx just a little.

"You should have said that."

"As if you gave me time to say anything. But enough pleasantries. For Derrick to call me means they are in trouble. Is Akira alive or not?"

"She's alive, but not herself. She's been," Nyx paused, "injured."

"I need to talk to her."

"We'll take you, but she might not talk to you."

"I don't care if she talks to me. I just hope she can do what needs to be done."

Charlie led them to the break room. Akira wasn't there. "Wait here. I'll get Ms. Akira."

L. Linda walked to the espresso machine, admiring it for a moment. "Does it work?"

Nyx said, "It works."

"May I? It's been a long night."

"Help yourself. I assume you can run it."

"Don't be silly." L. Linda found powdered milk and chocolate and went to work. A few minutes later, blowing steam from the mocha's surface, she walked to Nyx, holding the cup out for Nyx to see. "I'm trying to make a fern leaf with the foam."

Nyx glanced at the cup. "That's pretty good."

"Do you think? I want to make one for Derrick when he gets back."

Nyx said nothing.

L. Linda sipped, then smiled. "I needed something lovely after everything that's happened in Potterville."

"What's happened in Potterville?" Antonio asked, pulling out a chair for L. Linda.

"More robots came. Threatened to kill people. Martinez killed one," she looked at Red, scooted a chair out for him with her foot, "Mr. Fletcher ran over the other one with his truck, not one of his big trucks, but with the Dodge diesel 4 X 4. I didn't see it because I was on the coast saving Derrick." She took a drink.

"Saving Derrick?" Nyx asked.

"Yep. Derrick, Miriam, Rebekah, and Anna. Did I mention they found Anna? Well, duh, they must have, because I saved her. Oh, and a guy named Mike. Someone tried to blow them up but missed."

"Is Derrick safe?" Nyx asked.

"Was safe, but he made me leave. He's not safe now or I wouldn't be here. He should have let me stay with them."

Red said, "So, the people in Potterville are safe? Are they still at the jail?"

L. Linda set the mug down. "Heavens no. They are neither safe nor in the jail. I convinced them to move, and good thing because an assassin arrived as I was getting the last people out. Martinez killed the assassin." They didn't need to know that L. Linda beaned the assassin with a can of paint or that Martinez survived because of her instructions on—how to greet an assassin and live to tell the tale.

"Where are they now?"

"I guess I can tell you. They are at Mr. Fletcher's shop."

"Gramps let them into his shop?" Red asked. "Things must be as bad as you say."

"Worse."

"How could things be worse?" Nyx asked.

"He'll figure out the assassin failed soon. Then things will get much worse and quickly."

"Worse how?" Antonio asked.

"He will send more assassins, or he might just use the military."

From the doorway, a soft voice asked, "Are my parents okay?" Akira stood just inside the door—hair wet.

L. Linda said, "They are okay. For now."

"Why is she here?" Akira asked, pointing at L. Linda.

"We asked the same question," Nyx said and then added, "She says Derrick called her."

In a voice much softer than previously used, L. Linda said, "Hi, Akira. I heard you were injured. Derrick called me and I talked to Miriam. She is worried about you."

"Miriam asked about me?"

Miriam had not asked about Akira, but L. Linda wasn't going to say that. Derrick needed help, and Miriam thought Akira was the only person who could do what needed to be done. L. Linda had seen how Akira looked at Miriam, and L. Linda had figured Akira out quickly enough after arriving in Potterville. So, Akira's connection with Miriam was vital here. Akira's inclinations made no difference to L. Linda. She was only concerned about Akira doing what Miriam wanted.

"Miriam is in trouble. He almost killed her earlier."

Akira gasped.

Antonio said, "Wait. Can we back up? You said the military, as in, send troops to Potterville?"

L. Linda said, "Not likely. More apt to send a missile."

"Bomb the entire town? That's crazy," Antonio said.

Nyx said, "It's not. Remember the silo."

L. Linda looked as if she wanted to say something but did not.

Nyx said, "You keep saying he. Who is he?"

L. Linda looked at Nyx with an expression telegraphing impatience, but with a gentle voice, she said, "Prime. It must be Prime."

"What did Miriam say exactly about me?" Akira asked.

L. Linda stared at Akira, taking a long drink. "Miriam didn't have time to chat. She needs you to set up an open channel on as many satellite antennas as possible, but transmit nothing, zilch, nix, nada. Just wait for her signal. Can you do that?"

Akira looked at Charlie.

Charlie said, "Antonio and Red got one antenna working earlier. That's all we have."

Akira said, "I can do it. I hope it's enough."

11

MIRIAM STUDIED THE IMAGES FROM the satellite. Rachael wasn't kidding. The resolution was improved, and the vehicles were identifiable, even in black and white. A move right out of James Carver's playbook.

Miriam said, "Just as I feared."

"Why is a New America missile in Mexico? It doesn't look as if they are ready to fire because they are pointing north."

"They are ready to fire. Carver is going to bomb New America to justify attacking Mexico."

"That's crazy."

"I don't disagree, but Carver has done it before. North Korea didn't drop a nuclear bomb on Sacramento. Carver did. And the United States missiles didn't malfunction. They hit their intended targets."

"How could you possibly know that?"

"I've already said too much."

"Oh, my God. You've seen the missile silos."

Miriam stared at Rachael, wondering what she knew about the silos and not wanting to divulge more information. "We don't have much time. Get Derrick and Harley here. Then tell me how we get a message to our friends."

"I assume you know their location."

"Not exactly. How precise do we have to be?"

"The narrower the band, the better. Less likely to be intercepted and more likely to be received in its entirety."

"Can you use GPS coordinates?"

"That's how it's done. You can point to a map, and I'll figure the coordinates."

"You didn't say how accurate the target needs to be."

Rachael shrugged. "We could start with a five-mile radius, then go wider if needed until we get a hit."

"How will we know if they received it?"

"I'll embed a ping in the message. The system will bounce the ping back to us."

"But we won't know if it's them. Is that correct?"

"True."

"Sounds risky."

"Agreed. Not as risky as staying here."

Miriam nodded.

"I can encrypt the message. Then no one can read it without the key."

"They won't have the key."

"I can send the key with the message."

"I'm confused. If the wrong people get the message, they'll have the key."

Rachael said, "Right. Unless we include a security question to get the activation key."

"That works. How long will it take to develop the encryption and the key?"

Rachael said, "Under optimum conditions, a few weeks."

"Huh?"

"Relax. You said how long to develop it. I already have both."

"Don't do that to me. So, how do I write the message?"

"Just plain text, then I'll encrypt it."

"How long will that take?"

Rachael said, "Not long. It's copy and paste. It will take longer to determine the GPS coordinates."

"35°58'14.7 N 118°32'18.2 W."

"You're not serious?"

"Why would I joke about that? Besides, I don't see the humor. To be honest, I'm having trouble seeing humor in anything now, and that's not a good sign."

"Can you write those coordinates down? And are you sure?"

Miriam grabbed a notepad and pen. "I'm sure. The five-mile radius should work. If not, try ten and then fifteen. Is there a computer I can use to write the message?"

Rachael rolled her chair to the next terminal, logged on, and opened a word processing application. "There you go. I'll get to work on the rest."

Miriam scooted her chair to the computer, thought for a moment, and then typed:

```
We are in a town. Prime is watching us using
a satellite. Prime bombed a car full of kids
trying to leave. We can't escape, but we must
get out of here because the military will
have us surrounded within hours. The town has
about 100 people who must be evacuated.

Now accepting ideas of how you might rescue
us.
```

```
Encrypt   your   message   before   replying.
Instructions for that are included.

Miriam
```

Miriam pushed her chair back.

Rachael looked over. "Done?"

"For now. I assume we can go back and forth."

"Yes, but remember, we have little time."

"Understood. Let's see what their first response is."

"We need a question for the encryption key," Rachael said.

Miriam thought for a moment. Who to best answer? Nyx, Akira, Red, or Antonio if they were all still there, if they were awake, if they were alive. Charlie, but Charlie could be docked. It had to be something that wouldn't give Rachael too much information.

Question: Charlie's best friend until I showed up?

Answer: Jane.

"That's it?" Rachael asked.

Miriam nodded.

Miriam startled when the door flew open, smacking the wall. Harley rushed in, and Derrick was right behind him. "How's it going?" Harley asked.

"We were just about to send a message to Miriam's friends, and we found something else you need to see."

"What did you find?" Derrick asked.

Miriam said, "Show them."

Rachael held out one hand, focusing on the computer before her. "Let me get this sent." Less than a minute passed. "There." Within seconds, the computer sounded a ding. "They got it."

Miriam said, "Someone got it."

"What do you mean, 'someone got it?'" Harley asked.

Rachael didn't respond, but motioned Derrick to the monitor. An image appeared. "We found this."

"Missile," Harley said.

Miriam said, "Fifty miles south of the border."

Harley said, "Can't be. Those are New America vehicles."

Rachael said, "Correct. Tell them, Miriam."

"It's a tactic James Carver has used before."

"You mean Prime?"

"Same difference. Prime is (or was) James Carver. What you've been told about the Greatest War is a lie. North Korea didn't drop a nuclear bomb on Sacramento, and the United States missiles did not malfunction. They hit their intended targets," Miriam said.

Harley stared at Miriam. "What are you saying?"

Rachael said, "She's saying Carver launched all three ICBMs. He didn't end the Greatest War. Carver started it."

"That makes little sense. Why would he bomb his own country?"

Miriam said, "I don't have that all figured out yet, but for one reason, it made him look good, allowed him to declare Martial Law, and set himself up as emperor."

"You're saying he plans to launch those missiles against his own country?"

"That's *exactly* what I'm saying."

12

AKIRA HAD FINISHED MIRIAM's REQUEST received via L. Linda Maxton, regarding the satellite link and sat staring at the monitor, perhaps seeking proof Miriam was alive. Nyx stood off to one side of the room, not feeling any better about Akira's mental condition. If Miriam didn't send something personal to Akira in her response, Nyx feared it might send her friend into a deep funk, even deeper and funkier than Akira had been since exiting the treatment chamber.

Perhaps so deep, Nyx would never find Akira. Perhaps Akira would never find herself.

Although she could not be sure, Nyx thought Akira was getting worse, not better. At least she was alive, but Nyx missed her friend and felt alone, like she had when her father had disappeared years earlier. Not quite the same, but it almost felt the same.

"What's taking so long?" Akira asked no one in particular.

Nyx glanced at Antonio and shrugged.

L. Linda stood on the other side of the room, leaning against a desk, watching silently. Pushing herself upright, she walked over and sat next to Akira, rubbing her shoulder. "How are you doing, sweety?"

"Don't call me that."

"You know me, always saying something weird. They said you got injured. What happened?"

"I don't want to talk about it."

Red said, "There was a problem with the reactor…"

L. Linda interrupted. "As in nuclear reactor?"

"Yes. Anyway, a water valve needed replaced. Derrick and I worked on the valve, and Akira volunteered to go into the reactor control room."

Antonio stepped behind Akira. "She didn't just volunteer. She insisted she was the only one who could do it."

L. Linda said, "She was right, you know."

Red said, "Anyway. There wasn't a new valve, so Derrick and I had to build one. But I messed it up. It wouldn't fit. I took too long and—well, Akira got too much radiation."

Antonio said, "Red, it wasn't…"

Akira spun around in her chair. L. Linda startled, pulling away, as did Antonio. Akira said, "I never want to hear this story again."

Red said, "I'm sorry, Akira. It's my fault."

"Bullshit. Stop saying that. I was in the control room. Maybe I could have prevented what happened, but I didn't know any more about what I was doing than you did. You fixed it. You saved Potterville. I'm alive. End of story. Can we move on and focus on Miriam and the others?"

Red nodded. "I'll make it up…"

Akira stood, arms straight at her side, fists vibrating. "I swear I'll kick your ass if you say another word. I'd be dead along with everyone else had you not been here. End of story. Got it?"

Red nodded, fighting back tears. "Got it."

Nyx had never seen Akira talk to anyone like that. It was disturbing, yet Akira was protecting Red, in a way. Nyx didn't know what to think of the outburst. Perhaps it was an improvement, but something told Nyx it was not.

Charlie said, "We are receiving something."

Akira sat and spun back to the computer.

"What does it say?" L. Linda asked.

Akira said, "It's just some boxes." She clicked on one that read: message. The message read: encryption application and then another box that said: open. She clicked on it, and a dropdown menu appeared. In the dropdown, there was one question.

"Charlie's best friend until I showed up."

Charlie said, "Jane."

Akira typed in Jane.

A new window appeared that read: click here to run decryption. Akira clicked, and Miriam's message appeared. Everyone leaned in and read.

After a few moments, Nyx asked, "What are we going to do?"

L. Linda said, "They could walk out. Perhaps the satellite can't see individuals. That's their best chance. The town's people are on their own."

Akira whispered, "Miriam didn't mention me."

L. Linda said, "Miriam mentioned you when she called." L. Linda didn't say it was that Akira might be dead. That didn't seem like a good thing to say. Whatever had happened to Akira scrambled her brain. That much was clear. Akira might not be of much help and could prove a liability.

Antonio said, "I agree. Tell them to leave on foot. When they get away from that town, they can call L. Linda again. While they are walking, we can work on a plan to pick them up."

Nyx said, "I agree, too. Akira, do you want me to write the reply?"

Akira slid the keyboard to Nyx.

Red said, "You need to read that message again."

Nyx said, "The message is clear."

"None of you seem to understand what it says."

Nyx stared at Red for a moment. "You might be right. I have a history of poor decisions."

Red frowned. "All I'm saying is that Miriam didn't ask for advice. She asked how we could rescue them. That means we gotta do something, not give advice about what they should do. What if we are wrong about the satellite not being able to spot them walking?"

"Good points, but what can we do?" Antonio asked.

Red thought for a moment and then said, "If we had a military transport plane, we could get them all."

"Who would fly it?" Antonio asked.

Red glared at him.

Charlie said, "Transport aircraft are in hangar number 2."

Red said, "We saw the hangar, but I didn't see any transport planes. Just helicopters and fighter jets."

"I am aware of your travels within the complex. I am also aware of your unauthorized flight of a rotary aircraft, which included damaging one."

"Sorry about that."

"I did not anticipate you would try to fly it," Charlie said and then added, "Do they teach that at your school?"

Antonio said, "We tried to stop him."

"They don't teach it at school. I had flown that model using a simulator."

Nyx added, "That's a computer game."

"I understand flight simulators. Humans here used them to train pilots. However, I'm unfamiliar with computer games."

Red said, "But I didn't see a transport plane."

"Because you were in hangar number 1. Hangar number 2 is at ground level, built into the mountain."

"That makes sense."

Nyx sighed. "Red, you've never flown a transport plane. You've played a computer game. You'll kill yourself."

"I got no death wish. On the simulator, I've flown a couple of transport planes, and they are not as difficult as a helicopter. Well, mostly not as difficult." Red looked at Charlie. "What models?"

"There are several models for specific operational needs. Do you anticipate needing a large or small transport?"

"Let's start with large. Miriam said 100 people, but not how many vehicles."

"Red flew a helicopter?" L. Linda asked.

Akira said, "Red, you're crazier than I am. Why would you try to fly a helicopter?"

Nyx thought she detected a slight smile on Akira, but it faded.

Red shrugged. "I don't know. Look for Derrick and Miriam. Get our families out of Potterville. I just wanted to help."

Akira looked at L. Linda. "Are you sure my parents are, okay?"

"They were when I left. But Red's not wrong. They need to get out of Potterville."

Antonio paced the room. "How are we going to help everyone?"

Red said, "L. Linda, you're the only one who knows what's happening in Potterville, and you've seen Derrick. Who do we help first?"

"I have not seen Derrick in his present location, but definitely Derrick first," L. Linda paused, glancing at Akira, "and Miriam. My dad can take care of Potterville for now."

Antonio stopped. "No disrespect, but your dad works at the hardware store."

"He also works part time at the convenience store."

"It's not as if he has experience dealing with assassins."

L. Linda said, "He didn't always work at the hardware store. We are off topic. Miriam needs an answer."

"What are the large transports, Charlie?" Red asked.

"There are five Lockheed C5 Galaxy aircraft."

Red whistled. "Those are huge. We could fit several vehicles and a lot of people into one, but they need a large airstrip. Plus, I've never flown one on the simulator."

"There are also four Boeing C-17 Globemaster III aircraft. Data indicates they were preferred for short and undeveloped runways."

"I've flown those."

Nyx said, "Red, you haven't flown anything! You've played a computer game. It's too dangerous."

"I'm not asking you to go. I flew the helicopter, which you also said I couldn't do."

"Red, we don't want to lose you," Nyx pleaded.

"Like I said, I don't have a death wish. If I didn't think I could do it, I wouldn't. If you got another idea, say so."

L. Linda raised her hand.

"What? Nyx asked. "We aren't in school."

"Just a couple of teeny questions. How many people does it take to fly one of those globe-whatevers? Just two other minor little issues. How long have they been sitting there, and what makes you think they can still fly?"

Red said, "I need a co-pilot and a loadmaster. The loadmaster operates the ramp to get vehicles and such in."

"So, who's the second pilot?" L. Linda asked.

Charlie said, "I can serve as co-pilot. I have downloaded the operational data. In addition, if there's time, Red can practice in the simulator. All aircraft receive regular preflight maintenance. QR-3 robots can prepare an aircraft for takeoff."

"Have we forgotten about the satellite and Prime killing the kids in the car? I assume a giant cargo plane is easier to spot than a car," Antonio said.

L. Linda said, "I can fly the Prime aircraft and might be able to intercept incoming missiles."

"Might be able to, does not inspire confidence," Antonio said.

"Got another idea? I'm all ears."

Akira said, "Send a message to Miriam. Tell her what we are thinking and see what she says. There might be 100 reasons this won't work, and if that's the case, we are wasting time discussing it."

Nyx said, "Good thinking."

Staring straight ahead, Akira said, "Thank you."

Nyx's fingers stabbed at the keyboard. "Finished. What do you guys think?"

```
Miriam,

Red thinks he can fly a transport plane to
get you. How many people and what vehicles
need transported? Is there a place to land?
And here's the biggy—what about the
satellite?

P.S. Akira is here and says hi.

Nyx
```

Akira stared into the middle distance. Nyx glanced at her, then encrypted the message and hit send.

13

Friday, April 9, 5:05 a.m.

DERRICK WALKED TO THE WINDOW AND THEN back to the computer desk. They had not received a reply from the Base, although the ping—whatever that was—indicated someone had received the message. Since a satellite was monitoring them, the message might have been intercepted. A missile might be headed toward them right now. The more he thought about it, the more he regretted sending a message.

Worse, Prime might know Nyx's location, and Derrick could not protect her. He might never see her again. The thought had crossed his mind, but it was always because he didn't make it back, not because she didn't make it out. Why did he let her get involved in this? He should have left town the first time he saw her from his condo window.

Had he left then, she'd be safe now.

"Would you sit or stand or do something besides pace?" Miriam asked.

"Let him pace," Rachael said. "I'm about to join him. What's taking them so long?"

Miriam said, "I don't know. Are you sure they got the message?"

"I'm sure someone got it."

"Why haven't they responded?" Miriam asked.

"You keep asking the same question as if my answer might change." Rachael refreshed the computer screen. "We should have given them more information."

Derrick paused. "More information might have put them at greater risk. It is better to keep it vague until we know they got it. We provided too much information. We should have just asked something to confirm it's them."

Rachael said, "Let's assume the message reached the right place. It is nighttime, so maybe they're asleep."

Miriam said, "That's true. If that's the case, the military will have us surrounded before they wake up."

A rap came at the door. Derrick cracked the door, then opened it.

Harley walked in, followed by six kids, two girls, and two boys, plus Anna and Rebekah. "Sam's doing a fantastic job. The oil and gas are almost hooked up to the sprinklers. I've transferred control of the defense field to this computer." He waved at those who accompanied him, already removing parts from a bank of servers. "These guys are pulling hard drives. Are we making any headway here?"

Miriam said, "We sent a message but haven't received a reply."

"Aren't we forgetting something?" Derrick pointed up. "The satellite. They will spot us regardless of how we try to leave."

"I haven't forgotten." Miriam looked at Rachael. "I'm hoping you have an idea. I don't know enough about satellites. Any thoughts? Can we—I don't know—destroy it, or blind it?"

Rachael turned away from the computer. "I've put three satellites into motion. Two above the one monitoring us and one below. If we bounce static between the two above and the one below, it should blind Prime's satellite."

"What's your confidence level of it working?" Miriam asked.

Rachael shrugged. "About 80%."

"Is that the best you can do?" Derrick asked.

Miriam said, "Do you smell that? I had gotten used to the oil, but it seems ten times stronger. It's making my eyes water."

Harley said, "They must have started pumping oil and diesel."

Derrick said, "Wasn't it supposed to go through the sprinkler system?"

"It will, but we also decided to use the fire suppression hoses to spray the underground tunnels and such."

"Is that safe?" Derrick asked.

"It is not, but it will make a hell of a fireball when it goes off."

Derrick nodded. "How long before everything is ready?"

"About an hour."

"How long before the military is here?"

"About 90 minutes."

"Narrow window." Derrick looked at Rachael. "How long before those satellites are in position and is there anything you can do to increase our odds of successfully blinding Prime's satellite?"

Rachael turned back to the computer, and then, glancing over her shoulder, she said, "Best position, about an hour, but they should be close enough in 45 minutes to start jamming. I can try to boost the signal. We will get the best result if we wait until they are in the optimal position."

Derrick said, "Have everyone ready in 45 minutes."

"But we haven't even decided what vehicles to use."

"Have school buses and a couple of pickups loaded with the hardware you're taking. Have enough water for two days."

Harley nodded. "I'll be right back."

Harley stepped out. Derrick didn't know why he left. Maybe just to give instructions. Maybe it was something else. Thinking about it only made Derrick worry, and he already had enough of those.

The computer sounded a beep. Miriam spun around. "An incoming message?"

Derrick rushed to the computer. The message read:

```
Miriam,

Red thinks he can fly a transport plane to
get you. How many people and what vehicles
need transported? Is there a place to land?
And here's the biggy—what about the
satellite?

P.S. Akira is here and says hi.

Nyx
```

Miriam said, "Akira's alive, but something is wrong."

"What do you mean?" Derrick asked.

"I expected Akira to write the message."

"Good point." Derrick agreed. Computers were Akira's thing. However, he didn't say just seeing Nyx's name caused a warm feeling in his chest. He so wanted to see her again, which made his next decision even more agonizing.

Harley came through the door. "Did I miss something?"

Rachael said, "Their friends answered."

Derrick said, "We need to respond. How many people and what vehicles? They are bringing a transport plane."

"How in the hell did they get that?" Harley asked.

"I can't tell you that," Derrick said.

"Who's flying it?"

"Guy named Red."

"He's a pilot?"

"Not that I'm aware of. He is a high school student and defensive lineman, but if he says he can fly it, I believe him," Derrick said.

"I don't know what fits in an airplane," Harley said.

"Let's start with numbers. How many people?"

Harley looked up, counting on his fingers, and mouthing numbers. "Total of 112. That includes you guys."

Derrick said, "Then you're taking 111. How many can fit on the bus?"

Miriam said, "Wait. How do you get 111?"

Derrick said, "I'm not going. Someone must stay here and detonate the bombs. If you can rig a time delay on the explosions, that would be great."

Miriam said, "I'm staying too."

From behind a wall of computers, Anna said, "I'll stay. Miriam, you go."

From the other side of the room, Rebekah yelled, "No way, Anna. You're going with us."

"I'm not."

Derrick said, "We don't have time to argue. I'm staying. Everyone else is leaving."

Anna stepped into the open. "You're the one arguing. Have you forgotten we have to deal with the missile launcher in Mexico?"

"I haven't forgotten. That's why I would appreciate a time delay on the detonation. Create a diversion while I slip out."

Nist and Atwood walked in. "What's going on? We can hear you from down the hall."

Harley said, "A minor disagreement."

Derrick said, "Dimensions of the bus?"

Harley scratched his head. "I'll have to measure it."

Derrick said, "Best guess. Then measure, and we'll update them if necessary."

"I'd say 10 to 11 feet tall, 9 feet wide and about 40 feet long. We have a smaller one that's about 30 feet long. Two pickups will hold the hardware."

Derrick motioned to the computer. "Send them that. Tell them we're ready in 45 minutes."

14

TEN MINUTES PASSED THAT FELT LIKE as many hours. Charlie had taken Red and Antonio to the Globemaster C-17 flight simulator. Red would practice take-offs and landings. Antonio would learn to be a loadmaster. Nyx had little confidence they could do it. However, Charlie would be on board and could fly the aircraft because Charlie knew everything about it, having downloaded all the information. Akira sat silently, staring at the computer monitor.

The tension between them felt like a substantial charge of static electricity waiting for one of them to touch a doorknob.

"Do you think he can do it?" Akira whispered.

"Can who do what?"

"Red. Do you think he can fly the plane?"

Nyx took a deep breath. This was the first time Akira had spoken since the guys left. Afraid she might say something that would trigger Akira, she just said, "Maybe."

"He fixed the reactor."

Nyx nodded. "He did. He flew a helicopter, but not far." Nyx hesitated. "He crashed one too."

"He fixed the reactor."

"He feels terrible, you know."

"Why?"

"He blames himself for hurting you."

"He shouldn't."

Just then, the computer beeped notification of an incoming message.

```
We are dealing with the satellite. We have
just over 100 people, a school bus roughly
11 feet tall, 9 wide, 40 long, and four
pickup trucks. I'm sending you the GPS
coordinates. Be here in 45 minutes. We'll
load fast and leave.
```

Nyx whistled. "Forty-five minutes. That's not much time. Charlie? Can you hear me, Charlie?"

"I hear you."

"They want us in 45 minutes."

"I read the message."

"Is that doable?" Nyx asked.

Charlie said, "We are ready to roll the C-17 out of the hangar."

"How's Red doing?" Akira asked.

"He is well, to the best of my knowledge," Charlie said.

Nyx said, "I think she means in the simulator."

"He has crashed twice on landing, but he has taken off with little difficulty."

"But you can fly the plane, right Charlie?"

"I can navigate and assist with other functions."

Akira looked at Nyx.

"But you could fly it, right?" Nyx asked again.

"I think not. They did not design the aircraft for a robot. They designed it for a human. We are—different."

Nyx leaned back in her chair. The computer beeped again.

Charlie said, "We have the coordinates. Red has completed his last simulation, and we are going to the aircraft. I shall lose contact with you after we are airborne."

"Did Red manage to land the aircraft?" Nyx said.

Charlie did not respond.

"Charlie, did you hear me?"

"I heard you."

"Answer me."

"We've stopped at a computer in the hangar flight control office. I'm pulling up a map of the area so that Red can see the landing site."

"Charlie."

"Charlie, answer me. Has Red successfully landed the aircraft in the simulator?"

"Charlie!"

* * *

Nist and Atwood pulled up chairs, but before either could say anything, a knock sounded at the door. Todd stuck his head in and motioned for Harley. After whispering in Harley's ear for a moment, Harley said, "Professor, could I speak with you? Privately."

Atwood said, "No time for privacy. These folks know pretty much everything about us. So, just out with it."

Harley walked to Atwood. "It's Point, sir." Harley paused.

"Yes, Point, our Seattle contact. Go on then. I heard we are preparing to leave," he looked at his watch, "good lord, in less than 35 minutes. Sounds impossible."

Harley said, "It's Brogan, sir."

"And?" Atwood gave him a hurry-up signal.

"He's dead, sir. Cliff Haskins is now the Commander."

Atwood nodded. "Well, that is unexpected. Too soon, but it is what we hoped would happen. Any assessment?"

"Q says it's too early to tell."

"Yes. That makes sense. Thank you. Now, bring Lloyd and me up to speed."

"There's something else, sir,"

Atwood moaned. "What is it, Harley? Chop chop."

"Haskins is coming here." Harley paused. "To lead the troops in Mexico."

Atwood turned white.

❋ ❋ ❋

Nyx looked around the room. "Where's L. Linda?"

Akira said, "Perhaps she went with Charlie."

"Charlie? Is L. Linda with you?"

"She is not. Just a moment. Ah, she is near the Reactor Staging Area."

"What in the hell is she doing there?"

"I do not know. However, if I were to speculate, I'd say she's going to the Prime aircraft as she proposed earlier."

Nyx shook her head. "That girl is out of control."

Akira said, "She's trying to help."

"That weirdo is going to get herself killed."

"She's odd but calling her a weirdo is mean. She saved Miriam—and Derrick. I assume Derrick's life still has some significance to you, even if the others do not."

"What's that supposed to mean?"

Akira said, "Figure it out."

"Look, I'm sorry about a lot of stuff, but I'm not putting up with your crap. Sure, I care about Derrick, but I also care about the rest of them. Miriam, Rebekah, Red, Antonio. All of them." She paused, her chest heaving. "I still care about you, whether you like it or not."

15

L. LINDA HAD GLANCED AT THE MAP SHOWING Derrick's location when Charlie left to fetch Red and Antonio. Slipping out of the room, she intended to arrive first to support Derrick's extraction. Red would either be airborne or smoldering wreckage before she could takeoff.

She drove the electric cart with the accelerator pedal smashed to the floor, which wasn't as exciting as one might think. Golf carts are not fast, even glorified military ones. Only an idiot could crash it, and she was a lot of things, but not an idiot, although she'd admit many people thought she was odd or worse.

L. Linda was okay with that.

***

A Globemaster III C17 was sitting in front of the hangar door with the engines running when Red, Antonio, and Charlie arrived. Red didn't know how it got there but assumed black robots that Charlie called QR-3s moved it there. *Things are about to get real,* Red thought, sucking in a breath as Antonio and Charlie climbed into the aircraft. Antonio turned right toward the loadmaster's control platform. Charlie turned left, navigating sideways up a narrow staircase. Squeezing up the stairs wasn't much easier for Red. Pilots back in the day were wide receiver size, not lineman size.

A gigantic door slid open. The sky was turning pink in the east. Red donned a pair of sunglasses the previous pilot had left on the console. After a hasty pre-check, and despite three failed landing attempts, Red pushed the thrust lever forward, spinning up the four turbofan engines until the massive aircraft rolled forward on its own power. The jet was moving. Red's mind was reeling.

Red had told Antonio he could not go after the last failed landing simulation. Antonio said neither Red nor Charlie could operate the load deck from the cockpit, so Red relented because they didn't have time to argue. They had to get in and out of that town fast before the military arrived. They'd be lucky to get away without being shot down. The military would not be expecting a decades-old Air Force transport plane, so perhaps they wouldn't be carrying surface-to-air missiles, but Red wouldn't bet on it.

Jimmy Priest's flight simulator—a computer game, according to Nyx—fired missiles at military planes, as well as creating other challenges during flight simulations. Fighter jets had evasive maneuvers and anti-missile defenses to deploy. Cargo planes had none. Red finally admitted his flight training was limited to the simulator here—a real cockpit with actual flight controls and gauges. The simulator here pitched and rotated. It felt like a real aircraft. Controls operated with hands and feet the same as the C17, not images on a computer screen activated by moving a cursor. Nyx was right—Jimmy's flight simulator was just a game.

Red was firmly belted in the seat of the Globemaster. This was no game. Anti-aircraft weapons would not be a virtual threat. Those would be real as well. That the aircraft had United States Air Force markings might cause the military to hold fire but relying on that wasn't much comfort. That his flight training consisted of playing a computer game didn't provide much comfort either.

Although the simulator duplicated the cockpit, now the aircraft responded to his input, which felt distinctively different from the simulator. He heard the engine's throaty whine, smelled the jet fuel, and felt the power reverberating through the plane. Red felt thrilled and terrified simultaneously.

Charlie said, "Correct to the right."

Red said, "Working on it."

"That is evident, but you went too far left, then too far right. I have scanned all available information and cannot find the zigzag pattern for runway taxiing."

"I'm not doing it on purpose."

"I see. Then why are you doing it?"

"Because I don't know how to fly an airplane. I shouldn't be doing this. You and Antonio need to get out. It's too dangerous."

Charlie said nothing for a moment. "Too far left, sir."

"I know that."

"Just fulfilling my co-pilot duties, sir."

"Stop calling me sir. That's my grandfather."

Charlie said, "Perhaps it would be easier to drive straight if you were on the runway, Captain."

"Runway! All I see is sand."

"Oh. I see. The runway is 25 yards south. That is to your right, Captain."

"I know which way is south. I'm not stupid."

"I am sorry, Captain. I did not mean to imply you were of lesser intelligence than a typical human."

"Stop calling me that. Just call me Red."

"I will call you Red when we are out of the aircraft. I have researched all available documentation, and you are the Captain of this aircraft."

"I'm just a stupid kid." Red guided the aircraft onto the runway that Charlie could see hidden under the sand. "That is much better. Charlie, seriously before I takeoff, I want you and Antonio to get out. I'm not a pilot. I couldn't land in the simulator, so there is little chance I can land the real thing."

"Then why are you here, Captain?"

Red shook his head. "Because I couldn't sit here doing nothing."

"You are risking your life to save your friends."

"They aren't even my friends. I just met Derrick. I don't know Rebekah or Miriam."

"You have known Akira, Nyx, and Antonio longer."

"Much longer. We grew up together."

"So, you are close friends?"

"Not really." Red paused. "We didn't hang out."

"Hang out?"

"Do things together."

Charlie said nothing for a moment. "Turn left 90 degrees in 3, 2, 1."

Red made a hard left turn.

"Fifty yards, then another 90-degree left. That will put you in the center of the runway for takeoff."

Envisioning a football field, Red estimated 50 yards, then turned left. Charlie said nothing until Red stopped the aircraft.

"Well done, Captain. Are you too warm? You are sweating. Humans sweat when they are too warm. There's an air vent just there." Charlie pointed.

Red studied the controls. "I'm kinda busy. You're the co-pilot. Open the vent for me."

"I am not designed to operate things made for humans."

"Just do it. That's an order."

"Very well." Charlie stood, still bent at the waist. Reaching over Red's head, he grabbed a small round air control nozzle, crushing it in his fingers. "Oh, my. Look what I've done." Charlie sat. Pieces of plastic fell from his hand.

"At least I'm getting more air," Red said.

Charlie said, "I have instructed QR-3 robots to clear this runway. That will make landing easier when we return."

"Thank you. It's time for you to get out. Take Antonio with you."

"What if Loadmaster Morales refuses?"

"He's not a loadmaster. He's a junior at Potterville High School. Drag him out if you must. That's an order."

"If you are not the Captain, what makes you think you can give orders?"

Red shrugged. "It worked before."

"You mean when you ordered me to break the air nozzle?"

"Yeah. That."

"Ill-conceived orders often fail. You should ask Loadmaster Morales if he wants to get off the aircraft."

"Fine." Red keyed the microphone. "Antonio? Are you there?"

"I'm here. Why aren't we moving?"

"I stopped so you and Charlie can get off the plane. Charlie will meet you at the door." Red looked at Charlie. "There. Satisfied?"

Antonio's voice came over the radio speaker. "Are you on again about the simulator?"

"Just get off the plane. Don't make me drag you off."

"Good luck with that. I secured the door. Now, stop talking and start flying."

"Antonio, please get off the plane. I can manage alone. According to Charlie, I'm the Captain, and you both gotta follow my orders."

"I guess you'll have to court-martial me when this is finished because I'm not leaving. Our friends need help, and there might not be time for you to get them on the plane and out of there. I'd never forgive myself if—well if they don't make it because I wasn't there."

Red said, "I can hardly live with myself after what I did to Akira. I can't risk your life. Please, Antonio, get off."

Charlie let out a little squeak, not unlike someone crying who didn't know how to. "That—I think the term is—breaks Akira's heart when you say it."

Red said, "Akira isn't herself. I know she gets upset, but it's true."

Charlie said, "It's not true, and it's not just what Akira says. It's what I feel."

Red turned, staring at Charlie.

Charlie keyed the radio. "Antonio, this is Charlie. I must also be court-martialed upon our return because I'm not leaving either. Red is the Captain of this aircraft, but I am disobeying his orders."

Red frowned. "You just keyed the microphone."

"Keying the microphone was required for communication with Antonio."

"But you didn't break it."

Charlie glanced up at the air vent control he had crushed. "Oh. Right."

Red said, "Explain. That's an order. Can you follow that one?"

Charlie stared out the window. "I broke the vent on purpose."

"Why?"

"So, you would not ask me to pilot the aircraft."

"You can fly the plane? Trade me places."

"I cannot. It would not be safe."

"It would be a hell of a lot safer than me flying it."

Charlie didn't respond.

Red unbuckled his safety harness. "Trade me places."
Antonio's voice came over the radio. "What's the holdup? Let's go!"
Charlie shook his head. "I can't. Don't ask me again. I'm not okay."
"What happened to your voice?" Red asked.
Charlie said, "It's not me talking. It's Akira."

* * *

L. Linda wanted to explore the engineering building because its name fascinated her beyond measure, but her investigation would have to wait. It might have to wait a lifetime, or more accurately stated, until another lifetime if reincarnationists were correct in their views regarding the afterlife. Instead of exploring, she ran to the warehouse, raised the roll-up door, and dashed to the Prime aircraft.

Conducting a preflight check was probably standard operating procedure for anyone trained to fly the machine, but she had neither training nor time. Red was probably already in the air if they made it. If not, she and she alone had to get Derrick out of that desert town. If possible, she'd get Miriam too. Rebekah and Anna only if it didn't cause any delay. The others? Well, the others were on their own.

Most likely, she'd only extract Derrick, and there was a good chance he'd make the trip unconscious because he would not willingly leave the others. She didn't like using violence, but one must do what is required sometimes. That was a concept rooted in her worldview, not because she wanted it, but because it was reality. Otherwise, she wouldn't be alive to save Derrick in the first place.

Without a checklist, without a warmup, L. Linda blazed out of the warehouse at a speed no one would have recommended. Leaving the roll-up door open, which posed risks of its own, she pointed the aircraft straight up and out of the canyon, then flew close to the ground. She couldn't stay at this low altitude above populated areas, but she didn't want to be spotted close to the hidden canyon. She saw enough to understand why Derrick didn't want anyone to know about it.

If there had been more time, perhaps they could have found a way she could communicate with Red. This rescue would have been easier if they also had communication with Derrick. This was flying blind. Well, not blind. She could see outside the aircraft using several methods, including sonar, radar, and infrared, all with telescopic enhancement. Still, blind in the sense that she didn't know where Red was or how he was doing and until she saw the jumbo plane, picking up its passengers. If there was no plane, she'd know they didn't make it.

If she found the town—too many ifs for her way of thinking. She didn't like it.

Just focus on the objective, she thought. *Get Derrick out alive. Then go from there.*

L. Linda did not understand it would prove more complicated than it sounded.

* * *

Red keyed the microphone, "Antonio, you'd better come up here."

Antonio said, "For the last time, I'm not getting out."

"It's Charlie. Something's wrong with him."

A moment later, Antonio appeared at the cockpit door. "What's wrong? We should be in the air."

Red nodded. "A minute ago, Charlie sounded weird. Then he said it wasn't him but Akira. He broke that," Red pointed, "on purpose because he didn't want to fly the plane. He can fly the plane, but he's been lying about it."

Antonio stepped behind Charlie, touching his shoulder. "Hey, buddy. What's happening? We need to leave. If you can fly the plane, that would be best, but we need to go."

Charlie raised his head. "I cannot. I'm not safe, and I'm getting worse."

Red said, "Explain it to us. Maybe we can help."

"You can't help. Akira, part of her at least, got stuck in my memory. Memories, but mostly emotions. I cannot process emotions. At first, they were floating, but they found each other somehow. I tried to file them, but they won't stay put. Akira—the part inside me—is sad. There are scared parts, parts I think you call love, a few happy parts, but mostly sad. She's, I think the word is, despondent."

"How despondent?" Red asked.

"Self-destructive."

"Suicidal?" Antonio asked.

"Yes. I fear she might force me to fly into a mountain. I can't control it. I may have to shut down."

Red said, "Akira has been saying she doesn't feel right. She certainly isn't acting normal."

"Can you fix her, Charlie? Get both of you back in the treatment machine, perhaps." Antonio said.

"I do not know. Everything I did was untested. This is my fault. Everything is my fault." Charlie hung his head, making the crying-like noise again.

Red looked at Antonio.

Antonio shook his head.

Red put his hand on Charlie's shoulder. "Charlie and Akira, if you can hear me, we need to go. You're going to be okay. We gotta get Miriam and Derrick, plus an entire town of people. But as soon as we get back, we'll get you two to treatment and get this fixed. Okay? I'm going to fly the plane. I need Charlie to help. Can you do that? Can you let Charlie help?"

Antonio added, "We all love you, Akira." He paused, "You too, Charlie. We're going to make this right. Somehow."

Charlie looked at Red and then turned to Antonio. "You promise?"

Simultaneously Red and Antonio said, "Promise."

And with that, Charlie's light grew a little brighter. "Captain, you are cleared for takeoff."

Antonio said, "I'm headed to my post."

Charlie provided a steady list of monotone instructions, which Red followed to prepare for takeoff. The familiarity of the terms and Charlie's monotone voice calmed Red a little. Charlie's dialog would be meaningless had Red not played the C17 computer simulation at Jimmy Priest's house. Perhaps the computer experience wasn't a complete waste of time.

Lined up on the runway, or at least where Red assumed the sand concealed it. He took a deep breath and thought about something Coach Browning had said once. *"The guy lined up across from you is just as talented and determined as you are. He might be stronger, more experienced, and meaner too. The only way to win each snap is to believe you can. If you believe you can't, you'll be right 100% of the time."*

That's why Red believed he could pilot this aircraft. Doubting himself meant they'd all die. "Ready for takeoff?"

Antonio's voice came over the headset. "Loadmaster ready."

Charlie said, "Co-pilot ready."

With that, Red pushed the throttle forward. The plane moved and then sped up, jolting them as it swayed over the sand-covered runway.

The speed indicator spun as the massive jet accelerated. Watching where he was going seemed unnecessary because there was plenty of desert between them and the mountains, and he couldn't tell the difference between the runway and the desert. When they reached take-off velocity, Red engaged the flight control system to raise the nose of the aircraft, pressing him into the seat. Everything disappeared except the sky. Red lost orientation with the ground but focused on the aircraft's instruments.

Charlie said, "The trajectory of the aircraft is too shallow. We will hit the mountains in 45 seconds. Increasing the climb rate is recommended."

Red's heart pounded in his chest. The once distant mountains grew increasingly large. He pulled up on the yoke, and the nose of the jet rotated skyward. He breathed easier, confident they would miss the mountains at this angle.

Charlie said, "Airspeed too slow. Aircraft will stall in 35 seconds. Recommend increasing speed."

Red reached for the thrust control and missed it. Fumbling for the lever, he found it and increased the thrust. With the thrust of the four jet engines, the ground grew distant below them.

"Adverse flight conditions resolved," Charlie said.

They were airborne.

Red leveled the plane. "Are we good, Charlie?"

Charlie said, "Yes. Flight deck 6,153 feet, airspeed 375 knots."

Red said into his microphone. "This is your Captain. Rescue One is airborne and en route to extraction."

16

ATWOOD HAD TURNED AN UNPLEASANT SHADE of ashen gray when he heard Cliff Haskins was the Commander of the military. Derrick assumed this Haskins fellow was more ruthless than most to cause such an adverse reaction in Atwood, who, until now, seemed unflappable. Troubling because Prime was problem enough.

Derrick looked at Harley. "Are all your people ready to go?"

"Getting there," Harley said.

"What do you plan to do with the two soldiers?" Miriam asked.

Harley said, "They're in the jail." He shrugged. "I guess they can just stay put."

Rebekah said, "I thought you were going to destroy the town."

"Yep. It will go up like the biggest bonfire ever."

Atwood said, "We aren't going to kill those boys."

Harley said, "They'd kill us given a chance."

Atwood said, "We aren't them."

"Then what should we do with them?"

Atwood said, "We could release them when we leave. They can join up with their mates when they arrive."

Derrick said, "That's just another way to kill them. Prime won't reward them for letting us escape."

Miriam said, "There's no guarantee we have a way out."

"She has a point," Harley said, and then added, "I'm not convinced you have a schoolmate who can fly a transport plane. If he gets it off the ground, and if he lands it without crashing, I still don't give us high odds of a successful escape."

Derrick said, "He'll be here, and you'll be fine."

Atwood said, "I'm not leaving. Lloyd, you go with the others."

Nist stared at Atwood. "And just what do you intend to do?"

"Stay here. I have to see Cliff. It might be my last opportunity," Atwood said.

Nist said, "And what do you hope to accomplish?"

Atwood shrugged. "I'll try to convince him to come with me."

Nist shook his head. "That will not happen. Better to give Haskins more time."

Atwood said, "If we are successful in our escape, he won't have time. Prime will kill him."

Rebekah said, "Back to the soldiers. What are you going to do with them?"

Harley said, "Well, we can't take them with us. We can turn them loose, wish them the best of luck."

Derrick said, "Why not ask them what they want?"

Harley glared at Derrick. "Are you crazy?"

Atwood looked at Harley. "No harm in asking them. Have someone bring them here."

Derrick said, "Give them civilian clothing and bring their uniforms."

Harley stared.

Atwood nodded. "Not a bad idea."

Harley said, "Mind filling me in? I lost something in the translation."

Atwood said, "We could take them with us, and then when we land, they can go their separate ways. Go home, go start a new life, whatever."

Derrick said, "And I need a uniform." He looked at Atwood. "I'm not going with the others. Maybe I could help you with this, Haskins guy, but I don't understand why you want to speak with him."

Atwood said, "He's, my son."

Rebekah said, "That's awkward. Does he know you're here?"

"He only just learned that he has a father—other than the man who raised him—a few hours ago." Atwood looked at Derrick. "You need to go with your friends. I'll be fine."

"I'm not staying because of you. I have other work to do."

"What other work?" Atwood asked.

Derrick looked at Harley. "You haven't told them?"

"Haven't had a chance."

"Tell us what?" Nist asked.

Derrick said, "There's a New America missile launcher 50 miles south of the border. Prime plans to launch a missile at a New America city to justify starting the war."

"That's crazy," Atwood said.

"He's done it before," Miriam said. She looked at Derrick. "I'm not going either."

Derrick shook his head. "You guys go. I'll handle this."

Anna said, "I'm staying to help Derrick." She glared at Derrick. "It's not open for discussion."

Rebekah said, "Then I'm staying too."

Harley plopped into a chair. "I'm staying. Someone's gotta blow this place up."

Nist said, "This is unacceptable! That means I also must stay."

Atwood said, "Not going to happen. Someone needs to get our people resettled and carry on the mission. You're the only one who can do that."

Nist said, "But…"

Atwood cut him off. "No time to argue."

Derrick said, "Take Doc, Marie, and Mike with you. They have no place to go, and it sounded like you could use a doctor. And I have an additional request."

"What's that?" Atwood asked.

"Don't hold them as prisoners. Let them go if they don't want to stay with you."

Nist nodded. "Works for me."

Todd pushed the door open, and the two soldiers, Plotter and Evans, shuffled into the room, dressed in faded t-shirts and jeans, hands and feet bound with zip ties. Todd tossed the uniforms on a nearby counter.

Derrick said, "Cut them loose."

Todd said, "You don't give orders here."

Harley gave a halfhearted wave. "Just do it."

When the boys were free, Derrick motioned them into chairs. "We have little time. A plane is coming to get everyone. We must decide what to do with you two. We could leave you behind and you can surrender to the military, but I don't recommend it. It would be a death sentence."

"How do you figure?" Evans asked.

"You were assigned to watch us. They will blame you that we escaped."

Evans said, "If you get away."

Derrick remained impassive. "We will, and you won't last long if the military finds you."

"What are our options?" Plotter asked.

"You can go with the town's people, and they will release you when the plane lands. You can go wherever you want. Go home. Go someplace new. Start a new life."

Plotter said, "If I had a place to go, I wouldn't have joined the military. I don't want to kill people in Mexico."

Evans said, "I don't have anywhere to go either."

"You can go anywhere together. Start a new life. Trust me, it's possible," Derrick said.

"Why can't we stay with you guys?" Plotter asked.

Derrick said, "You mean with the people who live here?"

Plotter nodded.

"Not my decision, but I doubt that's a possibility." Derrick paused. "Trust. It would be difficult for them to trust you. What's to say you wouldn't give their location up, hoping for leniency for yourselves?"

Plotter swallowed. "I understand." He looked at Atwood. "Please, sir. My brother joined the Resistance after I enlisted in the military. Had I known he was going to do that, I would have stayed at home and tried to help him. He's the only family I have left. You can keep me locked up until you verify my story."

Atwood looked at both boys and then at Nist. "What do you say, Wizard? It's your show now."

Nist said, "Don't talk like that. You'll find us, Corbin. We'll start over together." Then Nist studied Plotter and Evans. "I don't know. What do you think, Harley?"

"You're asking me? I'm just a kid myself."

Nist nodded, not an agreement sort of nod, but an 'I'm sad to hear you say that' sort of nod.

Harley stood and walked around the soldiers. When he stopped, he stared at Atwood and then Nist for a moment. Then he leaned down, staring Plotter in the face. "If you do anything to hurt the people of this town, I'll hunt you down and kill you. Do you understand?"

Plotter nodded.

Harley turned to Evans, but before he could say anything, Evans said, "I understand, and I won't let you down."

Harley straightened, pausing for a moment. "Well, shit. Let's give them a chance."

Derrick smiled.

Nist said, "Harley, when this is over, remind me it's high time I let you sample my beer."

Harley said, "I won't forget. Time to get everyone to the vehicles." He looked at Derrick and added, "That plane should land any second."

17

THE C-17 WAS ON COURSE TO THE RESCUE SITE. Red took a deep breath. The rushing air from the vent Charlie had busted cooled his face. He wished Miriam and Akira knew they were airborne, but he had no way of communicating with them. Not that the Base didn't have communications, but because they did not have time to determine if New America military personnel could monitor their radio traffic. The radios still worked despite being abandoned for decades. Charlie was responsible for that. When he reactivated—after his supervisor, mentor, and creator did not return—Charlie took it upon himself to continue Jacob Truman's work. Charlie also made many parts of the Base operational, including aircraft. Had Charlie not done that, they would not be flying, and the others wouldn't have a chance. Thirty-three years ago, had Charlie docked as usual, he would not have reactivated. Had Derrick not punched Marcus Carver, they would all be in Potterville right now, dying of radiation exposure.

So many events had happened by chance, but those events now gave Red an opportunity to save an entire town, but only if he could land and get the plane back in the air.

How many chances were left? Perhaps all the luck had been used up getting this far. Red sensed good fortune was running out.

"Landing gear up?" Charlie asked in a calm voice.

"Shit. I forgot," Red said, turning to Charlie and giving him a weak smile. The landing gear doors clunked as they closed. "Yes. I mean, Roger. They are up now."

"Who is Roger?" Charlie asked.

"It means yes. I don't know if military people actually say it. I heard in a movie."

"We are not in a movie."

"True, but I like saying it," Red said.

"Understood. I suggest we descend to a lower altitude. My research indicates we might avoid radar detection. Plus, we don't have far to fly by aeronautical standards."

Red descended to the elevation Charlie had determined was best. "I want to fly in straight over the main street and land. We should have enough room to land and take off. Let's hope they are ready to load. I don't want to be there when the military shows up."

Charlie said, "Roger, Captain."

Antonio's voice came over the headset. "Can I assume we made it, or is this just where I'm stuck in the afterlife?"

Red smiled. "We are A-OKAY and en route. Just be ready on that bay door."

Antonio said, "Will do."

"Roger."

Antonio asked, "Who's Roger?"

Red said, "That's what you say if you mean yes. You say, Roger."

"Like in the movies?" Antonio asked. "What do I say if I mean no?"

Red looked at Charlie.

Charlie said, "Say negative, Loadmaster Morales."

Antonio laughed, "Roger that, Co-pilot, Charlie. We got to give you a last name, Charlie."

Charlie said, "I would like that."

18

FOR THE PAST 45 MINUTES, THE SILENCE HAD been deafening. Nyx and Akira stared at the monitors. Nyx wished Charlie were here. At least he gave her someone to talk with. In the monitor's reflection Akira's face appeared, stonelike to the extent she hardly resembled the girl Nyx knew. Nyx wanted to say something but feared another verbal assault. So, she said nothing.

Finally, Nyx could stand it no longer. "Are we still jamming the satellite?"

Akira said, "You're not jamming anything."

Nyx sighed. "Is the satellite still jammed?"

"Yes."

"Radios?"

"Also, yes."

Well, so much for conversation, not that she expected much, but a few words would have been nice. Nyx took a deep breath, trying to think of a question that couldn't be answered yes or no. That should not have been difficult, but she drew a blank and made a statement instead. "I hope they made it. I wish we had communication with them. It's killing me not knowing. Yet, if things don't go as planned, I'm not sure I can handle knowing."

Nothing.

"I'm thinking about dropping out when this is done."

Akira looked at her. Glared was a more accurate description and then turned back to the monitor.

Nyx said, "I'm exhausted. No sleep, in I don't know how long. I'm going to make myself a coffee."

When Nyx left, Akira was still staring at the monitor, hardly acknowledging her leaving. Nyx thought about getting a soda instead of coffee, but her last soda had tasted metallic, so she stayed with her original choice. The expresso machine took a few moments to heat, during which she ground fresh coffee, which had kept remarkably well in the vacuum-seal bags. The aroma carried her to a better place, but only for a second or two. She made fresh milk, if one could call it fresh when made with powder and added chocolate. Although it felt like a waste of time, she made Akira one as well, not because she thought one mocha would change how Akira felt, but because Akira needed to be alert if the others needed her help.

They need Akira, not me. No one needs me, Nyx thought.

When Nyx returned, she slid a steaming cup in front of Akira.

"What's this?" Akira asked.

"A mocha."

"I didn't ask for a mocha."

"True. And I didn't ask if you wanted anything, but I made you one. Drink it or not, doesn't matter."

Akira didn't move for several minutes, but eventually she picked up the mug and sipped. "Thanks."

"No worries. You need to stay sharp in case they need help."

"I'm okay."

"I didn't say that you were not."

Akira sipped and then set the mug on the workstation. "What did you mean about dropping out?"

Nyx shrugged. "I don't know. Everything. School, student council, track. Everything."

"Why would you do that?"

Nyx drank but didn't respond for a few minutes. "I'm kidding myself. I shouldn't be making decisions with the council. The council affects people's lives. I'm not qualified to do that. I can run at the high school level, but I won't be able to compete in college. If I'm not going to college, there's no reason to be in high school. Mom works two jobs trying to keep me happy. I'll get a job, so she doesn't have to work so hard. Soon as I'm able, I'll move out. She doesn't want me there."

Akira spun around to look at her. "I'm the one with the scrambled brain. What's your excuse?"

"No excuse. I'm just accepting reality."

"I must have been in the treatment chamber when this new reality happened. Fill me in."

Now it was Nyx's turn to stare at the monitor. "You know. You were always too nice to say anything. I appreciate how you tried to spare my feelings, but I've accepted it now. Time to move on before I do more damage."

"What in the hell are you talking about?"

"I killed my dad, and you know it."

19

RED ALTERNATED BETWEEN SCANNING THE instruments and the landscape. Lacy-white clouds slid by just outside the cockpit. As the plane banked, the ground below them filled the right-hand windows. Blue sky filled the windows on the left. After a few moments, he completed the turn and proceeded due west. He had been flying the massive aircraft for 20 minutes, and it had not fallen from the sky. They were on a direct approach to the desert town from the east, and the highway was directly below them. It occurred to him that in a perfect world, he would feel confident.

But it wasn't a perfect world, and that fact circulated in Red's mind like a whirlpool in a toilet. Round and round. Earlier, he had convinced himself that he could fly this aircraft because he'd played a few games on a computer. He had also persuaded himself that his purpose to save the others was pure of heart. Now he felt equally sure he could neither pilot the aircraft nor that his reasons were noble—what a bunch of crap.

To be truthful, he didn't know what he had been thinking.

Charlie was the reason the plane was on course. However, Charlie had said nothing since the last path corrections. Red glanced at Charlie every few seconds. Charlie was not only silent. It was as if Charlie had died. Only the faint glow of his effervescent-blue eyes indicated he was still operational, at least to some degree. Red wanted to say something but feared Akira's memories or emotions were causing Charlie's eerie silence. Plus, Red didn't want to deal with Akira. He had hurt her enough already.

Red wanted to help Akira. Or perhaps he was just trying to soothe his conscience because he was responsible for almost killing her, and although Charlie had saved her, it seemed as if neither Charlie nor Akira would ever be well again.

So, why were they 5000 feet over the desert somewhere in Arizona or Southern California? Charlie would know their location, but Red didn't ask. This question, among many questions, occupied Red's thinking the most. And the answer wasn't what Red wanted to believe or admit, but it was there just the same, and it wasn't a good reason to risk Antonio or Charlie.

Red wasn't here only to help. He was trying to fill a deep void in his own life. Red's father had left when Red was in the first grade. He didn't say why.

He didn't even say goodbye. Red went to the kitchen to eat breakfast that morning, unlike other kids who hated mornings, especially school days. He loved them because it was about the only time he saw his father.

He and his father ate breakfast together every morning.

Until that morning. The day before Red's seventh birthday.

That morning, his father wasn't at the breakfast table. No bowl of cereal was waiting for Red either. Instead, his mother was there crying. She rarely joined them for breakfast. His mother never told him where his father had gone. She just said, "You're fixin' your own breakfast from now on. Eat and go to school." And with that, she left the room.

About a year later, his mother remarried. This man was nothing like his father. His life did not improve.

Red had been trying to fit in ever since.

Jimmy Priest befriended Red shortly after that, which didn't help Red's social standings. So, this wasn't about bravery, duty, or even being a team player. It was about trying to prove he was worthy. Getting people killed wouldn't improve his feelings of inadequacy unless he died along with everyone else.

That was the best he could hope for.

"Do you see it?" Charlie asked.

Red leaned forward. "See what? The road? Yes, we've been flying over it for ten minutes."

"Not the road, the town."

Red squinted. "Is that what it is?"

Charlie said, "If you cannot see the town, you probably cannot see the 15 military vehicles headed toward it."

"Crap. How far are they from the town?"

Charlie calculated. "Ten miles."

Red took a deep breath. Feeling sorry for himself would not get this done. The aircraft accelerated. "Hang on."

"We should reduce speed," Charlie said.

"No time for that. How close can you estimate the altitude we must be to not hit a building with the landing gear extended?"

Charlie said, "Not remarkably close, I'm afraid. You'll need to be 2017 feet above sea level."

"That seems extremely low."

"The town is at 1988 feet above sea level."

Red said, "Understood. What is the margin of error?"

Charlie said, "Our velocity is increasing. You should slow down for landing. Unless you've changed your mind."

Red said, "You haven't answered my question. What is our margin of error?"

"I can only estimate 99.5% accuracy at this speed and distance."

"What's .5% of 2017?"

"Approximately 10 inches.

"Close enough. Be ready to lower the landing gear on my mark."

"On your mark?" Charlie asked.

"When I tell you."

"Very well. Are we going to slow down?"

"At some point, yes. I can see them now. Looks like they are stopped except for one vehicle going on ahead. Can you see how many people and what weapons the first vehicle has?"

"I see three heat signatures. There is a .50 cal. machine gun mounted. One heat signature is at the gun."

"By heat signature, I assume you mean person."

"That is correct."

"Three thousand feet."

The jet blasted over the convoy, 1100 feet overhead. Red keyed the microphone. "Loadmaster. Be ready and hang on. This is going to be a hard landing."

Antonio said, "Roger. What's happening? It feels like we sped up and then descended."

"Roger that. Going in hot because there's military just outside of town." Red paused. "Antonio, thanks for being here. It means a lot to me. I wish I could tell you this is going to work out."

Antonio cut him off. "Just land the friggin' plane. No time for getting all teary-eyed."

Red said, "Now, Charlie."

Charlie said, "Landing gear down."

"Hang on." Red descended, cutting the throttle, raising the nose, and lifting the flaps, which felt as if he'd hit the brakes, thrusting himself and Charlie forward. The safety harnesses held them tight. The buildings rushed by below them. At the edge of town, the tires smacked the road, bounced once, and then Red applied the brakes, extended all the flaps, and engaged the reverse thrusters, gluing the aircraft to the asphalt.

Twisting in his chair, Charlie said, "I believe you damaged a chimney."

"I'll send them a check."

Red keyed his microphone. "Lower the ramp."

"We are still moving," Antonio said.

"Lower it! We'll be stopped soon enough. Then get those people on board."

When the massive plane stopped moving, Charlie said, "Are you okay, Captain?"

"Am I still alive?"

"Yes, sir. You appear to be."

"Then I'm great. Why do you ask?"

"I understand why they call you Red, but at the moment, you are extremely pale."

"Is it a good look on me?"

"Not particularly."

"I'll get some sun when this is over."

Charlie made a weird clicking sound. "I believe you made a funny."

Red looked at Charlie with a slight smile and keyed the mic. "How's it going, Antonio?"

"I got an incoming bus with four pickup trucks following. They have people crammed as tight as possible."

"Do you see Derrick or Miriam?"

"I do not. They must be in the bus."

Antonio had just secured the bus when something smacked its rear bumper. He ran around the bus and studied the bumper but saw nothing unusual. Then, another clank and a hole appeared. Glancing toward town, he saw the Humvee coming fast.

Antonio waved his arm for the next truck. The Humvee was still some distance. Sand drifts caused it to bounce, making it hard for the guy with the machine gun, but someone was bound to get hit by the bullets spraying the airplane.

Antonio motioned people out of the vehicles and hollered, "Take cover!"

People scrambled from the bus and pickups, pressing themselves into nooks or using the vehicles as shields.

The second truck hit the ramp and then the third.

Antonio keyed his radio. "Red, get us out of here. They are shooting at us!"

A blast of hot gas from the jets caused dirt to boil behind the C17. The plane started to move. The ramp dragged on the asphalt, covering the last pickup with a shower of sparks.

Antonio raised the ramp a few inches. The fourth truck was just a few feet from the plane but could not get on. The jet was speeding up. Antonio lowered the ramp, and it hit the ground, showering the truck with sparks again. Antonio bumped the control, the ramp just inches off the ground now. He waved frantically for the truck, but it was losing ground.

Antonio hollered into the microphone. "Slow down. We still have a truck to load."

The plane slowed more than a little. Perhaps massive jets do nothing in small increments. The truck's front tires hit the ramp, launching it a few inches into the air. When its rear tires contacted the ramp, it rocketed forward, smacking into the back of the truck in front of it. Antonio pushed the up switch, raising the ramp. Bullets were now striking the aircraft at a steady rate.

Antonio screamed into his microphone. "GO, GO, GO!"

He had not secured the vehicles and wasn't exactly certain how it was done. However, two young guys started doing it before Antonio could react. They seemed to know what they were doing, so he let it go. The aircraft pivoted skyward. Antonio grabbed a nearby railing, holding on tight.

Charlie said, "They are shooting at us."

"That's not nice," Red said.

"It is not. Technically, this is not our aircraft. Fortunately, the QR-3 robots can repair it."

"I feel better already."

Charlie said, "Unfortunately, we cannot clear the bluff in front of us."

Red said, "Tell me something I don't know."

* * *

L. Linda had pointed the Prime aircraft southwest in the general direction of the desert town. From 40,000 feet, she used the tele optics, hoping to spot the place. She saw scattered towns. A few looked abandoned, many did not. None looked like the place where Prime had Derrick trapped. She should have paid closer attention to the GPS coordinates. That was a stupid mistake, and mistakes, stupid or otherwise, get people killed. When she saw mountains again, she concluded she had flown too far north and east.

That's why she wasn't there to provide protection.

When she arrived, L. Linda saw a giant jet lifting off, smoke trailing from one engine. She scanned the town, surprised to see the heat signatures of several people still there. Perhaps they didn't have time to get on the plane. She brought her aircraft around for a better look at those few souls who remained there for what purpose—she couldn't imagine.

She saw a man running across a street, followed by another. Too far out to recognize anyone, but she was sure she knew neither of them. Derrick and Miriam had a certain way of walking. She could recognize it. It was a walk that came with training that turned people into lethal weapons. Part muscle tone and balance, but mostly an attitude of superiority that the individual seldom recognized in themselves.

Suddenly, the optical system fluttered, losing focus, returning, and then flickering again. *Jamming the satellites. Good work, Akira.*

* * *

Had he gotten to know Derrick on a more personal level, which would never happen because they were not friends, Red would have learned they shared something—the ability to slow stuff down. Although Red wasn't a Test Subject, had not been trained since early childhood like Derrick, and could not slow things to the same extent, he still had some ability to do so. That's what happened next.

Charlie said, "The aircraft cannot clear the plateau. You must land immediately."

"I can see that, and no can do. Military. Bullets. Remember?"

"But we will crash. She is frightened, and I don't know how to help her."

"Who? Akira? The one in your head?"

Charlie said, "Yes."

Red said, "I got this, Akira."

In a softer voice than usual, Charlie said, "I trust you, Red."

In his normal voice, Charlie said, "We cannot make it."

Red said, "Hang on." Keying the radio, Red said, "Loadmaster. Get everyone clear of the vehicles and make sure no one is on the plane's left side."

Red did not wait for a response from Antonio. There wasn't time. Before the jet lifted off, Red already knew it would not clear the plateau. He already knew what he must do. He had done this same maneuver in the simulator. Not the real simulator at the Base, but on Jimmy's computer game. He'd attempted it many times.

He learned it flying fighter jets. Not real fighter jets, computer fighter jets. Computer fighter jets could perform this maneuver.

Cargo planes could not. Game over.

Red didn't have a choice. He had to make it work.

he had done it before—once—on a computer game.

Red increased the throttle and banked hard left. The jet rotated 90 degrees. Red expected a significant bump when the vehicles fell against the side of the cargo bay, but it did not happen. Either Antonio did a miraculous job of securing the cargo, or Red's understanding of physics was worse than he thought.

Warning bells filled the cockpit, and red lights appeared all over the instrument panel. At least that part was the same as the computer game.

Charlie said, "The aircraft is not capable of this maneuver."

"Landing gear up!"

Red heard the landing gear retracting. He should have told Charlie to do that sooner. This was going to be close, even if he was successful. If he was not, everything would end suddenly.

An odd thought occurred to Red. What would happen to Charlie? He might not die like the rest of them. Perhaps Charlie would remain aware but be scattered in pieces, unable to move. Just lying there waiting for his power to run out? This new body did not need recharging daily. Part of Akira would remain with Charlie. Alone and afraid.

Red returned the jet to a horizontal position, but still in a steep climb with the thrust at full power, pressing him into the captain's chair. Glancing over, he saw Charlie staring straight ahead, gripping the edges of his seat, the hard composite material breaking in his grip. Red hollered, "It's going to be close."

A thud sounded.

The jet shuddered.

* * *

The Humvee that had been shooting at the cargo jet circled back toward town. The convoy, still miles out, was moving forward. L. Linda didn't check to see if Red cleared the plateau because it was certain he would not, and she didn't want to see it. Her anger grew because she could have prevented it had she been here sooner. She had pinned her hope on Derrick King. Not just Derrick, but Miriam and Anna as well. Three Test Subjects were more than she'd ever dreamed of. Now, it was just her. Jason would help, but she wouldn't allow it. He had already done more than she could have ever imagined, and she would not let him take part in what was certain to be a suicide mission.

Such is life, at least, her life.

Scanning the town again, she spotted a man partially hidden behind a brick building, waving a white flag. That seemed odd. Zooming in, adjusting the focus, she saw the man. He wore a tweed sports coat, which seemed strange given the temperature and the situation. She scanned the shadows, spotting another man concealed in a doorway. Despite the advanced nature of the aircraft's optics, the darkness prevented her from seeing his face. But she didn't need to see his face to know who it was.

Derrick King, what in the hell are you doing?

20

CORBIN ATWOOD WAS A MAN OF SCIENCE, NOT given to rapid-fire, ad hoc decisions, especially when such decisions had a high probability of getting people killed. Circumstances didn't allow for contemplation, research, or debate. The kid who had caused the problems in the first place had dictated the plan, and no one had been able to alter the conversation. That didn't mean Atwood had a better idea. He had none.

So, Atwood conceded Derrick King's plan, although he felt the scheme would fail. At least the rest of the town had gotten away, at least they got on the jet, but he did not see if the plane had cleared the plateau. However, when it came to strategies, Atwood never thought a teenager would fly a military cargo jet here. So, there was that.

But this plan seemed crazier than a teenager piloting a military cargo jet.

It went like this. Atwood would lure his son close to the alley. Just the commander and no others. Atwood doubted his son, Cliff Haskins, would have believed what Stanley Mires, the man Prime called Quigley, had told him. Even if Haskins believed it, there was little reason to think he'd be interested in a father he'd never met.

Then, if he could lure Haskins away from the other soldiers, Atwood merely had to convince the Commander of the New America Military to send the unit away and join the Resistance. Then they'd drive into Mexico, overpower the soldiers guarding the launcher, drive said launcher back across the border, and hide it. Atwood had added disarming the missile as his part of the plan. Derrick made it sound easy. Very matter of fact, like let's meet for lunch tomorrow.

However outrageous Derrick's scheme sounded, Atwood agreed for one reason. It was his only hope to save his son. And he planned to save his son, even if it was only for today.

A young soldier aiming a rifle at Atwood eased across the sand-covered street, sweat streaming down the kid's face. "Keep your hands where I can see them and step into the open."

"Easy, son. I mean you no harm." At the edge of the building, Atwood lifted his arms higher. "I'm unarmed. I need to speak to your commander. Alone."

"That's not going to happen. Now, move into the middle of the street. Last warning."

"Don't do anything rash. I'm unarmed, but that doesn't mean everyone is."

"What does that mean?"

"It means there are rifles trained on you and your commander. We don't want to hurt anyone. I only want to talk to your commander. See if we can strike a deal."

The kid didn't know what to do with that information. "We don't make deals."

Atwood chuckled. "We are Ravagers. That's all we do is make deals. I get it. It's unlikely we have any material things the military needs, but we have valuable information. How about it? Tell your commander the old man wants to have a word with him. That's all. Seems like a fair trade for your lives."

"We can flatten this town if you try anything."

"Be my guest. Save us the trouble."

"What does that mean?"

"Don't you smell that?"

"Yeah. It smells awful, like old gearbox oil."

"Did you notice it's getting stronger?"

The soldier nodded.

"It's not old oil. It's new oil, unrefined, and there's a lot of it. We are routing it through the fire suppression system, giving every inch of these old buildings a thorough coating of oil, diesel, and gasoline. Once we've pumped those 600,000 gallons into the buildings, we will put a match to it. Not an actual match—a bomb. This place will blow sky high, and most of you are within the blast zone."

"I don't believe it. You'll kill yourselves."

Atwood nodded "You're right. But, as I said, we hope to strike a deal. Just contact your commander and tell him I want to talk. No harm in asking, right? His name is Cliff Haskins. Tell him I knew his mother."

The kid looked as if this was the most significant decision he'd ever faced. Keying a microphone attached to his vest, he said, "The guy here wants to talk to Commander Haskins."

Derrick remained hidden in shadow. He had a radio and an earpiece, through which Harley provided an update—most of the unit was in town now, and three of the seven vehicles were atop the defense bombs surrounding the town, buried in the sand.

The soldier said, "He didn't say, but he knows the commander's name. He said he knows Haskins's mother."

Atwood said, "What did he say?"

"They didn't tell me."

Atwood said, "I don't have all day."

"If you haven't noticed, you're surrounded."

"I noticed. But here's the problem. I see what you can do. You can't see what we can do."

"We can call in air support."

"That would be a mistake. They can't get here fast enough," Atwood said.

Atwood impressed Derrick. He sounded more confident than Derrick felt.

Several silent minutes passed. Derrick resisted the urge to peek at Atwood and the soldier. Harley spoke into Derrick's ear. "Someone is walking toward Professor. It must be Haskins. Why would he come here? This is a small operation someone of lower rank could handle. He looks too young to be commanding the entire military. However, the age of these soldiers makes me think they're all just kids."

Derrick couldn't respond, nor could he see what was happening.

"Commander Haskins?" Atwood asked.

"Yes, sir. I'm here to search this town."

"On what premise? We are not the enemy. We are New American citizens."

"You're Ravagers and we have information you are harboring people wanted for high crimes against the country."

Atwood whistled. "Sounds serious. Tell you what. Let us speak privately. I'm sure we can strike a deal."

"Who was on that aircraft, and where did it come from?"

"Man, you ask a lot of questions, and we haven't even started our negotiations."

"We don't negotiate. Just hand over the fugitives. We mean no harm to you."

"Forgive me if I have misgivings about trusting the government. As you might suspect, we're an operation that's —well, let's just say, off the radar. However, we have much to offer you, and I'm certain you'll agree once we've spoken privately."

Haskins didn't reply.

"Come now. You have our little town surrounded. What's the harm of us chatting for a few minutes? If we can't reach an agreement, you go about whatever you intended to do." Atwood paused. "The information I offer might not mean much to you, but Prime would find it extraordinarily valuable."

Haskins hesitated and then looked at the soldier. "Private, return to the Humvee. If I'm not out in 15 minutes, move in."

"Yes, sir."

Derrick heard footsteps shuffling through the sand, more noise than typical. Atwood was exaggerating his movement to ensure Derrick was ready. Unnecessary, but Derrick appreciated Atwood's attention to detail.

Haskins said, "Stop. Where are you going? I did not agree to leave sight of my troops."

Still walking toward Derrick, Atwood said, "I thought speaking in private implied out of earshot and out of sight. I do not know what technology you might have that could allow our conversation to be monitored."

"What difference would that make?"

"I assure you. It will make a great deal of difference."

Derrick could see Atwood now. Haskins was so close Derrick could smell his aftershave and see his shadow. Haskins was close enough, but not yet time. Professor hoped to talk Haskins into going without a fight. Derrick wasn't optimistic.

Atwood stopped. "If it makes you more comfortable, will this do?"

"What is it you're offering?"

"What I have is extraordinarily valuable. It is priceless."

"Nothing is that valuable. Everything has a price."

"Even you?"

"What does that mean? I'm not for sale. I serve my country."

"You serve Prime. The fugitives you are looking for are children. Have you given any thought to why Prime is afraid of three kids?" Atwood waited for a response, but Haskins said nothing. "Cliff, I offer you a new life. A new beginning and a better way."

"I'm happy with my life. If you haven't noticed, I've done rather well."

Atwood said, "Indeed. I'm proud of you. But I was even prouder when you contacted the Resistance. Quigley told you about Prime's plan to justify a war with Mexico by bombing New America."

Haskins didn't respond right away. "You shouldn't say things like that. Even an accusation would put me under investigation."

"Does that mean they are monitoring our conversation?"

"They are not. They can't."

"Why not?"

"Our radios are not working properly. Do you know anything about that?"

"Perhaps, but we don't have much time."

Haskins said, "True. Besides, you know nothing about me."

"Oh, but I do. I know a great deal about you."

"I don't believe you. This is all some sort of trick."

"Son, this is no trick."

"Don't call me son. You call me Commander Haskins."

"I'll do no such thing. I refuse to call my son, commander. This isn't how I hoped we'd meet. Cliff, I'm your biological father."

21

L. LINDA COUNTED THE HEAT SIGNATURES, representing people remaining in the desert town. She knew one was Derrick. One was the man in a tweed suit. The other a soldier of some high rank, she assumed. In addition, she counted four others. Anna, Rebekah, Miriam, and someone unknown. Why were they still there? It made little sense.

Not that L. Linda didn't want to know what happened to the cargo jet. She did. Spectators were drawn to disaster like moths to a flame, bees to a flower. People couldn't resist. Car accident, fire, or fight, it was all the same. They pretended it was awful, yet they stared at it. L. Linda understood. She had the same instinct, but she had seen enough horror for a lifetime.

Resisting the urge wasn't difficult.

It was for that very reason she had taken on the persona of L. Linda Maxton, a person who did not exist in any universe, including this one. But she liked it. More than liked it, she loved it.

Of course, it could not last. Soon L. Linda would have to die. Her true self was required. Her true self would not likely survive, and she was okay with that. If her enemy was destroyed, she would die happy. That was all that mattered.

That Derrick, Miriam, and Anna were still alive increased her odds of success. They might die also, and she regretted that, especially Derrick, but she couldn't change the situation any more than she could prevent the sun from rising in the east.

But she was still human.

So, she activated the rearview camera to see the cargo jet wreckage. Just for a moment. No need to dwell on it.

But the wreckage wasn't there. She scanned the plateau. Nothing. *How in the hell did you do that, Red?*

22

FLYING OVER THE VAST CALIFORNIA desert, Red thought about how little he'd seen of the world. It seemed odd this thought came to his mind, and he could have contemplated his lack of travel to a greater extent if it were not for the slow but steady loss of hydraulic pressure displayed in one of several gauges. Charley had not mentioned it, so it was probably nothing.

Red's heartbeat had slowed, his breathing near normal again. The takeoff was anything but easy. The sand-covered road had looked flat, but it was not. Accelerating toward the mountains, the jumbo jet jerked and shuddered, making it difficult to hold the controls. Red had put the aircraft into a steep climb but intuitively knew they could not clear the plateau, so he tried a maneuver he had only completed once successfully, and only on a computer game. The vehicles should have toppled to the side of the aircraft, ensuring his attempt would fail, but he never felt the cargo shift. He did not understand how Antonio secured the vehicles so fast. Red wasn't sure Antonio even knew how to, but somehow, the load had not moved, and Red had pulled off the impossible.

Red looked for a place to land so they could get people off and return to the Base. "See anywhere to land?"

Charlie said, "Negative. I've been watching our instruments. I've noticed a drop in hydraulic pressure."

"I noticed that too. Is it a problem?"

"At the rate we are losing pressure, it will be a problem in 93 minutes and 11 seconds."

"Then we'd better land soon."

"Roger that," Charlie said, and then added, "I love saying Roger."

Red gave Charlie a slight smile. They passed over a small town. Not much there to speak of but not abandoned like the place they had just left. A few green round fields indicated farming activity. More brown circles revealed even more failed operations. A lone highway extended into the distance. "This highway looks promising."

Charlie peered ahead. "It does. However, might I suggest the airstrip?"

Red craned his neck. "I don't see an airstrip."

"It's coming up. On our left. Ease to the left about ¼ mile off the highway."

Red banked left, then straightened. "Almost perfect. You can make minor adjustments when the strip comes into view."

"Glad you're with me, Charlie."

"I'm pleased to be of assistance."

"Are there planes on the airstrip?"

"None visible. Perhaps in the hangars."

In the distance, Red saw the airstrip. Not an airport. It occurred to him that people flew small planes to airstrips like this at one time. The country must have been so different back then whenever—'back then' existed.

Keying the microphone, Red said, "Loadmaster."

Antonio replied, "Loadmaster, here."

"We're landing momentarily. Be ready to unload. Have you spotted Derrick and the others?"

"Negative. It's been a little crazy back here."

"Understood. Great job securing the vehicles."

"Don't thank me. Two guys jumped on it immediately. They knew what they were doing, and from your flying, it was a good thing they were on board."

The landing strip was suddenly much closer than Red had expected. It wasn't perfect, but it was in better condition than landing on the sand-covered road.

Charlie said, "Airspeed is too fast."

"I see that," Red said.

"Perhaps we should abort and come back around."

"Too risky. People have spotted us. We just don't know who. We've got to get these people off the plane and get back in the air ASAP."

"Still a little too fast."

"We'll make it."

"There might not be enough runway."

"Hang on."

Charlie said, "A safety harness secures me."

The plane bounced once and then hit hard. Red engaged the braking systems, forcing the plane to remain in contact with the surface. Not great, but they were still in one piece. However, the end of the runway was approaching faster than the aircraft was slowing. The fence disappeared under the nose of the plane, followed by the sound of twisting metal, and then the jet stopped dead. "Shit. I hope the landing gear isn't damaged" Speaking into the microphone, Red said, "Antonio, get those folks off the plane. I'm on my way."

Antonio said, "First truck is already moving. The same guys who secured the vehicles are working fast."

Red looked at Charlie. "Stay put. Run the checklist. I'm going down to see Derrick and the others, check the landing gear, and figure out how we'll get turned around."

Charlie said, "I should come with you."

"Negative."

"But I may be of some help." Charlie paused. "I am eager to see Miriam. Does that seem odd? Because I'm a robot?"

"Not odd at all. We're all excited to be together again."

"Then I should come."

"Negative."

"Why do you not want me to come?"

"Duh. Robot." Red smiled. "Explaining why kids are flying an ancient United States military jet will be difficult enough. Explaining you would be impossible."

A Derrick King Novel, Book 6

23

AKIRA SAT, STARING AT THE COMPUTER monitor, saying nothing.
Nyx understood. Nyx had never told anyone about her responsibility regarding
her father's death. She hoped maybe finally telling someone might help. It
didn't. And Akira didn't react. She said nothing. Maybe Akira already knew.
Knew all along but was too polite to confront her about it. That was probably
it.

Nyx didn't want to be here. She didn't feel like being anywhere.

"You didn't kill your father," Akira said, still staring at the monitor.

"I did."

"Your father left. He thought he could give you and your mother a better
life. He was wrong."

"He left because of me," Nyx said, fighting back tears.

"What makes you say that?"

"I was never satisfied. Always whining about something. Clothes, our
house, our food, everything."

"You were just a little girl. Little kids don't understand."

"Had I not been that way, he would not have felt desperate to do
something."

"He loved you. But he was conned. It wasn't your fault."

"You don't know that. You don't know what I was like. You don't know
anything about it."

"Actually, I do."

Nyx glared at her.

"My mother told me about what happened. I didn't want to say anything
because I was afraid it would make you feel worse."

"How could I possibly have felt worse?"

"Knowing about your dad. He wasn't the smartest guy." Akira paused.
"He had talked about becoming Chosen before you were born."

Nyx said nothing for a few minutes. "You're just saying that."

"I'm not. It's true. Everyone knew."

Again, Nyx fell silent. Finally, she said, "So everyone thinks my dad was a
fool. That must mean they think I'm an idiot."

"I should have told you sooner. I knew it made you sad, but I didn't realize how twisted it all was in your head, but I'm going to clear it up right now. All you have to do is listen and believe me. Deal?"

Nyx nodded.

"People loved your dad. He was a good man, but naïve. A preacher came to town and convinced a bunch of people he had a direct connection to the Chosen and could get people there if they trusted him. Once he had identified the followers he could con, he did just that. He convinced them to give him all their money, and he'd get them into a Chosen community. He told them it was a done deal, and the money was just to cover moving expenses."

"And my dad, did it?"

"He did. Then he felt guilty about it. He was the only one who went back to the preacher to ask for his money back."

"I suppose the preacher refused."

"The preacher was gone. Left town. Disappeared. Rumor was that he went to Reno. Your dad went to Reno to get his money back. He called your mom from Reno, so she knew he made it that far. That was the last she heard from him."

"Do you know what happened to him?"

"I don't, but it's one of three things: he found the preacher and the preacher killed him or he didn't get the money back and could not face the humiliation, so he went somewhere to start a new life."

Nyx stared at Akira. "You said three things."

Akira took Nyx's hand. "Number three, he failed and took his own life. I'm sorry. None of those are answers you wanted to hear. Here's the thing. People don't think badly of your dad, and they think the world of you and your mom. Don't feel like you're a burden to your mom. She is so proud of you. You are her world."

Nyx said nothing for a moment. "Thanks for telling me and for being such a good friend." She paused. "For caring."

"I didn't tell you because I care. I'm sorry, but I don't care. I don't feel anything. I'm just flat. Charlie took all my emotions."

Nyx felt a loss for words. "Then why did you tell me all that?"

"Because you had it wrong. I don't like wrong, because that's me right now. Besides, it was time you understood it correctly."

"I see. Well, thanks." And with that, Nyx fell silent again. She had a lot to process. She appreciated what Akira told her. She had always believed her father was either dead or simply left them, but she did not know the reasons. Her mother never told her about the money, and she had been too young to know what her father did outside the home. However, now was a poor time to process the truth about her dad. It was all just too much. She'd been overwhelmed with it all and feeling sorry for herself. Self-centered just like when she was younger, complaining about things to her parents. She was never satisfied. That wasn't a bad trait when it came to track. Always striving to be faster, stronger, better. But it would destroy her if she didn't learn to balance the rest of her life.

And the rest of her life sucked at the moment. She was worried sick about Red and Antonio. She didn't know Miriam and Rebekah well, but she was still worried about them. She'd never met Anna but that didn't mean she didn't care. She even worried about Charlie, and he was just a machine.

Then there was Derrick. With him, it was different.

Her feelings for Derrick made little sense. Over the last few weeks, she'd been infatuated and furious with him. But now, she wanted nothing more than to hug him as if she would never let go. She would feel safe and loved, at least for a moment.

For a moment, before she told him it was over between them.

Derrick deserved better.

Akira whispered, "I wish we knew something."

Nyx wasn't sure if Akira wanted a reply or was just talking to herself. Nyx said, "Me too. Are we still jamming the satellite?"

"Yes, but I don't think we can continue much longer."

Nyx said, "Crap. It was a crazy idea in the first place. It won't be difficult for the military to find a cargo jet. They'll shoot it down or track it back here. If they make it back here, which is unlikely."

Akira said, "Sorry I brought it up. You're making me feel worse, and I didn't think that was possible."

"That's me, isn't it? Mom should have named me Debbie Downer."

"What's happened to you? This is not the Nyx I know." She paused. "Are you still angry with me? Look, I'm sorry for what I said earlier"

"You don't need to be sorry. You were just telling the truth. I get it."

Akira turned back to the monitor and said nothing for a few minutes. "What I said was true, but also not true."

"Okay," Nyx said, drawing the word out until it was clear it was not okay.

Akira turned to her. "I'm talking about Derrick."

"Oh. I didn't know we had changed topic."

"More stuff I need to straighten out with you. So, here's the thing. I was mad when Derrick came to town. I had a crush on him clear back in grade school, but he didn't even know I existed. Then he came here and didn't even recognize me, despite helping him in school and trying to flirt, but I'm terrible at that. Flirting that is. I'm a nerd. Then you see him, and it's love at first sight. So, yeah, I was mad and hurt, but not really at you. I was mad at Derrick…"

Nyx cut her off. "I'm sorry Derrick didn't remember you. That must have hurt. He's a jerk sometimes."

"Stop interrupting me. I was mad at Derrick, but mostly I was mad at myself…"

"We all make mistakes…"

"I swear to God if you interrupt me one more time, I'll knock you into next week."

Nyx stifled a giggle, then burst out laughing.

Akira glared at her. "What's so funny?"

"I'm sorry. Nothing. It just struck me as funny. Knock me into next week. Sorry. It's just—I don't know, so much pressure."

"Tell me about it. Try having your brain scrambled."

Nyx stared at Akira. "I'm sorry."

"Stop saying that. Derrick is rubbing off on you."

Nyx nodded. "I've been selfish. I've been absorbed with my problems."

"Well, get a grip," Akira said.

Nyx felt her heart racing. "I can't do it."

"You can't do what?"

Nyx raised her arms. "This! I can't do this. What are we supposed to do? Antonio and Red and even Charlie, in a cargo jet? What were we thinking about letting that happen? They don't have a chance. If they don't crash, the military will shoot them down. An assassin went to Potterville to kill our families. What if Prime or whoever sent the first assassin sends more? What if our families are killed before we get back? What were we thinking about with Derrick and Miriam? Why did we even come here with them?"

"Slow down," Akira said.

Nyx sobbed. "I can't do it. I can't lose my mom and Derr…"

Akira slugged her in the arm. "I said stop it. Falling apart isn't going to change anything, and it isn't helping."

Nyx rubbed her arm. "That hurt."

"When this is over, you can fall apart. But not now. I need you. I'm a mess if you haven't noticed. It's not that I disagree. We could lose everyone. Then it would just be us two remaining to do whatever we need to do about this entire situation."

"But what can *we* do?"

"I don't know, but if we lose everyone, I'm damn sure going to do something."

Nyx continued to rub her arm. "I didn't realize you could hit like that."

"Yeah, well, I can. And I'm going to hit you even harder if I hear you blame yourself for what happened to your father again. That was not your fault. He loved you and was trying to make a better life. He got conned. You may never know what happened, but know this: it's the same people, the same system."

"What do you mean?"

"The same people, person, system who killed your father is trying to kill us. The system is screwed. We've always known it, but we couldn't do anything about it. Sure, we've made Potterville a better place. We've carved out our own small space in the world, but it's small and fragile and probably wouldn't be tolerated if New America found out."

Nyx said, "You're right about that. But they might not let us have our little space after this."

Akira glared at her. "I agree. That's why we must fight back."

The rage in Akira's eyes scared Nyx. "But what can we do?"

"If they take everyone from us, then we take from them.

"What are you saying?" Nyx asked.

Akira's stare grew cold. "I have nuclear missiles."

24

CLIFF HASKINS'S LIFE WAS ABOUT TO CHANGE. He just didn't realize it yet. The change would be unwelcome and involuntary. Commander Haskins might not recognize his days were numbered, or perhaps he did. He knew a cargo jet had lifted off, taking the inhabitants of this settlement with it and would soon learn his small military presence was doomed. In the life of Cliff Haskins, this would prove memorable. If he survived. That was yet to be determined.

Derrick took a step closer. Haskins turned as if to defend himself. It was a natural response, although unwise. Corbin posed no threat. Derrick, on the other hand—

Haskins said, "That's close enough."

"I mean you no harm. It doesn't have to come to that, but you need to come with us."

Haskins chuckled. "Look around, kid. You're surrounded."

Derrick nodded. "True. However, that doesn't give you the advantage that you assume."

Corbin motioned Derrick to stop. "Mr. Haskins, you know about the missile in Mexico. Quigley told you. Help us stop this."

Haskins said nothing.

Allowing Haskins time to mull this over was a luxury they could not afford. Derrick said, "Tell your troops to pull out. Then come with us. That way, no one gets hurt."

"For a kid, you sure talk tough."

Atwood said, "He's giving you good advice. Let's not make this difficult. I'm sure your mother taught you right from wrong, and allowing Prime to start a war is immoral, and if Prime does, you can't be a part of it. Gloria would tell you I'm right."

Sweat ran down Haskins's face. "You don't know my mother."

"Son, I'm your father. You know how that works. Right? I didn't know about you until your stepfather was killed. I attended his funeral. Eric Haskins was my best friend in high school. I was furious when I learned about you. It tore me up that Gloria didn't tell me. I didn't get a chance to be your dad. However, Gloria wasn't wrong. I wouldn't have become a professor. I wouldn't have ended up here. We have done important work in this little town. Now, we are thrust into a situation where we can do something extraordinary. We can prevent a war. Save millions of lives. And we can do it together."

"You're crazy. Even if I believed you, which I don't, how can we stop it?"

Derrick said, "Professor, we need to go."

Atwood nodded. "Cliff, tell your troops to leave. Derrick is right. No need for them to get hurt."

Haskins shook his head. From Derrick's experience, limited as it was, that meant Haskins was not yet swayed, and they were out of time. What Derrick could not predict was Haskins's response following the first explosion. Derrick had been monitoring Harley's transmissions with the control center. One vehicle had stopped on top of a buried explosive. The soldiers had taken up positions behind it. Harley would fire a few rounds into the Humvee, hoping the soldiers would seek alternative cover before he detonated the first bomb.

Haskins might tell his troops to fall back, or he might tell them to attack. The military unit was small, but it was still heavily armed. The town was not. Only Atwood and Harley stayed to join Miriam, Rebekah, Anna, and himself.

Raising his right hand, Derrick said, "Sorry, time's up."

An automatic weapon opened fire from a rooftop. It was a sound like no other, not like the movies. The shots rang out loud, and the bullets whistled through the air until they hit metal. Then a deafening explosion. The ground shook. Atwood ducked. Haskins keyed his microphone attached to his collar as he reached for his gun. Both moves logical but disastrous.

Derrick hit Haskins once, causing him to crumple to the ground.

Atwood caught Haskins before he fell. "That was unnecessary," Atwood said.

Derrick moved behind Haskins, grabbing him underneath both arms. "It *was* necessary. Help me get him to the truck."

Not waiting for Atwood, Derrick dragged Haskins toward the parking garage behind them. Shots rang out from above as Harley fired on the soldiers. Derrick hoped Harley didn't kill any of them. Probably kids like the two on the mountain.

The lack of time and resources prevented the formulation of a plan that guaranteed an effortless exit. Getting Haskins to order the troops' withdrawal was the best-case scenario. But Haskins was unconscious, and the shooting had started. The next option was to shoot their way out. Derrick hated that option, which was Harley's idea.

Derrick and Atwood carried Haskins to one of the two vehicles inside the parking garage. Both were lifted four-wheel-drive pickups with .50-caliber machine guns mounted on tripods. Where they had acquired such weaponry was unknown to Derrick. They had one last chance to avoid this course of action. The odds were low but worth trying.

"We need him awake," Derrick said.

"We should restrain him first," Atwood said.

Derrick shook his head. "We don't have time. Either he stops this, or many people will die, and we could be among the fatalities."

"If he won't cooperate, you'll knock him out again."

"True." Derrick gave Haskins a light slap on the cheek. "Hey. Wake up."

Atwood grabbed Derrick's wrist before he could slap Haskins again. "Stop. Let me do it."

Still cradling Haskins's head, Atwood pulled a small packet from his pocket, tore it open, and waved it under his nose. "Cliff? We need you. Wake up, son."

"What's that?" Derrick asked.

"Ammonium carbonate, Smelling salts." Atwood held it under Derrick's nose.

Derrick jerked away. "Why do you have that?"

Atwood shrugged. "For occasions like this, which seemed like a reasonable expectation given the circumstances."

Haskins shook his head, brushed his hand under his nose, and glanced around, trying to clear his thoughts. "What…"

"I hit you. Sorry. Do you hear all the gunfire? Lots of people are going to die unless you order them to pull out."

Derrick unclipped the microphone from Haskins's shirt, holding it out to him.

Haskins looked at Atwood.

"He's right, son. I know this is a lot to take in but do the right thing. Tell those kids to pull back."

Derrick said, "Tell them to get at least five miles away from town. This place is going up with a big explosion, and no one will want to be closer than that." Technically, the soldiers did not need to go that far for safety, but Derrick did not want the soldiers to see them drive out of town.

Atwood said, "Do it. Like it or not, you're coming with us—no reason for anyone to get killed. Prime is going to kill you if you stay. I will not let that happen. Not today."

Haskins sat up. Keying the microphone, he said, "This is Commander Haskins. Fall back. I repeat, fall back immediately. Get at least five miles from this place as fast as possible. It's going to blow up. They have it rigged." He sat there a moment, thinking, and then keyed the microphone again and said, "It's a suicide mission. Get the hell out of here!"

25

AFTER DESCENDING THE STAIRS, RED WOBBLED, then leaned against the fuselage, trying to calm his nerves. And his stomach. He had believed he could fly the aircraft. Now, he wondered what was wrong with him. He took off and landed. Took off again, pulling a crazy stunt that worked, but crazy just the same, while taking fire from the military. He didn't want to try again. The front landing gear was probably damaged from this less than perfect touch down. Too many risks already.

His luck was bound to run out.

He glanced behind the plane. Two trucks had already backed out, people milled around, waiting for the rest of their friends to unload. Red didn't know where they were, somewhere east of the nameless town he had seen. He didn't even know how long they had been in the air. Everything was a blur.

He could have killed these people.

He could have killed his friends.

Well, they were not friends. Were they?

Feeling as if he could hold whatever was left of breakfast down, he headed toward the ramp. Derrick King was not his friend, but Red was excited to see him, Miriam, and Rebekah. He had not met Rebekah's sister, but he was glad they found her.

Four pickup trucks set on the tarmac as a school bus backed down the ramp. The bus was packed full. People stood in the aisle, even sat on the entry/exit steps used to load and unload. The pickup cabs were crammed with four or five people and another seven or eight sat in the pickup bed. That's probably why he had not spotted Derrick and the others. The bus was too full. That's all it was.

A man wearing a green shirt and a tan corduroy blazer walked toward Red.

Holding out his hand, the man said, "My name is Lloyd Nist. The kids call me Wizard. I hoped to speak with the pilot. Thank him for rescuing our little town."

Red grasped his hand. It felt reassuring to see an adult. "I'm the pilot, sir."

"Please. Wizard or Lloyd. The landing was a little rough, but you got us here safely and for that we are grateful. However, you look too young to be flying such a plane. Although the soldiers Derrick captured were high school age."

"Derrick captured soldiers?"

"Yes, he did. Well, he and Anna."

"Anna, as in Rebekah's sister?"

"I believe that's correct. Hard to imagine. She is just a little thing, about Miriam's age, but I saw her take down our head of security with my own eyes. Where did you get the plane?"

Red stared as people scrambled out of the bus. "I can't say. Speaking of Derrick, where is he? I don't see him. I don't see any of them."

"Then you don't know?"

"Don't know what?"

Nist scratched his head. "They didn't come with us."

Red felt heat rising in his cheeks. "They what? We risked our lives to rescue them."

Nist shrugged, "Well, you rescued us."

"Where are they?"

Nist said, "I can't say for sure. The four kids, our head of security, Harley, and my protégé Corbin Atwood, stayed behind. As you saw, the military had the town surrounded when we left. However, if all goes as planned, they'll be on their way to Mexico by now."

Red threw his hands up. "Mexico? Why in the hell would they go to Mexico?"

Nist studied him for a moment.

Antonio stepped from the ramp. "What's going on? Where's Rebekah?"

"They didn't come. They're headed to Mexico. That is if the military doesn't capture or kill them, I suppose." Glaring at Nist, Red added, "Do I have it right?"

Antonio sank, plopping his butt onto the ramp. "Mexico? They don't speak Spanish. Rebekah never said anything about speaking Spanish. They can't get across the border. I don't understand. Why?" Antonio found it difficult to reconcile his reactions and certainly wouldn't attempt to explain them. Fear and sadness best described his feelings upon hearing that Rebekah wasn't on the plane. Antonio felt ashamed that he felt relieved that Derrick had not made the trip. It was not the first time Antonio wished Derrick King had never arrived in Potterville.

Nist said, "Well, I guess I can tell you. I mean, obviously, you know more about Derrick and Miriam than we do. They went to prevent a war."

Red said, "You're not serious. How could they prevent a war?"

Nist glanced around. "Well, we discovered a mobile missile launcher near the Mexico border."

Red said, "Okay. So, that sounds bad, but it still doesn't answer my question."

Nist said, "They are not Mexico's. They belong to New America."

Red nodded. "Prime is going to bomb his own country to justify a war."

Nist said, "You don't sound surprised."

"I am not."

26

NYX TRIED TO BUSY HERSELF BUT HAD NO skill set equipping her for this situation. On the other hand, Akira had been hunched over a keyboard, smacking keys as if each stroke devastated a bunker in which Prime hid. Beyond not knowing what to do, Nyx felt sick. Worried about Derrick. Worried about Red and Antonio. Worried about Akira.

Beyond worry, Akira scared Nyx. Was she trying to launch nuclear missiles? If she was, Nyx had to stop her. But without the others here, what could she do? Hit her over the head? Nyx had felt relieved when Akira set up the satellite link. Nyx had hoped the connection with Miriam might help restore Akira's memories. On a positive note, Akira had tried, in a rough sort of way, to ease Nyx's thoughts about her father. But this was still not Akira. Not the Akira she'd known for years. Not by a long shot.

Nyx could make coffee. That was one skill she possessed. Not the L.-Linda-Maxton-coffee-making skill level, which created an avalanche of concerns Nyx did not need, but she could make coffee. She could do that.

In the kitchen, Nyx found a QR-3 robot standing motionless, eyes dark. "Excuse me. Mr. Robot, can you make us breakfast? Hello?"

Nothing.

"Charlie would make us eat."

At the mention of Charlie's name, the robot's eyes lit, turning its head toward her.

"Charlie wants us to eat."

With that, the robot began gathering pots. Nyx shrugged. "Thank you, I guess?"

At the espresso machine, Nyx made two mochas, trying her best to make art with the foam. She was shooting for hearts this time, thinking about making one for Derrick when he returned. One looked like a lopsided clam having a bad day, and the other was just a blob of foam. Although L. Linda had only worked at Donna's Bistro a few days, she had learned to make fantastic latte art and even created a new drink she named a DK Double Honey. L. Linda had made a perfect heart shape in one she brought to Derrick. The girl was weird, but talented. It was a strange name for a coffee drink, to Nyx's way of thinking. *What does that even mean? DK Double Honey—Oh, shit.*

Sliding a mocha, bearing the pathetic clam in front of Akira, Nyx sat beside her.

"I didn't ask for another coffee."

"I know." Nyx thought for a moment. "I wanted one, so I made one for you. Plus, I don't know what else to do. You don't have to drink it if you don't want."

Akira glared at her and then went back to pounding at the keyboard. Nyx sipped her coffee. The scent of bacon drifted into the room. "The robots are fixing us breakfast."

"I didn't ask for breakfast either."

"Charlie would make us eat."

"Charlie's not here."

"True. He's out with Red and Antonio, risking his life to help our friends."

"He's a robot. He doesn't have a life."

"Red and Antonio do."

"I didn't ask them to do that either."

"True. They took it upon themselves. I understand Antonio. It's obvious he has feelings for Rebeka. But to be honest, I don't understand Red. Why is he doing it? He doesn't even like Derrick."

Akira glanced at Nyx, gave her head a little shake, and then returned to the keyboard. After a few minutes, Akira took a breath, sat back, and picked up the mocha. Staring at her drink, she said, "What's that supposed to be?"

"I was shooting for a heart, but it looks more like a sad clam. I have no artistic talent."

"It takes practice." Akira took a sip.

"L. Linda was making art in her drinks right away." Nyx took a deep breath. "She even invented a drink. She called it a DK Double Honey."

"I remember. Remembering isn't my problem. It's putting stuff in context that's hard." Akira paused. "The worst part is that my feelings don't match my memories. That's not accurate. I don't have feelings, but I sort of remember what I should feel about things," She paused, "and people."

Nyx felt probing Akira's thoughts was dangerous. Exploring her own thoughts was not much safer. "So, L. Linda, she's good at a lot of stuff, isn't she? I mean, she's kinda weird, but she gets stuff done. She found Derrick and the others and saved them. Then Derrick called her and told her how to find us."

"Derrick called her, but Miriam told her how to find us."

Nyx thought for a moment. "DK Double Honey is a weird name for a drink, don't you think?"

Akira sipped. "It serves a purpose."

"Does it? What do you think it means?"

"By the look on your face, you've already figured it out."

Nyx stared at Akira for a moment. "Should I be worried?"

"Yes. You should be worried about a lot of things, but DK Double Honey should not be at the top of your list."

***

Soldiers scrambled to the vehicles that were not yet damaged. Bombs exploded as if in a choreographed dance designed to usher them away from the town. Miriam rather enjoyed triggering the bombs, and she planned to detonate them all. No reason to leave explosives, which could pose a risk to people in the future. So far, she did not think any of the soldiers had been killed or injured. Derrick wouldn't be happy if there were. So, she set them off as close to the vehicles as possible, hoping the soldiers believed a miracle had spared them. Knowing she was the miracle made her smile.

The unit followed Commander Haskins's order, racing out of town, disappearing into the distance. Miriam was the last one out of the building. The fumes from the oil and gas were overwhelming. With the military now clear of the explosives, she put the last of the plan into motion. They had less than five minutes to get out of town. It would take her three minutes to reach the others.

Exiting the building, Miriam saw two trucks waiting. She jumped into the back of the last truck and screamed, "Go!"

They were a mile and a half from the town when a bomb exploded. Miriam saw the windows blow out, followed by a puff of smoke from each opening. When the sound reached the truck, the boom caused her to cover her ears. Seconds later, a black cloud engulfed the building.

Then the rest of the town exploded in a massive fireball.

***

The school bus followed the four trucks to the highway. It wasn't much of a highway because no cars had gone by since they had landed. Perhaps there wasn't much traffic on this road, or maybe the town's folk saw the military plane land and wanted nothing to do with it. Either worked for Red. He wanted to get away without being discovered.

Antonio looked toward the front of the plane, and the chain-link fence twisted under it. "Do you think it's damaged?"

Walking toward the front of the plane, Red said, "I was afraid to look."

The chain-link fence had wrapped around the front landing gear. Antonio didn't know what the landing gear was supposed to look like but was sure it didn't look right.

Red stood on the fencing, forcing it to the ground so he could move in closer. "It's messed up."

"How are we going to get the plane untangled? Even if we can, is it safe to fly?" Antonio asked.

Stepping out from underneath the fuselage, Red said, "I don't have answers to either question." He pointed toward the road. "I'm not sure what we're going to do about that either."

A tractor appeared in the distance. Red was already walking toward the road. Antonio jogged a few yards to catch up. There was no rush. Tractors are not fast. When his father was home and not working somewhere else following the crops, Antonio helped him in the fields, so he knew about tractors. Although it was still half a mile away, Antonio felt confident the tractor was too small for the job.

The tractor crawled along. Heat waves rising off the road, distorting the image of the man and machine. The tractor rolled to a stop when it reached where Red stood. It had no cab like larger tractors. The diesel clattered softly at idle.

The man took off his cap and scratched his head. "Holy crap. What's happened here?"

"We had a minor emergency. Had to land. Runway was too short," Red said, hoping the man knew nothing about old military transport jets. The length of the runway wasn't the problem. Red's lack of training on a C-17 Globemaster was.

"Is everyone okay? Where's the pilot?"

"I'm the pilot."

The man frowned. "You look too young to be a pilot. I know the military has waived the age requirements of late, but still. Besides, that's an old plane. Says United States Airforce."

"Right. It's surplus. I'm flying it to my uncle's place in Kansas. We'll salvage it there. Sell the parts that can be repurposed and cut up the rest for scrap metal."

"If you say so. Seems you're risking your life when the government will suck up most of what you make with taxes and fees."

"Got to make a living somehow." Red paused. "We need help getting the plane off the fence. Your tractor is too small. I doubt it will budge it."

The man stepped on the clutch and put the tractor in gear. "You got that right. I know a guy. I'll see what I can do." He pulled a cellphone from his coveralls as he drove away.

Antonio said, "You think he's calling someone with a bigger tractor or the cops?"

Red started back toward the aircraft. "Who knows?"

"So, what are we going to do?"

"You're the smart guy. What do you suggest?"

Walking beside Red, Antonio said, "Do you know where we are?"

"Not exactly. Arizona, I think. Charlie can tell us."

"We should ask him."

Red said, "What difference does it make?"

"I don't know. Just trying to figure out how to get back to Nyx and Akira. I wish Rebekah and the others were here."

"Wishing ain't gonna make it so."

Antonio said, "I don't have a suggestion. We can't leave the jet. It might lead someone back to the Base."

"I wasn't suggesting we leave it. I'm just open to ideas," Red said.

"We could set it on fire. Put holes in the fuel tanks, put a match to it."

Red said, "I said open, but that seems extreme. Plus, how do we get back to the Base?"

Antonio shrugged. "I don't know. Walk? Get a ride?"

"Walk? In this heat? And what do we do with Charlie?" Red asked.

"Good points."

"I guess that leaves flying back," Red said.

"We've circled back to 'how do we get off the fence and turned around?' We do have to turn it around, right?"

"We do. You forgot the part about the damaged landing gear."

"I didn't forget. So, back to my original question. What are we going to do?"

Red stopped at the jet's loading ramp. "We start by finding a large pair of wire cutters so that I can cut the fencing from the landing gear. Check the cargo area."

"Why would a plane have wire cutters?"

Red shrugged. "Basic tools. A heavy-duty pair of pliers. You've been on a farm. You make do with what you got."

"And what are you going to do?"

Red motioned toward a hangar. "See if I can get inside. If anyone still uses it, they'll have tools. Maybe even an airplane we could borrow."

"You're going to break into the building and steal an airplane?"

Red put his hand on Antonio's shoulder. "It wouldn't be the first airplane we've borrowed."

27

FAR ABOVE THE INFERNO, A PRIME AIRCRAFT flew lazy circles, from which L. Linda Maxton had watched buildings explode like dominos. Two pickup trucks raced south as black smoke billowed behind them. The military unit had stopped four miles east of town and could not have seen them leave. Derrick and the others must be in those pickups. What in the hell are they doing?

Why didn't Derrick go with Red and Antonio? Her lack of understanding was exasperating. Infuriating was a better word. But what really chapped her butt was that Derrick had taken Nyx Belos to a secret military base. It was like rubbing salt into a fresh wound. Nyx got to Derrick first, and L. Linda didn't understand how it happened. L. Linda spotted Derrick in his window even before he left the condo. She did some research and had suspicions about this new kid in town. She was there the day he asked Donna for a job. After he left, she pleaded with Donna for a job. Even volunteered to work for free. Donna didn't need, nor could she afford to hire two people, but let her work in trade for a tab. She started working the same morning as Derrick. She had set it up perfectly.

Except Nyx already had her hooks in him.

L. Linda still couldn't believe it.

Nyx had little time for boys. At least, that's what she had been telling people. L. Linda figured it was just another break from her boyfriend. It wasn't unusual—not for Nyx.

So, why Derrick?

Of one thing, L. Linda was confident: she could not let Nyx ruin this. It was her one shot, long shot though it was. L. Linda had been through too much to let puppy love ruin her scheme. It couldn't happen. She wouldn't allow it.

Back to the present.

L. Linda wanted to follow the pickups and Derrick. She could provide protection and help them do whatever they felt was more important than escaping. Begrudgingly, she admitted their mission must be vital, but there were other things to consider. The military unit would contact their headquarters, if they hadn't already, and explain the situation, which might trigger a full-scale operation.

Red and Antonio might still be in a humongous aircraft that would draw attention. That could lead the enemy to the Base, which would not be good. Not good at all.

A full-scale operation might also find two pickup trucks south of the burning town. Also, not good.

Stopping the military unit rose to the number one priority.

L. Linda turned the aircraft toward the fleeing band of soldiers. She had searched for the aircraft's weapons, and having found a few options, she looked for an explanation of each weapon's capabilities but found none.

"Hey, computer! What weapons does this thing have?"

No answer.

"Damn it. Answer me."

Nothing.

"Crap."

L. Linda scanned the inside of the aircraft, or rather a holographic display by which the pilot, which was her, flew the thing. Robots had flown this one to Potterville. She wondered if robots wore the headsets or if everything just happened in their heads.

Focus.

In the corner of the holographic display, were the words Sentry 3.

"Hey, Sentry!"

Nothing

"Hey, Sentry 3."

A female voice said, "How may I help you?"

Why is it always a woman's voice?

"Can you access the aircraft weapons?"

"That operation is not available. Only the pilot and copilot can operate the weapons system."

She wondered if the robots could fire the weapons. Probably. The computer probably recognized the robots as authorized pilots. She wondered what the computer thought she was.

"Do you know what the weapons do?"

Nothing.

"Sentry 3, do you know what the weapons do?"

"Affirmative."

"Which weapon is best for destroying vehicles on the ground?"

"All three weapons can destroy targets on the ground. Only the pilot and copilot are authorized to activate weapons."

Well, that doesn't help.

"Sentry 3, do you know who I am?"

"Sentry 3 does not recognize the human."

"I am the pilot."

"Sentry 3 does not recognize the human."

"Then who is flying the aircraft?"

"The human is flying the aircraft."

"And what does the pilot do?" L. Linda asked.

"The pilot operates the aircraft."

"And I am doing what?"

"Operating the aircraft."

"Correct. I am flying the aircraft. Therefore, I am the pilot."

"Updated. Sentry 3 recognizes the human as the pilot. How may I be of assistance?"

"Thank you. I'm glad we got that straightened out." L. Linda felt a bit conflicted, and she didn't like it. Part of her just wanted to wipe that unit from the face of the Earth to ensure they carried no message back to their leaders, who would then relay the information to her enemy.

Part of her wanted to stop them without killing them.

That comforted her, just a little, knowing she had maintained a shred of humanity in the madness.

But she didn't like it.

It was weak.

This was no time for weakness.

Then something occurred to her. They might have sent a scout back. What if the scout saw the two pickups leave town? If not, for sure they saw the cargo jet. They shot at it. However, if they didn't see the pickup trucks, they would assume everyone escaped on that plane.

Think!

If they think Derrick escaped on the jet, they'll focus on finding the plane, which means they won't search for pickups.

L. Linda flew over the military unit, far too high for them to see or hear the aircraft. The unit remained stopped about five miles from town. Just sitting there. *Why would they stop there? Perhaps they were following orders.* She remembered seeing a soldier walking toward the man with the white flag. Derrick hid in shadow. *Did you kidnap a commanding officer, Derrick? Bold move.*

Focus.

"Hey, Sentry 3. Can any of the weapons disable a vehicle without killing the people?"

"Yes, the Kinetic Cannon can penetrate armor. By targeting the heat signature of a motor, a vehicle can be disabled without harming the passengers."

Okay. That's an option.

But doing that would signal her presence, and that would not be good. She needed this aircraft. She was sure of that. They could find her with the satellite once they get clear of the two relics Akira and Miriam positioned to cause interference.

Destroying their satellite moved to the top of the 'Things L. Linda must do before lunch list. "Hey, Sentry 3."

"How may I be of assistance?"

"Locate satellites above us."

"Locating satellites. There are three satellites above the aircraft."

"Can you tell how old they are?"

"Analyzing."

"Two were built 87 years ago, and one was made 12 years ago."

"Bingo."

"Sentry 3 does not understand, Bingo."

"Yeah, neither do I. How high is the newest satellite?" L. Linda asked.

"The Prime Corporation Nexus 14 is 509.9995043 kilometers above the earth."

L. Linda sighed. "In miles, stupid computer."

Nothing.

"Sentry 3, how far in miles, please?"

"Prime Corporation Nexus 14 is 316.899 miles above the Earth."

"How high can this aircraft fly?"

"Kilometers or miles?"

"Can it fly higher in kilometers than miles?"

"No. The altitude is the same in either measurement."

"Miles, stupid machine."

Nothing.

"Sentry 3, in miles."

"This aircraft has been certified to reach an altitude of 90 miles."

L. Linda shook her head. "Does that mean it could go higher?"

"It is possible, but structural integrity has not been tested above 90 miles. The aircraft that reached 90 miles sustained hull damage. Traveling above an altitude of 50 miles is not recommended."

L. Linda said, "Not helping. What is the farthest a weapon on this aircraft can reach?"

"That has not been tested."

"Speculate."

"Sentry 3 does not understand speculate."

"It wasn't a question, stupid computer. Guess. Can one of these weapons reach the satellite at 90 miles?"

"Sentry 3 does not guess."

L. Linda took a deep breath. "Can Sentry 3 estimate?"

"Affirmative. Sentry 3 can evaluate data and make estimations.

"Sentry 3, estimate if an onboard weapon could destroy the satellite if we flew to a height of 90 miles."

"Which satellite do you want to destroy?"

"The newest one, please."

"Prime Incorporated owns the newest satellite."

"Yes. That's the one."

"In theory, the Kinetic Cannon could reach that satellite."

"I need specifics."

"The Kinetic Cannon fires tungsten projectiles at a rate of 1200 rounds a minute, in 15 shot bursts with a muzzle velocity over Mach 5. Because the bullet travels fast enough to escape the Earth's gravity, it could hit the satellite."

"What are the odds of hitting the satellite?"

"Less than one percent."

"Not good enough. What else we got?"

"Perhaps the Laser."

"We have a Laser?"

"Correct. That is why Sentry 3 suggested the Laser."

"How far can it reach?"

"It can reach the moon, but it would cause no damage at that distance. It would create a red dot covering approximately 50 miles."

"Doesn't sound promising. Sounds more like a flashlight than a weapon."

"The moon is 238,900 miles from Earth."

"How close would we have to be to damage the satellite?"

"That has not been tested. The atmosphere distorts, reflects, and absorbs the laser beam, which reduces its range. However, the atmosphere ends at the Kármán line, some 62 miles above the earth."

"How far can it damage stuff in the atmosphere?"

"It can damage most surfaces ten miles away."

"But above the atmosphere, it could reach farther. Correct?"

"That is correct, in theory. It has not been tested."

"Perhaps we'll test it then. How many times can it be fired?"

"That depends on the aircraft's power supply."

"This is taking too long. If we flew up 90 miles, how many times can we fire, and will it destroy the satellite?"

"The Laser would likely cause significant damage to the satellite, in theory. However, climbing to an altitude of 90 miles will exhaust most of the aircraft's power supply. The aircraft could fire twice and retain enough power to return to Earth within safety protocol margins."

"What are our chances of destroying the satellite with two shots?"

"Forty percent."

"Screw safety protocols. What if we fly to 80 miles? How many shots could we fire?"

"The aircraft could fire three surges."

"What's the odds of destroying the satellite?"

"Forty-five percent."

"Not good enough. How many surges can we fire at 90 miles? Total. Using all the aircraft's power."

"The aircraft could fire eight surges."

"And the odds?"

"The estimated success increases to 94.5 percent, but the aircraft will not..."

L. Linda talked over the computerized voice. "I'll take those odds."

28

Friday, April 9, 9:15 a.m.

THE SUN HAD RISEN WELL ABOVE THE EASTERN horizon, and heat waves shimmered on the runway. When Red returned to the aircraft, he didn't see Antonio. However, he heard what sounded like cursing, except in Spanish, coming from the front of the jet. Antonio would be found there. Red carried a bolt cutter with three-foot handles, strong enough to cut a padlock of no small significance. Antonio tugged on a section of fencing crumpled in the landing gear.

"What ya doing there, little buddy?" Red asked.

"Very funny. Come help, you big ox."

"These are for men, but you should still be able to use them." Red held out a pair of gloves.

"You've turned into a comedian. What gives?"

"It's sinking in. We're lucky to be alive. A condition which may not last, so I'm enjoying the moment." Red studied the fencing bound in the landing gear, cut through some wires, and then with one hand, pulled a piece free, tossing it to the side.

Antonio held up a pair of linesman pliers. "These work, but you've got me beat."

"What happened to your head?"

"A piece of fencing came free and smacked me." Antonio wiped at the wound. "I think it's stopped bleeding though."

Red studied a sizable chunk of fencing balled up under the landing gear. "I'll start cutting this free, but it's going to be tough pulling it out. Get Charlie."

"You think that's safe? I mean, explaining the plane was hard enough."

"We'll work fast and keep our eyes peeled. The only vehicle we've seen was that tractor. If we see anything coming, Charlie can hide inside."

Antonio left and soon returned, with Charlie following. Red had cut the fence in half, leaving a three-foot section that looked like a nest of snarled hair bonded to the landing gear.

"How can I help?" Charlie asked.

Red dropped the bolt cutters, grabbed the fencing with both hands, planted his feet, leaned back, and pulled, his face turning red. The fencing didn't budge.

Breathing deeply, Red said, "Charlie, a little help?"

Charlie motioned Red out of the way and walked halfway around the rat's nest of steel, studying it for a moment. "I see the problem."

"And?" Red puzzled.

"It is caught in the landing gear."

"No kidding."

"What is a kidding?" Charlie asked, then said, "Oh, based on the context, I assume it means joking."

"Close enough. Sarcasm. Can you pull it out or not?"

"No need for hostility, Red Badowski." And with that, Charlie grabbed the fencing with one hand, the stiff chain-link wire crumpling as if it were made of silk thread, and with a firm jerk, ripped it free. Holding it in the air, Charlie said, "I do not think this can be easily repaired."

"I don't want it repaired." Red pointed to the desert beyond the fence. "Just toss it out there."

Charlie carried the gnarled fencing out from underneath the aircraft and then tossed it, sending it 20 yards into the air and 40 yards into the desert.

"Holy crap," Antonio said.

"No shit," Red agreed.

Charlie said, "Would you like to free the other piece of fencing?"

"That is exactly what I want to do," Red said, adding, "Let me cut it first."

Charlie said, "I can do that." Charlie lifted his arm. A bright red beam of light burst from Charlie's palm, sending a shower of sparks as he cut through the fencing.

Red tossed the bolt cutters to the ground. "Don't need those anymore." Red went to the landing gear, studying it from all angles.

"What do you think?" Antonio asked.

"It's bent up for sure, but it's in one piece."

Pointing, Antonio said, "Damn. Look at the size of that tractor. That farmer wasn't lying. He knew a guy."

Red said, "Charlie, hide."

"Where would you like me to hide?"

"In the plane."

"Very well. And how long would you like me to remain in the aircraft?"

"For God's sake, until we come to get you."

"Very well."

Charlie walked toward the stairs at the front of the plane. The huge tractor exited the highway onto the tarmac, not more than a quarter mile away.

"Can you move faster, Charlie?"

Charlie turned. "I have the capacity to move with significant speed when required."

"Can you do it now? You need to hide."

"May I ask what I am hiding from?"

Red put his hands on his head. "From the farmer!"

Charlie turned. "Is the farmer driving that large machine?"

In unison, Red and Antonio hollered. "Yes!"

"In that case, I must move quickly."

In the blink of an eye, moving with more grace than seemed possible, Charlie disappeared into the plane.

Red looked at Antonio. "Unbelievable."

Antonio said, "Agreed. On several levels."

The huge farm machine rolled to a stop near the jet's ramp. The diesel engine pulsed. A man in faded gray overalls, covered with dust and stained with oil, climbed down from the machine. Brushing off dirt, the man said, "Wow. Clancy said it was a big plane, but I ain't never seen such a thing up close. I saw one like this up north near the airbase once." The man moved to see the tail section better. "This here is an old plane, although it looks much like the one, I saw. But this dates to the old United States. Where are the pilots?"

Red said, "I'm the pilot."

The man laughed. "Good one." Extending his hand, he said, "My name's Hank."

"Red."

"Antonio."

Both boys shook the man's hand.

"Whoever flew this thing didn't know how to land it proper. Who's going to pay for that fence?"

Without hesitation, Red said, "My uncle will take care of it."

"And where's your uncle?"

"Kansas."

"Is he the pilot?"

"He's not. I am. He's in Kansas. Runs a salvage operation. We're taking the plane there. He bought it from a surplus sale. We had a problem, had to land."

"What sort of problem?"

"Hydraulic." Red pointed.

Antonio hadn't noticed before, but one wing shimmered with oil.

"That why the pilot hit the fence?"

"Yep."

Hank said, "You got it fixed?"

Red said, "We do."

"We do?" Antonio asked.

Red threw Antonio a look. "You think your tractor can pull us back?"

"I reckon it can. But what about paying for the damages?"

"Sooner we get home, the sooner my uncle can get things taken care of."

"Your uncle's not here?"

"No. Like I said, he's in Kansas."

"Where's the pilot?"

"I'm the pilot."

"Not funny anymore. I saw a big guy. Bigger than you even getting into the plane. He the pilot?"

Red looked at Antonio. "Yeah. He's the pilot."

"Can I talk to him?"

"He doesn't talk to people."

Hank cocked his head. "And why's that? I think there's something fishy going on. Your uncle didn't buy this plane, did he? He stole it. He some sort of fugitive? Maybe a drug runner." The man in glanced into the cargo bay. "It's empty."

"We are not drug runners."

"But it's stolen. Isn't it?" Hank scratched his chin. "You're with the Resistance. Ain't that right?"

Antonio was the smart one. He was the student council president, but this was how he did with Nyx. He had sat back, saying nothing, until he vetoed their vote. Red thought, *I wish you'd take over now, Antonio.*

"I can't talk about that," Red said, then paused before asking, "Are you in the Resistance?"

Hank smiled and then winked. "Can't say. Now, let's get you out of here. There's a military base nearby, and I suspect they have already heard about this plane."

"They have aircraft?" Antonio asked.

About time you helped, Red thought.

"Helicopters. It's an infantry unit. Foot soldiers. Tanks and trucks and such." Hank climbed into his tractor. Pointing to a ridge a few miles in the distance. "Here come the soldiers now. We'd best hurry if you're with the Resistance."

Red stepped to the side to see around the tractor, then said, "Crap. Antonio, raise the ramp. We got to get out of here."

Hank spun the tractor around and backed up to the aircraft. Red lifted the heavy chain from the hitch and attached it to a hook on the jet. Red hollered, "Take up the slack, then see if it will move."

Hank was already easing forward when Red called out. He had pulled stuff before. With the chain tight, Hank raised the throttle and eased the clutch out. The chain grew taut, and the motor grunted, and then the front of the aircraft snapped free of the remaining fencing. Red gave Hank a hurry-up signal. When the jet had moved far enough to where Red thought he could turn it around, he motioned for the tractor to stop.

Red unhooked the chain and draped it back on the tractor. "Get clear. We gotta go!"

Hank gave Red a salute, put the tractor in its highest gear, and headed to the exit. The military could catch the tractor if they went after him. It wasn't as if the tractor could outrun them unless Hank could drive places the military could not. More likely, the soldiers would come after the aircraft.

Red ran to the stairs and scrambled into the cockpit. "Where's Antonio?" Red engaged the starter motors.

"Mr. Antonio is in the cargo bay."

"Tell him to secure everything and get up here. Fast!"

Charlie called Antonio on the intercom system, relaying Red's instructions, and then said to Red, "You have not completed the preflight checklist."

"No time. Cross your fingers."

Charlie manipulated the fingers of both hands, finally pointing both index fingers straight out and then making a cross. "My fingers were not designed to cross. Will this suffice?"

Red glanced at Charlie. "Just an expression, but yes, that'll do."

Antonio climbed into the cockpit and stared at Charlie. "What's he doing?"

"Crossing his fingers. You should do the same but get strapped in first."

Turning back to the controls, Red pushed the right throttle forward, pivoting the enormous jet, but overshot the mark. The aircraft moved in a zigzag toward two military vehicles with flashing lights that had driven onto the far end of the tarmac.

"Hang on!"

The thrust of the four engines pushed Antonio into the seat. "You don't think they'll shoot us, do you?"

"I hope not. They don't know who we are."

The vehicles set side by side. Two soldiers exited, carrying rifles.

"Can we make it?" Antonio asked, craning his neck to see over Charlie.

Red asked, "Can you answer that question, Charlie?"

"The front landing gear should clear the vehicles. The vehicles will fit inside the span of the outside landing gear."

"I hope you're right," Red said.

A bullet hit the cockpit window, causing a spiderweb but glancing off. "Assholes!" Red shouted.

"So much for them not shooting at us," Antonio said.

The sound of bullets striking the aircraft mixed with the roar of the jet engines. The nose of the jet rotated skyward. Red raised the landing gear just as they left the ground. Objects on the ground grew smaller as they rose into the sky. Red took a deep breath. Studied the console and made adjustments.

"Do you think the plane is damaged?" Antonio asked.

"It must be. That's not the important question. Will the damage cause it to fall out of the sky? That's the question you should ask."

"You're not much comfort," Antonio said and then added, "but great job. Three takeoffs and two landings. One more landing and you're officially my number one hero today."

Charlie said, "One more landing will not be possible."

Red looked at Charlie. "What does that mean?"

"Perhaps I should have mentioned this earlier, but you were in a hurry to leave."

"Mention what?"

"Stress fractures to the front landing gear will cause it to fail upon touchdown. The aircraft cannot land. It can only crash."

29

WITHOUT A DOUBT, THIS WAS THE FOOLHARDIEST act L. Linda had ever considered doing, and she had done some crazy shit. But taking an aircraft, she knew nothing about into orbit was by far the winner in L. Linda's book—*Crazy Stunts for Fun and Profit.*

The aircraft's visual control now contained a red square showing the satellite's location. "Okay. Here we go," L. Linda said.

The detached voice said, "You must put on the flight suit."

"What flight suit?"

A door, not unlike a gym locker, popped open, revealing a suit, complete with a helmet like an astronaut might wear. She had not noticed the locker thing previously, which caused her to realize how little she knew about the aircraft. She knew practically nothing. She knew it was angular shaped, flat black, and had a large, gray capital P on each side. It flew, but how it achieved that was neither apparent nor like any other aircraft she was familiar with. It belonged to Prime, not the military. That Prime had all the best stuff didn't surprise her. What did bother her was not knowing how much stuff Prime possessed that the rest of the world didn't.

"No time. We aren't staying up there. Just firing off a few rounds, then back we come, quick as our little spaceship will carry us."

"Before running out of oxygen at the Kármán line, the acceleration will render you unconscious. The suit protects the pilot from the g-force as the aircraft accelerates to 25,000 MPH."

"Okay. I'll put on the stupid suit. But don't take my picture. I don't want the kids at school to see me in this stupid thing." L. Linda slipped out of her jeans and into the suit. "Not that it's a bad look. It's just not me. Know what I'm saying?" L. Linda fastened the helmet and moved back into the pilot's seat. "Are we ready now?" L. Linda asked.

There was no response.

L. Linda aligned the red square in the display, which now appeared in the face shield of her helmet and pulled the control back. But nothing happened.

"Hey, Sentry 3."

"How may I be of assistance?"

"Can we go now? Launch. Go. Scram. You know, go blow up the satellite?"

"Technically, we will not blow up the satellite. Instead…"

"Shut up and go. Is that simple enough?"

"As you wish. However, I must issue this warning: Warning, flight plan A to reach 90 miles above the Earth will deplete the fuel supply."

"Stop wasting time. Go!"

The aircraft pivoted, then shot into the sky. The shaking felt as if the machine would tear itself apart. The g-force beyond anything she had imagined. Even wearing the suit, she felt on the verge of blacking out.

The voice said, "20,000 feet, 25,000 feet, 30,000 feet, 45,000 feet, 55,000 feet, 100,000 feet. Altitude now 20 miles, 30 miles, 50 miles. Nearing the Kármán line, in five, four, three, two…"

The sky, or at least the visual representation of the sky in her virtual reality-style headset, changed from blue to black. L. Linda Maxton had traveled to space. *Take that, students of Potterville High.*

The voice said, "Warning. Fuel supply at 25 percent. Initiate return flight."

L. Linda said, "No. How long before we reach 90 miles?"

"In three, two…"

L. Linda had the satellite's location in the crosshairs. She tapped the firing button five times. "Return flight, NOW!"

The aircraft slowed and did a slow arc. Earth filled her display. "Beautiful," she whispered.

The display flickered.

Then everything went black.

30

THE ROAD MEANDERED THROUGH JOSHUA trees and cacti varieties unknown to Derrick. He and Miriam were in the bed of the lead pickup truck. Atwood drove, and Commander Haskins sat in the passenger's seat. Harley drove the other truck, and Anna and Rebekah rode with him. From the town, plumes of black smoke billowed into the sky. The road curved left over a knoll. Atwood pulled to the side of the road. Harley stopped behind them.

Atwood got out, hands on his hips, staring at the raging fire that consumed their town, his face etched with sadness. Harley walked to Atwood and threw his arms around him. They had lost their home. Not just a home, but all they had worked to accomplish. And Derrick had caused it. Death and destruction followed him everywhere. Previous to this only Paul Jorgensen had died. But others had been killed now. The thought caused his stomach to rise into his throat.

Derrick walked to Atwood. "I'm sorry this happened. It's my fault."

Atwood released Harley and then did something unexpected. He put his hands on Derrick's shoulders and then hugged him. "Son, you didn't cause this. Prime did. This starts with Prime and ends with Prime. The sooner you understand that, the better."

After a moment, Atwood pushed Derrick away but held him at arm's length. With a firm tone, he asked, "You got that?"

"Yes, sir." Derrick wanted to believe this.

Haskins walked around the front of the truck.

Atwood released Derrick and turned to Haskins. "I wasn't there when you grew up, and for that, I am truly sorry."

Haskins said nothing for a moment. "You didn't know about me."

"I didn't. I would have married your mom if she would have had me. Apparently, she wanted something else."

"My guess is she wanted you to stay in school. She wanted you to succeed, to become something. Looks like her sacrifice paid off."

Atwood said, "Eric was a good man. I assume he was a good father."

"He was. I have no complaints."

Atwood said, "You're free to leave. I won't force you to go with us. I'm afraid that while I may have saved you from the fire," Atwood motioned toward the thick black smoke, "I have not put you in a tenable situation. Prime will kill you if he finds you. I'm certain of that. And it will be difficult to hide, although I'll do my best to help if you want to disappear. And I'll understand if that's your decision."

Haskins said, "And what are you going to do?"

Atwood shrugged. "The only thing we can do. We are going to stop that missile. Hope that will prevent a war."

"Let's say you're successful. I mean, it's highly doubtful you'll succeed, but let's say you do. How long do you think that will forestall war? Prime intends to extend his empire to the tip of South America and then conquer Canada. Stopping the launch will only delay the war. It might not even do that. Prime might invade without firing the missile."

Atwood nodded. "You're not wrong. Let me put it another way. If we can stop the missile, we'll at least have saved the people Prime was going to fire upon."

Derrick said, "Neither of you needs to come. We can handle it. Go. Find your people. Start your lives over."

Miriam said, "He's right. You two go. If we could have a truck, that's all we need."

Haskins said, "You're just kids. You don't have a chance. There will be a unit assigned to protect that mobile launcher. They are trained and armed."

Harley said, "We have weapons."

"With what?" Haskins asked.

"Two 50 cal. machine guns, two sniper rifles, and some explosives."

Haskins whistled through his teeth. "You've got to be kidding me. You can't get your hands on shit like that."

Harley shook his head and motioned toward where the town once stood. "Yet."

Haskins nodded. "I see your point."

Harley said, "I'm going. Professor, you, and your son, take a truck and find the others. They'll need you to reestablish. Your work is too important to risk."

Atwood looked at Haskins and then at Harley. "I can't let you do this alone."

"I'm not alone. I've got this lot." Harley motioned toward Derrick.

Atwood's expression went from sad to tormented as he turned to Haskins. "Son, if you come with me, we'll find our next town. We can build it together."

Haskins looked at Harley, then to Derrick, then to the three girls standing behind them. Then he looked at Atwood. "I accept that you're my natural father, but I can't go with you."

Atwood hung his head and nodded. "I understand."

"Let me finish. I can't go with you and let these kids try to stop the launch by themselves. I swore an oath to protect my country, not to protect Prime. You go. If we make it back, I'll find you."

Atwood looked up. "That's not gonna work. We're all in this together. Unfortunately, it's likely none of us make it back."

Part Two

1

Friday, April 9, 9:15 a.m.

IN THE MOUNTAINS OF OREGON, A SOLITARY man eased along a steep section of the Pacific Coast Trail, descending into the Columbia Gorge. Through the trees, he caught glimpses of the small community of Cascade Locks. It would be the first town he'd entered since leaving home. He had been hiking, which was more like running, for eight days, which felt more like eight months. Mostly he'd stayed on the Pacific Coast Trail, except for a few detours to lower trails due to snow. The last two days, he had been breaking trail through knee-deep snow. Now each step required careful placement to avoid slipping in the mud and taking a nasty fall. An injury could prove fatal.

Eight days had transformed the man. His hair was shaggier than he'd ever worn it, his beard untouched, his clothing soiled. Leather boots—new when he started, now well worn, scuffed, wet, and caked in mud—looked like he'd owned them for years. Everything about the man's clothing and gear looked a bit ragged, yet everything was new nine days ago.

The day it happened.

The day he left.

The journey had been difficult for a man who had never hiked a mountain trail. He had been conditioning himself for three years, because it was three years ago that he decided to escape, and at the time, his departure date was unknown. It remained unknown until April 1. However, he had decided on his method of escape, which had to be unpredictable, contrary to his nature, and entirely untraceable.

Not only did he have to escape, but he also had to disappear, never to be seen again.

Traveling the trail this time of year posed problems. Since he did not know when his departure day would come, he had prepared for a winter hike. If it was a snow year—they still happen from time to time—he might have to camp at the snowline for two or three months before continuing North. It could still snow at the higher elevations in early April, but this year was drier than normal, and it was normally pretty dry here. However, a storm had dropped two feet of snow a couple of days ago, slowing him down, but until then, he had made good time.

Making good time was critical. Being farther from home than was reasonably possible might keep him off the radar screens. That was the only thing that would keep him alive. Staying alive was important to him. He still had some things to accomplish. But he would do them in a new life. His previous life ended the day Prime discovered Derrick King was no longer in Potterville, California.

2

STANLEY MIRES, THE MAN PRIME CALLED QUIGLEY, had been in his office for two hours, trying to determine what was going on in the California desert. The satellite pictures had stopped coming, and communications from the military unit where Commander Cliff Haskins had gone had ceased. It surprised Stanley that Prime had not called for him, although he was not disappointed. Prime would be furious, not knowing what was happening. Being in Prime's presence wouldn't be safe for anyone, even those not involved in the situation.

Stanley's reprieve from Prime's wrath ended when a mechanical voice boomed over the loudspeakers. "Quigley! Get in here."

Entering Prime's office, aromas of fresh coffee and bacon filled Quigley's nostrils. Prime had ordered breakfast. Prime did not eat, not in the same manner as regular people, so the food was for Quigley.

Breakfast was not the good omen one might assume. Warm gestures were not something Prime did. Instead, it was often a last meal, although the guest typically never got a single bite of it. It was as if Prime wanted to make the person's death as painful as possible. Merely snuffing out a person's life wasn't enough.

"Good morning, Quigley. Do sit and eat."

"Yes, sir. Thank you, sir." Quigley sat, sipped coffee, spread peach jam on toast, then took a bite. If this were to be the day he died, he would get one bite, denying Prime the chance to kill him before he tasted the food.

"You seem hungry this morning."

"Yes, sir. Thank you, sir." Quigley picked up a piece of bacon, holding it for a moment to allow Prime an opportunity to electrocute him. After what happened last night, Quigley was looking forward to ending his employment here.

"I trust you have been monitoring our operations in the California desert."

"Yes, sir. I've been attempting to, but we are not receiving any information."

"Why is that, Quigley?"

"The technicians don't know for certain. They suspect a solar flare."

"Call for a satellite technician. I want to hear this explanation in person. Also, have Pacific Edge send an aircraft to that town to determine what is happening there."

"Yes, sir. Right away, sir. I can do both tasks in my office."

"Stay. I want you here when the technician arrives. We'll hear the explanation together."

"As you wish."

Quigley sent a text to the IT group requesting a satellite technician and then ate—confident his appetite would soon wane.

3

COLLINS SAT IN JACK'S SHOP, DRINKING COFFEE that had grown cold and bitter. He had been awake for hours, hoping L. Linda would return before her father got up, arguing with himself about not awakening Jason earlier, often standing to do just that, only to sit again. *What good would it do other than to cause Jason to worry?* Jason couldn't change things. The girl was gone, and that was that.

And Collins didn't know what to do about Jack. Jack was instructed to sink the aircraft in the lake. Instead, he brought it here and told L. Linda about it. If Jack knew she was going to take it, well, that might be a crime. Then what was he supposed to do? Arrest Jack? Put him where? In jail?

Lori Martinez wasn't the only one ready to resign from this stinking job.

The sun had been up for a couple of hours, but he understood why people were still asleep. It had been a long, unpleasant night, and he doubted anyone had slept well. However, he decided it was time to face two unpleasant tasks. First, tell Jason Maxton his daughter had left in the Prime aircraft. Second, confront Jack about not sinking the aircraft as instructed. After that, perhaps he would toss in the towel, gather anyone who wanted to leave Potterville, and hit the road.

Walking as quietly as possible, Collins worked his way to the back of the shop, which was an old warehouse, to a 1952 Chevrolet, five-window pickup. Jason and L. Linda had slept in the back of the old truck. Collins knew where each family had made their beds. He didn't realize they had not all remained in the beds they'd made.

Collins eased to the pristine pickup, the glossy paint reflecting the exit door sign. That L. Linda's spot was unoccupied came as no surprise. However, Jason was also missing.

Collins shook his head. "What is wrong with those two? Damn it. He's probably looking for L. Linda."

Working his way back toward the front office where Jack had made his bed on an old couch, Collins stopped to check on Lori. It was not the first time he'd stopped here, at a mid-seventies Lincoln Continental convertible, but it was the first time he found the car empty. "What the hell?" *Probably needed the restroom. Now, she's probably looking for me.*

Lori wasn't at the front of the shop in the makeshift break/lunch/meeting area they had devised by setting up a couple of folding tables and a few chairs. Here, Collins stopped sneaking and marched straight toward Fletcher's office. The heat rose in Collins's face as he remembered L. Linda wouldn't be missing had Fletcher just finished the job like he'd been told. Throwing the door open, Collins stared at the couch. Empty. "Where in the hell is everyone?" Collins murmured.

When Collins exited Jack's office, Browning stood at the sink, filling the coffeepot. Spotting Collins, Browning said, "I could smell this paint remover clear across the shop. You weren't drinking this crap, were you?"

"No. Well, yes. But I wasn't getting much down."

Browning finished putting coffee into the filter, flipped the switch, and turned toward Collins. "We'll have fresh in just a..." Browning stopped. "What's happened? You look mad as hell."

Collins took a deep breath as he sat. "L. Linda's gone."

"Gone? Gone where?"

Collins said, "I do not know. Jason is gone too. Plus, Jack's not in his office." He paused. "Lori is not in her spot either."

"Maybe they ran to get some stuff from home," Browning said.

Collins said, "I heard something last night at the far end of the shop. When I opened the bay door, I saw L. Linda get into a Prime aircraft. I pounded on the outside, but she flew away. I couldn't stop her. I have no idea where the others are. I've been up all night, and I haven't seen or heard anyone else moving."

"Where did L. Linda get a Prime aircraft?" Browning asked.

"It must be the one Jack was supposed to put in the lake."

Browning shook his head. "What was he thinking?"

"Good question. I meant to ask him just now."

Browning brought two mugs, sitting one in front of Collins.

Collins stood. "I'll get Lori a cup. She should be here soon. She must be in the restroom."

Browning set his mug down. "Sit back down. I just came from the restroom. She's not in there."

4

UPON DESCENDING INTO THE GORGE, the Pacific Crest hiker found a small campground, a waystation for those traveling the trail. There was one tent at the far end, but he saw no activity. Perhaps they were still sleeping or maybe in town getting supplies. The man stopped, eased his pack to the ground, and sat at an old wooden table made with thick slabs of bare wood scarred by deep cracks from age, moss growing on the edges, and here and there a few flecks of dark green paint.

For a moment, the man just sat, soaking in the forest. The temperature was in the sixties but comfortable, and the air was damp and clean and scented with pine.

Except for the areas deforested by massive wildfires, the entire journey had been more beautiful than he'd ever imagined. Having spent his life indoors, doing scientific experiments, pouring over research papers, testing theories, and trying to please a boss with an unquenchable hunger for power, he'd never spent much time outdoors except running on the beach for the past few years. The beach was his training ground, conditioning for this. But running on the beach and running with a pack in the mountains were two vastly different things. Still, the conditioning made it possible.

His pants were muddy and wet from the knees down. His boots were soaked, and his feet numb. He pulled dry socks and pants from his backpack, placing them on the table. With his boots unlaced, he put his right toe on the heel of his left boot, trying to force it off. He had just started to apply pressure when his calf spasmed with a painful cramp.

Rubbing his leg but avoiding a skinned knee, he wondered if he might have set a record for getting here. He had covered about 646 miles, from mile post 1510 to 2147, in eight days. He thought that might be a record, but he'd never know. Six hundred and forty-seven miles. The first day, he ran on pure adrenalin. After that, he settled into a grueling pace. He climbed as fast as he could, trotted on downhill slopes, and ran when the trail was flat. He started moving before sunrise and continued after sunset. A full moon allowed him to continue well into the night. Camp meant climbing into his sleeping bag. No fire, no cooking. Just power bars and water from streams, using purification tablets to prevent illness. Eight days, eighteen hours a day, four and a half miles an hour, 646 miles. An insane and punishing pace that only terror could sustain. That he was here seemed impossible, even to him. He hoped it would seem impossible to others.

This was the first town he'd been in since leaving, skirting around every town he neared. If his theory was correct, they'd never suspect he would be hiking, and if they thought he was hiking, they'd never believe he could get this far so quickly.

Only the initial part of his escape was in a vehicle. The hiker did not know the man who picked him up. He had not been in an automobile since that day. He almost missed that ride because he was locked in his home that morning. After breaking the lock on the door, he told his wife to check on their daughter while he went to see what was happening.

That was the last time he saw his wife.

That was part of the plan.

Was she still alive? The question had crossed his mind more than he'd like to admit. He had loved her once, but no longer. For many years they had been like-minded, eager to please, hoping to be the team with a breakthrough. She remained focused on those early shared ambitions, but he had changed. It hurt knowing she was dead or helping them hunt for him.

After several cramped muscles and a few odd positions, he had both boots off. Both socks bore splotches of blood from blisters. He studied the nearby tent. Still no movement. He didn't know how people behaved in situations like this, but assumed modesty often gave way to necessity, so he stripped off his wet jeans and underwear. It was possible his clothing could be salvaged with a couple of wash cycles. He had no practical experience with cleaning soiled clothing. Clean clothing was necessary before interacting with other people plus a shower, but he'd have to make do with a change of clothing and keep his distance from others as much as possible. With clean socks and jeans donned, he pulled a clean sweatshirt over his head. He had one pair of shoes, so the wet boots went back on his feet.

He wondered if his clothing would be stolen if he left them to dry. Although it was difficult to imagine anyone would touch them, he did not know how desperate people were in a town like this. He had encountered a few people on the trail, most of which he spotted far enough away he could hide until they were gone. The few he couldn't avoid seemed pleasant enough. Pleasant meaning, they had no interest in him.

It had rained last night. He'd pitched his tent under a tree and caught rainwater in a pan, but he couldn't start a fire, so for dinner he ate his last power bar. Cascade Locks had been his planned first stop since he'd studied the maps left in his backpack and he had provisioned his food exactly right. He found it hard to believe he'd made it this far, but he was here and needed supplies.

After more deliberation than seemed worthy of the issue, he decided to leave the wet and soiled clothing, which proved a more difficult act than he'd imagined. At the edge of the campground, he turned to see if they were still there. One might assume he had formed a bizarre attachment to those clothes because of how many miles they had traveled together. There was truth to that, but mostly it was because of how hard it was to obtain them. Everything he owned, he now carried with him. It had taken him three years to gather it.

The hiker's plan had started with a few innocent conversations with a computer technician, expressing mutually agreed upon dissatisfactions regarding their lot in life. They first met in the pub, shared a beer, which turned into a few beers and then a ritual every Thursday. It took the hiker six months to build trust and then one day, because the hiker felt he had to tell someone, he told the technician about his thoughts of getting out, leaving it all behind. To his amazement, not only did the hiker feel freedom unlike anything he'd ever experienced, but doors started opening as well.

During the entire preparation for his escape, he only met two people—a schoolteacher and the computer guy. Still, he avoided details with them as much as possible. His discussions with the teacher were vague and always done in passing on the streets of their small town, but the computer technician always seemed aware of those discussions, so the hiker knew they talked to each other as well. The plan was simple: walk, avoid towns, north to Canada. Because he would be hiking, he never researched hiking gear, trail systems, clothing, or anything associated with his escape while at work. It was important that he leave no trail, not even a hint, to follow. So, others did the work, gathering clothing, camping gear, food, and maps. That last day, and to his amazement, a stranger risked his own life by driving him out-of-town while all hell was breaking loose. He'd never know who they were or be able to repay them. That part troubled him. If he lived long enough, he'd try to help other people. That's what he told himself.

At a road leading into town, he paused. It was just after ten o'clock, according to his watch. He needed to restock supplies, but first, he wanted a meal and hot coffee: find a café, sit in the corner, avoid eye contact, eat breakfast, get supplies, and vanish. That was the plan.

Stick with the plan.

Traffic was light, not unlike the foot traffic on the Pacific Coast Trail, except the sightings of others here were counted in minutes instead of days. He crossed the street. One block to the north, he saw train tracks and the Columbia River. To the west, a bridge spanned the river, the State of Washington on the other side. Something about Washington sounded like safety. Possibly because Washington's northern border was with Canada. There was no guarantee he could cross that border, but that was his plan. Safety waited for him in Canada.

Just a few more weeks.

He came to a dilapidated building with large roll-up doors and lots of windows, but the glass was so dirty he could not see inside. He climbed the stairs. It looked like a restaurant on the second floor, but it was dark. A sign on the door said closed. He wondered if that meant closed permanently, or if it was open at some point in the day.

Back on the ground floor, he cupped his hands over his eyes and peered in. The inside looked nothing like the outside. It was immaculate. Huge shining, stainless-steel tanks lined the back wall. A guy was washing the floor with a hose. So much water, it was hard to imagine. He looked for a sign on the building or near the street. He saw where one had been, but it was gone. Broken or stolen, he didn't know. Maybe they couldn't afford to replace it or perhaps replacing it didn't matter. Everyone in such a small town knew what they did here, but he did not. He had seen nothing like this.

"Can I help you?"

The voice startled the hiker, causing him to jump. "Sorry. I'm not looking for any problems." Waypoint for hikers, someone had scribbled that on his map. The Pacific Crest Trail came to this town because the bridge was the only way across the Columbia River for miles and linked to the trail on the Washington side. But he didn't know much about the trail, who used it, or if the town welcomed hikers. Perhaps they did not.

"Relax. I'd say you just came off the trail." The man pointed.

"Yes. I did. I need supplies."

"By the looks of you, a good meal wouldn't hurt either."

"I hoped to eat in town."

"We aren't open just yet."

"I saw you were not. I'll be going. I didn't mean to cause you any concerns."

"Aren't you curious about what we do here? I mean, most folks are."

The man hesitated. He was curious but wasn't looking for conversation. Not that he didn't want one, but the less he said, the safer. "Well, to be honest...."

"We brew craft beer. Few of us left, you know, what with the drought and such."

"That is interesting. We don't have those where I'm from."

"Where are you from?"

Crap. Why would this guy ask that? It's almost like he knows something. But that's impossible.

The hiker motioned back toward the trailhead. "South. Worked in the fields. I'm headed to Washington. Heard I could find work in the vineyards."

The man nodded. "Ah, you're headed to Yakima."

The hiker was not headed to Yakima and didn't know if they had vineyards there. "Uh, yeah, maybe. Is that the best place to find work? It doesn't have to be vineyards. That just sounded better than regular fieldhand employment, but I'll do whatever."

The man studied the hiker for a moment. The hiker feared he was about to ask another question, but the man said, "It's early for beer, but I have coffee, and we make root beer as well. Our kitchen staff is prepping for lunch. They could fix you a hamburger. How about it? My treat."

Although he didn't want entanglements or further conversation, his hunger overrode his reluctance. "I have money."

The man offered his hand. "My name is John."

The hiker said, "Scott." Not true, of course. He had an identification card that looked as authentic as the ID New America had issued him, except this card said his name was Scott Key. In his first night's campfire, he'd burned his original ID and clothing. He was Scott Key for the rest of his life, however long that might be, which wouldn't be long if his plan failed.

"Glad to meet you, Scott. Follow me." John trotted up the stairs to the door where the closed sign hung in the window and stepped inside. "The washroom is down the hallway. Wash up. I'll have you a hot cup of coffee when you return."

Scott slid his backpack to the floor just outside the door, gave a single nod, and proceeded to the washroom. After cleaning up the best he could, he returned, and true to his word, John had a steaming cup of coffee waiting for him. Scott picked up the coffee and roamed around the dining area, part of which overlooked the brewing operation. Where he lived, there was no brewery. Scott never thought about where the beer was produced. There were two beers and one brand—Carver and Carver Light. There wasn't much difference between the two as far as Scott could tell. Both smelled and tasted a bit like canned corn. He didn't care for beer, but on the rare occasions when he could leave work, he'd stop at a pub for a beer or two. He drank alone until he met the computer guy, then it became their clandestine meeting place where they sat in the back in a dark corner. He never felt it was entirely safe. That feeling would soon intensify.

John struggled up the stairs, carrying a small glass in one hand and two plates balanced in the other. "I hope you don't mind if I join you."

Before Scott could reply, John put the plates on a table, both of which contained a hamburger and golden-brown French fries and smelled wonderful. Maybe the aroma *was* wonderful, or perhaps it smelled wonderful because he'd been eating power bars and trail mix for the last eight days.

John sank into a chair and motioned for Scott to sit. The liquid in John's glass was black as night, unlike anything Scott had ever seen. Before Scott could speak, John raised his glass and said, "I said it was too early for beer, but this is the first pour of our new porter recipe. Small batch, you see, as a test. Not too early for a wee sip."

John held the glass under his nose and then raised it. "Nice malty aroma with a bit of roast and opaque, but clear. Head looks right." He took a sip, nodded, and took another. "I think we nailed it. I've been tweaking this recipe for years." He took a drink. "Yep. This is it. This is what I've been looking for. I'll pour you one of these later if you stop by." John indicated his porter.

With his mouth full, Scott said, "This is kind of you."

"My pleasure, but it is just a burger and fries. You're my first hiker this year. We get a few. I look forward to it every year. We don't get many visitors in Cascade Lakes, so meeting folks traveling the trail is a nice diversion. They say a lot of people used to hike the trail. It runs from Mexico to Canada. But you probably know all about that."

Scott knew little about the trail. He didn't know it started at the Mexico border, but he knew it went to Canada. He also knew he was probably not the first hiker on the trail. While he had not seen many people, he had seen a few. "I don't know much about it."

John studied Scott for a moment. "Looks like the trail has gotten to know you."

Scott didn't reply, taking a bite of his burger. What does John mean by that statement? Is this some sort of trap? Having swallowed, Scott said, "I don't understand."

John chuckled. "Looks like you've met the trail up close and personal. I suspect you haven't looked in the mirror, but you have a black eye and scratches on your face." John glance down. "But you know about your knee because blood is soaking through your pants. I assume you have a nasty abrasion hidden underneath."

Scott took a deep breath. "Yeah. Steep section a couple of days ago. It had snowed during the night, and the next day the trail was slick. I fell a few times."

"You need to get a proper bandage on that. I'll see to it before you leave. Have you seen many on the trail?" John asked.

Scott said, "Not many."

"Yeah, not many. They trickle through. Like I said, legend has it many people used to hike the trail. Do the entire thing, border to border. Just for the fun of it. Can you imagine that? People with enough time and money they could hike over 2500 miles just for fun. They say the old country was a failure, but that's not something people can do today. Kinda makes you wonder, doesn't it?"

Scott felt certain the question was a trap sprung and baited. He took a sip of coffee. "Like you said, just a legend."

"I said that, didn't I. Still, makes you think. People nowadays use the trail for three reasons: they don't own a vehicle, and they are running from something or to something." John studied Scott again. "My guess is you are all three of those things."

"I'm just looking for work," Scott said.

"Most folks are hunting for a job. They always say that. They've heard it's better somewhere else. I suspect they never find it any better than the place they left. But I think they leave out the part about running from something. What are you running from Scott? The law? Bad marriage? Kids? Perhaps all three."

Scott thought for a moment. "I'm running from the heat."

John dropped his burger and burst into laughter. "And you're headed to Yakima? It's already been over 100 degrees there and it's only April."

"I didn't realize that. But I'm used to working in the heat."

John gave his head a slight shake. "I suppose that's true in a manner of speaking. Well, it's a tough life, isn't it, Scott? But I don't need to tell you that. When did you start?"

Scott caught himself before he said eight days, not that John would have guessed he'd left from Carpinteria eight days ago. Nine hours spent in the back of a truck to Castella, where he got on the Pacific Coast trail. No one would believe him if he'd said that. "About three weeks. I've lost track of time."

"Where'd you start from?"

Scott said, "Near Fresno."

"Strawberries?"

Scott said, "Come again?"

John glanced at Scott's hands and then said, "You must have been picking strawberries. That's the early crop there. Takes a lot of labor. I have a cousin down there. We don't get strawberries here, except what we grow in our gardens. Strawberries go to the Chosen. Them assholes get all the good stuff."

Scott nodded. John was correct about that. Scott got all the good stuff as a scientist working in a Chosen Community, or at least, that's what he was told. But the hamburgers here tasted better, although he seldom ate hamburgers, except occasionally at the pub. Hamburgers and fries are commoner food. However, here, in this small commoner town, both tasted delicious, causing Scott to wonder how many other things the Chosen and their servants had wrong about the outside world.

John continued. "Damn Chosen, SOBs. They want my beer—all of it. We gotta make that Carver crap. It's mandatory to have a license. But they wanted the craft stuff too. So, I brewed a special beer. I call it crap-in-a-kettle, but we sell it as a New America Light Ale named Heaven." John laughed. "It's awful. We use the cheapest ingredients. The stuff stinks, but they buy it because, bad as it is, it's still better than the Carver crap. I make good beer for regular folks like you. You understand that what I'm telling you is all off the record. The authorities don't know I brew stuff they don't get."

Scott nodded. Friendly as he seemed, John made his feelings about the Chosen clear. John would turn hostile if he knew who Scott was and what he had done, who he'd worked for, and about the children. Scott felt confident this friendly fellow would cut him up and feed him to the fish if he knew about the children. Scott wouldn't blame him.

Eat, get supplies, cross the river, and keep moving toward Canada. Stick with the plan. That's the only way.

"What's your plan, Scott from Fresno?"

"Like I said, I'm headed to Yakima to look for work."

"I mean, what's your plan today?"

"Get supplies, cross the river, keep moving."

"You're looking for work?"

"Yes."

"How about a change of plan? Go down the street to the Cascade Inn. Ask for Jerri. Tell her John sent you. She'll rent you a room at a reduced price. We have a little deal under the table, if you know what I mean."

Scott did not know what John meant but assumed it was something like how he got his clothing and gear—under the table. "I wasn't planning on staying."

"I heard you. That's why I said it's a change of plan. Look, no offense, but you need a shower, and you must have clothing that needs to be laundered. You could use a good night's rest."

Scott wasn't sure where to go on this. He could agree and still sneak out of town. It wasn't as if John would go looking for him on the trail. "A night in a bed is tempting."

"There you go. Come back here for dinner, say 8:30. The rush, if there is one, will be over by then, and we can sit, drink a couple of beers, make plans for the next week or so."

Scott felt a sudden urge to run. "Make plans?"

"Yes. You need work. I need help for a few weeks."

"I appreciate it, but I need to keep moving."

John put both palms on the table. "So, you have said, Scott from Fresno, but here's the deal. Things have happened that you want to know about."

Scott felt as if he should bolt for the door but could not.

John leaned over the table. "Someone escaped from Pacific Edge." John looked around, although they were alone. "I'm in the Resistance. I don't share that with strangers, but we are no longer strangers. Are we, Scott from Fresno?"

Scott said, "I don't understand."

John stood but never broke eye contact. "I'll see you at 8:30, Scott from Fresno. I have information for you."

5

QUIGLEY WATCHED AS PRIME PACED THE office, waiting for the satellite technician to arrive. Prime's face, at least in this version, was incapable of frowning or smiling, although Quigley didn't think Prime ever experienced happiness beyond whatever pleasure killing people gave him. Still, Prime's impatience grew exponentially with each passing minute.

On his first day of employment, his first sight of Prime had turned Quigley's stomach. Prime did not call him Quigley back then. That came weeks later. Prime didn't rename assistants until it appeared they might survive awhile. Many didn't last long. This was the third replication of Prime since Quigley's employment here. How many were made before that? Quigley didn't know. That first body was a mix of mechanical and human parts. The face had been removed from a person. However, tubes and wire snaked from the back of Prime's head into the sides of the face to circulate a polymer compound replicating blood to keep the skin alive. Prime said there were other parts of the male Test Subjects under his plastic exterior. This variant had been designed so Prime could eat actual food, but it didn't go well. It did not go well for the people who created that variant either. It was the first execution Quigley witnessed.

Prime was angry and hungry. Hungry because Prime had not consumed real food in many years. Angry because he was Prime. Prime was eager for the next modification. It was to be revolutionary, but failed experiments had delayed its implementation. The creator of New America didn't like delays.

Several laboratories scattered across the country, like the one in Pacific Edge, strived to meet Prime's demands. Quigley knew few details about the labs. He only gathered that among other things, they tested drugs, experimented with medical procedures, grew body parts for incorporation into Prime variants, tested psychological manipulation, and trained assassins.

However, one laboratory in Dallas did something different: they created humans. The purpose of those humans was unknown to Quigley. Three of those humans had been moved to Pacific Edge several years ago. Recently, one had been exiled and two had escaped, and Prime wanted them back or dead. Prime always gets what he wants.

There had been four-legged and four-armed versions before Quigley arrived. He had not seen these, and that was some consolation. The second Prime variant, while Quigley had been here, was almost identical to the first, sans the human face. Too many problems with the skin, and the scientists were no closer to solving the eating problem. That version was supposed to be temporary but lasted several years before the current one replaced it.

Of course, this was just the Seattle version. Quigley didn't know if the other Prime variants in the other facilities were the same.

The current variant in Seattle, the one Quigley was watching, stood on two legs, and had two arms. This one was slightly taller than the average man and had a mechanical face that was covered with a skin-like plastic. However, it had an exposed human torso, hairless chest and abdomen covered with clear, no doubt bulletproof, laminated polycarbonate.

Quigley wondered about the reasoning for the design on several levels. Since this version also could not eat, Quigley could not imagine what purpose the human part served. The human part bothered Quigley the most. Not because of how it looked, but what it represented. It had once been a person: a son, perhaps a husband, maybe a father.

One thing the three variants had in common was they were all Prime. That didn't change. The way Prime did things remained the same. The human pieces did not make Prime more human.

Quigley did not look forward to the satellite technician's arrival because the technician would not live long. Based on Prime's mood, it would be a painful and messy death. Prime could have robots clean the mess, but it would likely be left to Quigley. Prime liked to test his assistants' willingness to do anything. That happened a lot recently, and he did not know why.

A chime rang, indicating someone in the elevator was requesting access to the Penthouse. A woman's image appeared on a monitor dedicated to security cameras. he recognized her as the satellite technician. The security team had already cleared her and forwarded her file information, which Quigley had reviewed.

That the technician was a woman surprised and bothered him. She would have been Chosen because commoners don't rise to such positions. He was not opposed to women in such a position, although it was unusual. women were not encouraged to pursue college other than to find a spouse if they had not been picked during the Choosing in high school, and going on to a career, in anything other than teaching or nursing, was rare. Being at a level to represent any field before Prime, rarer still. He had not witnessed a woman in Prime's presence other than cleaning the Penthouse, and even then, Prime typically left the room.

Would a woman survive long enough to answer Prime's questions? Unfortunately, he would soon find out.

Quigley went to the elevator. A small woman stepped out, dark hair cut short, black-rimmed glasses, and of middle eastern ancestry. Quigley smiled, not because he knew the woman or felt confident about her future, but because he could do little else. Her last moments on earth should be no worse than necessary.

He offered his hand, and she took it. Her hands were soft, but her grip firm. She held his hand and said, "I'm Ava."

Quigley said, "Pleased to meet you." She continued to hold his hand. Inexplicably, he felt his heart rate increase.

"I am here to see Prime."

Quigley detected no fear or awe in her voice. Instead, she sounded confident. He did not know if that was a good thing. "Do you have questions before we enter?" Quigley asked. "I understand that—well, let's just say this is a distressing experience for most people."

"Is it? You seem relaxed," Ava said.

"I've worked here for many years."

"Yes. It shows. Yet, I sense anxiety." She rubbed the back of his hand with her thumb. "Not to worry, Mr. Quigley. I have met Prime at its other locations."

Quigley nodded. Unable to form a clear thought, he said, "Shall we?"

Before Quigley could make an announcement, Ava opened the door and marched in. "Hello, Prime. You requested my presence. I hope this doesn't take long. I need to catch a flight to New Mexico, and you know how infrequent flights are."

Prime said, "This won't take long. Why do we not have information from Southern California?"

"I told you in the e-mail. We've lost contact with the satellite."

"Don't use that tone with me. I want details."

"No tone intended, but I don't know what happened to the satellite, or I would have told you in the e-mail. That's why I'm going to New Mexico to the VLA." She turned to Quigley. "That stands for Very Large Array. It's the best place in New America to study satellites and other things in space."

Quigley nodded.

"You don't have to explain things to Quigley. He's just an assistant."

"I understand Mr. Quigley's position. You do not need to explain it to me."

"Why don't I have images of that town in the desert?"

"I told you. We can't communicate with the satellite."

Prime said nothing.

Quigley expected a bolt of electricity, or perhaps Prime would kill the woman himself. No one spoke to Prime in this manner and survived. Not in Quigley's experience.

Although it might get him killed, Quigley asked, "What do you think caused the problem?"

Ava said, "That is a good question. I wish I had an answer. It could be many things. At first, we thought it was just interference. Perhaps a solar flare. We used to monitor those but stopped decades ago. Other countries still do, but we are not permitted to communicate with them." She glanced at Prime. "That makes it difficult to know many things."

Quigley was amazed that Ava was still alive.

Prime said, "A solar flare? That doesn't sound feasible. What other theories?"

Ava took a deep breath. "It could be anything from other satellites to a system failure. That's why I must go to New Mexico."

Prime said, "I need to know what is going on in that desert town."

"You have military people there. Ask them."

Prime did not have the ability to make expressions, but Quigley believed he could feel the wrath emanating from the man/machine.

Prime said, "I have not heard from them. Communication is down."

Ava nodded. "They were using the satellite to bounce transmissions."

Prime said, "What about other satellites? We have other satellites."

"We do. But it takes time to move them into position."

"You said other satellites might cause interference."

"Correct. Other countries have satellites, and there's old junk floating around. We've asked for funding to clean things up several times, but it's always denied. Now, perhaps you can see why it's important."

Prime waved her off. "Do those old satellites still work? Perhaps you could use them. I need answers, and I need them now." Prime pointed to a computer. "See if you can contact an old satellite. Succeed and live another day."

"Either you're looking for an excuse to kill me, or you know less about satellites and computers than I imagined. I can't contact a satellite using your computer. I need to be in New Mexico at the VLA."

"I've had enough of your insolence. I have other people who will gladly take your position."

"How many people understand the old technology, or the computer code in the old satellites?"

"Quigley will do that research to find those people."

"I'll save him the time and trouble. I'll tell you. There is one person, and her name is Ava. I am the only one who knows the old technology. Do you want to know why? I'll tell you why. Because I think we should clean up the skies above us before they rain down hunks of metal on us, but you keep denying the funding to do so."

Prime started toward Ava. If Quigley could destroy this manifestation of Prime, he would do so now, even though it would bring about his death and end his mission.

Ava held out her hand. "Would you like to hear something interesting?"

Prime stopped. Perhaps confused by Ava's unwillingness to cower.

"Go on then."

"I have a theory about the lost communication."

"I'm listening."

"I think satellites interfered with the signal, but not because it was a random crossing of paths. I believe someone moved satellites there on purpose."

Prime said, "Koreans. It had to be them. Russia still wants parts of Europe, and our alliance remains. But since Korea has moderated and made friends with other countries in Asia, they are no longer the firm allies they once were after the Greatest War."

"Perhaps. You need me at VLA to determine that. However, I think the satellites only caused the initial signal loss. Here is the rest of my theory. I believe the satellite is gone."

"What do you mean, gone?"

"Destroyed."

"Who has that capability?"

"That, Prime, is the question. If you want to learn the answer, I suggest you let me catch that plane."

Prime remained silent for a moment, as if conferring with the other Prime locations, and then said, "Quigley, arrange a private flight for Ava on my aircraft." Prime paused. "Whichever aircraft will get her there fastest."

Part Three

1

Friday, April 9, 9:17 a.m.

THE SUN HAD RISEN IN A BLUE sky. Heat waves shimmered across the vast desert sand. Too hot and too dry for much to survive. Even the mountains stood like lifeless giants. It made sense to build a military base here, especially one to keep hidden.

Nyx had taken the stairway to the surface and then run to the mountain that concealed the hangar, sat in a shaded nook, and was soaking with sweat. Potterville got hot in the summer, but nothing like this. She didn't know what the temperature was—120? It felt as if she had stuck her head in an oven. The shade helped, but she felt sure she was sunburned, even though it only took her about five minutes to run here. She didn't want to run back. She'd be sunburned for sure if she did, so she sat, hoping to see the giant jet appear in the sky.

Then she could go into the hangar and stay out of the sun.

Then she could greet Red and Antonio upon their successful return.

Then she could run to Derrick and throw her arms around him.

But there was no plane in the sky.

So, she sat. Waiting.

Minutes clicked off as the sun rose. Still no planes, no jets, no anything. How long would it take? How far did they go? How fast did the plane fly? She didn't know but made calculations and considered many circumstances that might explain why they had not returned. None of them sounded right.

Something had happened to them.

Now it was just her and Akira.

And Akira wasn't herself, not even close.

2

NINETY MILES ABOVE THE EARTH'S SURFACE, an angular black aircraft floated in a manner that would appear to be aimless. It was not. A dead satellite began a slow orbital decline 150 miles above the aircraft. Eventually, it would reenter the Earth's atmosphere and be incinerated. The black aircraft would reenter the atmosphere much sooner. There was a slim chance it would not burn up and a slimmer chance it would land successfully. That the pilot would survive, slimmer still.

3

NO ONE HAD SPOKEN FOR SEVERAL MINUTES. Red checked instruments, twisted knobs, flicked switches, and occasionally tapped a gauge. Antonio didn't know what any of it meant. He wondered how much Red understood. They had rescued the people from the desert town but left Miriam, Derrick, Anna, and Rebekah behind. Miriam, Anna, and Derrick were unique in ways Antonio didn't understand. Test Subjects, they said, but he didn't know what that meant. Miriam's mind worked in ways he couldn't comprehend. He had witnessed Derrick's superhuman annihilation of the soldiers at the school. Prime robots had come to Potterville searching for Anna Ford. To some extent, he understood that Anna, Miriam, and Derrick felt an obligation to do something. What they needed to do was unclear.

But why did Rebekah go with them? She was just an ordinary girl. Well, not ordinary, but not a Test Subject. Why didn't she get on the plane? Why did she choose the others over them? Over him?

Of course, they had no way to land the plane.

So, there was that.

No longer able to stand it, Antonio said, "Uh, what about the landing gear? That's a problem. Right?"

Charlie said, "The flight instructor manual details procedures for landing with the landing gear up."

"So, we just do that then. Right?" Antonio asked.

Charlie said, "Unfortunately, the manual also recommends a water landing if landing without the landing gear. Such a landing on dry ground is not recommended."

Antonio thought for a moment. "We could find water."

Charlie said, "That is an option."

"No water near the Base," Red said. "Besides, we won't be able to change course much longer."

"What?" Antonio asked.

"We are losing hydraulic fluid on the right side. They must have hit something."

Charlie said, "The aircraft has redundant systems. Perhaps we can reroute something."

Red said, "I've already tried. It gained us some pressure, but we are still losing fluid. Eventually, it will be gone. Then we don't have the controls needed for landing, even if we had landing gear. Besides, we can't make a gear-up landing because the front gear is now stuck, partially retracted. It would be impossible to land it."

Antonio said, "So, we're dead."

"We can jump," Red said.

"Very funny," Antonio said.

"With parachutes, idiot," Red said.

"Oh. I had not thought of that."

"How did you get elected student council president?" Red asked.

"My charm. Or perhaps my good looks. Nope, must be that I'm humble."

Red said, "I'm bringing us around on a bearing that will take us close to the Base. We parachute and walk the rest of the way. It'll be hot, but I hope to get us close."

"What about the jet?" Antonio asked.

"It's going to fly until it runs out of fuel. What's the range on the remaining fuel at our current speed?" Red asked.

Charlie said, "Approximately 2,145.45 miles."

"Can't you narrow it down?" Red asked.

"I can, but I will need precise data on winds speed, cruising altitude, and aircraft speed. I based my calculations on current speed and conditions."

"Joking, dude."

"Oh, I see. Ha, ha."

"Can we be serious?" Antonio asked. "Myself included."

Red said, "We have that technology. How about making yourself useful by finding parachutes? Get two for the big guy here." Red motioned to Charlie.

"I saw chutes in the passenger section. I'll be right back," Antonio said.

A few minutes later, Antonio returned laden with four parachutes, which he piled by the entrance. He peered out the window over Red's shoulder. "Where are we? This doesn't look right."

"We are flying northeast of the Base. The plane will be on a southwest course to ensure it's over the ocean when it runs out of fuel. No one gets hurt. No one knows about it except the soldiers who shot at us."

"And they'll be looking for something they can't find," Antonio said. "I like it. If we survive jumping out of the airplane."

"Nothing to it. Jump out, pull the cord."

"It doesn't scare you?" Antonio asked.

"Scares the crap out of me. But it beats the alternative."

The plane banked left.

Red said, "It won't take us long to be over the Base."

"I forgot to ask. Who's flying the plane after we jump?" Antonio asked.

"No one. I'll set the auto pilot to increase altitude just after we jump so the plane clears the mountains. You and Charlie go to the cargo bay. Get your parachutes on. Lower the ramp. I'll be down soon."

"Don't keep us waiting."

"No worries. I plan to be back for lunch."

"Always thinking about food," Antonio said.

"Better than thinking about jumping out of an airplane."

"Good point. At least we aren't ditching a perfectly good airplane."

Charlie said, "The aircraft is perfectly good for flying, just not for landing."

Red and Antonio stared at Charlie for a moment.

Red asked, "Charlie, did you just make a joke?"

"Yes. Since you did not laugh, I documented it as unsuccessful and will analyze the plausible reasons it failed while plummeting to the ground."

Antonio and Red erupted, laughing.

Charlie said, "Further analyzation required."

4

L. LINDA FELT THE SAFETY HARNESS, tighten against her shoulders. The cold permeated her flight suit. She didn't understand what had happened. It was pitch black, and she didn't know where she was. Her thinking was cloaked in a thick fog. She only knew her future was bleak and short.

However, she had accomplished something others had not. New America did not send people into space, and according to the media, never had. They blocked, cleansed, or otherwise banished any history of the United States having a space program and said anyone saying differently was fake news. New America liked saying fake news a lot. L. Linda believed other countries had space programs, sent people into orbit around the Earth, had a station on the moon, and sent people to Mars. She only knew this because of what the Resistance posted online. The Resistance might not be organized, but it was persistent.

The Resistance was good at making banned information available. Still, it was best to download stuff before New America found and destroyed those sites. Although New America didn't have a space program, and had not supported L. Linda, she had traveled to space. But the Resistance did not know about it, so her accomplishment would remain unknown. No one would believe her anyway.

L. Linda was also persistent, but persistence wouldn't help here. Her time was up, but her life had not been a complete waste. She'd saved Derrick once, getting him out of a literal box earlier. Perhaps she'd helped him again by destroying a satellite. She didn't know if the satellite was out of commission, and she'd never know if her sacrifice helped.

Derrick would never know what she did or tried to do. Worse, he'd never really know L. Linda Maxton. And that was a shame, or perhaps a blessing. To be honest, she didn't know if she could have told Derrick everything. Now she didn't have to make that decision.

It made her sad, not because she believed she'd live a long life or find happiness or any of the regular stuff kids her age dreamed about. It made her sad because she always thought her life would end in violence. That she'd go down fighting.

Instead, she'd run out of oxygen or freeze to death long before this metal coffin burned in the earth's atmosphere.

That made her sad.

5

Friday, April 9, 9:55 a.m.

THE ROAD TURNED, CLIMBING A STEEP GRADE. At the top, Harley pulled into a turnout that overlooked the valley, where he got out and sat on a rock wall. They all joined him and, for ten minutes, watched in silence. Black smoke boiled into the sky. Even here, the acidic smoke burned Derrick's eyes, and he felt the heat from the flames, or maybe it was just the sun beating down as the temperature soared.

Derrick said, "We need a plan."

No one spoke for a few minutes. Then, still staring at the inferno that was once his home, Harley said, "We'll need a passport in Mexico."

"Like a government identification?" Miriam asked, then added, "There's no way. There's a bounty on us, remember? Plus, we don't have time. We must find another way."

"Not a passport from the government. New America doesn't allow travel to Mexico, and Mexico guards the border to keep us out. I mean a statement from someone in Mexico confirming we have a business transaction. In our case, it means exchanging goods or services related to ravaging operations."

Derrick said, "You make it sound like a business rather than an illegal operation."

Harley shrugged. "It's the business we're in. Besides, any travel into Mexico is illegal."

"How do we get this passport?" Derrick asked.

Harley said, "No idea. Generally, Mexican buyers usually come to us. We only initiate contact if we have something unusual. Now, we have nothing to offer. Plus, they would never let us in with the weapons, and we can't attack the New America military without weapons."

Derrick turned back to the blaze.

Getting across the border would be difficult.

Bringing the .50 cal. machine guns, problematic.

Taking out a mobile missile launcher, unlikely.

Derrick felt eager to leave, but sensed Professor Atwood and Harley needed more time to process the loss of their town. Harley surprised him when he said, "It's pavement for the first 50 miles, and then we'll take a dirt road that will become little more than a trail. We'll be close to the border then, but not a border crossing. No one gets in that way. We use unofficial crossings."

"Then why bother with a passport?" Derrick asked.

"It reduces the odds of the cartels killing us."

"Cartels?" Derrick asked.

"Criminal gangs. Not many anymore, but they still patrol the border in the unpopulated areas, which is where we'll need to cross."

Derrick stared at Harley for a moment. This sounded less promising with each passing second. "Then how do we get in?"

"We make our own road." Harley walked to the lead truck and climbed behind the wheel.

Derrick gathered the soldier's uniforms and tossed them out.

"What are you doing," Miriam asked.

"On second thought, getting caught with New America military uniforms seems like a bad idea," Derrick said.

Soon they were speeding down an uninhabited road through an uninhabited desert. Harley drove the lead truck, the theory being that anyone watching them approach might recognize him and hold their fire. Anna rode in the back with the machine gun, hidden but ready. Rebekah sat with Anna. They had some catching up to do.

Atwood drove the second truck, and Haskins sat in front. They had even more catching up to do than did Rebekah and Anna. Derrick and Miriam rode in the back of the truck, also with a machine gun on the floor under a tarp. Derrick needed time with Miriam, and this might be the only chance he would have for a while.

It could be the last time ever.

Sometimes reality eliminates good possibilities, leaving one with few good options and none of them ideal—most, undesirable.

The wind whipped his hair, which had grown much longer than it had ever been. Gone were the days when he trimmed it daily with a Barber-Bot™. The enhanced color had faded. The tips were still nearly white, but the recent growth was brown and much darker than he'd remembered it being before he had changed the color. His eyes, no longer ice blue, were reverting to their natural color, which was hard to describe: kinda blue, kinda grey, kinda green. He hadn't considered what people thought as his appearance changed, but now realized it served as a constant reminder: he was not the person he had claimed to be. Part of him wanted to get a haircut, at least removing the near-white tips, but another part wanted to keep it as a reminder of his transformation. Another part wanted to keep them because—well, he thought it looked kind of cool.

They made a sharp turn to the right. Derrick and Miriam both lifted off the bed of the truck a couple of inches as it left the road. Atwood slowed to a crawl. It was difficult to see. Dust swirled, enveloping them. Derrick waved the dust from his face. Not that it helped. "I've been thinking."

Miriam said, "Glad to hear it."

"Can we be serious?"

"We can try."

Derrick shook his head. "I've been thinking about Father and Mother."

"You mean our Keepers?"

"Do you think about them?"

Miriam said, "I try not to."

"Me too. Most of the time. Still, sometimes I think about them." He stared into the distance, swaying with the motion of the truck.

"I recommend you stop doing that."

"Stop what?" Derrick asked. "Thinking about them?"

"Duh."

Derrick said, "I wonder about the other Test Subjects as well. What do you suppose happened to them?"

"You don't want to know."

"You know? Tell me. What happened to them?"

Miriam took a deep breath. "They didn't make it."

"Didn't make it where?"

"Out of the program."

"Oh…" Derrick's voice trailed off. "They were deconstructed?"

Miriam nodded. "That's what they call it. A living dissection is a more accurate description."

"I figured that was the case, but I hoped to be wrong. Why did they do that? I don't get it."

Miriam shrugged. "I didn't get that deep into the files. That's how they do it. That's all I know."

"Why didn't they kill us? Why were we allowed to continue?"

"One of our Keepers talked them into continuing the test outside the facility. I don't know which one. I only read a couple of e-mails. Moving us to Pacific Edge was a first, and we were supposed to remain confined there. Prime didn't approve your exile. That's why they went to Potterville to bring you home."

"When they offered me a pardon?"

"Correct."

"What about Anna?"

"What about her?"

"Why did they let her live with Rebekah?"

"I don't know. The Keeper who convinced them to continue the experiment said Anna was just a control. A Test Subject outside of our environment."

Derrick said, "By outside our environment, you mean not living with Keepers?"

"Pretty much."

"So, Mother and Father kept us alive? Do you know why? Maybe they, I don't know, cared about us?"

"Only one wanted to keep the experiment going. The other wanted it to end."

"It must have been Mother. She was distraught when they exiled me."

"She was upset, but I don't think it was about you."

Derrick said, "I don't understand."

"It's just a feeling. I suspect she was upset about the situation."

"Because I was exiled?"

"Yes, and no. Upset, they exiled you, yes, but not because of you. Because she feared what would happen when Prime learned about it."

"You think Prime was aware of the experiment?"

"I do."

"You think it was Father then?"

"Father convinced them to exile you."

"The Tribunal wanted me to stay in Pacific Edge?"

"They wanted you dead."

"Oh." Derrick paused. "So, you think Mother wanted me dead?"

Miriam nodded.

Derrick said nothing for a moment. "There's something else. As memories return, I can't account for school days. It was as if I only went to school a couple of days a week."

Miriam nodded. "Same for me. I think we were training. Training during the nights and certain days, except for a few days a week when we were in school. They used hypnosis to make us forget about the days we were not in school."

"What about the other students? Our teachers? Rebekah, Anna, Jana Somersworth? Why didn't they ask where we were?"

"Good question. We'll ask Rebekah. During the nights, Anna trained with us, but she was in school during the day when we were gone." Miriam thought for a moment. "I have a question. How many girls were on your list for The Choosing?"

Derrick thought for a moment. "Twelve. No, ten."

"Can you name them?"

Derrick stared at her. "I cannot. That's crazy. Isn't it?"

"Not really. How many kids went to Pacific Edge Academy?"

"Upper classes? I don't know. About 700, I guess."

"You had four girls on your list. Do you remember their names?"

Derrick's eyes darted from side to side. "That can't be right." He thought for a moment. "Something is wrong."

"Nothing is wrong. Who do you remember from your list?"

Derrick said nothing for a moment. "Jana and Rebekah."

Miriam nodded. "That makes sense. You liked Rebekah best, but they told you to choose Jana."

"Told me?"

"Using the 1984 chip."

"Oh. I was really in a fog, wasn't I?"

"That's one way of saying it. They created your memories. There were 47 students at the academy."

"That's impossible."

"You probably remember the building as huge."

"It was huge." Derrick stared at her, then said, "It wasn't. Was it?"

Miriam gave her head a slow shake.

They continued in silence for several minutes until Derrick asked. "Why the training? If we were supposed to be killed at the end of the experiment, why train us to fight? That makes little sense."

"I don't know. I've puzzled over it myself."

Atwood hit the brakes, coming close to a stop.

Derreck grabbed the side of the truck's bed as it jerked and bounced over the rough trail, littered with large rocks and deep holes. Atwood had faded farther behind Harley, waiting for the dust to settle. "Perhaps the Keeper that kept the experiment going arranged it?"

"Probably."

"Are there other Test Subject projects?"

"Yes, but I didn't have time to study them. I have all the files saved on the flash drive Allen gave me."

"You don't know what they were trying to accomplish in our test?" Derrick asked.

"Only in general terms."

"And?"

Miriam shrugged. "Control people using the 1984 chip for one."

"For what purpose?"

"I don't know." Miriam paused. "Perhaps to develop workers Prime could trust more than regular people."

Derrick stared into the distance. "To do things that normal people wouldn't do. But the experiment failed?"

"It didn't fail. They thought it was a success while we were in the facility. You were the primary Test Subject. They manipulated you to act differently than the rest of us."

"But I attacked a staff member."

"Because they dialed up the anger stimulus and reduced the constraint control. They wanted you to do that."

"If it was a success, why would they kill us?"

"To complete the study. Measure organic changes. Determine what worked so they could replicate it."

"But you said I failed," Derrick said.

"Outside the testing facility. When you hit Marcus Carver, you looked perfect until then."

"I'm confused."

"You're not alone."

"It doesn't seem to bother you."

"It bothers me, but I have the files. I'll understand it when I have time to read them. Maybe Father arranged the training, hoping we could be put to work for Prime without growing another generation. Maybe he thought it would mean more money or a big promotion or whatever reward people like him get for successful work."

Harley had stopped on a ridge overlooking a valley. Atwood rolled up behind him as dust swirled around the truck and a breeze blew it back upon them.

Derrick waved his hand in front of his face. "I think Father had other reasons."

"Such as?"

"In case we got out of Pacific Edge."

"What do you mean?"

"So, we could protect ourselves, perhaps do more than that."

"Now *you're* talking in riddles."

"Father told me a riddle just before Paul showed up. He said maybe I could make a difference. Make a difference in everything. I didn't understand. But now, it's happening. We could make a difference—in everything."

6

ONE THOUSAND FEET ABOVE THE MOJAVE desert, a C-17 Globemaster cargo jet banked left, turning toward an abandoned military base near Death Valley. The pilot wished he had not sent the copilot with the loadmaster. The copilot could have plotted the precise course and timed their jump so they would land within feet of their destination. The pilot could only guess based on the route he'd flown since depositing their cargo—a bunch of people they didn't know—on an airstrip somewhere in Arizona.

The unlikely pilot, a high school kid, had the C-17 burning along at a respectable 350 knots, which was just over 400 mph. He'd have to slow down to 150 to parachute but shortening the time to their destination was critical. Part of the aircraft's hydraulic system had failed, and the aircraft's flight integrity was iffy.

Plus, he was hungry.

Red slowed the aircraft to 270 mph and engaged the autopilot. The flight path was not what he had hoped. With general knowledge of the map and their original coordinates saved in the system, he had planned on flying north over Nevada and then south toward their destination. That would create the longest flight path, so the aircraft would run out of fuel somewhere in the South Pacific.

It became clear it wouldn't work because he would lose the ability to steer the plane before he could cover the distance needed to establish the desired course. He settled on a path that would get them close to their destination, but not close enough, given the heat in the desert. Walking to the Base would be difficult. Perhaps Charlie could find the hangar, but even that wasn't guaranteed.

The bottom line, even if they survived the jump, they might not survive the desert.

With the course set, Red throttled back the engines. The plane slowed, but without the ability to change the flaps, it wasn't slowing quick enough, which created two problems. First, their airspeed would be faster than recommended for a parachute drop, and two, they were approaching the drop site too fast. He'd have to race to reach the cargo bay, and he'd not been there before. A wrong turn could cost time, and time wasn't on their side. To complicate matters further, he'd never put on a parachute before.

Red fought through narrow stairs and doorways as he struggled with the parachute. When he arrived in the cargo bay, the noise was deafening. Antonio wore earmuffs and a parachute. Communication would be impossible. Charlie wore two parachutes, one on his chest, another on his back.

Red yelled, "We are going too fast, but we have to jump soon!"

"What?" Antonio asked.

Red couldn't hear him but could read his lips. Red lifted one of Antonio's earmuffs. "Too fast."

Antonio gave him a thumbs up. Red shook his head.

Looking at Charlie, Red said, "Too fast, but we gotta jump. Do you know where we are?"

Charlie shook his head.

"Shit." Red looked at his watch. According to his calculations, if one could call them calculations, guessing was a more accurate term. They had to jump in 30 seconds. Red could not estimate their speed. They had slowed, but the plane was still slowing, which meant they were still going too fast.

Red didn't know what would happen when they jumped. Perhaps the parachutes would be torn from their bodies. He thought they'd need to free-fall to slow down so the chutes wouldn't be ripped to shreds, but he didn't know how long they could free-fall at 1000 feet.

Red decided to wait ten seconds before pulling the ripcord. He had no reason to think that was long enough and feared it was too long.

Red counted to ten with his fingers and motioned to pull the ripcord.

Charlie shook his head. With both ripcords in his hand, he made a jumping motion and tugged the cords.

Red shook his head, mouthing ten.

Charlie made a jumping motion and tugged the cords.

Red held up five fingers, then tugged the cord.

Charlie shook his head again, walked to the edge of the cargo bay, and jumped.

7

Friday, April 9, 10:00 a.m.

L. LINDA AWOKE, SHIVERING IN THE COLD, wondering if this was what death felt like, thinking if it was, it sucked. A distant, metallic voice said, "Reentry sequence initiation in 60 seconds."

She blinked but couldn't see anything. Either the aircraft was completely dark, or she'd gone blind.

Still wearing the flight suit, L. Linda wrapped her arms around her chest. "I'm freezing."

The detached voice now sounded inside her flight helmet. "Temperatures inside the cabin will rise when the aircraft reenters the atmosphere. Failure is possible."

"Failure of what? The aircraft? The controls? Can you be more specific?"

"Correct. All systems may fail."

"Where are we?"

"On course, as ordered."

"As ordered? Remind me."

"Returning to the last coordinates before going into orbit. However, the aircraft does not have sufficient power to return to that location."

"Then where are we going?"

"As close as possible to the previous location near the California Coast."

"What does that mean: Near the coast?"

"The location is over the ocean, near the coast."

The aircraft jolted as if it had hit something.

The voice said, "Reentry sequence initiated."

L. Linda tightened the straps of the harness, pulling her firmly against the back of the seat. The aircraft lurched side to side and up and down. "How long will this take?"

"Unknown. This aircraft was not tested for these conditions."

"Best guess."

"Guessing not a program component."

"How about an estimate?"

"Estimated 90 seconds to impact."

"Impact?"

"Power insufficient for a proper landing."

"Sounds fantastic."

The machine did not reply. Perhaps it was programmed to ignore sarcasm. The aircraft continued to jostle her from side to side. She grew tired from trying to hold her head straight, fearing a severe jolt might separate it from her body at any moment. She grasped the arms of the chair with all her strength. Her determination to remain calm faded as the ship's hull glowed red.

A haze of smoke filled the cabin. Even inside her helmet, she smelled the acidic odor of burning metal and melting plastic. So, this is the end? Not at all how she'd pictured it. Not that she had dreams of a quaint white house with a white picket fence, where she'd grow old with the love of her life, drinking iced tea and waving to neighbors passing by on their evening stroll. She had not pictured that, but not this. Helpless.

She wanted to see the end coming. With tears running down her cheeks, she said, "Can you show me outside?"

"Outside cameras damaged."

"Is there no other way?"

"Transparency is achievable but is not advised."

"Do it. Let me see out."

In front of her, the aircraft's hull became transparent but glowed red, with flames leaping from the sides. It was difficult to see through the haze of smoke, which crept into her helmet, or perhaps the air supply was compromised. Her eyes burned, and she fought to stifle coughing.

But at least she could see it coming.

Nothing but water.

With any luck, the crash would kill her. She had not considered drowning. Didn't like the idea—too much swimming, too much trying to stay alive.

Being eaten by sharks wasn't appealing either.

Perhaps she could instruct the autopilot-computer-thing to drive into the sea in a manner that would ensure instant death, but before she could think of a way to say it, she saw the water rushing up to meet them. Instantly, explosions happened all around her, and bags enveloped her, cushioning the blow's violence, as if she was in a giant bounce house.

The aircraft hit again. Then again. She couldn't see anything.

Finally, the aircraft stopped. The bags deflated. The transparency was fading, but she could see they were half-submerged. Water seeped in through the damaged walls. She fought out of the restraining harness and struggled to shed the flight suit. "Open the door!"

The machine did not respond, and the doors did not open.

With the helmet off, she coughed violently, and her eyes stung and blurred with tears. She rushed toward the exit door, and in the last fading light, she spotted a red button with the words EMERGENCY HATCH. She smacked the button. The door cracked open a few inches. Water flooded in.

She tried to slide the door. It didn't move.

Water rushed in up to her waist. Drowning in the ocean didn't appeal to her. Drowning in this box appealed even less.

L. Linda wedged herself into the door's frame, bracing her legs against one side and her back to the other. She pushed with all her might. The angle made it difficult, reducing the force she could exert against the door, but it moved, if only an inch or two. On one hand, movement was good, well received, a great thing to have happened. On the other hand, it allowed more water to rush in, causing the aircraft to sink faster.

She had seen this scene in dozens of movies. Water rises until only inches remain for the person to take one last breath before the hero swoops in and saves the would-be drowning victim. Or the would-be victim miraculously saves herself. L. Linda had no faith in the first scenario, so it was save herself or die.

Wedging herself against the hull and then placing her feet against the door—like lifting weights from a squat, except horizontal and underwater. She pushed and felt the door move just a little. Swimming up out of the water, she had two feet of airspace. It was shrinking fast. After taking a breath, she tried to force herself into the doorway again, but the water rushing in made it difficult. Her feet slipped off the door. Her lungs burned, but she got back into position. They left the entire rushing-water-difficulty-thing out of movies.

The door moved an inch, but the opening was still too narrow.

The entire door would soon be underwater.

One last breath before going under in a last attempt to escape this coffin. If she failed, that was the end of it. No one would know what happened to her—not Jason, not the kids at Potterville High, not Derrick King.

L. Linda took one final breath. Just like in the movies. She dove under the water and forced her way into the opening. Just like in the movies. Then she got stuck. At least this part wasn't like any movie she remembered.

L. Linda twisted and fought and panicked. She didn't like panic. It wasn't something she'd felt often. There was that time when she dropped a carburetor jet from her 175 cc Honda, fearing she'd never find it. Even during her alarm, she knew she could find another jet in Jack Fletcher's boneyard.

This was different. This was pure terror.

Light drifted down from above. Air was just a few feet above her. A few feet were all she needed to breathe again. Funny how she took breathing for granted until she couldn't. Then it became pretty important. Urgent even. So, her squirming and pushing and twisting intensified to a new level. A serious level. A frantic level. She shed the flight suit as quickly as possible, hoping that losing that by losing that bulk, she could slip through the small opening.

The steel door dug into her skin as she forced herself into the narrow opening. Buttons were torn from her shirt. A shoe came off. *Not going back for that.*

Then suddenly, like a hotdog squirting from a ketchup and mustard slathered bun at a cookout, she was out.

Swimming hard to the surface, ten feet—that felt like miles—she found air. Sweet, wonderful air.

She bobbed on the surface, for a few moments, treading water. Her breathing and heart rate slowed. Now for the next problem. She was in the ocean without a boat. She could swim, but she didn't even know which direction to go. The panic had subsided a bit as she went from the notion of drowning within seconds to drowning within a few hours.

Or becoming shark food.

Sometimes her imagination wasn't her best friend.

So, what now, L. Linda Maxton? On the bright side, you're still alive. The water is warm. That's a plus right there. And the crashing waves sound soothing.

Crashing waves.

L. Linda had never been in the ocean, so she didn't know if one would hear crashing waves in the open sea. She spun 180 degrees and, less than 50 yards distant, she saw waves rolling onto a sandy beach.

The aircraft-robot-thing had landed close to the coast, just as it had said.

8

ANTONIO AND RED WATCHED AS CHARLIE'S parachutes opened, the chutes held, and the robot, still in one piece, floated toward the desert sands. Charlie must have known something Red did not, but there was no time to contemplate it because, with each passing second, they got farther from Charlie. Finding each other would become increasingly difficult, and they did not need another problem.

Red grabbed the ring on the ripcord, looked at Antonio, nodded, ran down the ramp, launched into the air, and immediately pulled the ripcord. Everything seemed fine until the chute opened, jerking Red to a sudden stop, like driving a car into a concrete wall at high speed. The harness straps dug into his skin, and he felt sure they would snap and send him plummeting to the Earth.

But they held.

He twisted, turning to find Charlie, and searching for Antonio. Charlie landed about a mile away, but he could not see Antonio. Perhaps Antonio was hidden behind his parachute. Perhaps Antonio was too scared to jump. *I should have tossed that little squirt out of the plane first.*

Red spotted the C-17 headed southwest. That gave him a sense of direction. Studying the horizon, Red picked out landmarks for guidance. The Base was to the north. How far north and the exact direction were unknown. They were in serious trouble if Charlie didn't know how to find his home.

It felt as if he were floating into an oven, growing hotter with each passing second. The ground rushed toward him. Red had seen people parachute in movies. Some hit the ground, tucked, and rolled. Some touched down and walked as if they'd just reached the bottom of a staircase. He decided to tuck and roll. It looked easy, not unlike something he might do in football.

As it turned out, it was nothing like football.

To say that Red timed the landing poorly would be an understatement. He bent his knees slightly to absorb the contact, but the ground came faster than he'd anticipated. Rather than tuck and roll, he crumpled and smashed. Face-planted, knocking himself unconscious.

Red heard someone yelling his name about the same time he became aware of hot sand burning his face. He tried to roll over but failed.

Antonio shouted, "Red! Are you okay?"

"Do not move him." Charlie came to Antonio's side, dragging his two parachutes.

Red groaned. "I think so. Give me a minute." He rolled over.

Antonio said, "Charlie, rip off a piece of the parachute so I can wipe away some dirt and blood."

Charlie did as Antonio asked, handing him an evenly torn piece of cloth.

"I don't suppose anyone brought water?" Antonio asked.

"I would go for a cold soda," Red said.

"I meant to wet the rag," Antonio said, wiping blood from Red's face. "I don't see any bad cuts. It looks like most of the blood came from your nose. I think it's broken."

Red pushed himself to a seated position. "Is it a good look or a bad look?"

"Not sure yet. Too much dirt."

Red said, "Help me up."

Charlie said, "You should not move until I have evaluated your condition."

Red started to stand but stopped when he reached one knee. "We need to get moving. Someone might have spotted the plane."

Antonio offered his hand.

Red said, "Charlie, do you know where we are?"

"We are in the State of California, in what used to be called Death Valley. Death Valley was a National Park in the old United States but was abandoned when James Carver formed New America. President Carver incorporated many National Parks into his corporation, but not Death Valley."

"Great information. But I meant, do you know how to find the Base?"

"The Base, as you call it, is approximately 15 miles, 2450 feet northwest."

Red said, "Approximately?"

"I could be off by a few inches one way or the other."

"Fifteen miles is close enough. Let's go." Red took a step, wobbled, then stopped, raising one hand to shield his face. "Damn, it's hot."

Antonio said, "Walking at a brisk pace, we'll cover three miles an hour. It will take us over five hours. I don't think we can make it in this heat, and it's going to get hotter."

"What choice do we have?" Red asked, then added. "We could run. Ten-minute miles would get us there…" He counted on his fingers. "Uh, well, we'd get there faster."

"It would take us over two hours. We can't run in this heat. Especially without water. We'd never make it."

Red said nothing for a moment. "We need to hide the parachutes." He stumbled toward a pile of rocks, dragging his chute. When he reached the rocks, he loosened the harness, letting it fall to the ground, then he reeled it in and gathered it into a ball.

Charlie said, "I shall fashion head coverings for you both. That will give you protection from the sun."

Antonio said, "Thanks, Charlie, but I'll be okay. I work in the fields on the weekends. I'm used to being in the sun." He pointed at Red. "But the fair-haired boy needs one for sure."

Red said, "A parachute hat. I like it."

Charlie said, "Mr. Antonio, you may be accustomed to the sun where you live, but there is no such thing as being accustomed to this heat."

Red stuffed his parachute into a gap and tossed a large rock on top of it. "Do you know the temperature, Charlie?"

"It is 115 degrees. The temperature could reach 127 degrees today."

Antonio whistled. "On second thought, make me a hat."

Red sat on a rock. "Maybe Charlie should go to the hangar and come back with a vehicle."

"That might work." Antonio turned to Charlie. "How fast could you get to the Base?"

"I could get there in 45 minutes."

"Problem solved. Let's stretch out one of these parachutes for shade while Charlie gets a vehicle." Antonio started to unfurl his parachute.

Charlie said, "That will not be possible."

Antonio stopped. "But you just said…"

"I recall what I said. However, at my top speed, I will run out of power in 15 minutes and 27 seconds."

Red said, "I wish you could be more precise."

"Very well, 15 minutes and 26.3356 seconds."

"I was joking."

"I see. Further analysis required."

"I thought you didn't need to dock as often in the new body," Red said.

"Correct. However, the high temperature requires additional cooling, and that is draining my power supply."

"How long will your power last if we walk?" Antonio asked.

"Power conservation is much better when walking. Power will last 4 hours and 33.5678 minutes."

Antonio sat down beside Red. "We're screwed."

9

Friday, April 9, 10:47 a.m.

EVEN IN THE SHADE, THE HEAT BECAME unbearable, forcing Nyx underground, where she lingered in the cool passageways, studying machinery, supplies, tools, and weapons as she worked her way back to Akira. Something had happened to Red and Antonio, meaning something happened to all of them. She should get back to Akira but was taking her time. Akira might have learned something, but Nyx wasn't sure she wanted to hear it.

Plus, Akira frightened her. Suppose something happened to the others. That left just the two of them, and Akira wasn't herself. Still, Akira was more capable. Nyx was one small problem away from curling into a fetal position in a dark corner. She could not face losing another person in her life. She had lost her dad, and then her mother had grown distant.

When Nyx finally arrived, Akira sat staring at a computer monitor, Nyx paused at the door. After a few moments, Akira said, "Are you coming in or what?"

Nyx hesitated before walking to the workstation and plopping into a chair. "Something must have happened to Red and Antonio. They have been gone too long."

"Fair assessment."

"Have you learned anything?"

"Like what?"

"About Antonio. About the town?" Nyx paused. "You know—anything."

"Like whether I've become normal?"

"I didn't say that."

"You should have. It's a fair question."

"So? Anything?"

"A couple of things."

"And?"

"The town they were in is burning."

Nyx gasped. "Did they get out?"

"I don't know. Maybe. I'm still learning how to operate the satellites. I didn't get pictures, but I saw the heat signature. The entire town went up in flames and fast."

"What do you think that means?"

Akira shrugged. "Most likely, the military blew it up."

Nyx remained silent for a few minutes. That might be the last loss she could handle. She wasn't sure. "Maybe the town's people blew it up themselves."

Akira glanced sideways. "Why would they do that?"

Nyx shrugged. "I don't know. Throw Prime off track? Destroy stuff they didn't want the military to find? Maybe I'm grasping at straws."

"The last one sounds right."

"Anything else?"

"Yeah. The satellite we were blocking is gone."

"Moved?"

"Did I say, moved? It's gone. Poof." Akira closed and opened both hands as if signifying an explosion.

"Oh. What happened to it?"

"If I knew, I would have told you."

Akira still wasn't herself. She was never gruff. Always calm and courteous. The girl who made tea to calm others. This was not the Akira she remembered. "Do you have any theories?" Nyx asked. "About the satellite?"

"I do, but first, there's someone missing who you don't seem concerned about."

"I'm not following you."

Akira rolled her eyes. "Derrick. You haven't mentioned his name."

"I'm afraid to." Nyx paused. "Back to the satellite. You were about to tell me your theory of what happened to it."

"I was?"

Nyx said, "What do you think happened?"

"I think L. Linda happened to it."

"She should be back too. I kinda forgot about her."

"Not surprising."

Nyx knew Akira wasn't herself. Knew it was up to her to remain calm and supportive, but she fired back. "What is that supposed to mean?"

"Nothing. Forget it," Akira said.

Nyx took a couple of deep breaths. Changing the subject, even though she knew the answer, she asked, "How are you doing?"

"I'm alive."

"I'm worried about you. You're my best friend."

"Am I?"

"You know you are. Sorry, I don't know what you remember. I'm telling you. You're my best friend. You have been since grade school. I hope you'll remember at some point."

"I remember."

"Good."

"Not necessarily."

"I don't understand."

"I remember too much. Everything, as far as I can tell. No blanks."

"That sounds good to me."

"But no filters. Just facts."

"Okay," Nyx said, drawing the word out.

Akira stabbed at the keyboard.

"Are you mad at me?" Nyx asked. "Is it still about Derrick?"

Akira stopped typing, staring straight ahead. Then, turning to face Nyx, she said, "Yes, but not about what you think. Yes, I was hurt that you didn't notice I liked Derrick. I saw chemistry between you two. I get that. Sure, a best friend ought to notice, but you didn't." Akira paused. "I guess I'm mad at myself. Yeah, I'm mad that Derrick didn't remember me. But mostly, I'm mad at myself."

"Whatever for?"

"Because I let you get away with things. I have never said anything about things you do. No one does."

"Afraid of me? What did I do?"

"Maybe I'm wrong, but I'll bet I'm not."

"Wrong about what?"

"Have you told Derrick about you and Antonio?"

Silence.

"Just as I thought."

"Why don't you mind your own business," Nyx snarled, storming out of the room.

10

Friday, April 9, 10:55 a.m.

COLLINS PACED, CHECKED HIS WATCH, and then paced more. Everyone was awake now. Browning's kids were bored and hungry. Alice did her best to keep them occupied, but she was running out of activities. Perhaps no activity would prove successful under such circumstances. Collins had wanted to look for Maxton, Fletcher, and Martinez, but Browning talked him out of it. In the first place, Browning said they were not together, so it wasn't like finding one found them all. Second, they were probably all fine, just doing errands they felt were important. Third, Browning's kids needed Collins's protection.

Collins hushed the room. A noise outside. He heard a vehicle's motor go silent, followed by car doors slamming shut. Collins motioned everyone to hide and remain silent. He got behind a steel beam and aimed his gun at the door. The doorknob turned, slower than one might expect if it were one of the missing three.

The door eased open a few inches, then stopped.

Collins pulled the trigger halfway through its cycle and then paused. If it wasn't Fletcher, Maxton, or Martinez, it was most likely an assault. The door wouldn't stop a bullet, and if he hit the first person before they burst inside, he might stand a chance of stopping them. Unless it was a platoon of soldiers. There was no stopping that. But if he was wrong—

The door squeaked as Martinez pushed it open with her back, her arms laden with two paper bags.

"Where the hell have you been?" Collins holstered his weapon and motioned the others to come out of hiding.

Maxton entered next, carrying two large black cases, not unlike suitcases, but they were not suitcases. "Don't yell at Lori. It was my idea."

Lori set the bags on the table. "Don't believe him. I was headed out the door when Jason stopped me."

Fletcher came in next. "What's the fuss?"

Lori said, "Bill is upset that we left, just as I predicted."

"Didn't take a genius to figure that out. No offense. Just saying." Fletcher hung his denim jacket and cap on hooks near the door.

"Jack, we need to talk," Collins said, the anger in his voice evident.

"I suppose we do. Go ahead then."

"In your office."

Fletcher said, "Just say what you got to say. Won't change anything going to the office. Everyone's still going to hear you, I reckon."

Collins stared at Jack, glanced at Lori, and looked as if he wanted to say something. Perhaps he hoped Lori would intervene, but she stood with her arms crossed as if demanding that Collins behave. "I gave you a lawful order to get rid of that aircraft. Instead, you brought it here."

"Yep."

"That's all you have to say for yourself?" Collins demanded.

"For the moment. We done, or you need to blow off more steam?" Fletcher asked.

"We are not done, not by a long shot."

Lori said, "Bill."

"Not now, damn it."

Browning said, "Bill, it might be best to cool off a bit."

Collins said, "Cool off! Jack, you didn't just keep the aircraft, you told L. Linda about it!"

Fletcher said, "That is true."

"Why in the hell did you do that?"

"She asked."

"She asked and so, just like that, you showed her?" Collins asked.

Fletcher folded his arms. "First, I didn't show her. I told her it was in the back."

Collins said, "Same thing, and you haven't answered my question."

"Which question? Why I kept it, or why I told her?"

"Both."

Jack relaxed, walked to the coffeepot, and poured himself a cup. "I told her because she asked. L. Linda is as stubborn as they come. Smart too. She knew I wouldn't have put that thing in the lake."

Jason said, "He's right, you know."

"Why isn't it in the lake?" Collins asked.

Fletcher said, "Too important and too valuable."

"Money? That's all you were thinking about?" Collins asked, throwing his hands up.

"Not money. Value. Two different things."

Collins said, "L. Linda is gone. Do you know that? Left in that damn machine."

"I suspected as much," Fletcher said.

"You're some piece of work, Jack Fletcher. You don't seem to care one bit about her."

Jack sat. "Bill, I'm only going to say this once. You're mad at me. I get that. But don't accuse me of not caring about L. Linda. Say that again, and I'll get pissed, and you don't want that."

Collins shook his head and paced from one side of the area to the other. Jason Maxton stood with his back to the counter, leaning back with his arms folded. Collins looked at Jason. "You're rather calm. Am I the only one here worried about your daughter?"

Jason said, "It's not that I'm not worried, but with all due respect, Sheriff, I don't think you've grasped the gravity of the situation."

"I know we have five kids missing and now six. I know that!"

Jason said, "Let's start with Lori. Maybe you should ask her why we left."

Collins glanced at Lori. She didn't look the least bit happy, but he wasn't sure if it was because of how he'd spoken to Jack or something else. "Why did you leave, Lori? I was worried when I realized you were gone."

"There was a little dead body problem. Remember? The woman I killed. The one who tried to kill me. The one who killed Paul Jorgensen, Jimmy Priest, and his parents?"

Collins looked down. "Right. What did you do with her?"

"I took her to the coroner and told him to get the Priest family. I told him the investigation into Paul and the Priest family was closed. The woman who called herself Pixie murdered them."

"I'm sorry, Lori. I should have taken care of that last night."

Jason took his glasses off and stepped away from the counter. "Bill, sit down."

"But…"

"Sit."

"Now look here…"

Browning spun a chair out. "Hear him out, Bill."

Collins sat. Lori stood behind him. Whether as support or to whack him should he say the wrong thing, he did not know.

Jason rubbed his hands together. "Where to start? Let's try to put this in perspective…"

"I have things in perspective," Collins said. Lori put a hand on his shoulder. A friendly warning, he assumed.

Jason said, "Let's rewind to them exiling Derrick and Miriam escaping from Pacific Edge. Those are facts, even if we don't know the reasons."

"Derrick hit a Carver kid," Collins said. Lori put a hand on his other shoulder.

"Agreed, but we don't know everything there is to know. Remember, Miriam said they were Test Subjects and Pacific Edge planned to kill them."

"How do you know that?"

Jason shook his head. "It should be obvious, but it doesn't matter. Pacific Edge wants them back, and that's logical. But then Prime showed up. Not Prime itself, but aircraft and robots, far beyond any technology we were aware of. When Prime showed up, the military and Pacific Edge security disappeared. Think about that for a moment. Until those aircraft came here, folks thought Prime was a myth. At most, some sort of council for the Ones. Then Prime sent an assassin. She killed four people in this town, and it would have been more had it not been for L. Linda."

Collins patted Lori's hand. "Let's be clear. My deputy killed the assassin."

Lori said, "Jason is right. I'd be dead had L. Linda not helped me."

From amid the cars in the shop, Samantha Patel said, "L. Linda saved us too. You should have seen it. It was not unlike what Derrick did with the soldiers."

Collins said, "Now, Samantha, let's not get carried away."

Allen Patel stood. "She speaks the truth. What L. Linda did was amazing. We'd also be dead if not for her."

Collins said, "Explain to me how L. Linda can be like Derrick. She's lived here for, how long, 15 years? We all know L. Linda. She's smart," he paused, "but kinda odd. She's not athletic, and beyond her mechanical skills, I'm not sure what she does."

Jason said, "Less than five."

"Less than five, what?" Collins asked.

"We've been here less than five years."

Collins looked at Browning. "That can't be right. I feel like I've known L. Linda forever."

Browning shrugged. "I do too, but Jason is right."

"L. Linda intended to blend in—me too. You need to understand. The L. Linda you know, is the person she wants you to know."

"What's that mean?" Collins asked.

Jason waved him off. "That's not important. Back to Prime—has Prime's importance not dawned on you? There is nothing more powerful than Prime in this country. Perhaps no more powerful force in the world."

Collins said, "Come now, Jason. You're sounding a little wacky."

Jason walked closer. Collins noticed he looked different without glasses. But it wasn't just the glasses. Jason had lost the nerdy-looking zippered windbreaker he typically wore, and his loose-fitting shirt did not conceal a lean, muscular frame Collins had not previously noticed.

Collins tried to stand, but Lori held him in the chair. Collins said, "If Prime is so powerful, why are you not more concerned about L. Linda? You should be mad as hell at Jack. If he'd gotten rid of that aircraft like I said, she'd still be here."

"I said before. I'm concerned about L. Linda, but I'm not mad at Jack. Jack did the right thing. That aircraft is valuable, not in dollars, but because of its capabilities. Besides, it's not Jack's fault L. Linda is gone. She would have left with or without the aircraft."

"How do you know she would have left?" Collins asked.

"For God's sake, Bill. She rode that little Honda to the coast. She found Derrick and the others and saved them."

Collins took a breath. "Good point. Even so, she doesn't know how to fly that thing. She could be killed."

Jason said, "I trust L. Linda. She wouldn't have taken it if she couldn't fly it. That wouldn't make much sense, would it?"

Collins thought for a minute. "Why do you think she would have left without the aircraft?"

"Because she's trying to help Derrick… and the others."

"But she could kill herself trying. And that damn aircraft is the reason."

Jason walked to the table where Lori had deposited the paper sacks and removed food containers from the Bistro. With his back turned, he said, "You still don't understand. Prime wants Derrick and Miriam dead, which means Prime wants everyone connected with them dead. You're right about one thing: L. Linda might not survive. What you fail to understand is that there's a real possibility none of us do. At least L. Linda is fighting back, and I'll be damned if I'm going out without a fight."

11

CHARLIE EXAMINED THE PARACHUTE and then ripped it. He handed Red and Antonio a rectangular piece of the fabric, neatly torn with a semi-circle on one end and square-edged on the other. Then he measured and snapped the cord that attached the parachute to the harness. Red recognized how effortlessly the machine broke the cord.

Handing each boy, a piece of fabric and string, Charlie said, "Head coverings."

Antonio said, "You are correct. This fair-haired boy needs it. Put it on, Red. I'll tie it for you."

"I've got nothing to prove, and I hate getting sunburned. Thanks, Charlie."

As Antonio snugged the cord around Red's head, Charlie said, "Mr. Antonio also must wear the Shemagh. The color of your skin matters not to the sun."

"Charlie, can you shut down to save power?" Red asked.

"I can."

"How does that help?" Antonio asked as Red tied his cord.

Red said, "We make a slip using the parachute, and the harnesses will make it easier to pull."

"Pull?"

"I didn't mumble. Charlie gets on the slip, powers down, and we drag him. When we get close enough that he has enough power to reach Base, he powers up and goes for help."

"What do you mean: Goes for help?"

"I suspect by then, we won't have enough strength left to make it to the Base," Red said.

Antonio said, "I don't like the sound of this."

"I'm open to suggestions."

Charlie said, "I do not like the idea either. However, having analyzed our situation, it is the best option."

Antonio said, "We could wait until dark. I can run to the Base when it's cooler, then come back and get you both."

"Without water and shade, you might not survive until dark. Plus, it will be difficult finding the Base in the daylight. Nearly impossible in the dark," Charlie said.

"Then it's decided. Charlie, can you fashion the slip, so we have equal distance to the chute?"

"I can do that."

Charlie took two harnesses, wound the cords together, and stretched them out on the desert sands. "That should do it." Charlie walked toward them. "I can power down, but you will have to push this"—he touched a small panel, which flipped open—"and then touch this button."

"At least that part is easy," Antonio said.

"It might prove more difficult than you imagine. If you wait too long, reaching the stage of heat exhaustion, you're thinking will become cloudy. If you wait until heat stroke begins, you won't survive."

"You're just bubbling over with cheery thoughts." Red pointed. "Get on the slip and power down. It's getting hotter, and I want a cold soda."

Charlie did as Red requested.

As they put on the harnesses, Antonio asked, "How will we know when we are close enough to start Charlie?"

Red said, "Count our steps."

"You can't be serious."

"Then we have to guess."

"Guess wrong, and none of us make it?"

"No wonder you're council president."

They stretched the cords tight, leaned into the harnesses and started moving forward. It was not unlike pushing a sled on the football field, except they pulled it rather than pushed it.

"We should have Coach Browning set this up using the sleds. It's good exercise. I won't have to lift weights today," Red said.

"Do you take anything seriously? Does anything get you down?"

Red didn't say anything for several minutes. "Yeah, there are things that get me down, but nothing I can do about them."

"What sort of things?"

"Mostly how people treat each other."

"Oh? Got an example?" Antonio asked, then added. "Something bothering you now?"

"Maybe."

"What?"

"You don't want to know."

"Try me."

They marched on 100 yards. Both were soaked with sweat. *This isn't good,* Antonio thought. *We'll be dehydrated in no time.* "I wish we had some water. We should have got some in the town."

"We couldn't. We barely got out of there," Red said.

"So, what's bothering you? I mean, we might not even make it back. You might as well get it off your chest."

They drudged on another 50 yards. "I've wondered something. But it's kinda personal. You might not want to get into it. It's not like we are close friends."

"Are you kidding, bro? We might die out here together. It doesn't get much closer than that."

Red said nothing.

"Come on. Out with it. Don't keep me hanging here."

"Does it bother you? Nyx and Derrick. I mean, she went after him right away, and, well, it's not been that long."

Now it was Antonio's turn to be silent. They slogged on for what felt like an hour.

"How far have we gone, do you think?" Antonio asked.

"No clue. Feels like five miles, but I'm guessing less than a mile."

Antonio said, "So, back to your question. It wasn't easy. It bothered me a little. But Nyx and I parted on okay terms. She's free to date whoever she wants."

"Just that easy, huh?"

"I didn't say it was easy. You know how it is."

"I don't. I've never had a girlfriend. Who would be interested in a big dumb lummox like me?"

"The only part you got right is that you are big. You're a smart guy. I'm the lummox for not seeing that until now."

"If it wasn't easy watching Nyx and Derrick, why did you help him from the beginning?"

"You mean like help him find his locker and such? Hey, that's my job, remember? Plus, I knew nothing about him and Nyx at the time. I'm not even sure when that all started."

"But you kept helping him. I saw it. You kinda had his back. You and Malcolm. I don't get Malcolm either. Helping someone like Derrick doesn't seem like something he'd do. Did you have something to do with that?"

"I may or may not have had a conversation with Malcolm about Derrick."

"I still don't understand."

Antonio said, "I'm student body prez. That's my job. Looking after people."

"I guess. But it still seems there's more to it than that."

They plodded another silent 100 yards before Antonio said, "Okay. You're right. I had noticed the attraction between Derrick and Nyx. So, I guess I was doing it for Nyx. You know, trying to make her life a little easier."

They marched on. Antonio noticed his shirt was drying out. Another bad sign. He glanced at Red. His shirt was even drier. He did not know how far they had gone but was sure it was not far enough to awaken Charlie.

Antonio said, "Why does it bother you?"

"I don't know. I guess I want to believe that Nyx is a good person. I want to believe you're a good person too. And Rebekah seems like a nice person and kinda innocent in this entire thing."

"Now I'm confused. How does Nyx liking Derrick make her a bad person? I know you don't like Derrick, but how does, you know, them dating or whatever make Nyx a bad person?"

Red said, "Derrick is a lot of things. He lied to us. He was Chosen. But he is as naïve a person as I've ever met."

"Still lost over here."

"Really? Do you think Nyx has told Derrick about you and her?"

"No idea."

"I don't think so. He seems oblivious to any of that."

"Your point?"

"I hope she's not using Derrick to make you jealous."

"Oh. I had not thought about it that way."

"Yeah, right. I also hope you are not using Rebekah to make Nyx jealous. I can imagine how much that would hurt Rebekah. If that were the case, I wouldn't see you as the same person I have always admired."

Nothing else was said.

They struggled on into the desert.

12

AS L. LINDA SWAM TOWARD THE SHORE, a figure appeared at the base of the cliff near a trail that led to whatever town or village was nearby. She had spotted him coming down the path and wondered how much he'd seen. Had he seen the aircraft? She didn't know if that was good or bad but thought it would mostly be bad. Explaining the machine wasn't something she wanted to do. The wrong person might wonder if a reward existed for anyone seeing the aircraft and a bonus if the pilot was also captured. She would soon find out just how *wrong* a person this was.

She had lost a shoe trying to squeeze out of the sinking Prime aircraft, which was another thing she hated to lose—the aircraft, not the shoe—and the other she kicked off swimming in the surf toward shore. Socks soon followed, apparently lured to a life at sea rather than sticking it out with their owner. L. Linda didn't mind losing the socks. She'd be better off barefooted than stocking-footed, but she was a little pissed about the shoes. She liked those sneakers.

She'd lost a few buttons on her shirt as well. When she stood, she checked to see just how naked she appeared before walking through the surf to the boy now standing on the shore. She had one button left, enough to cover most of her wet t-shirt, which had become somewhat transparent.

"Hello," L. Linda said, approaching the shore.

"What are you doing here?" the kid asked.

"Swimming," L. Linda said.

"You're not from around here," the kid said.

"You know everyone around here?"

The kid said, "Pretty much. It's a small town. What's your name?"

"Janice. What's your name?"

"My name is Tom. What are you doing here?"

"I just told you. Swimming."

"Where are you from, Janice?"

L. Linda pointed. "Up the coast."

"Pacific Edge? I don't think so. Three girls escaped, and they've locked the place down, including the service town."

"Do you live in the Pacific Edge service town?" L. Linda asked, hoping to steer the conversation in a new direction.

"I do not. I live in a small village just up there." He pointed toward the cliffs rising beyond the beach. "So, where are you really from?"

L. Linda thought for a moment, wondering why he was so interested in her origin. "Okay. You got me. I'm from Fort Hill, but I'm here visiting friends."

"Who's your friend?"

L. Linda said, "You ask a lot of questions."

"There's been some weird stuff going on here lately." He pointed to the cliff half a mile to the north. It looked like a huge chunk was blown out of it. "I heard an explosion. Early yesterday morning. I was still in bed. Heard it was a Prime aircraft, but I don't think that's true. Prime is a myth."

"I don't know anything about that."

"I didn't say you did. Who's your friend?"

L. Linda said, "You probably don't know her. Her name is Samantha."

"Samantha Patel? Must be—she's the only Samantha I know."

Crap.

"Yes. Samantha Patel."

"That's strange."

"How so?"

"Because the Patel family has gone missing. All of them. They left right after those girls escaped from Pacific Edge."

"I have to get going." L. Linda started to the south, hoping to walk around the kid. She didn't have to answer his questions.

Tom stepped in front of her. "Slow down. We're not finished here."

"I'm done. I need to leave."

Tom lifted his shirt, revealing the handle of a large knife, protruding from a leather sheath. One that might be used to skin a deer.

"Are you threatening me?"

"Not yet. You're kinda cute. How about we negotiate?"

"Negotiate what?"

"Me letting you leave."

"Am I under arrest or something?"

"Let's say—or something."

Tom's tone had changed. He sounded menacing or at least his best attempt. He wasn't a big guy, not compared to Red Badowski. Now there was a big guy. This kid was more the size of Antonio Morales, but not as fit, not that it mattered. Tom wasn't nervous and that gave her the feeling this wasn't new to him. He had threatened people before. Probably girls. Probably used that knife.

L. Linda said, "Look, I've had a long day already. I'm tired. I don't want problems. Just let me leave. I won't go to the police or anything like that."

"What's in it for me?" Tom slid the knife from its sheath.

How about you get to live? "You get to walk away with no worries. What you've done in the past isn't my concern. I've got bigger things to be concerned with."

"You're funny. I get to walk away? I'm walking away regardless of what happens to you. What do you mean, my past isn't your concern?"

L. Linda should not have said that. She knew it but had done it anyway. She really was tired. Her thinking wasn't as clear as it should be for this sort of thing. "I didn't mean anything. Just saying, let me leave, and you have nothing to worry about."

That wasn't entirely true. If she lived long enough, she'd do some digging into unsolved crimes here, specifically missing girls. If she found any, and she was certain she would, then she'd come back and deal with this scumbag. But right now, he was not her priority.

"I have nothing to worry about either way. So, I see no reason to let you walk away. There's no fun in that for me."

You just can't let it go. Big mistake, but your choice. "What fun did you have in mind? Perhaps I'm not as unwilling as you think. You're kinda cute," *in a serial killer sort of way,* "so maybe there's less to negotiate than you think."

She envisioned the wheels turning in his head. The more she watched, the more confident she became she was not his first victim. Probably his fourth victim. His father must be important, and therefore, Tom wasn't worried about becoming the target of an investigation. He had killed all his victims, and no bodies had been discovered. His methods worked, which increased his confidence. However, he had not encountered a would-be victim who showed an interest in his macabre intentions. The sparkle in his eye said he was interested in something new.

"What are you thinking?"

L. Linda took a step toward him. This did two things: it created a sensual mix of danger and intimacy unlike anything he had experienced. Second, it brought her closer to killing range for one or the other of them. L. Linda had not yet decided how this would end. She only knew she was not interested in getting cut.

"I'm not your first. That's good. I like men with experience. But I've never met a man willing to take it all the way. How about you, Tom? Do you take it all the way?"

Tom hesitated. He wanted to tell her now. He sensed her excitement. "I take it all the way, baby."

L. Linda said, "I mean all the way. That would really turn me on. We could do it together. Would you like that? But there's just one thing."

"What's that?"

He was beyond interested now.

"I gotta know you're careful. I don't want to get caught. I don't want to go to jail. And I want someone who won't get cold feet or wimp out at the last minute. How can I be sure you won't wimp out, Tom?" L. Linda took half a step closer.

Tom looked uneasy for a moment. Thinking this through. He repositioned the knife in his hand. Could he have found his soul mate? Perhaps he'd fantasized about it but never considered it a possibility. Tom wasn't the brightest bulb in the room. Otherwise, he would have recognized this was a ruse. But he had that big knife, and she was just a girl. He'd killed girls before. Girls were not a threat.

"How do I know I can trust you?" Tom asked.

"The danger is exciting, isn't it, Tom? Are we talking the same language? I want to kill people. I'm not sure you can do that. We can have sex with them first, if that's what you like."

Tom swallowed, struggling to believe his luck. Someone who shared his twisted perversions.

"I like that a lot," Tom said, with a quiver in his voice.

"How many, Tom? How many have you killed?"

"Three."

"Did you rape them?"

"Two of them. One tried to run."

"No, boys?"

"Just girls."

"Could we do, boys?"

"Oh, yeah. I'd like to."

"Where did you hide them? That's important if we do this for a long time."

"In the ocean. I sink them with rocks."

"You have a boat?"

"No. Over by the cliffs."

"How do I know you're telling the truth and not just fantasizing?"

"I can show you. It's low tide, and you can see them if you know where to look."

"Oh, Tom. Show me. Show me the bodies."

Tom pointed. "You go first."

"We haven't reached an agreement yet, Tom. You go first. I'll follow."

Tom thought about it for a moment.

"Don't think, Tom. Just go with me on this."

"How do I know you won't try to run?"

"I'm barefoot. I'm sure you noticed. I can't outrun you with no shoes. I probably couldn't with shoes. You also have the knife, remember? Besides, I want to see them. I want to be with you, Tom. But we'll have to learn to trust each other, right? Here's our first step toward a beautiful, trusting relationship. You go. I'll follow."

"Okay. But don't try anything." Tom held up the knife. "I'll kill you just like the others."

"It excites me when you talk about killing."

Tom turned and walked northeast toward the cliffs. L. Linda had lied to Tom. She could outrun him shoes or no shoes. But she had to know if he had killed three girls. That would determine how this played out. Tom didn't know it yet, but if he had killed those girls, they would be his last.

When they reached the rocks, Tom looked over his shoulder. "Be careful on the rocks. It won't be as easy as walking on the sand. If it hurts too much, we'll have to come back after we find you some shoes."

"I'll be okay." L. Linda stepped gingerly, placing her feet carefully. It was all an act. Her feet were tough because she went barefoot all the time to keep them that way. Effectively used, bare feet make excellent weapons.

When they reached the edge of a rock ledge at the base of the cliff, Tom stopped. "Come over here. I can see them."

L. Linda stepped to the edge, but not at Tom's side.

He pointed up. "You can't see from up there, and there's no path, so there's no reason for people to come. I tossed the first one into the sea, but the next morning when I checked, she was back on the beach. I dragged her up here, put rocks under her clothing, made sure the rocks were secured, and then pushed her over the side. She sank straight down." He pointed. "That's her in the white shirt and blue pants."

The shirt was white, except for the dark-red stains. "How long has she been down there? She looks so peaceful. I want to swim down and touch her."

"Six weeks."

Tom was so impressed with himself that he had not considered a flaw in his method. The clothing would deteriorate. The bodies would resurface. L. Linda saw the girl's bloated body straining against the cloth. She won't stay down there much longer.

"What if someone were to see them? You seem confident. Like you would not be a suspect. Is your father like the mayor or something?"

Tom chuckled. "You're kinda right. Not the mayor. He's the pastor at the Church of the Doctrine. I'm a deacon. They'll never suspect me."

"But your father would protect you if they did?"

"He would not. He's working hard to be Chosen. Becoming Chosen is more important to him than I am. That's for sure."

Despite Tom's unskillful handling of the knife, it was still deadly. Three girls at the bottom of the ocean would attest to that. Taking a knife away isn't as easy as they made it look in the movies. The best defense in a knife fight was a gun. L. Linda didn't have a gun. She had two bare hands and two bare feet. Being an unarmed opponent against a knife-wielding maniac was never a good way to go. Jason had encouraged her to train more, but she always felt she'd have time for that later.

Later was now.

She was as ready as she was going to get.

13

Friday, April 9, 11:00 a.m.

HARLEY STOPPED THE LEAD TRUCK NEAR a fenced area containing massive electrical components. Although the site looked derelict, one side of the fencing buried under a mound of dry round weeds, perhaps it still functioned, because Derrick could hear buzzing and felt a slight tingle in the air. Wires stretched from the components to giant metal towers, where they joined more wires that stretched to more towers, extending into the distance in both directions until they disappeared over the horizon. Harley walked to the driver's side front wheel on his truck, leaned over, changed something, and then did the other side. Then he walked to Atwood's truck and did the same thing. Harley spoke briefly to Atwood, but Derrick didn't hear what was said.

Moving again, Derrick asked, "What was that about?"

Miriam said, "Do I look like a truck mechanic? He changed something, but I don't know what or why, but I suspect we'll find out."

They found out soon enough. Harley turned left. There was no road, just a small gulley with a sandy bottom. It looked like it carried water in heavy rain, but Derrick found it hard to believe it had ever rained here. Maybe it did occasionally. Perhaps that was years ago. The heat became unbearable. Derrick used his shirt to shield the sun and motioned Miriam to scoot into his shadow.

It was slow going. Dereck could have walked faster. The possibility of getting stuck in these sand washes did not appeal to him. "I wonder how far it is to the launcher?"

Miriam said, "About 35 miles."

"Have we crossed into Mexico?"

"I don't think so."

"Harley said the launcher was 50 miles south of the border."

"He did. Fifty miles if we stayed on the road. Apparently, he decided against that approach."

"How can you know how far it is?"

Miriam shrugged. "I don't understand how. I just can."

Atwood followed Harley into a smaller gully. The truck struggled over rocks and ruts in the sand. Twice Derrick thought they were stuck, but after

Atwood rocked the truck back and forth, they were moving again. The walls of the ravine rose on both sides. After turning a tight corner, Atwood stopped. Derrick stood and saw Harley had also stopped. Harley motioned Rebekah and Anna to follow.

Atwood and Haskins exited their vehicle. Derrick remained in the bed of Atwood's truck. Harley, Rebekah, and Anna were walking toward them.

Atwood said, "What's up?"

"I thought we should talk. Mexico is just over the rise." Harley pointed. "The valley on the other side is Mexico.

Atwood said, "I didn't know we'd be in this rough a terrain."

Harley said, "I thought it best. Mexico is probably watching everything closer than usual. They may even have eyes on these sand washes. No guarantees we won't be spotted."

"What if we are?" Atwood asked.

"That's one thing we should discuss," Harley said.

"So, what if we get caught?" Rebekah asked.

Harley said, "Good question. I'm open to suggestions."

Miriam said, "Tell them we are lost."

Harley said, "I was thinking the same, but if we are lost, why would we stray off the road into such difficult terrain? It doesn't make sense."

"Good point," Miriam said.

Rebekah said, "Do we need two answers?"

"Like a good answer and a stupid one?" Harley asked.

"No, smart ass. For depending on who finds us: New America or Mexico."

"Oh. Good thinking."

Haskins asked, "How about we are running from drug dealers?"

Harley nodded. "The Mexican people would understand the danger of New America Drug cartels."

"Can we use the same reason for the New America military?" Rebekah asked.

Haskins said, "No. New America would just turn us over to the closest cartel."

Everyone stared at him.

Haskins shrugged. "The cartels all have agreements with New America military and police."

Atwood said, "Students."

Derrick said, "I don't understand."

"You are students searching for archaeology or paleontology sites."

"I'm not familiar with those terms," Derrick said.

"Science. Archaeology is the study of human history, and paleontology is the study of plants and animals, both primarily focused on prehistoric artifacts."

Derrick looked puzzled. "Prehistoric?"

"Dinosaurs and such," Atwood said.

Derrick had never heard of dinosaurs but decided to not ask for further clarification.

"Can they be both?" Haskins asked.

Atwood thought for a moment. "Best to be one or the other. As a history professor, I would be most convincing as an archeologist. This area was once filled with Native Americans until the Spanish invaded. We are out looking for ruins."

"Native Americans?" Derrick asked.

"Yes. The indigenous people who lived here before Europeans invaded," Atwood said.

"But the Chosen's ancestors were here originally," Derrick said.

Everyone stared at Derrick.

Derrick glanced down. "That's another lie, isn't it?"

Miriam said, "Professor, you're forgetting something."

"What's that," Atwood asked.

Miriam pointed at Haskins. "How do we explain him?"

Harley said, "Good point. I didn't think to grab extra clothing."

Haskins unbuttoned his shirt, tossing it to the ground, and then pulled out his wallet, removing anything that might identify him by name or rank. "My pants are military but can be purchased in a surplus store. The white t-shirt isn't unusual."

Harley said, "So, if it's Mexican authorities, we are running from drug dealers, and if it's New America, we are students. What school are we from?"

Atwood said, "the University of Arizona. Let me do the talking."

Miriam said, "One question. Would New America allow students to look for proof the Chosen were not the original people here?"

Atwood said, "They would not. We are looking to ensure any such evidence is destroyed."

"Is that believable?" Rebekah asked.

"It is not only believable. It is routine." Atwood paused. "Where is the launcher?"

Harley said, "About 40 miles southeast."

Miriam said, "Thirty miles if you could go straight."

Harley nodded. "Sounds about right. This sand wash ends up ahead. Typically, they end in a box-end canyon or a steep, narrow, rocky ravine, but this one is just a hill and a straight shot to the top of a ridge. From there, we drop into a dry lakebed, where we'll cross two highways. Not much traffic this time of day because of the heat."

"Understandable," Atwood said, then added, "We should have brought water."

Harley reached behind the truck's seat, pulling out a damp canvas bag. "I remembered. Go easy though. I have another canteen in my truck, but that's all of it."

"Thank God, or whoever we should thank for water," Rebekah said, grabbing the bag and taking a drink. "It's colder than I expected."

Harley said, "It's the bag."

"I don't understand," Rebekah said.

"Right. We'll hang them on the mirrors. They will be even colder next stop," Harley said.

Rebekah handed the water to Anna. "That makes no sense."

Atwood said, "I agree, but it works. Wizard came up with it. He tried to explain the science to me once, but to be honest, I couldn't follow it."

"Were you an actual professor?" Miriam asked.

Atwood chuckled. "I taught history. History according to New America."

Miriam nodded. Images of the empty missile silo and the targeting of Sacramento came to mind. "That seems a common theme."

Before taking a drink, Derrick looked at Haskins. "What about your military unit?"

"What about it?" Haskins asked.

"What will they do next?" Anna asked.

"Why is that important?" Haskins asked.

"They were looking for us. That makes it important to me. There are a lot of moving pieces here. Where are they going? Who are they communicating with? Do they know we got out? If they know you left with us, they'll be tracking us, so they might figure out where we are going and alert the missile launcher. They might have moved, and we'll never find them. Or they might move up the launch time, and we'll be too late."

"Is that where your head has been? It seemed you weren't paying attention to what I was saying. I was just talking to myself, wasn't I?" Rebekah asked.

"I heard every word. I can listen and think." Anna paused. "So, what will they do?"

Haskins said, "Hard to know for sure. First, we could not communicate with the main unit or with command."

Miriam interrupted. "Because a satellite was blocked?"

Haskins stared at her for a moment. "Something like that. How did you know?"

"It doesn't matter. Go on."

"Our communications were limited. Unless the satellite is back up, they can't contact command. Prime may not know what happened."

"What will the unit do?"

Haskins shrugged. "Hard to say. They were all young, inexperienced soldiers."

Derrick said, "Expendable. First wave. Like the two kids on the hill."

"You know about them?"

Atwood said, "We captured them. Well, Derrick and Anna captured them."

Haskins looked from Derrick to Anna. "These two?" Then Haskins's face paled. "Were they in the town when it…"

Atwood said, "They were not. They wanted to go with us. Well, with the others."

"But how did these two…"

Miriam said, "Not important. Back to what the military unit might do."

"They will stay put for a while. They will probably send a scout back to survey the town. Even five miles out, they heard the explosions and saw the smoke. They must think I was killed. I doubt they saw us leave. Eventually, they'll rejoin their unit at the border."

"Maybe Mr. Haskins should return to his unit," Rebekah said.

"What good would that do?" Miriam asked.

Rebekah shrugged. "I don't know. Help us somehow. It's just a suggestion."

Atwood said, "He can't. Prime will kill him. Prime might already have put out a kill-on-sight order."

"When was the launch supposed to happen?" Derrick asked.

"They are probably waiting for orders. Until Prime hears about what I found in your town. However, the troops are in place. It would help to have the unit back, but it's small, so it wouldn't make much difference. Under normal circumstances, Prime would wait until I was there to oversee the battle, but he either thinks I'm dead or wants me dead. Prime won't wait to have a commander there."

"Which means?" Miriam asked.

"He could launch at any moment."

"Any idea where the missile will strike?" Derrick asked.

Haskins said, "I do not know, but if I were to guess, I'd say either Potterville or Pacific Edge."

"Why there? It's not fair," Rebekah said.

Haskins said, "I hate to say it, but you kids are the reason. Prime wants you, and everyone connected to you, dead."

14

THE MOIST AIR CARRIED THE SCENT OF THE SEA, and the crashing waves were like nature's lullaby. The cliffs and the waves lapping at the rocks created a landscape any artist would strive to capture. An idyllic place where lovers might cement their everlasting commitment to one another. The only things preventing this spot from earthly perfection were the bodies of three dead girls and a kid with a knife.

L. Linda stared at the bodies. Perhaps knife-boy Tom thought she was eager to add more, dreaming of how they might do it together. But she wasn't thinking about that. She was thinking about how he would look down there with them.

She was thinking about her next move.

Knock him out and roll him off the cliff. Perhaps he'd drown. Even if he didn't, she could escape. Save her own skin, but if Tom survives, more girls will die. There must be mothers and fathers, sisters and brothers, and friends, perhaps lovers, all wondering what happened to these three. The girls deserved final resting places where their loved ones could visit. They did not belong at the bottom of this cove.

Tom also deserved things.

One thing was pain.

A lot of pain.

L. Linda was not naïve. This wasn't the movies. This fight wasn't choreographed. That knife was no prop. Kicking the knife out of his hand was an option. Perhaps sending it into the sea. Safer for her, but she needed that knife to pin the murders on Tom. Another problem: it might not work. He might manage to hold on to the knife. And if she tried to kick the knife out of Tom's hand, he might suspect she didn't plan to help him kill more girls.

Separating the ligaments in his knee, causing it to bend in ways nature never intended, was her best bet. Excruciating pain reduces one's effectiveness in a fight. He might drop the knife, curl up in a fetal position, screaming and crying. That was one scenario. The other was that he might strike wildly with that big blade. Even a novice can get lucky. She could not afford to get hurt. At best, it would be damn inconvenient, at worst, deadly.

The clock ticked. Time to act before Tom got antsy. Before Tom started to rethink his situation.

A thinking Tom. could be a dangerous Tom.

L. Linda turned, smiling. "This is so exciting. Are you excited, Tom?"

"So, excite…"

Tom didn't get to finish his sentence. L. Linda leaned away, drawing her knee into her chest, and then snapped her leg straight, causing Tom's knee to explode backward. Before Tom hit the ground, she repeated the motion, aiming at his other leg, but missed the knee and broke his femur. Tom screamed, swinging the knife wildly as he collapsed.

Fortunately, Tom missed. Now, he wasn't going anywhere. Sweat rolled off his reddening face. He gritted his teeth, swinging the knife back and forth in ever-decreasing strokes. It turned out he was tougher than she had anticipated. Still, he looked like he might pass out, but she didn't want that to happen. Not just yet.

She wanted to chat.

He continued to swing the knife half-heartedly. He didn't realize he was making this easier. She caught his arm on a backswing, twisting his arm so his palm and elbow pointed upward, forcing his face into the ground. The knife fell onto the rocks. Then she delivered a blow to his elbow with all her weight.

His elbow, like his knee, was now bent in a new direction. His scream did not cover the sound of tearing tendons and cartilage, but the screaming was getting old, so L. Linda punched him, breaking his nose, and knocking him unconscious.

While Tom took a little nap, she worked quickly, arranging small rocks to fashion an arrow pointing toward the cove and the words: "Tom killed them." Then she worked the knife into a fracture, so it stood straight up, easily seen.

When Tom stirred, L. Linda was sitting on a rock nearby. He groaned, tried to move, and then collapsed.

Looking at her with hatred in his eyes, Tom said, "I'm going to kill you."

"Your killing days are over. You can try in prison, but they won't put you with girls. They won't give you a knife, either.

Tom tried to crawl toward her, causing his legs to twist in ways Mother Nature never intended. He screamed. Looking down, he saw his feet were tied together with shoelaces. He tried to reach his ankle but fell back, panting. "I'll get you for this."

"Give it up, Tommy. I don't think your femoral artery is torn, but your broken bone could cut it. If that happens, you'll bleed to death before anyone finds you."

L. Linda stood. "What does this fit?" She held out a key attached to a fur rabbit's foot.

"That's mine!"

"It looks like a Honda key. Where is it? Don't make me come over there."

"Screw you."

L. Linda started toward him. "Have it your way."

Tom held up his hand in surrender. "Don't. Take the trail. First road to the right is Elm. House next to the church." Tom paused. "Five-fifty Honda. It's in the shed."

"Does it run?"

Tom nodded.

"Sweet. I'm glad we met, Tommy."

15

AS THEY BAKED IN WHAT FELT LIKE A FURNACE, the sun climbed into the clear blue sky. The water bag made another round, and ideas were shared. Derrick listened, hoping someone would have an idea better than his. He thought Miriam would have a plan, but she had said nothing. Harley talked the most. Sometimes making suggestions, often interjecting why a plan wouldn't work.

Derrick marveled at the cacti and the rock formations. The entire landscape stood alien, desolate, and foreboding, yet beautiful. He did not know why he found it interesting. Then he drifted, daydreaming about traveling here when this was over. Perhaps on a motorcycle, which he equated with freedom, although he'd never ridden one. Maybe L. Linda Maxton could teach him to ride. He wondered what had happened to her. She found Akira as requested. She was probably eating lunch the robots had prepared and chatting with Akira and Nyx. By now, Red, Antonio, and Charlie might have returned.

Everything at the Base was probably fine.

Probably.

"Derrick. Derrick! Earth to Derrick!"

Derrick turned to the group. "Sorry. I drifted off."

Harley said, "No kidding. I was saying, I hope you have an idea. We are evenly divided between two plans. Care to weigh in on which sounds best to you?"

"Uh, sure. Well… Sorry, what are the plans?"

Miriam shook her head. "Seriously? You haven't been paying attention at all?"

Derrick repeated. "What are the options?"

"Commander Haskins says it will be a minimum number of soldiers, mostly privates, mostly new," Harley said. "Probably one sergeant, perhaps a corporal as well. Two drivers. The sergeant and corporal might be in a different vehicle. They might have a lead vehicle plus one bringing up the rear. However, there's an equally good chance they only have two vehicles. The strategy is to keep the unit small. Less likely to be spotted. Mr. Haskins says they will have one or two troops posted as lookouts."

Derrick nodded. "So, what's the plan?"

"Plans," Miriam corrected. "One plan is to position ourselves some distance from their location. Do reconnaissance, determine how many troops, and locate the lookouts. Take out the lookouts like you and Anna did last night. Rebekah and I would set up the machine guns as close to the site as possible, just in case. Atwood and Haskins would drive in. Haskins would then determine the best course of action. He might tell them the mission is scrubbed or reset the launch coordinates, sending the missile into the sea."

"Second option?" Derrick asked.

"We mount a machine gun on each truck and come in hot. We should be able to wipe them out before they can react."

"What about the lookouts? They will have rifles."

"Anna thinks she can take them out with the .50 cal. Either that, or we take cover until we get them with a rifle."

Derrick stared at Miriam for a minute, and then asked, "Which plan do you favor?"

"Plan B. I don't want to kill people either, but it's faster. I'm afraid we've already wasted too much time. I keep fearing we'll see a missile streaking through the sky."

Derrick said, "I agree. We have wasted too much time."

Harley said, "So, which plan are we doing?"

"Neither."

"Neither?" Harley asked.

"Correct. The first plan takes too long. Not an option. The second plan kills too many people. Snipers will pick us off before we reach the site. Also, too much gunfire. We will have the Mexican Military on top of us before we can escape."

Miriam said, "At least we could prevent a war, even if we don't make it out."

"Not necessarily. Mexico might consider a missile launcher south of the border as an act of war. Plus, Prime will invade whether or not the launch is successful."

"Are you suggesting we do nothing?" Miriam asked.

"I am not. I'm just saying we aren't doing either plan."

"You have something better?" Harley asked.

"Not much better. But it's what we are going to do."

"Since when did you take charge?" Haskins asked.

"Right after I heard your plans. Here's what we will do. Miriam and I are going to drive right up to the launcher. We'll drop Anna and Rebekah off before we reach the site."

"Unbelievable. Not going to happen that way. I'm the Commander. I make the decisions, and I'm going. If they have not been in communication with command because of the satellite problems, I can simply take charge."

Derrick said, "Or you could order them to arrest us. You save the day. They launch the missile. Prime gets its war. You save your butt."

"I won't do that. You'll have to trust me."

"I don't have to trust you. But if I decided to trust you, you still aren't going with us. You, Atwood, and Harley need to find the rest of your people."

"I don't understand," Haskins said.

"If we all go in and fail. Then all hope of preventing this war is lost, and there will be no one who knows the truth. The Resistance information is vital, and the information regarding how the war started must be included. In addition, if we are successful, you and Mr. Atwood must stop things from spiraling out of control."

"You lost me. If you're successful, why would things spiral out of control?"

"Never mind. I'm getting ahead of myself." Derrick paused. "If we stop the missile, the next thing is stopping Prime.

Haskins said, "I appreciate your confidence, Derrick, but you can't stop Prime. Prime's assistant made that clear to me. Prime exists…"

Derrick held up his hand. "In several places. We know that."

"Seven places, to be exact. Quigley, that's the assistant, said he could be replicated quickly. So even if you could get by security and stop one Prime, it would be replaced almost immediately. Plus, that's just at one location," Haskins said.

Miriam said, "We are off topic and there's no time to debate this."

Haskins said, "Regarding the launcher, your plan won't work. They are not going to just let you drive up."

Derrick said, "They are kids. We are kids. We race up and tell them drug dealers are chasing us. Before they have time to think about it, we'll disable them and reset the launcher."

"What about the lookouts?" Haskins asked.

Derrick said, "They will be watching for attacks, not babysitting the soldiers. With luck, we'll launch the missile toward the ocean and be gone before they know we were there. End of story."

"It's suicide," Haskins said.

"You might be right. That's why you must survive, as well as Anna and Rebekah. If things go wrong, Anna and Rebekah can escape, perhaps find you. Someone must carry on." Derrick glanced at Rebekah, hoping she understood that 'carry on' meant someone had to get back to the Base.

Haskins said nothing. His jaw muscles flexed as if he were chewing on tough leather.

Miriam said, "Derrick's right. This is our best option."

Rebekah said, "I don't like it. The suicide part especially."

Miriam smiled. "You knew the job would be dangerous when you left Pacific Edge."

"Very funny. I had no idea it would get this bad."

Anna said, "Rebekah doesn't need to go. I can handle it with one machine gun."

"Who will rescue Rebekah if we don't make it?" Miriam asked.

Anna said nothing.

Atwood said, "Cliff, did you see Prime in Seattle?"

"I did."

"Is that when Quigley told you about me and the missile?"

Haskins nodded. "Driving me to the airstrip shortly after I talked to Prime."

Atwood looked at Derrick. "If you go after Prime, you'll have to destroy entire facilities. There can be no survivors, but, if possible, start in Seattle and get Stanley Mires, Prime calls him Quigley, out."

Miriam said, "Quigley must be the Resistance person you said got close to Prime?"

"Yes. He has paid an extraordinary price. He knows more about Prime than anyone. Save him if you can. He is our most valuable resource." Atwood paused. "He deserves to survive after what he's done."

Haskins looked at Atwood. "I can't believe what I'm hearing. They have a half-baked plan to stop the launch, and you're thinking they can stop Prime. I must be missing something."

Atwood took a deep breath, his shoulders slumped. "I'm not optimistic. Just saying, I hope Mr. Mires makes it out."

16

IT FELT AS IF THEY WERE WALKING IN AN OVEN. The sweat that blurred Red's vision earlier had stopped. He vaguely remembered a discussion in health class about heat exhaustion and heat stroke. The first dangerous, the second deadly. Twenty minutes ago, he felt nauseous, but he kept it together. Antonio was not as lucky, puking up what little liquid he had in his stomach. They needed Charlie to finish the trek to the Base, but Red feared they were not close enough to activate Charlie. If Charlie didn't make it, they were dead.

That's when Antonio stumbled and fell.

Red rolled Antonio over. His brown skin had turned bright red. He was in serious trouble. The machines at the Base could save him. Maybe. But Red felt confident they could not bring him back to life if he died out here. Red carried Antonio to the parachute, positioned him next to Charlie, and covered him as best he could.

Sliding his arms through the harness, Red pulled the cables tight, dragging both friends through the sand. The pull didn't seem much different from what it had been. Antonio had not helped much the last 20 minutes, and he added little weight compared to Charlie. Antonio's condition had changed so gradually that Red hadn't noticed it. He should have been paying closer attention to Antonio and made him get on the parachute sooner. Antonio should have said he was in bad shape, but he'd pushed on until he dropped. Such was his nature.

The heat waves made it difficult to focus on the landmarks Charlie had identified to keep them on course. Occasionally, Red glanced back to see if the drag marks were straight or if he had veered off course.

Red sensed that he would soon collapse. Whether it was a good decision or not, he might never know, but Red decided to jog.

He picked up the pace. It occurred to him that if he passed out, failing to activate Charlie, they would all die. So, he concentrated on his breathing, heart rate, and vision.

That's when he saw Rebekah jogging alongside, crying.

"What's wrong, Rebekah?"

"It's Antonio."

"He'll be okay. We'll make it."

"It's not that. He made up with Nyx, and Derrick doesn't want me. He never did. No one wants me," Rebekah sobbed.

"That's not true. You're beautiful and smart. And…"

Red stumbled, collapsing face-first into the sand.

Then everything went black.

17

L. LINDA MADE HER WAY UP THE TRAIL toward town, which turned out to be more of a village, and almost deserted. The windows were boarded on half of the homes. She wondered why people had abandoned the place. It seemed like a beautiful place to live unless one hated the ocean, which was something she could not imagine. Perhaps someday she would live by the sea, but this would likely be the last time she saw it. That made her a little sad, but at least she'd seen it. Even swam in it. So, she had that.

A church stood on the corner. It had a sign in the yard that read: Doctrine Study, Wednesdays 7:00 p.m. The house next to it was a large two-story, freshly painted, and seemed out of place among houses with boarded windows and those with only the last remains of paint clinging to weathered wood. A poor town where only the preacher seemed to earn a decent living. She envisioned the fervent sermons, where the preacher exhorted people to give their money to obtain Chosen status. Don't covet earthly goods but eternal life, where they could walk on golden streets. Or keep their money and face eternal damnation.

She did not want to see this preacher, father of Tom-the-killer. But perhaps meeting the preacher might be best—even fun. Perhaps she would lead him to his son, show him the dead girls at the bottom of the cove, and then break the preacher's legs. The man must bear some responsibility for his son becoming a killer.

Still—rather than attempting to take the motorcycle undetected, getting permission would be best. If the preacher-daddy saw her stealing it, he would call the police. She didn't need the police. The girls in the water required the police, although it was too late for them, but not for other girls who might cross Tom's path one day. Much better if the police were chatting with Tom rather than looking for her.

She walked straight to the front door of the white two-story home. Thinking about her lines and knowing this needed to be one of her best performances. If she failed to convince preacher-daddy, she would be forced to hurt him too. She could see no other options.

She knocked and heard movement inside. The door opened. An old man, hunched, bespectacled, balding, wearing a sweater, faded black slacks, and plaid house shoes, opened the door.

"May I help you?"

"Hi. Are you Tom's dad?" L. Linda asked.

"I am, but Tom's not here."

"Tom is near the beach on a rocky spot overlooking a cove. I just left him." Which was true although not altogether accurate.

"I wondered where he went. He's supposed to be mowing lawns today." The man shook his head. "I have to force him to get anything done. He thinks people should pay him, but I ask you," he waved his hand, "does it look like these folks have money?"

"Here's the thing. I came to see Tom's motorcycle."

"You what?"

"Tom's motorcycle. He has one, right? I want to buy it."

"He's selling it?"

"That's what he told me. I hope he wasn't playing a trick on me. Kids do that sometimes." She paused. "They make fun of me. Call me weirdo and stuff like that."

"Child, don't you believe them. You have a kind heart. I can see that in your eyes."

L. Linda said, "You're joshing me."

"I'm not. It's a gift…" His voice trailed off.

"And a curse?" L. Linda asked.

"That it is."

L. Linda stuck out her hand. "I'm Carisa Howe."

He looked her over, pausing at her bare feet. Raising his head, it was as if he had just now seen her. "My goodness, child! What has happened to you?"

"I was swimming, and a wave tossed me onto the rocks. I'm fine."

Taking her hand gently, not in a handshake but in a manner unaccustomed to her, the preacher said, "My pleasure to meet you, Carisa. Such a pretty name. I'm Tom Farrer, Tom Sr. You're not from here. I know everyone in this little town."

L. Linda looked around. "Nothing like I imagined. It's such a beautiful place. It seems like it should be, I don't know, just more. You know what I mean?"

Tom Sr. nodded. "It's a shame, isn't it? This was a vacation spot once. Decades ago, mind you."

"What happened?"

"Well, New America happened. The Chosen happened. Folks don't have money for vacations, which means no work for people here. A few fishermen just hanging on, but the fishing isn't any good nowadays. They say it was once a wonderful place for fishermen, but not in my lifetime. Still, they try. It's in their blood. And, well, it gives them a bit of freedom, and that's no small thing, is it?"

L. Linda felt confused. This wasn't the man she envisioned. Intrigued, she asked, "You're a preacher? Doesn't everyone want to become Chosen? Isn't that what it's all about?"

Tom Sr.'s eyes shifted from one side to the other as if spies lurked nearby. "Can I trust you with something?"

Why would this man say something to a stranger that must be kept secret? More confused than ever, she said, "You can trust me."

"I don't teach the Carver Doctrine," he whispered.

"What do you teach?"

"The forbidden religions. Not just one. I teach the common threads. The things that make us better human beings."

L. Linda felt stunned for a moment. She didn't know such people existed. Why wasn't this man in Potterville? Had Jimmy Priest followed his teaching, he'd still be alive. The teaching Jimmy believed was based on simple greed. Not money, because people didn't get rich, but craving to be Chosen, and with that came wealth and elevation above the commoners. Commoner was a bad word in Potterville, but it was accurate. That's all they were—commoners. A synonym for trash, which is how the Chosen saw them. Jimmy acted superior but saw himself as trash. That's why he longed to become Chosen. To rise out of the despair of his life. L. Linda hated Chosen wannabes like Jimmy. Because of their ignorance. No one ever earned their way to becoming Chosen. It was just a con. A way to control the commoners.

"I didn't know such things were taught," L. Linda said.

"It's forbidden. It's the advantage of living in this little village. I know everyone here. I trust them."

L. Linda glanced at the house. "Well, looks like you do okay."

Tom Sr. shook his head. "The paint. I begged them not to do it. The people painted it. I told them to save their money for something useful. Or if they wanted to paint, start with their own houses, and do mine last. It was the one thing I've said that they disregarded. I went to the Pacific Edge service town to see my sister. She fell sick. Died. When I returned, well, they'd painted it. Can't be unpainted, can it?"

"I'm sorry about your sister." L. Linda wasn't just sorry about his sister. She was sorry about his son. Not the part about breaking Tom's legs, no, that part she didn't regret even a little, but sorry because knowing what his son had done would crush this man's spirit. And that made her sad. The world needed more men like this.

L. Linda gathered herself. "Can I ask you a question?"

"Of course."

"What do you see in your son's eyes?"

The man cocked his head to one side, staring at her for a moment. "I don't see kindness."

"What do you see?"

"Evil."

L. Linda didn't know if one could see good and evil in a person's eyes, but he wasn't wrong. However, he'd missed the mark with her. She didn't have a kind heart. She wasn't sure she even had one. Sure, she had a muscle that pumped blood, but that wasn't what she meant, and she was about to prove it. "Could I see Tom's motorcycle?"

"I should wait until he gets home. I can't believe he'd sell it. Don't get me wrong, I've told him to get rid of it. It's prideful. I mean, it's not a great-looking machine. To be honest, it's downright pitiful, but people in these parts don't have motorcycles. Too frivolous. They can hardly afford to put fuel in their old fishing boats. Not unusual for someone to tow a neighbor in because they ran out of fuel."

"He told me he found a better one but needs to sell this one first."

Tom Sr. shook his head. "I should have known."

"Anyways, I can't wait for Tom. I gotta go soon. If I don't buy it, I gotta catch a ride home."

"Hitchhiking isn't safe for a young girl." Tom Sr. sighed, "Follow me."

She followed him to a shed. He slid the door open and pulled a dirty sheet off the machine. He wasn't lying. She'd seen better examples in Fletcher's junkyard. Paint so faded she couldn't tell the original color. The handlebars were bent, one side up, the other down. The seat had rotted, leaving just an inch of crumbling foam. No fenders. No gauges. If it ran, she'd be amazed.

"Will it start?"

Tom Sr. shrugged. "I guess. Tom rode it yesterday. Just tore up and down the street. Rubbing it in that he had the only motorcycle in town, I suppose."

L. Linda grabbed the handlebars and started pulling it out.

"Be careful. You've got no shoes. You'll injure yourself."

"Don't worry. I get that all the time. I should have worn shoes, but I'm barefoot so often I kinda forgot. I'm a bit ditsy sometimes. Anywhos, I'll be super careful, and I won't go far." She hated lying to the man, but Potterville wasn't far, was it?

"You forgot shoes?"

"Like I said, ditsy."

It looked no better in the sunlight. However, she gazed at the four exhaust pipes converging into one. An honest-to-God four-cylinder machine. She'd dreamed of owning one. Unfortunately, Tom had not treated the motorcycle much better than the girls he'd killed and dragged to the ocean. He had been brutalizing the bike more than showing off.

L. Linda tested the front brakes. Inserting the key, she said, "Tom gave me the key. I'm just going to take it for a little spin. In the meantime, you might want to check on Tom. I thought he'd be here by now. There were three girls on the beach. I hate to say it, but I think you should get down there."

Tom Sr. shook his head. "Say no more."

She twisted the key. The green neutral light glowed softly. Not enough battery to use the electric starter, which didn't surprise her. Still, she had hoped to avoid kickstarting it.

She had not lied about often going barefoot. She walked to school, carrying her shoes, and worked out in their garage barefoot. Tough feet made excellent weapons if she ever needed to use them, and that preparation had paid off with knife-boy Tom. But bare feet, even tough ones, were not suitable for starting motorcycles.

As Tom Sr. reached the sidewalk, he turned. "You be careful. And watch those pipes. They'll burn you."

She gave him a thumbs-up. When he was out of sight, she took Tom's helmet off the sissy bar and pulled it on. It was open-faced and too big, but better than nothing. The temperature was in the mid-seventies, but she didn't know the disposition of the machine, so she positioned the choke at the midway spot, stood on the left foot peg, and gave the kick starter a solid push with her right foot.

The motorcycle gave a slight cough, then at the end of the stroke, it kicked back. It hurt bad, and tears welled in her eyes.

But L. Linda Maxton wasn't a crier. She had not shed a tear in many years. She might have made an exception if the kickback had a bit more kick to it.

She was angry with herself. She had positioned the center of her foot on the kick starter, which was the most likely place to break a bone. A broken foot would not be good at this point. Not good at any point, really, but if she were going to break her foot, this was not the time. Too many mistakes. Well, it wasn't all bad. A satellite was out of commission, and Tom Jr.'s killing business was in foreclosure.

She hoped.

Tom's father should call the police, but what if he didn't? What if he decided to protect his son? Tom Jr. might say that she had killed those girls and then injured him when he confronted her. What if Tom Sr. sent the police after her? She should have thought this through more carefully. It all came down to whether Tom's father believed his story.

Even more reason to rocket out of here, although the 550 was no doubt incapable of rocketing. She should have checked the gas in the tank. There was no reason to think knife-boy Tommy had much money for fuel. However, it didn't matter. She would go however far the gas would take her. She had no money. If she was lucky, it had enough gas to get to Potterville. If not, she hoped it got her far from here. Then she'd find other transportation. One step at a time.

First step, start the motorcycle.

She opened the choke, and twisted the throttle open, and then, using the ball of her foot, she stood and put all her weight behind a forceful stroke of the starter.

The engine roared to life. She blipped the throttle a few times. The motor hesitated and spit. Not as finely tuned as her little 175, and much louder as if the muffler was but a hollow shell, the inside rusted away to nothing, or perhaps knife-boy Tom had gutted it.

She clicked the transmission into first gear and eased the clutch out. Soon she was speeding down a city street. The people were probably used to Tom racing down the road, so nothing new. Although the exhaust was loud, she could hear the timing chain slapping, sounding as if it could break at any moment. In addition, the drive chain sounded as if it were permanently kinked in half a dozen places and could derail at the slightest provocation.

She wasn't sure how far this village was south of Pacific Edge, and she didn't want to find out. The road would still be closed where they blew up the aircraft and almost killed Derrick and the others. So, she headed inland into canyons that twisted and turned and intersected with other roads, mostly unmarked. Houses scattered here and there, some empty, some not. None looked like a good stop for tea or a pair of shoes.

L. Linda had thought shoes were the least of her worries. She had second thoughts now. The motor and exhaust pipe's heat were worse than she imagined. She positioned her feet as far out on the foot pegs as possible, but that wasn't good enough. She had to hold them out in front of the bike to cool them. Burned feet were as bad as broken feet. She should have stolen some shoes.

18

Friday, April 9, 12:10 p.m.

IN AN OLD HOTEL, IN CASCADE LOCKS, Oregon, a man lay on a bed staring at the ceiling, contemplating the water stains, and his decision to stay in town today based on a stranger's request. A lady at the hotel had spotted him walking up the street, met him in the parking lot with a key, and pointed him to a room. She said John had it covered. This was a mistake. Scott knew that, but the bed felt good and a hot shower, assuming they had hot water in this place, would seem like a slice of the afterlife promised to the Chosen.

A beer sounded fantastic too after spending the last eight days pushing himself beyond exhaustion, scanning the sky for hovercraft, and watching the trail for Pacific Edge security. However, he would pass on the beer. He couldn't stay here. Even this room felt like a grave mistake, violating every rule he'd established for himself. No stopping, no talking, no phones, no messages. Keep moving. Get to Canada. Plead for asylum.

He stood a chance if they granted him asylum, but even there, he still faced a substantial risk of being assassinated. If Canada rejected his application and deported him, he'd face an agonizing death.

Being in this room, despite knowing the danger, showed weakness in his resolve. He'd never make it at this rate. Convincing Canada to grant him asylum seemed like a long shot at best. A dream. A fantasy. A hallucination. Perhaps he should just remain Scott Key. Go to Yakima or wherever it was that vineyards grew. Get work on a farm. That wouldn't be such a horrible life. He was used to long hours but not doing physical labor. After this hike, however, he'd be well conditioned to be a laborer. He'd fit right in: tanned, weathered, in need of a shave, and shower. No one would be the wiser. No one would know his real name.

New plan.

One problem. Apparently, John at the brewery knew his name and had been watching for him. John knew about Derrick and Miriam. Scott wanted to know about Derrick and Miriam, but they were no longer his concern. He had to accept that and move on. He'd kept them alive well beyond their expiration dates. That was all he could do. They were in trouble, but they were never supposed to live this long. He'd bought them a few years.

All he could do.

Yet this John fellow knew who he was. How did that happen? Scott knew about the Resistance, but he wasn't a member. Not that he didn't support them. He believed they were doing important work. But the Resistance couldn't change anything. No one could.

On those long, hard days on the trail and on those chilly nights, shivering in a sleeping bag, he often fantasized about how Miriam and Derrick might change things. This helped him feel better about his work. His work got people killed. No question about that. After this fiasco, many had died because of things he'd done or, sometimes, not done. The Pacific Edge Tribunal Chief Justice was probably dead, if not the entire Tribunal. Certainly, the people who had helped Derrick in Potterville had paid the price.

Scott had assumed Miriam was dead.

She'd engineered a scheme to escape. The near drowning must have been a ploy. Just a part of a more elaborate plan that included locking him and his wife in their observation room and crashing the Pacific Edge computer system. Apparently, she was even smarter than he realized.

His wife was dead. Probably. She stood a slim chance of survival if she helped find Derrick. But that only postponed her death. Prime would kill her when she was of no further value.

She had cried the day they exiled Derrick. But there were no tears for Derrick, only for herself. She hated keeping Derrick and Miriam alive. It didn't start out that way. He had convinced her that keeping the experiment going was to their benefit, and that Prime would understand when they presented their findings. Prime didn't support self-initiative, but when Prime saw they had perfected a body he could inhabit, he would understand why their work was vital. And because the bodies would burn out fast, compared to his hybrid existence, they would have to create a constant supply. That insured a long life with top benefits. Perhaps new bodies for them as well. After all, they knew the secrets.

Worst-case scenario, if Prime was unsatisfied with the new body for itself, the Test Subjects were perfect candidates for close assistants. Finding people 100% trustworthy was difficult. Impossible was a better term. Even now, Prime might have people from the Resistance infiltrating its inner circle.

But things had changed. More accurately stated, Scott had changed.

He had developed feelings for Derrick and Miriam. That wasn't supposed to happen. His wife wanted to end the experiment several times, arguing they had enough data, adding it would be their heads if Prime learned the Test Subjects were still alive. In addition, the next generation was ready to begin trials, and they needed to be at the test facility.

But he had kept going. Just one more experiment, he would say.

Then came the experiment with Marcus Carver. Marcus felt honored to be part of an experiment for a Prime project. He didn't like Derrick or Miriam, making it even more satisfying. Marcus wasn't going to hit Miriam. He would not risk being the one to be punished. And Scott had guaranteed Marcus that Derrick would do nothing. They didn't explain why they were so confident. They had been bombarding Derrick for weeks with control thoughts via the 1984 chip. His every move and decision had been controlled, from how he criticized Miriam to steering his decision for the Choosing, steering him away from Rebekah Ford and toward Jana Somersworth.

Everything was under control.

Until it wasn't.

Scott took a deep breath. No changing it now. He hoped for the best for Derrick and Miriam, but there was nothing more he could do. Beyond that, he had a keen interest in staying alive. That was the priority for everyone, wasn't it? In the spirit of staying alive, getting out of here was vital. He should not have come to this hotel. John, the beer maker, may have already turned him in for a reward. Security might be headed here right now.

Just a quick shower, and he'd hit the road.

Scott sat on the edge of the bed. Every muscle complained. He had not stopped for first aid supplies. The blisters on his feet oozed pink liquid under the bandages as he pulled them off. White in the center and red around the edges, he assumed they were mildly infected. Under normal circumstances, an easy fix at the clinic. Under normal circumstances, he would have never developed blisters on his feet. Maybe on a finger, maybe on a thumb. Next, he worked on the bandage on his knee he had crafted from a t-shirt and strips of duct tape. He had large square bandages in his kit, but none big enough for this wound. Pulling at the tape's edge, hurt like hell, tearing out hair and scabbed skin. Slow wasn't the way to go on this. With a quick jerk, the bandage came off and flew across the room. It took all of Scott's will power to not scream. Tears filled his eyes. Blood trickled down his shin. He had worked hard getting into physical condition for this hike. It was essential and got him this far. However, it had not prepared him for just how demanding the journey would be or the toll it would take on his body.

With steam rolling out of the shower, Scott eased in, expecting his wounds would protest violently to the hot water. He wasn't wrong. Gradually the pain subsided but never left. Still, he didn't want to leave the hot water and may not have had it not suddenly turned cold.

Dressed, he laid down. Just for a moment, then he'd move on.

He'd be on the trail in Washington soon.

Just a minute longer on this bed.

Then sleep overcame him.

19

RED DRIFTED IN AND OUT OF CONSCIOUSNESS. He felt sure someone had set him on fire. Lying on the ground with his head turned, his vision was blurred, and he could only see sand. It felt as if something was crusted on his face, but he could not move his hand to brush it away. A taste of iron filled his mouth.

Blood.

Desert.

I'm in a desert.

We jumped out of an airplane....

Not possible.

Dreaming.

Must be dreaming.

Antonio? We were together. Wait, Rebekah said Antonio was with Nyx. Where is Rebekah? He had to find her. Too hot here for Rebekah.

Red rolled over. That took all the strength he could muster. The sun lit his face like a blowtorch. He raised his hand to shield his eyes. "Antonio? Are you there? I need help."

But Antonio didn't answer. Marshalling himself, Red sat up. Cords stretched from where he sat to a white sheet of some sort.

Parachute.

Antonio.

Charlie.

It was coming back to him now. They did jump from a plane. A C-something or another. Rescued people.

But not Derrick.

Mexico. Red didn't understand Mexico.

Charlie. They shut Charlie off. Why would they do that? He couldn't remember.

The sand burned his hands and knees as he crawled to the parachute. Pulling back the cloth, he saw Antonio's face. Bright red. Not good.

Red uncovered Charlie. Why was Charlie covered? He didn't remember doing that. How to turn Charlie on. He couldn't remember that either. Everything seemed cloudy. Where's Rebekah? She might remember.

But Rebekah wasn't here. Was she? He didn't think so. A hallucination. He was in dreadful shape. Antonio was worse.

"Must start, Charlie." Red probed the machine for a button. The metal was hot. Finally, a section depressed. The robot's eyes lit.

Charlie stood. "Where are we?"

Red collapsed. "Don't know."

Charlie pulled Red onto the parachute and then kneeled beside him. "Oh, my. You need medical attention. Get help. Batteries low. I remember. But issues. Back soon."

Charlie covered Red and Antonio. "Pull them? No, not enough power. Issues."

And with that, Charlie left, sort of running, sort of jumping. Each stride covering ten yards, he was moving fast.

It took Charlie less than two minutes to cover the first mile. His stride went from ten yards to seven yards to five yards. The second mile took four minutes. Five yards now, the third mile took eight minutes.

Now he was walking. A warning sign flashed before his eyes, but that was just happening in his computer brain.

OVERHEATED.

FAILURE IMMINENT.

In the distance, he saw the hangar doors in a depression carved into the mountain. "Must go on."

Charlie tried to force himself forward. Robots were not programmed to have a will of their own. This came from Akira. Akira's thoughts and memories had intermingled with his programming when he overrode the medical unit to heal her. As his artificial intelligence evolved, he had attempted to understand emotions.

One might have thought Charlie had emotions, but he did not. Only in an analytical sense. These were Akira's emotions. Charlie had known they were there since he disconnected from Akira's treatment. He tried but failed to process them. They threatened to overwhelm his logical way of thinking. So, he had gathered them and locked them in a file, hoping that someday he could pull one at a time, analyze it, understand it, and perhaps make it his own.

With his system failing, the emotions seeped from the locked file. Love, friendship, loyalty, pain, sorrow, loss. Charlie felt all of Akira's emotions.

All of them.

Too much.

Must go on. Must save them.

Too much.

One hundred yards from the entrance, Charlie stopped.
Teetered, then fell.

A Derrick King Novel, Book 6

20

Friday, April 9, 12:10 p.m.

AS THE SCENTS OF GASOLINE, OIL, STALE exhaust fumes, soup, and pastrami mingled together, the friends of the absent children ate in silence. Jason Maxton's last words seemed to have driven home the reality of their situation. His daughter had stolen a Prime aircraft with the sole purpose of saving those missing high school students. Potterville, a quiet town, was now a place where an assassin had killed four people.

Their student council could not save them.

Their adult council couldn't save them either.

The sheriff could not protect them.

Potterville had become Prime's enemy.

Coach Browning pushed the rest of his sandwich to his eldest son, Terrance. "You still hungry?"

"Not really," Terrance said, taking a bite of his father's half-eaten sandwich.

Browning looked at Collins. "I gotta think about my family. I want to help, but they come first. Sorry, but I can't stay here given the risks."

Collins started to say something, but Jason Maxton cut him off. "Where would you go?"

Browning shrugged. "I don't know. We lost everything in the fire, but we still have the van. We'll just drive until we find something."

"You won't make it far." Jason stuck a potato chip in his mouth as he stood.

"What makes you the expert?" Browning asked, the anger or frustration in his voice evident.

Jason said nothing as he picked up a black case he'd carried in earlier. He walked to a workbench, set the case down, then clicked the latches. Picking up black pieces of metal and plastic, he assembled a rifle within seconds.

Collins stood. "What the hell?"

"Sit down, Sheriff," Jason said. "With all due respect, the situation is out of your league. I'm taking over."

Browning said, "I'm confused."

From the office doorway, Jack Fletcher said, "Best listen to him."

Collins said, "You know something, Jack?"

"Nothin' specific. I know L. Linda didn't just roll into town on the pumpkin truck. Makes sense that Jason hasn't always been an accountant or whatever he claims to be."

Allen Patel said, "I've been quiet too long. We must rise to the challenge. The Resistance will help us. They're the only ones who will."

Lori Martinez said, "Jason, are you in the Resistance?"

With his back turned to the group, assembling another weapon, Jason said, "Not officially."

Patel said, "I am in the Resistance. I have contacts here."

Collins said, "I assumed as much, Allen."

Lori said, "Jason, what do you mean? Not officially."

Jason turned, holding a rifle with a thick barrel and a huge scope. "At this point, we are all in the Resistance."

Collins said, "Jason, mind explaining who you are exactly?"

"I mind. Let's just say Jack is correct. I have not always been an accountant."

"And L. Linda?" Collins asked.

"Let's leave her out of it. I thought we had a future here, but not likely now. I hoped L. Linda could just be the weird girl you all know."

Browning said, "Well, she still has me baffled for what it's worth. So, what's the plan?"

Jason said, "Right from your playbook, Coach."

"Jason, you're as weird as L. Linda. I'm confused."

Jason said, "You can't just play defense. Waiting to be found isn't going to cut it." Loading bullets into the rifle, he said, "Let's play some offense."

21

UNDERGROUND IN A MILITARY GYM, a solitary girl ran laps. She had been running for 30 minutes. Sweat-soaked her gym clothing, a drab green t-shirt, and jogging shorts, both found in the women's locker room. Nyx Belos ran to clear her head. It wasn't working. Too many swirling thoughts.

Too many contradicting emotions and too much fear.

In the shadows, someone watched her run, also suffering from too many swirling thoughts but lacking the contradicting, or possibly, clarifying emotions.

Akira Nakamura had been best friends with Nyx since grade school. Akira remembered how it happened. She had asked Nyx to be her girlfriend, but not in the way other grade-school girls were friends. Akira had not yet learned her feelings for Nyx were different and frowned upon by some. Those hateful people's thinking was driven by The Doctrine of the Chosen and the Doctrine of the Followers, which were the same except the Chosen lived in fortresses walled off from the commoners. Followers were just commoners, wishing they were Chosen.

Instead of shunning Akira, like most, Nyx explained. Instead of avoiding her, Nyx protected her.

It made perfect sense why Nyx was closer than a sister. What didn't make sense is why Akira felt nothing for Nyx. Not love, not friendship, not jealousy, not hate.

Earlier, Akira had blown up at Nyx. It seemed like anger, created from jealousy, but it wasn't that. It was confusion. It was logic.

Everything Akira had said was true. Well, she didn't know Nyx's motives. That was conjecture. Akira lined up all the logic and decided she must hate Nyx.

As her thoughts slowed and became more orderly, she realized something.
She felt nothing.
Just memories.
No emotion tied to any of them.
She had become like a robot.
The machines had healed her but had stolen her emotions.

Watching Nyx, Akira tried to feel something but could not. She remembered emotions, but that wasn't the same as having them. Akira did not know if she could function without feelings.

Didn't know if she wanted to.

Akira tried to hate the machine called Charlie for saving her, changing her, but she couldn't even do that.

But she needed to talk to Nyx. Antonio, Red, and Charlie had been gone too long. She should be worried, but she was not. It was just a fact.

Nyx was probably worried.

That was just a fact too.

Stepping onto the track, Akira stood in Nyx's lane as she turned the corner.

Nyx stopped, breathing hard. "What is it?"

Akira said, "They've been gone too long."

"I agree. But which ones are you referring to? We have more than one group missing. Well, L. Linda isn't a group, but she's still missing."

"Are you worried?" Akira asked.

Nyx said, "Worried sick. Aren't you?"

"I understand I should be, but I don't feel worried. It's weird. Who are you worried about most?"

"What kind of question is that? I'm worried about all of them," Nyx said.

"Who is number one?"

"I don't know. Derrick, I suppose."

"Must be nice."

"What must be nice? I told you already. I didn't mean to steal Derrick from you."

"I know that."

"Then what do you mean? There's nothing nice about it," Nyx said.

"Nice to be worried."

"I'm not sure I understand."

Akira said, "No time to explain. We need to do something."

"Like what? I don't know what to do or where to begin."

Akira said, "Maybe go outside. Find something that runs and go look."

Nyx stared at Akira. "Go look. In that vast desert? That's your idea?"

"Best I've got. I'll use the satellites. See if I can learn anything."

"That's dangerous. You said we shouldn't use the satellites."

"We used them once."

"Right. Because Miriam told you what to do. It was a onetime transmission."

"Maybe not."

Nyx shook her head. "And I'm supposed to just drive around the desert?"

"Use your head. You've done it before. Take binoculars, scan the desert. Go straight out, stop, scan more."

Nyx signed. "Sounds hopeless."

"It might be hopeless, but it's logical."

"Explain."

"If Red and Antonio had problems, they would try to get here another way. That means they might be in the desert."

"Worth a try, I guess."

"Take water."

"Logical."

"Exactly."

Akira turned and walked away.

Nyx thought for a moment and said, "If I didn't know better, I'd say it's not just logical but hopeful."

Akira looked over her shoulder. "I have zero hope."

22

Friday, April 9, 12:25 p.m.

A SOLITARY PICKUP TRUCK SET PARKED ON a rock-strewn ridge. The sun had risen to its zenith, and Derrick assumed it was just past noon. Miriam probably knew what time it was, but he didn't ask. The sun's heat filled everything as if it had forced itself between each molecule, which he had only learned existed since attending school in Potterville. The thought of Potterville High School reminded him of how much he used to fear the commoners. Now he wanted to be back in Potterville, doing stuff with those he once feared, but he would likely never see the school again.

He and Miriam sat in the truck's bed. Rebekah and Anna were in the cab, waiting for Derrick's signal. The air shimmered, making the valley below unfocused. In the distance, a vast lake covered the valley floor. However, he felt sure the water wasn't real. How he knew this evaded him, but he remembered the hypnosis and how someone had hidden his memories and inserted commands. The hidden memory part worried him, and the implanted commands terrified him.

He had spent far too much time convincing the others to leave and go in a separate direction. After considerable debate, Harley, Atwood, and Haskins had agreed that finding their town's people, rebuilding their operation, and preserving history was their best option. Derrick felt relieved they were gone. At least they had a chance.

Although the heat didn't bother Derrick, which seemed odd, they did not have enough water to stay hydrated, and their situation required clear thinking and careful planning, but there wasn't time for careful planning. The missile could fly before they arrived, so they opted for a hastily concocted, half-assed strategy instead. Even well-planned operations go wrong, and this haphazard affair had little chance of going right. While driving here, Derrick had considered several scenarios, analyzing outcomes, and cons outnumbered pros ten to zero.

To make matters worse, random thoughts circulated with wild abandon, making it difficult to focus. One reoccurring image included—well, everything included Nyx—but this one bothered him most. He had not fully processed that Red had flown a cargo jet to the desert town. The military shot at the plane, but Red got it into the air. However, the aircraft may have been damaged, and people may have been injured. There was no guarantee Red could land it safely a second time.

Had Nyx been on the plane? Did a bullet penetrate the aircraft and hit her? Although he tried to block such thoughts, he failed. Nyx might be injured or dead. Breathing became difficult.

When he managed to block thoughts about Nyx, Potterville popped in. Prime will punish those who had helped him. Potterville could be under siege. He pictured soldiers marching through the streets, shooting people at will.

"Derrick!" Miriam slapped his shoulder.

"What?"

"You've drifted off again."

"Just thinking."

"It's hard not to worry. I've been thinking about Akira myself. I'm happy she's alive, but she didn't seem herself. You must be worried about Nyx. Do you think she was on the cargo plane?"

"I don't know. It wouldn't make sense. Would it?"

Miriam shrugged. "Are you sure this is the best plan?"

Derrick shook his head. "Not at all. We won't know until it's over."

"We have machine guns. We could go in shooting."

"That would mean a lot of dead people. We could be among them. If we don't stop the launch, many people will die. I just hope the soldiers are slow to shoot a bunch of kids." Derrick motioned Rebekah to open the truck's back window. After going over the plan one last time, he said, "Let's do this."

Rebekah started the truck and headed toward the valley. Once on the flat, they were in Mexico, according to Harley. Rebekah glanced back at Derrick. He nodded, motioning her forward. The plan was simple. Rebekah would cross the dry lakebed as fast as possible. They would come to a highway. Once on the road, she'd push the truck to top speed. When they reached the spot parallel to the missile, she would leave the highway and race toward the canyon where the soldiers had hidden the launcher.

They would make no effort to conceal their approach. The soldiers might have spotted them already because the truck created a massive cloud of dust. Anyone attacking would try to take them by surprise, not come storming at them. If they made it to the launch site alive, they'd beg for help. Claim drug dealers were chasing them. Just some crazy kids. No threat at all. At least, Derrick hoped that's how the soldiers would see it. Like he hoped Nyx wasn't on that airplane. Hope was not Derrick's preferred thing in which to place his confidence.

Objectively, they had no plan because they didn't even know how many soldiers were there. This was all they had. If they were not shot, they would spread out, which would give Derrick, Miriam, and Anna each two or three soldiers to attack. Rebekah would stay back, ready to use the machine gun if things went badly. Derrick had given her a crash course on the weapon's operation. She would not have to hit moving targets. She would concentrate the gun's fire on the control panels. Destroy them and end the missile strike.

If it came to that, it meant their time on earth had ended. He would not see Nyx again. She wouldn't even know what happened to him. For all she'd know, he ran. Abandoned her. Somehow, he felt this would hurt worse than if Nyx knew he died.

But that sort of thinking had to end. Despite how far-fetched this plan sounded, he had a marginally good feeling about it. It was crazy enough that it might work.

They intersected the highway. Rebekah turned right onto the blacktop and floored the accelerator.

Miriam looked at Derrick and shouted, "This is going to work!"

"I hope you are right!"

That's when he heard a siren.

Less than a mile behind them, a white and blue police car with spinning red lights was closing in fast.

23

JASON MAXTON FINISHED ASSEMBLING THE LAST weapon, and then he filled a clip with bullets, slid it into the pistol, and laid it on the workbench. Browning counted three rifles, one with an enormous scope and barrel three times the size of a typical rifle, two military rifles, five handguns, and two shotguns. Jason went out to the truck Jack had driven and brought in two more cases, struggling with their weight, displaying ripples in his arms and chest that Browning had not noticed previously. Browning realized he'd never seen Jason not wearing a jacket, even when it was hot out. Browning thought it was because Jason was a bit wimpy. Now he realized that wasn't the reason.

Collins sat at a nearby table, working his jaw, looking as if he might explode. Browning grabbed two sodas, sat, sliding Collins a cola. Collins started to stand, but Browning caught him by the shoulder.

Collins said, "Where in the hell did you get that arsenal?"

Without turning, Jason said, "That's unimportant."

"It's important to me. I am responsible for this town."

Jason turned and stared at Collins for a moment. "I understand, Bill, and I'm not trying to be difficult. It's unimportant because it doesn't matter at this point. Plus, I can't tell you where I got them."

"You mean you won't tell me?"

"That too."

"What do you intend to do?" Collins asked.

"Protect our town."

"I understand that's what you want to do, but how? You can't just start shooting people."

"I can if I don't know them."

"You don't know everyone in town."

"I may not know them personally, but I can recognize familiar faces. I know a stranger when I see one."

"We get people passing through, you know. You can't shoot people just because they don't live here."

"I know that."

"Back to my original question. What's your plan?"

"We are going to watch. We are going to listen."

Lori said, "Could you be a little more specific?"

Jason turned. "Lori, did L. Linda tell you what the assassin would look like?"

"No."

"Was there any doubt in your mind when you saw the assassin?"

"Well, I thought maybe she'd been in an accident."

"Was there any doubt, or was that just something you told yourself because you didn't want to believe she was a killer?"

Lori thought for a moment. "I knew she was the assassin."

"There you go. I'll tell you what to watch for. If you see an assassin, you'll know. But we won't just shoot anyone we suspect." He turned back to a case. "We'll use these first." He set four radios on the counter.

"I have radios," Collins said.

"Not like these."

"They look the same."

"They are not. These are a unique frequency and encoded. They can receive other signals, but the transmission from these radios can only be heard if you have a radio with the encryption chip, and I have all the radios with these specific chips."

Browning said, "Where did you get this stuff, Jason?"

Jason took a deep breath. "Let's just say in a previous life and leave it at that. Let's talk about assignments."

"Previous life?" Collins asked.

"I said, leave it at that. You already know more than I ever intended. If we live through this, L. Linda and I will move on."

"I hope that doesn't happen," Fletcher said.

Jason cocked his head, staring at Jack.

"I hope you don't leave. No reason to. I don't care where you're from or what you used to do. You are one of us now, and none of this needs to be repeated outside this room." Fletcher glared at the kids in the room.

Wide eyes and nods issued from them all.

"We'll see," Jason said, adding, "Who can shoot a rifle?"

Browning said, "I went hunting a few times when I was a kid."

Jack said, "I'm good with a rifle."

Collins said, "Since when?"

"Since I was a kid, and I got a freezer full of game to prove it. Shotgun too, but not so much with a pistol."

Collins said, "I might be the only one with much experience with a pistol."

Lori folded her arms. "Excuse me?"

Collins said, "Sorry. Lori qualifies with the pistol each year."

"I do more than that."

Collins looked at Lori. "What's that mean?"

"It means I go to the range twice a month."

"I didn't know that. Why?"

Lori looked down and then back up. "I was hoping to impress you at the next qualification. Plus, I might have to save your sorry ass someday."

Collins shook his head.

Jason said, "I assume you can shoot a shotgun."

Lori said, "Yeah, especially if it's taped under a desk."

Jason nodded. "That is apparent." He paused, then said, "We'll work as teams. Jack will take up a position in the clock tower with the sniper rifle. He can see most of the downtown from there. I want everyone in Jack's field of vision 90% of the time, meaning stay on the streets running parallel to the tower. When you're out of his sight, check the area before entering, then move quickly to where he can see you again."

"That limits us to downtown," Collins said.

"True. It's not a perfect plan, but there aren't enough of us to venture farther. It will be enough. An assassin will come downtown. That's where most things happen, plus the Sheriff's Office, the Bistro, and such are downtown."

Browning said, "the Bistro?"

"Yeah. It's a crossroads. Everyone goes to the Bistro, eventually. If you want to know what's happening in Potterville, go to Donna's, sit, and listen."

"Are we going to warn Donna?" Evie Belos asked.

"Yes."

Evie said, "I can shoot a gun." She looked around. "I grew up on a farm. Dad taught me to shoot varmints."

Jason said, "That's great. You stay here and protect the others."

"But I'd..."

Jason held up his hand. "It wasn't a request."

Jason laid out the details. "We all go to the library and access the tunnels. We'll use the tunnels to get to the courthouse. Jack goes to the clock tower, and Lori gets the animal control truck. It's less threatening than a patrol car. We will cover three-blocks each direction. Coach and Allen will be on foot, walking across the street from each other, staying on the same streets as Lori, trying to stay within eyesight of each other. Bill, you cover sections opposite of where Coach and Allen are."

Lori interrupted. "Three of us will be together, and Bill will be alone."

"I know, but Bill's the sheriff. Coach and Allen are not trained."

"Where will you be?" Collins asked.

"I'll be staying close to Donna's. That's the best central location, so I can respond if you see anything suspicious."

Browning said, "That means you're alone where you said an assassin is most likely to show up."

"Stay in eye contact with one another as much as possible. Radio checks every ten minutes or less. Questions?"

Lori said, "You were going to tell us how to spot an assassin?"

"Right. They will look like any ordinary person, except that the ordinary will be overdone. They could be old, or at least they'll look old. Or young. Male or female. They might even look like someone you know. Disguised."

"That's not very helpful," Lori said.

"Just be careful and radio if you see anyone you don't recognize or anything that looks suspicious. I'll head your way. Just let me take care of it."

"That's real vague," Collins said.

"Trust your gut," Jason said.

Allen said, "What if we have to do something before you get there?"

Jason stared at Allen for a minute, then scanned the room, looking each adult in the eye. "Don't hesitate to shoot them."

24

AIRCRAFT DESIGNED FOR MANY PURPOSES stood in straight rows in the massive hangar, but Nyx couldn't spot a vehicle she could drive into the desert. She should have gone to where Red found the helicopter yesterday, but she thought that would take longer, and she felt as if she were sitting on a bomb, and someone had already lit the fuse. She cursed herself for waiting so long to do something. It was clear something had happened. Red and Antonio should have returned by now.

Just another failure to add to her long list of failures.

Nyx saw a weird-looking machine used to move aircraft. It looked like an offspring from the mating of a farm tractor and a small truck. It did not look fast, but the dash lit when she turned the key.

As the roll-up door opened, heat poured in as if she was entering an oven. She did not realize how accurate that description was. A century ago, the world's hottest temperature was 134 degrees. It was already 145 degrees here and was neither the high for the day nor the hottest time of year. The world had changed.

Death Valley now lived up to its name. It was uninhabitable.

As soon as the door was high enough, Nyx raced from the hangar. The machine was faster than she expected. There was no speedometer, but she estimated its top speed was about 35 mph. She didn't know how far it would go. Like other vehicles here, it ran on a battery. She'd have to turn back before the power fell to 50%. This was another mistake because there were four-wheel-drive vehicles that ran on diesel in the underground hangar. Better choices. If she got stuck out here, she'd be no help to anyone.

But she would not have to go far. Half a mile from the hangar, she saw something on the desert floor. She kept the pedal to the floor, pointing the vehicle toward it.

One hundred yards and closing, she recognized what it was.

Charlie.

She locked the brakes, sliding to a stop next to the fallen robot. She kneeled. "Charlie? Charlie?"

Nothing.

She scanned the desert and could see Charlie's tracks. Jumping back into the vehicle, she started out again, this time with confidence they were out there, no doubt in trouble, perhaps dead.

Please be alive. Please! She pleaded but knew it would change nothing. She didn't think she could hold it together if she found Antonio dead. Why did she break up with him? Whatever it was, it seemed insignificant now.

She did some rough math in her head. At 30 mph, it took two minutes to cover one mile. But she had neither a watch nor a speedometer. She had a power gauge that showed 60%. To be safe, she should turn around, but she knew they were out there. Had to be. But how far? The cargo plane would be visible several miles in the distance.

Fifty-five percent.

Turn around.

She drove on, deciding when the gauge read 52%, she'd go back and get a diesel truck.

At 53%, she saw something that didn't look right. Half a mile out, something looked whiter than the sand. She pushed the pedal to the floor again. She had slowed a little, hoping to not consume the battery as fast, not knowing if that was a good or bad decision. If it worked, she would not take credit, it had been just a lucky guess. If it failed, she'd blame herself for another poor decision. It was how her brain worked.

Fifty yards out, she understood what she was looking at. It was a parachute with a lump and behind it drag marks. *Where's the plane?*

Stopping alongside the white cloth billowing in the breeze, Nyx bailed from the vehicle. She stared at the lumps. It was them. Had to be. She knew that.

But she didn't want to look at them.

She didn't want to see her dead friends.

After a moment that felt like hours, she pulled the cloth back. She saw Red first. His skin was dry and red. She kneeled beside him, lowered her cheek to his nose, and felt his breath.

Dashing back to the vehicle, she grabbed two bottles of water and then ran to Red, pouring some on his forehead and shirt. He moaned but said nothing.

"Red, try to drink." She lifted his head, pouring a small amount of water on his lips. A little trickled into his mouth. Fearing he might choke, she stopped.

Dreading what she might see next, she pulled the parachute off Antonio. He looked worse than Red, his dry skin red and blistered. She didn't check for breathing but poured water on his blistered skin and lips.

"Try to sip." She lifted his head, pouring water on his lips.

His lips parted, and she poured a little more.

Rasping, almost inaudible, Antonio asked, "What took you so long?"

"Can you walk?" Nyx felt an urge to kiss him but didn't. That would have been too painful for Antonio. And for her.

Antonio tried to move, then shook his head.

Nyx scanned the desert. The cargo plane was not visible. "Where's Derrick and the others?"

Antonio shook his head and moved his lips, but his voice was inaudible. Nyx thought he said Mexico, but that made little sense. Her heart sank. Where's Derrick? Why were they not all together?

"I can't lift you. I'll have to drag you."

She poured the rest of the water on Antonio's chest, used the other bottle to drench Red, and then covered them both with the parachute and tucked it in underneath them. She backed the vehicle to the harness, jumped out, and hooked it on the hitch. Back in the vehicle, she eased forward, taking up the slack.

She drove slowly. This was going to take too long. She remembered learning about this in health class. Both heat exhaustion and heat stroke were dangerous in Potterville summers. Especially for farm workers and others who had to be outside. Red and Antonio were no doubt suffering from severe heat stroke. They might die before she got them out of the sun.

They might die even if she did.

But they had the robotic medical unit. She needed to get them there, but Charlie was needed to get them in.

She sped up a little. The parachute held.

She sped up more.

The power gauge read 41%.

25

THE DIMLY LIT ROOM REFUSED TO COME INTO focus, as did Scott's thinking. He was not on the Pacific Crest Trail—it was too comfortable, nor was he in Pacific Edge—it was too dilapidated. As his thinking cleared, he remembered. He was in a drab old motel room in Cascade Locks, Oregon.

He should have been on the other side of the river by now. An old alarm clock near the bed said it was 12:35, although he did not know if it was accurate. He had no watch, no cell phone. Sleep wasn't part of the plan, but he was exhausted and had not slept long, so he didn't chastise himself. He wasn't expected for dinner until 8:30, so there was no rush. Unless John had turned him in. If that were the case, he was already too late.

Scott rolled out of bed and staggered to the bathroom, where he splashed water on his face. As his head cleared, he thought about John saying he had information. What sort of information? Something about Derrick, but that couldn't be right. He must have misunderstood. It was probably something about Yakima. Scott didn't care because he wasn't going to Yakima. Perhaps it was about the beer John brewed. Scott was more interested in the beer than he was in Yakima. In fact, Scott was tempted to stay until 8:30 to have a beer. Perhaps he could do that. Dinner and then leave. It would be dark, which wasn't the best for hitting the trail, but he'd traveled the trail at night until he was too exhausted to go any farther. But something told him waiting until after dinner wasn't safe. He wished he had a beer with breakfast.

Scott decided there was time to do his laundry. He didn't have many clothes. Probably just one load. He had never done laundry, but how hard could it be?

Then he'd pack up and leave. Nothing needed to be fixed today. Nothing was more important than his escape.

He dressed, gathered his clothing, and headed to the laundry. The lady who'd checked him in pointed it out, and said it was free. The washing machine looked ancient. On a cabinet were instructions held by yellowing transparent tape. With the laundry started, Scott returned to his room, where he dumped the rest of his backpack onto the bed. Easier to sort through stuff and reorganize here. He planned to slow down when he'd made it this far, beyond the range that Prime would use in search of him. However, he felt as much urgency as the first day he fled Pacific Edge.

Maybe Prime wasn't looking for him. Perhaps Prime thought he had committed suicide. That would not be a bad guess because it was a reasonable alternative to what Prime would do to him. In fact, Scott had given suicide serious consideration because he could control the method. He didn't have the luxury of assuming Prime would give up searching. Prime wanted to kill him. That's what he believed.

Scott wished he could turn the tables and destroy Prime, but he knew that was impossible. Prime existed in seven places, and each unit existed independently, but all the units were connected. These were secure locations with redundant servers that maintained Prime's existence. Destroy one, and you've accomplished nothing. Scott knew the location of six sites, but the seventh remained a mystery. No one knew where it was, and it was said the seventh could withstand a nuclear strike.

Though ending Prime's reign was essential, Prime could not be killed. The only way Prime's reign would end was a full-scale foreign invasion. Millions would die, and they would still not root out Prime's hidden location. But perhaps they could isolate and control Prime. At least for a while. It was a far-fetched notion that would begin soon. The world was fed up with New America, and they only needed an excuse to strike.

Because of Scott's status in the Test Subject Program, he had researched the world outside New America. Besides his medical and psychological degrees, he was a computer expert, and in his digging, he had stumbled upon an old system that created a virtual private network or VPN. James Carver had outlawed VPNs after the Greatest War to ensure internet traffic could be monitored for traitors. Traitors were defined as anyone questioning Carver's policies or deviating from Chosen Doctrine. Current technicians were just people capable of connecting a printer to a computer and had little actual computer knowledge, so the VPN Scott had developed went undetectable. Computer techs today didn't know such a thing was possible.

A few people could do programming, and since computers, phones, etc. had not changed in years, few programmers were needed. Those few were in a Chosen Community in Washington State, close to a Prime headquarters. In addition, there were advanced technicians in each Chosen Community to oversee technical operations.

A shared interest in computers created a rapport between Scott and the Technical Services supervisor in Pacific Edge. In a gradual process that took two years, their relationship blossomed into friendship, which became an alliance built on trust and shared values. AJ Patel helped Scott escape, and Scott helped Patel develop the VPN.

The VPN allowed the Resistance to become invisible online to New America Security (NAS). To keep NAS thinking they were rooting out the Resistance, he set up decoy accounts that were easily detected. Even then, given the ineptitude of NAS technicians, those sites would operate for months before being taken down. People downloaded lots of music and other artifacts from the old United States from those decoy accounts.

AJ focused on learning about Prime. Scott focused on learning about what was happening outside New America, and putting pieces together, Scott realized things were worse than imagined. Only he had all the details because he had not shared them with the others. He'd left Pacific Edge sooner than intended.

His mind kept churning about the past few weeks. When Prime learned Derrick had been exiled to Potterville, it drove Prime into a rage. Still, Scott kept Derrick and Miriam alive, by convincing Prime it was all under control, and the value of continuing the experiment under such adverse conditions was worth the risk.

However, when Miriam and Anna escaped, he knew they would not survive much longer. He had prepared to escape as well, but he had told his wife nothing. Not that he wanted to leave her. They used to agree on almost everything, finished each other's sentences. It wasn't her fault. He had changed, but she had not.

She had wanted all the Test Subjects terminated, fearing her reputation would be damaged if things went south. When the experiment with Derrick failed, and he smacked Marcus Carver, proving their controls had serious limits, she fell apart. She cried when Paul Jorgensen came to take Derrick to Potterville. But she wasn't sad about Derrick. She cried for herself, for the damage Derrick had caused to her career.

Scott didn't tell her about his plan because she would have turned him in. So, no great love lost, although it made him sad. Sadness fades when the alternative is a painful death, and he had no intention of dying. Not like that. Still, his odds of survival were slightly more than zero, and staying here wasn't increasing those odds even a little.

Scott needed to survive for two reasons: One, he liked living, and two, he had valuable information on a flash drive sewed into the liner of his backpack. The Resistance wanted what he had. Taking it gave him insurance with the Resistance. He didn't trust them. Not entirely.

He would give it to them once he was safe in Canada.

26

REBEKAH TURNED, GLANCING AT DERRICK. Derrick mouthed the word stop. A police encounter could not have happened at a more inopportune time. The canyon in which the launcher was hidden was only a mile farther south. By now, the New America missile unit might be watching them. Being stopped by a police officer blew holes in their story about drug dealers chasing them. Convincing a Mexican police officer to let them go seemed unlikely. Derrick felt sure time was running out.

Rebekah steered the pickup truck off the road and stopped. Derrick ensured the tarp was covering the machine gun, then pulled peaks in the canvas to conceal the weapon's shape.

Derrick held his hand out to Miriam. "Stay put."

Miriam followed him out of the truck's bed. "No way."

Rebekah and Anna joined them.

The police car stopped, angled toward the center of the highway. It was not what Derrick expected. The car looked new, the paint glowed, and the light bar sparkled. The police cars in Potterville looked old by comparison, with faded paint and a dull light bar. The officer spoke into his radio, then stepped out. He did not match Derrick's expectation either. Young, perhaps 30, and fit. His uniform was clean and pressed.

"Licencia y registro, por favor."

Rebekah said, "I don't understand."

The officer frowned. "Americans? Driver's license, registration, and passports, please."

Rebekah said, "I'll need to check in the truck."

"You're the driver?"

"Yes."

"Let's start with your driver's license."

"Uh, I don't have one."

The officer moved within a few feet of them. Derrick could take him out without difficulty, although he didn't want to. He didn't want everything to be about knocking people out just because he could.

"How about a passport?"

"I don't have that either."

"Why does she need a passport?" Miriam asked.

"The plates on the vehicle are from California. You look New American, and this is Mexico."

Miriam threw her hands to her face. "You're joking, right? Mexico? We had no idea."

"No idea? How is that possible?"

"We came across those hills," Miriam pointed, "off-road. We came upon this road and took it."

"Why did you go off-road? That's crazy in this desert."

Rebekah said, "A drug gang was chasing us."

"Why was a drug gang chasing you? Are you drug dealers?"

Rebekah glanced at Derrick.

Anna said, "No."

"Drug users?"

Rebekah said, "No."

Miriam stepped closer to the officer, causing him to turn away from Derrick. "We don't know why they were chasing us. Maybe they mistook us for someone else."

Derrick knew what Miriam was doing. She was setting the officer up to make taking him out easier. Derrick weighed his options. Lying had not served him well, and he was beginning to have a real aversion to it. He didn't want to hurt this guy. Derrick noticed a wedding band on the officer's left hand—a husband, perhaps a father. Then he noticed something else. The officer's name tag.

"That's not true," Derrick said.

Miriam glared at Derrick.

"What's not true?" the officer asked.

"Any of it, Officer Morales. I have a friend named Morales. Maybe you are related."

"Say, what? Do you think every Mexican named Morales is related? Just one big happy family, us Mexicans. Is that it? Or maybe you think I'm so stupid I'll say, 'let's be friends because you know a Mexican?' Is that what you think?" The officer breathed deeply and sweat formed on his brow.

"No, sir. I didn't mean anything like that. It was a stupid thing to say."

"And where does this friend live?"

"Potterville, California, sir."

"Potterville, California? What's his first name?"

"Antonio. He's not a close friend. We go to the same school. I'm new there, but Antonio has been nice to me. He's helped me a lot."

The officer stared at Derrick. The muscles flexing in the man's jaw, but his shoulders relaxed a little. "Antonio is my cousin. How is he?"

Derrick swallowed. "To be honest, I don't know."

"Care to explain?"

Derrick looked at Miriam, who was still frowning. She added a slight shake of her head.

"It has to do with why we are here. It's a long story, but here's the thing, there's a New America missile launcher in a canyon just there." Derrick motioned with his thumb.

"Hard to believe but go on. What does that have to do with you being here and Antonio?"

"Antonio and some other friends are helping us," Derrick paused, "with some stuff."

"Stuff having to do with a missile launcher?"

"Yes, sir. Well, sort of."

"Why would New America have a missile launcher in Mexico?"

"To start a war, sir. New America plans to bomb its own people and blame Mexico."

"Our news shows a massive military force on the border east of here. Bomb its own people, you say? I must admit, that sounds familiar."

"It does?" Miriam asked.

"Yeah. You know. The Greatest War. That's how it started."

Miriam looked puzzled. "What are you talking about?"

Now Morales looked confused. "The old United States dropped nuclear bombs on remote areas of Russia and North Korea. But it first bombed Sacramento, California. Then James Carver signed a treaty with Russia and North Korea. He looked like a hero, but he was not. That's how he overthrew the government. We learn about it in school. Everyone everywhere knows about it."

"They have kept that knowledge from people in New America. We just learned about it, but not in school." Derrick paused. "We learned about it the same way we learned about the missile launcher."

"Back to the launcher. Why would they send four kids to stop the launch? That's harder to believe than that a missile is in that canyon."

"We are the only ones who know about it," Derrick said, then added, "No one sent us."

"Well, I know about it now. If it's true."

"Let us go so we can stop them," Derrick said.

Morales thought for a moment. "I'm still not convinced. Plus, how are you going to stop soldiers? You're just kids."

Derrick said, "Drive up the road. Look for tire marks going toward the canyon. That should prove we are telling the truth. Then come back here. Let us go in. If we fail, you can call for help. If we are right, I hope you'll let us leave."

"How do I know this isn't a trick, so you can escape?"

"Can this old truck outrun your car?" Miriam asked.

Morales gave her a little smile. "It cannot. Tell you what, I'll drive down there and have a look. You stay put. But if I see anything, I'm calling it in. We'll let our military take care of it."

"I wish you wouldn't do that. Just come back and let us handle it," Derrick said.

Morales shook his finger at Derrick. "Just stay put."

Morales got into his car and drove south. Lights still flashing but no siren. Anna pulled binoculars from the cab and climbed into the back, scanning the horizon, then focusing on the police car. Derrick, Miriam, and Rebekah walked to the front of the truck.

Derrick saw the brake lights come on. "What's he doing?"

"Looks like he spotted something." Anna focused the binoculars. "He's getting out of the car."

Derrick could see him walking off the road a few yards, studying the ground. Then he crumpled and fell. "What happen?"

The report of a rifle sounded seconds later.

"Oh, my God! They shot him," Anna screamed.

27

THE HEAT WAVES MADE SEEING anything beyond 50 yards difficult. The heat was so intense Nyx couldn't breathe, and her skin felt as if it were on fire. Her shirt, previously soaked with sweat, was now dry. She wouldn't make it if she didn't get to the hangar soon. If she didn't make it, neither would Red and Antonio. The power gauge read 18%.

She glanced back, and saw that the parachute was still there, although Red was only partially covered. She eased up on the throttle but then pressed it back down. She'd cover Red when she reached Charlie. If, she reached Charlie. She had been driving toward a dark spot she believed was the robot. If it turned out to be a rock, she was screwed.

As the spot in the desert grew closer, Nyx saw it was Charlie. She sped up, angling toward the robot, hoping to bring the parachute up next to him. When she stopped, the parachute was within a yard of Charlie. Jumping from the vehicle, she stumbled, falling to her hands and knees. The sand burned her palms. She staggered to the robot on wobbly legs, squatted and slid her hands under Charlie's arm, then jerked her hand back. The metal skin was too hot to touch, even in the shade. Sitting on her butt, using her legs, she pushed with her feet and got the robot onto its side, and with much effort, rolled it onto its face. Another half roll got half of Charlie onto the parachute. To be certain Charlie wouldn't roll off, another quarter a roll would have been better, but Nyx didn't think she could do it. Back in the driver's seat, she started forward. Charlie's arm dragged in the sand, his body twisted, threatening to come off the parachute, but the cloth snagged something and held him. The power gauge was down to 9%, but the hangar door was within 50 yards. Nyx pressed the accelerator farther down while watching the makeshift stretcher.

A loud beeping started, and a red light on the dash flashed. The power gauge had fallen to zero. Twenty-five yards separated her from the hangar and the precious shade within. The beeping became a blaring horn. Two black robots appeared in the doorway, watching but doing nothing.

The vehicle slowed. She pushed the accelerator to its limit, but it made no difference.

Only 15 yards.

The vehicle bucked.

Then slowed more.

Ten yards.

It bucked again.

Five yards.

Nyx hollered, "Help!" But her voice was a mere whisper.

Neither robot moved.

The vehicle groaned to a stop just feet from the shade of the hangar. The blaring horn faded. She had exhausted every drop of the machine's battery. She whispered, "Help them."

Neither robot moved.

Nyx started to get out but fell back into the driver's seat. The horizon spun. She slumped forward. Everything went black.

28

WITH HIS BACKPACK SORTED AND REPACKED, Scott felt an urgency to leave, but he had laundry to finish. He considered packing his wet clothing and leaving. He would spread them out to dry once he was on the trail. With his backpack over one shoulder, he stopped, remembering he still wore the cleanest of his dirty clothing: shorts, a t-shirt, and flip-flops. The sun was shining, but maybe mid-sixties. He was not dressed for hiking.

It was just paranoia. Another few minutes wouldn't matter. Placing the backpack on the bed, he started for the door to put his laundry in the drying machine. He hesitated at the door, thinking about the flash drive containing the information he had gathered regarding James Carver and Prime, and the stuff he had stolen from the Resistance. It was his in the first place, but he didn't think the Resistance would see it that way. The information he had on Prime did not guarantee Canada would grant admittance or protection, but beyond what he could offer as a scientist, that information was all he had.

He opened the door and stopped. Two men stood waiting.

"Good timing. Scott, I presume." The largest of the two stuck out his hand. "I'm Rocky. John wants to talk."

"You startled me." The wheels turned in Scott's head. "I'm having dinner with John this evening. As you can see, I'm not dressed. My clothing is in the wash. I was headed down to dry them."

"You're fine as you are. Your clothing will be taken care of. We have a car." The man motioned to a pickup truck parked at the base of the stairs.

Scott said, "Tell John I will come as soon as my clothes are dry. It shouldn't take long, and it's not far to walk. Walking is what I do."

"He said now. Something has come up." The man brushed his jacket back, revealing a pistol. "Leave the backpack."

"I'll keep it if that's okay."

"It's not. Leave it. It'll be safe enough here."

Safe enough, given I will not live to see it again? "It stays with me," Scott said.

The man nodded and motioned Scott to the car. *So, this was it. He'd waited too long. John must have Pacific Edge security, State Police, or maybe people from a Prime Headquarters waiting at his establishment.* Scott took a deep breath. He saw no escaping this, but perhaps something would happen, and he'd attempt to get away, despite the abysmal odds of success. Escaping Prime was always a long shot. At least John was getting the reward rather than Scott's wife. That was a minor consolation.

The man motioned Scott into the middle of the cab. So much for the idea of jumping out along the way. The drive to the brewery took less than three minutes. One could see from one end of this town to the other. Above the trees, Scott saw the metal girders of what they called The Bridge of the Gods spanning the Columbia River. It wasn't the biggest bridge in the world by any measure, but it was impressive for reasons Scott could not quite put his finger on.

When they pulled up to the brewery, Scott saw four vehicles and seven people scattered among three tables on the deck. All appeared to have beverages, some had food, and everyone seemed relaxed, laughing, eating, and drinking.

The man said, "Follow me. John said to take you to his office."

Inside the large room containing several large stainless-steel tanks, Scott noticed two small wooden planks on the table, each held six small glasses filled with different liquids, from straw-colored on one side, each one a little darker until the last glass, which looked black.

John appeared, carrying two regular glasses, filled with a brown liquid with a foamy tan top. "Changed my mind. We'll sit here. I'd rather be here where the magic happens than in a stuffy office. That okay with you, Scott? All the guests are on the deck, and we need some privacy. I've told the hostess to keep everyone out of here."

John sat on one side of a long wooden table that looked like a tree sawn in half but covered with a clear, thick lacquer finish. A rich pleasant aroma that Scott could not identify filled the air.

John motioned to the six glasses. "These are the six beers we brew besides the Carver stuff, which we sell to New America but don't serve here. These six don't leave the premises." He held up a large glass. "And a soda we brew. Root beer. It doesn't leave the premises either. I've got wings and fries coming for us to share—a light lunch."

Scott put his backpack on the seat and sat across from John. "I was just doing laundry."

"I'm glad you had something to wear. People aren't accustomed to seeing naked diners." John laughed, then said, "I'd start here," as he indicated the lightest-colored beer, "and work to the darkest. Don't let the small glasses worry you. This way, we can see which you like best."

"I appreciate this, but…"

"I'm buying." John sniffed his first beer, held it to the light, then took a drink. "Like I said earlier, we brew Carver and Carver Light here. Have to because those are the only," John made air quotation marks with each hand, "legal beers. But I don't drink them. Maybe I already told you."

"How do you get away with making the other stuff?"

"Small town. Authorities look the other way. The country still needs beer, even if it's awful. Plus, officials get free beers when they are here. The good stuff. I wouldn't even wish the Carver crap on them." John laughed and took another sip.

Until setting foot in Cascade Locks, Scott didn't know other beers existed. Scott sipped the first beer. "It's interesting. I'm trying to say what it reminds me of. Grapefruit? Is there grapefruit in it?"

"Just hops, malt barley, and yeast, of course. You can't make beer without yeast. The aroma and flavor you're getting is from Cascade hops. I grow them here." John motioned toward the river but did not turn around.

Scott took another drink. "I could get used to this."

"Like I said earlier, perhaps that won't be as difficult as you think. You're looking for work, and I could use an extra hand." John started on the second beer.

"Why don't you sell this to the public? I mean, outside of here."

"New America prohibits it. You should know that. Did you think it was just in Chosen Communities, where only Carver products were sold?"

Scott caught himself before replying. "I know nothing about Chosen Communities. I'm just a fieldhand."

John started on his third sample. "This is my favorite." He set the glass on the table. "Scott, I don't mind calling you Scott. The name change, even here, is a good idea. Let's cut the crap. I know who you are. Here's the honest truth. I don't like your work. I'm talking about the Test Subject Program. Under normal circumstances, I'd toss you in the river tied to a rock. However, I understand you kept three kids alive. I'll give you that. It seems you have reconsidered your line of work. I'll give you that too, and if the change of heart is authentic, I figured you'd want to know what happened to the kids after you split."

John stopped talking when a woman in her mid-twenties arrived carrying two plates: one laden with golden brown French fries, the other with chicken wings coated with a reddish-orange sauce. John pointed to dishes on the plates. "Blue cheese dressing and fry sauce. Need anything else?"

Scott wanted to ask what fry sauce was but just shook his head.

John said, "Thanks, Jan. We are good for now."

When she left, Scott said, "I don't know those names," hoping he sounded convincing, praying John would decide he had the wrong guy.

John dipped a fry in the pink-colored sauce Scott was unfamiliar with. "Ain't gonna work, Scott. We have a mutual acquaintance. I know all about you. Here's the deal. I'm going to tell you about the kids. You're going to listen. When I'm done, we'll discuss what happens next."

Scott wanted to run, but he was still wearing flip-flops and gym shorts. John told him about Miriam's escape and Rebekah Ford going with her. Scott figured Miriam had escaped, but he didn't stick around for details. He didn't know about Rebekah. He was surprised to hear Anna followed them but dismayed they were separated. John gave some highlights of Derrick's time in Potterville. He explained that Derreck, Miriam, and Rebekah had found Anna, but Prime had been trying to kill them ever since.

"You don't look so good, Scott. Was it something I said?"

Scott stuck with his story. "You have the wrong guy."

"We'll need plenty of these." John pulled a napkin dispenser closer and then grabbed a chicken wing. "To be honest, you're pissing me off. You're Lawrence King, creator of the Pacific Edge Test Subject Program. Keeper of Derrick and Miriam King. But also, more recently, a member of the Resistance. You and AJ Patel created a VPN that allowed the Resistance to communicate without detection. After your involvement with the Resistance, you researched what was happening outside New America. We don't know everything you learned because you ran when Miriam escaped. We don't blame you for that." John wiped his mouth. "But the VPN stopped working just after Lawrence King disappeared. Seven days ago, to be precise. Now that, we do blame you for."

John picked up a chicken wing, dipping it in the blue cheese dressing, staring at Scott as he ate the meat from the bone. Scott was hungry a few minutes ago, but his stomach had twisted in a knot. He sipped his fourth small glass filled with an amber-colored beer. "I don't know what to tell you. I'm not who you think I am, but you can tell me your story. It seems I have no choice but to listen."

John wiped his fingers, sat back, and tossed the greasy napkin to the side. "You wouldn't be alive today if the Resistance had not helped you escape. You owe them. If the kids succeed in Mexico, it might delay the war, but Prime will invade Mexico anyway. We need your help, Scott. Derrick and Miriam need your help, and you owe them too. You owe them more than you can ever repay."

Scott said, "Prime is a myth. Most people don't believe it even exists. But let's say Prime exists. They say it cannot be destroyed. There's nothing anyone can do and certainly nothing I can do."

"Listen, this goes back to Carver and the Greatest War. Carver started it in agreement with Russia and North Korea. All three countries had to take a hit to make it believable, but Carver caused little damage to Russia and North Korea but destroyed a major city in the U.S. This isn't news to you because you discovered this information in your research. You told AJ Patel."

Scott waved his hand and picked up a fry. "Rumors."

"Did you learn the reason Carver started The Greatest War?"

Scott shrugged. "You tell me." He wasn't ready to admit his identity, but John had him pegged and his hope of evading the situation was fading fast.

"Carver needed to give Russia and North Korea major concessions to let him drop a nuclear bomb on them. Carver agreed to let Russia reclaim the Soviet Union countries, including East Germany, with future negotiations of further expansion. North Korea was allowed to take over South Korea and reunite the country."

Scott shrugged. "If you say so. What did Carver get?" None of this was news to him, but he tried to act as if he didn't buy into it.

"The ability to attack developing countries without repercussions. Other countries objected when such incursions occurred, but the Soviet Union and Korea threatened retaliation if other countries interfered with New America's military operations."

"Russia and North Korea's position makes sense, if it's true, which I'm not saying it is. But what was in that for Carver?" Scott asked, sniffing his fifth glass, a dark-brown color with ruby highlights.

"At first, it was all about money. Carver took over the military-industrial complex and needed wars to generate revenue. In other words, use up bombs, aircraft, etc., in wars, so he could build more. New America has been at war somewhere ever since Carver took over. The pattern was always the same. Start a war to stop some fictitious bogeyman, you know, gotta stop communism, weapons of mass destruction, on and on. Sometimes it was about obtaining natural resources, oil, coal, gold, and such. Other times, it was just using up a bunch of military resources and then pulling out."

Scott stared for a moment. "Okay, but if Prime owns everything, why does it need more money?"

"It wasn't just money. It was also power. Prime wants more. More of everything. There's no rhyme or reason to it anymore."

Scott picked up a chicken wing. He had never eaten a chicken wing but dipped it in the blue cheese dressing as John had. It was spicier than he expected, but he didn't react because chicken wings were apparently a commoner food, and something a fieldworker would be familiar with. "I can see how people might invent such a theory, but it proves nothing."

John shook his head. "There's more. Prime's treaties have fallen apart. The President has been pleading with Prime for change. New America must rejoin the world and change or else."

Scott shrugged. "Sounds like a good thing."

"Prime refuses. Prime is escalating things. Preparing to invade Mexico proves that. The Soviet Union and Korea are not the same countries they once were. Korea changed 50 years ago when the Kim Dynasty gave way to free elections. Korea is a world leader in many areas now, including human rights. The Soviet Union gave the countries it invaded after the Greatest War freedom to become independent and is now a partner with Europe. Both countries have declared the Greatest War treaty invalid and oppose any further New America aggression."

Scott drank some of the dark liquid, rich and roasty, hoping it would douse the flame in his mouth. He had not intended to drink the beer but felt obligated. He needed to keep his wits. Besides, he couldn't have resisted the beer. His resolve was fading. "Okay. Again, that sounds like a good thing."

"It would be if Prime would join the world, but he refuses. Every major military in the world is sending warships to both coasts. Canada and Mexico have huge deployments of World Peacekeepers in place. New America has antiquated weapons. Prime didn't want to invest money in research and development, so New America kept building the same old stuff that can't survive on a modern battlefield. The rest of the world has moved on. The rest of the world wants a real end to war. New America is the only thing preventing lasting peace. Other countries are just waiting for New America to do something stupid. Like, invade Mexico, for example. Then they will attack. It will take days, if not hours, to reduce this country to rubble."

John drank his last glass, stared at Scott, then, after a few moments, said, "They will destroy New America, but they won't destroy Prime, and when Prime retaliates, he could render the planet uninhabitable."

29

REBEKAH GRABBED A SECOND PAIR OF BINOCULARS, joining Anna in the truck's bed. Derrick sat on the rear bumper, bent over, with his head in his hands. Miriam sat next to him, put her hand on his shoulder.

Derrick said, "It's my fault. I killed him."

"You did not. You told him to let us handle it. He didn't listen."

"I should have disabled him. You moved him into position. I didn't do what I should have done. I'll have to tell Antonio his cousin is dead, and I'm responsible."

"If you had disabled him, and we went with our original plan, we'd all be dead, and they would have launched the missile."

Derrick said, "We knew the risk. He didn't."

"If they'd killed us, thousands would have died from the missile strike and millions in the war."

"Would you stop? Please."

"Stop what?" Miriam asked.

"People get hurt or killed because of me, and you always turn it around and say: If you hadn't done that, then this would have happened."

Miriam said, "I only say what's true. I'll let you know when you screw up. I don't understand it, but sometimes it turns out to be the best thing when you do the wrong thing."

Derrick said, "I'm sick of it."

Miriam said, "Me too, but we have a missile to stop."

Anna joined them on the tailgate. "Are you two, okay?"

Derrick said, "No," and Miriam said, "Yes."

Miriam said, "What's happening?"

Anna said, "Nothing."

"That's not good," Derrick said.

"Explain," Miriam said.

"It means they don't plan on being here much longer. They would hide the body and the patrol car if the launch were hours away. They plan on being gone soon."

"Then we need to move fast," Miriam said.

"We need a new plan," Rebekah said, standing above Anna.

"You're great at stating the obvious," Miriam said.

"Can you ever be serious? A man was just killed," Rebekah said.

"If I were to contemplate the situation's magnitude, I'd be curled up in a fetal position sucking my thumb."

Rebekah said, "Not a bad idea. I'll join you."

Derrick stood. "Anna, did you spot the sniper?"

"No."

"Then he can't see us."

"He might just have good concealment," Anna said.

"If you can see him, he's not visible from here." Derrick paused. "I trust you, Anna."

Anna smiled, just a little. "Thanks."

"Here's the plan. We drive across the lakebed to the mountain." Derrick pointed. "We head up the mountain together, except for Rebekah."

Rebekah said, "Hey, I'm going with you."

"We need you near the truck. When we are done, we'll signal you, and you come get us. It will save time."

"And what if you don't signal me?"

"You get out of here. Get to a town. Call Collins and convince him to evacuate Potterville. Then go to the Base and tell the others. You'll have to decide what happens next."

"I'll just pick you up when you're done," Rebekah said.

Derrick said, "Anna, Miriam, and I will get up to that sniper, take him out. Determine if there's another sniper on the other side, and if there is, take him out as well. We'll set up the machine gun within striking range of the launcher. Miriam and I will go down and take out the soldiers."

Anna said, "I should go to the launcher with you. I'm better at hand-to-hand combat than Miriam."

"True, but Miriam can figure out the controls to stop the launch."

"What am I doing while this happens?" Anna asked.

"You're manning a machine gun. If we have problems, you take them out."

"You want me to kill them?"

"Unfortunately, the machine gun only has one setting." Derrick took a deep breath and said, "Try not to kill us."

30

THE TRIP FROM KNIFE-BOY TOM's place to Potterville wasn't as pleasant as yesterday's ride. The heat of the desert and motor grew unbearable, and L. Linda was damn uncomfortable despite being on a four-cylinder motorcycle three times the displacement of her little 175. Her legs ached, but she had to hold them up and away from the motorcycle because the motor was too hot for bare feet on the pegs. She enjoyed the open-faced helmet, wind-in-the-face experience, until the first big bug smacked just below her eye. Bugs hit her feet as well, and large ones hurt like hell. She held the throttle open most of the time. She didn't know how fast she was traveling because there was no speedometer, but the speed was well below the 550's potential. The motor hesitated, coughed, and backfired. She felt sure it was firing on three cylinders instead of four. However, she knew it was traveling faster than her 175.

But it wasn't fast enough. She wanted to get off the infernal machine, find shoes, and wash the bug goo off her face. She had to get back to where Akira and Nyx were and find out why Derrick was not on that plane.

Back in the farmland, she rode past green fields of early crops. Leaves waving indicated a light breeze off the mountains, dropping the temperature as she grew closer to Potterville. She occupied the time thinking about turning this wreck into a decent motorcycle. Although she had not looked for a 550 Honda, Fletcher would have one in his motorcycle boneyard. But every time she thought about the 550, she also thought about knife-boy Tom, and when she thought about Tom, she saw three dead girls at the bottom of the sea. The 550 might not be in her future. More likely, it would become a pile of rubble after she took a cutting torch to it.

She hoped Tom's dad called the police and turned Tom in, but there were no guarantees, not even with people who portray themselves as righteous. As an odd girl in Potterville, invisible to many and dismissed by others, she saw things others overlooked, like the preacher of the white church on the corner of Main and 1st Street, who had many personal 'studies' with married women in his congregation. Sometimes knowing such things didn't improve her life and knowing about knife-boy Tom was one of those things.

Passing through fields, farm workers stared at the crazy person, with bare feet sticking out into the air, riding a rust-bucket motorcycle that spit, sputtered, and backfired its way toward Potterville. It was the most attention she had ever achieved while living here. Fortunately, she remained unidentified because of the helmet. She hoped.

While she loved riding, she'd be happy to get off this piece of crap. A cold drink would be nice, and shoes would be an improvement. She could go to her house for a change of clothing and shoes. Food would be great, but there was no time for cooking. A shower would be fantastic, but unlikely. Her father wouldn't be home, so that wasn't a problem. Learning how things were going for everyone at Jack Fletcher's shop was something she desperately wanted to do, but she could not afford to get hung up there, and they'd try to stop her from running off again.

Although it did not meet her needs, she decided to blast through town, go straight to the footbridge, cross the river, find the hidden entrance into the canyon that led to the Engineering building, and then get to where Nyx and Akira were. Running barefoot through the forest wasn't the best idea, but she'd be okay. There must be clothing and shoes in the complex. Nyx and Akira wore one-piece overalls with matching emblems, clothing for Base workers. She hoped there were other colors. Even there, she wanted to be different.

L. Linda hoped they had answers about Derrick. That's what she needed most.

She avoided most of downtown after spotting Lori Martinez in the animal control truck, skirting through an industrial area, mostly farm-related firms, mostly out of business. There were a lot of things out of business in New America. Nothing would change that anytime soon, even if drastic changes were made. But the economy wasn't L. Linda Maxton's concern. She had other priorities.

Settling score priorities.

Since the score couldn't be reconciled, she'd settle for a pound of flesh.

Arriving at the river, she allowed the motorcycle to fall against the embankment as she stepped off, pulled off the helmet, and tossed it to the ground. She would not need it again. She left the key in the ignition. If someone stole it, good riddance. It felt good to be off that thing. After picking her way up the bank, she ran to the footbridge about half a mile distant. If Jason saw the motorcycle, he'd figure it out, which she could live with. She trusted Jason. Pretty much anyone else wouldn't associate an abandoned old motorcycle with L. Linda Maxton, except Jack Fletcher. She trusted Jack, too.

Once across the footbridge, L. Linda maintained her pace along the trail into the meadow, where she turned left and slowed, watching her foot placements after leaving the trail. She did not need to poke a broken branch through her foot. Reaching the thicket at the edge of the meadow, she forced through a wall of wild bushes covered with ants, wanting to whack them but not taking the time to do so. Working at it now was just a waste of time. Time to waste was not a luxury to be enjoyed.

She'd plotted an accurate course, coming to a pile of rocks just as Miriam had described. Climbing halfway up, she paused and brushed at her arms, legs, face, and hair, scattering tiny black ants to the wind.

On the other side, she found a tunnel into the canyon that led to the engineering entrance. So far, so good. Once inside, she went straight to the electric carts and then drove to the Circle Transport. The trip there seemed much longer than the previous one, whether because the first trip was all new or because her distress had gone from anxious to hysteria, she did not know. What if the Circle Transport wasn't working? She doubted the electric cart could reach Nyx and Akira's location.

Charlie, the robot, should be watching, ensuring a transport was waiting for her, but perhaps since she had not confirmed a second invitation, things would be different this time. Nyx might block L. Linda from getting there. Only Derrick seemed to trust her, but Derrick wasn't there. L. Linda was accustomed to being ignored, familiar with being left out, and comfortable being the odd duck. It was the image she had created for herself. But that image would not work now. Unfortunately, she might have sabotaged herself.

Driving through a bay of military vehicles, yellow lights spun cylindrical beams of light. L. Linda wondered what that was about. Yellow lights meant caution. Caution in a place like this was worrisome, not that she needed another thing to worry about. Perhaps someone was trying to warn her off. Maybe it was something else.

A transport was waiting, the red and white medical one. The transport sped toward the Administration building. Again, the smell of death's decay turned her stomach when she passed silo number eight. She wanted to investigate and was sure it held secrets important to the history of this place and beyond, but no time for that now. Despite the speed at which this transport traveled, she felt time was running out.

Running out for what, or who, she did not know.

31

QUIGLEY STOOD ON THE ROOF OF PRIME'S Seattle headquarters building, watching as the angular black aircraft grew smaller, disappearing into the distance. A black robot piloted the aircraft, with a sole passenger on board, the satellite technician named Ava, who was going to the VLA in New Mexico to learn what happened to the satellite Prime had been using to find the kids who escaped from Pacific Edge. Prime was not accustomed to losing or even being challenged. The kids were probably dead, but their deaths were not confirmed. Prime could not communicate with Commander Haskins or anyone else on the border, and there was no information about the town where the kids were hiding. To say that Prime was livid was a gross understatement.

Quigley had not witnessed Prime in a situation like this, where so many things had gone wrong in what seemed like an orchestrated defiance of Prime's will. It frightened Quigley, yet he thoroughly enjoyed it.

Prime had grown more unpredictable in the last few years. Quigley expected Prime would kill the satellite technician, even more so because she was a woman. Prime had a low tolerance for everyone, but even more so for women. Prime had once been a man and felt superior to other people. The man who became Prime had been an arrogant narcissist, which was a benevolent description of James Carver.

James Carver had successfully conned many people, developing his own narrative that painted a different legacy than the reality of his life. It was as if an artist had painted an ocean landscape but told people it was a mountain, and those who looked at the ocean landscape, said they saw snow-covered peaks.

Industrial-strength deception. That was James Carver's true legacy.

Quigley had lingered too long, Prime would have grown impatient by now, and his delayed return would not lighten the mood. However, Quigley needed a quiet moment. The serene view of the city soothed him, despite knowing his interpretation was not in sync with the city's chaos. It was a desperate world down there. He knew that, but he could not change it. No one could.

His cell phone buzzed. Prime, no doubt, demanding to know his whereabouts. But it was not Prime. It was the President of New America. "Quigley, here. How may I help you, Mr. President?

"Yes, sir, I have relayed your messages. —

"Well, Prime has been busy and focused on other priorities. —

"Yes, sir. Right away, sir. I shall tell Prime immediately." Quigley ended the call and let out a long breath. This was a discussion he did not look forward to. Not that he looked forward to any conversation with Prime.

When Quigley returned to Prime's office, he felt sure Prime was near the end of his patience if Prime ever had any.

"What took you so long?"

Quigley said, "Sorry, sir. I received a phone call from the President."

"What does that fool want?"

"Same as previous calls. He wants to talk to you."

Prime waved him off. "I have no time for him."

"He said it's urgent, national security level urgent, sir."

"Everything is a national security threat to that idiot."

"He said Europe and the United Kingdom have massive naval fleets close to our Eastern Coast, and Japan, Australia, and China have ships off the Western Coast. Canada is amassing troops on our border."

"I've dispatched a message to the New Soviet Union and New Korea. They will strike soon to neutralize the threat."

"The President said they are standing down and will do nothing to stop an attack on New America if it invades Mexico."

"Lies. I have a treaty with the New Soviets and New Korea."

"New Soviets and New Korea will no longer honor the treaty, sir."

Prime said, "The President is weak. I've demoted him. We will crush Mexico and Canada and then the world. I have grown tired of the politics of it all. I will make the world better, as I have New America. That is my destiny."

Quigley remained silent, unsure of what to say. He could not change Prime's thinking. However, it sounded as if New America, bad as it was, was about to get worse. Perhaps the other countries could destroy Prime, but that seemed impossible, even with a full-scale war. While Quigley could easily dismiss Prime's stance as narcissistic ignorance, he felt certain Prime had a reason for feeling confident. How Prime could bring the world to its knees, he did not know. The problem was that he believed Prime could, and the world was about to find out.

"Excuse me, sir. Demoted the President?" Quigley asked.

"While you were escorting Ava to the flight deck and soaking in the views of Seattle, I dispatched agents to eliminate the president and those in Potterville who helped the renegade Test Subject, Derrick King. It appears the Test Subjects are dead, but those who helped them must pay for their arrogance."

Quigley took a deep breath. "Yes, sir."

Prime said, "We shall toast our success. Pour yourself a drink. Don't skimp. Get the good stuff. Whatever you'd like."

It was all good stuff. Although Prime did not, could not drink, everything in the room was the most expensive stuff available. The only time anything changed was when Prime learned of something more expensive or rarer than the existing items. Quigley poured 150-year-old Kentucky Bourbon, a generous portion, not because he wanted to celebrate with Prime, but because he needed a drink. More than one, actually.

Prime raised a make-believe glass. "To success."

Quigley raised his glass and then took a long drink. Prime didn't want to chat, nor did he want Quigley to enjoy the whiskey. James Carver might have spent idle time appreciating fine whiskey and chatting with friends, but those times were ancient history if they ever existed.

"Quigley, it's time for you to go."

Finishing the whiskey, Quigley said, "I shall be in my office then."

"I don't mean that, Quigley. Go to the flight deck. An aircraft is waiting. Don't bother gathering anything from your office. You need not take anything from here. Now, go."

And just like that, Stanely Mires' time as Prime's assistant ended.

32

WHEN L. LINDA ARRIVED AT THE ADMINISTRATION entrance, she noticed two crates a bit larger than a coffin. She remembered seeing them the first time she came but didn't stop to investigate. It did not feel like she had time to look at them now either, but she jogged over and read the label, which simply said A-series. A-series what, she did not know. She wanted to look inside, but she didn't have anything to pry the lid off, and it wasn't important. Finding Derrick was.

She ran through the halls. Confident she could find her way. First, she checked the break room. No one was there. The place had vending machines, but she had no money. These things were ancient and might not even take New America coins. She needed a drink, and a soda sounded fantastic, as did a candy bar and, better yet, some real food. Frustrated, she smacked a selection button on the soda machine. A can rolled out. *Fantastic!* She tried the candy machine and out dropped a candy bar. *Cool.*

Popping the can open, she poured half of it down her parched throat as she walked to the exit. In the hall, she trotted to where Akira had been, but the room was empty. However, on the computer screen was a video, or rather a live shot, of Akira pulling an unconscious Nyx from a vehicle. In the background was a large piece of cloth with three bodies, one of which was the robot they called Charlie. Red's size made his identification easy, which meant the smaller figure must be Antonio. A note on the desk read: I need help. We are in the hangar. Find us.

A map of the facility was displayed on a nearby monitor. After studying it for a moment, L. Linda dashed out the door. Instead of running toward the hangar, she backtracked to the break room, where she smacked the vending machine button labeled water. She didn't know what was wrong with them, but heat stroke was a definite possibility.

Gathering seven water bottles, she raced to the door, fumbling to work the latch. One bottle tumbled to the floor. She worked the door open and then used her foot to swing it out. With no attempt to retrieve the lost bottle, she ran toward the hangar as best one can carrying six water bottles. Remembering the route was easy. She took the stairs to the hangar, not trusting the elevator.

When L. Linda burst through the stairwell door, she could see Akira and the strange vehicle silhouetted against the white desert sand.

"What happened?" L. Linda asked.

Akira eased Nyx's head to the ground. "I don't know. I found them like this."

L. Linda opened a water bottle, dropped to one knee, and got Nyx into a semi-seated position. Cradling Nyx, L. Linda said, "Here, a little sip." Water dribbled from Nyx's lips. L. Linda tried again. This time Nyx opened her mouth, then coughed, choking. L. Linda said, "Go slow. No rush. I got you."

Akira said, "Something's wrong with Charlie."

L. Linda stared at her a moment. Nyx grabbed the water bottle, trying to wrestle it from L. Linda's hand. Pulling the bottle away, L. Linda said, "Let me do the work. You gotta take it slow."

"What about Charlie?" Akira screamed.

"First, we help our friends. They have heat stroke." L. Linda stopped. "Have you checked Red and Antonio? Are they alive?"

"I don't know. I think so."

L. Linda said, "Wet them down. Soak some cloth and put it on their foreheads."

"Where am I supposed to get cloth?"

"Holy shit." L. Linda pulled off what was left of her shirt, ripping it in two. "Use this. Hurry!"

Nyx sipped water, gradually awakening. Suddenly, Nyx leaned over, throwing up what water she had taken.

L. Linda stroked Nyx's hair from her face. "That's okay. You're in a bit of shock. Just a sip. You're going to be alright."

"Where's Antonio?"

"Over there. Akira is getting them wet, which will cool them down, but they need medical help."

"There's a medical unit here. The robots run it."

"And it works?"

"They fixed Antonio's knee and saved Akira from radiation poisoning."

L. Linda said, "They need help fast. We need wheelchairs or something. I'll send Akira."

Nyx shook her head. "Akira isn't herself."

"But she could get a wheelchair."

"She's useless. See for yourself." Nyx pointed.

Two bottles of water sat near Antonio's head, neither opened. Akira kneeled over Charlie, crying.

"What happened to her?" L. Linda asked.

"Her head's messed up from being in the treatment unit."

"And you want to put Antonio and Red in there?"

"No choice. Go help them. I'll be okay."

"Slow on the water. Got it?"

"Got it."

L. Linda ran to the big cloth, which turned out to be a parachute. What happened to the cargo jet, and where was Derrick? Only Red and Antonio could explain what had happened. However, they could provide no information. Red's face was bright red, and his skin was dry. Antonio didn't look any better, perhaps worse. L. Linda wasn't a doctor, but she'd had training, mainly to save herself.

She poured water over Red and Antonio, and then soaked the pieces of her shirt, placing a piece on each boy. She said nothing to Akira. The girl had gone mad, crying over a robot while three of her friends fought for their lives. Kneeling between Red and Antonio, L. Linda continued dousing them with water. Antonio puked. L. Linda rolled him on his side. "Sorry, dude, it sucks."

She knew Antonio couldn't hear her, but it didn't matter. No one had ever taught her to be a caregiver. She'd never witnessed it. Whenever she got sick, Jason didn't tend to her. He went to work and told her to take care of herself. Not that he didn't care. He didn't know how to care for anyone either. Besides, he knew she didn't need him. But, as much as she hated to admit it, she had needed him.

"Can you take a sip?" L. Linda eased Antonio's head up and poured a trickle of water into his mouth, afraid he might drown if he tried to swallow too much because his esophagus might be swollen shut.

Antonio coughed.

"More in a minute."

L. Linda looked up to see how Nyx was doing.

Nyx was crawling toward her.

"Shit. Akira!"

Sobbing, Akira said, "What?"

"A little help? Make Nyx stay put."

"I don't control her."

"Can you control yourself?"

"What's that supposed to mean?"

"I mean, your friends are dying. They need help."

"But no one is helping Charlie."

L. Linda wanted to slap her but said, "We'll help Charlie. I promise, but first, we must help Nyx, Red, and Antonio. Can you do that?"

Akira wiped her face with her sleeve. "You promise?"

"Yes. Don't worry. Charlie will be okay." L. Linda had no reason to believe that was true and didn't care for the most part.

"He's got to be okay. He just has to be. Charlie has part of my brain."

33

ANNA STARTED UP THE MOUNTAIN, having convinced Derrick to change their plan. Anna said the sniper would watch the launcher, which was south of the mountain. She would approach from the north. One person had a better chance of sneaking up than did three. Derrick argued he should go, but it was a short-lived squabble. Anna was the better climber and smaller, making spotting her more difficult. Her logic was sound. They had no time to waste. Even now, they might be too late. Derrick conceded, but that didn't mean he liked it.

Anna's plan was simple. She would climb the mountain. Disable the sniper. Derrick set no parameters defining disabled but said he hoped they didn't have to kill anyone. However, he agreed Anna would have to decide based on the situation. Derrick didn't like that either, but he was not responsible for putting a missile in Mexico to bomb a New America city to justify a full-scale war.

If they were lucky, the soldiers here were not significantly more capable than the two soldiers he and Anna had disabled outside the desert town. They all seemed to be kids, joining the army because it sounded better than other jobs available to them. The military wasn't a terrible job. Until the bullets started flying.

The snipers would have already shot the three of them if they were well trained and experienced. They had a sniper protecting the launcher, but who was watching the sniper? No one, apparently. They might have a second sniper on the opposite side of the narrow valley, but he would be focused on the soldiers below. If that was the case, Anna should be okay. If not... well, he didn't want to think about what-if scenarios.

He hoped this wasn't a mistake. Because memories had continued to return, he now remembered more about Anna. She was quiet in the Test Subject Program, and the keepers often ridiculed her to the point of being abusive. He had hit a tender in the back one day because of how he had treated Anna. Now, he realized it was part of the tests, although he still did not understand what it was intended to prove. He did not know if he had passed or failed that test. Maybe Miriam knew. He could ask, but he was not sure he wanted to know.

After they had left the testing facility, Anna went to live with the Ford family. He and Miriam remained under the direct supervision of their Keepers: Father and Mother. He did not know if the Fords were Keepers, but it seemed unlikely they were, but he didn't know. He thought Rebekah was just an ordinary kid. Not ordinary. She was incredible. Now that his thinking was not controlled by the Keepers and their 1984 chip, he realized his attraction to Rebekah was real, but he had planned to pick Janna Somersworth as his bride. Because they were directing him to do so. The 1984 chip controlled him. Yet, he broke free of it when he hit Marcus Carver.

He faced the uncertainty of his own memories and emotions. Since leaving Pacific Edge, he had made many mistakes and another just hours ago. He should not have let Rebekah come with them. She had insisted, but that didn't excuse him. She had no business here. He, Anna, and Miriam were Test Subjects, and Prime's property, not proper children who had parents.

He had made a mistake with Officer Morales.

He hoped he had not made a mistake sending Anna up the mountain.

* * *

Anna paused, gazing at the mountain, then back to the truck below. The truck was almost out of her line of sight. She was on her own now. The climbing wasn't difficult, but she had been moving fast, and she was breathing as if in a footrace. That was not the only reason she stopped. It was uncertainty.

No surprise. She had felt the same while ascending the mountain to disarm the soldier overlooking the desert town. The lack of confidence was not new to her. The Keepers instilled it in her. Anxiety, or something similar, was the testing they did to her. Derrick and Miriam, Number Six and Seven, saw how the Keepers treated her, but they didn't see it all. They didn't know what the Keepers did when she was alone.

The Keepers had wiped her memory of the testing facility and replaced it with a memory of being an orphan, adopted by the Ford family and fortunate to be Chosen, living in the safety of Pacific Edge. It made a perfect backdrop for insecurity. A child the parents didn't want. Despite her safe surroundings, she was always anxious, sleeping with her door locked and the lights on, afraid to speak out at school. Sometimes panic overwhelmed her for no predictable reason. She never told anyone. Now she knew they had continued testing her, using the 1984 chip. That's why she wanted to go up the mountain. Although her anxieties lingered, she wanted to crush them.

In hindsight, it seemed oddly wonderful that another former Test Subject, Miriam, had helped her break the mental barriers the Keepers created. When Miriam read a story at school about an ordinary girl, Anna thought the ordinary girl was her and was further convinced when the code Miriam described worked on the remote control. Anna's memories started returning without the virtual remote control she told Miriam and Derrick to use. However, the visualization helped her dig deeper. She hoped the same technique would help Miriam and Derrick access their memories. Remembering was the key to their future.

In school, Derrick and Miriam seemed like strangers, but she knew them better than most siblings know each other.

She understood.

Her worst fear wasn't the sniper.

It was Derrick.

*** * ***

Wiping sweat from her brow, Miriam said, "We should get in position."

Derrick glanced up and watched Anna disappear from his field of view. "Give her a few more minutes. They might have more snipers. If they see us, we could be dead before Anna is ready, which would also put her in greater danger."

Rebekah said, "I can't believe you let Anna go. To be honest, I can't believe any of this. I'm numb with non-believing."

Miriam patted her hand. "I get it. I struggle with it as well. Remember, until Anna told me how to unlock my memories, I didn't know my past, except what I read about us being Test Subjects. We are all doing the best we can."

Derrick said, "You're right. I should not have let Anna go. I keep making mistakes. It seems I can't make the right decision. My decision to let Officer Morales go got him killed. I may have sent Anna to her death." He paused, then looked at Rebekah. "I should not have let you come with us."

"Not your decision."

"I could have prevented it. Forced you onto the plane with the others. I should have left you at the Base."

Rebekah glared at him for a minute and then said, "We don't know if Red and Antonio are still alive," immediately regretting it. The thought had been circulating in her head but saying it might increase the possibility of the plane crashing.

Derrick said nothing for a while. "You're right. I just wish you weren't here."

"What's that supposed to mean?"

Derrick hesitated, then said, "I wish you were safe."

*** * ***

The mountain grew steeper, sometimes near vertical. Free soloing, no rope, no bolts, nothing to catch a fall. Unfortunately, a fall here would not be far enough to guarantee death, more likely broken bones. The result would be the same, except slower and more painful. Sudden death wouldn't be a bad thing. At least it would be over. Everything would become someone else's problem. However, it wasn't as if she had a choice. They had to prevent this war. It should not have become their responsibility, but it had.

More importantly, she had to protect Rebekah. Although she knew Rebekah wasn't her biological sister, it made no difference in how she felt, which seemed strange. She should hate Rebekah. Perfect Rebekah. Long-legged, athletic, beautiful Rebekah, with a crooked smile that melted most boys' and some girls' hearts. Unaware how she affected people, Rebekah breezed through life, or so Anna thought.

When she'd heard Rebekah up in the middle of the night, somehow, she knew it was not insomnia, so she followed Rebekah to Technical Services, but was careful to remain unseen. Why was Rebekah doing this? She was running from her perfect life. Anna didn't understand. That night, she wasn't prepared to escape, but wearing pajamas and house slippers, she had followed Rebekah, willing to face the commoner world, but refusing to be separated from her sister.

Anna's love for Rebekah wasn't logical. Not true sisters, and different in almost every conceivable way. Anna was short, blonde, shy, and afraid, a loser. Rebekah was her opposite. Derrick King was the only prize Rebekah couldn't attain. Anna saw how much Rebekah hoped to win Derrick's heart, and she saw the spark between them, but also knew he wasn't going to choose Rebekah. Rebekah knew it, too. At least Anna believed she did. Anna had seen the sadness in Rebekah's eyes when Derrick was with Jana Somersworth.

Anna hated how Derrick treated Rebekah until she remembered her past and started putting the pieces together. They were still controlling Derrick. Otherwise, he would have picked Rebekah. Anna was sure of that.

Reaching the mountain peak, Anna paused, catching her breath. Stealth was imperative now. She did not know the sniper's location. He might be 100 yards down the mountain, or he might be 10 feet from her. As she rested, her anxiety intensified, and she did not know what to do about it.

Anxiety caused her thoughts to run wild. She had gotten better at reeling them in, but it remained a challenge. And her thoughts were running berserk regarding Derrick. Much had happened with Derrick, Rebekah, and Miriam before she was reunited with them. Somehow, Derrick had become the leader. Anna didn't know if there was a vote, or if Derrick just took charge. Miriam was more intelligent than all of them put together. Miriam should be the leader. Why she was so smart, Anna didn't know. Anna wondered if Miriam was the center of the experiment: How intelligent can a Test Subject become? Anna and Derrick were the controls: How do controlled Test Subjects compare to one who is allowed to reach full potential?

So, yeah, Miriam should lead, not Derrick. That wasn't everything. Anna wondered if Derrick's decisions were the best. He was not following their survival training. They should have killed the soldiers on the mountain overlooking the town. Instead, Derrick not only let them live but allowed them to go with the town's people. Those soldiers might give up their location. Derrick might have sentenced the entire town to death by letting those two live.

Derrick should have killed the New America Commander. One rarely gets a gift like that. The Professor would have objected. Granted, it would be hard to see your son get killed, even one you didn't know. Derrick might have had to kill the Professor and Harley as well.

Derrick didn't want her to kill the sniper. He acknowledged she might not have a choice, but he made his preference clear. Derrick had admitted there were memories he could not access. Even if he was unaware of the reason for his decisions, he might still be carrying out instructions implanted using hypnosis. The longer she remained still, the more her thoughts ran wild.

The sun's intensity was unbearable, and the rocks were hot to her touch. Her clothing was soaked. The soldier would have water. She hoped he had plenty, because when he took his position, he had not planned to share it.

A small lizard scurried across the rocks, stopped, moved a few inches, stopped again. The lizard darted into a dark crack and returned with a small scorpion in its mouth. The more she thought, the more uneasy she felt. In training, they studied many predators. Predators did not give their prey second chances. The scorpion could sting the lizard, rendering it immobile, or worse, so the lizard strikes decisively, killing the scorpion instantly. Derrick's decisions, whether his own or guided by his Test Subject inclinations, could get them killed. Anna filed the lizard-decisive kill observation away.

Despite her misgivings, she was also trained to follow the leader's instructions. When she got off the mountain, if she got off the mountain, she'd corner Miriam to discuss Derrick. Try to convince Miriam to lead. Until then, she'd try not to kill the sniper. If there was a second sniper on the other canyon rim, that might change her thinking. Derrick gave no instructions regarding that scenario. He didn't have to. There were few options regarding a second sniper.

Her breathing had returned to normal, so Anna crept to the ridge and peeked over the edge. The soldier was 15 yards below. Open ground, no cover. Taking him by surprise would be difficult, but not impossible. Scanning the area with binoculars, she studied the launcher. The missile was huge. Three soldiers, two at a control panel, one walking from one vehicle to the other, checking something in his hand, probably a satellite communication device. He was waiting for instructions regarding the launch.

Looking toward the highway, she couldn't see the police car or the body. That meant a second sniper. The second sniper had shot the officer, not this one. This one laid under a small tent-like cloth that blended into the rocks. The average person would not see him, even using binoculars, but she was not an average person. Although the reason for their training remained a mystery, it was the only reason they had gotten this far and the only reason they might avert this attack. This was not the first time Anna had thought about this. She had found no answers for their training before, so she would find none now.

Easing back, she moved about 10 yards down the mountain, found a crevasse where she could lie flat, and hang her leg into the crack to look as if she might have broken it. She had to get the soldier on this side of the ridge because attacking him on the other side posed too great a risk of being seen by the other sniper. Granted, the sniper wasn't watching this ridge. The sniper was focused on the military unit and the pathway leading into its position. However, movement or noise might draw attention. She did not have enough training to dodge a sniper's bullet. No one did.

Once in position, she screamed. It was a stifled scream, hoping it would not carry across the canyon. She remained still, listening. She thought she heard the hiss of a radio keyed and the murmur of a male voice. Probably the sniper alerting the others he'd heard something and would investigate.

She could not see the man coming. Her head was uphill, so he'd not be in her line of sight until he was right on top of her. In addition, she kept her eyes shut because it was important he believed her to be unconscious. Best if he didn't have a weapon in his hand when she struck. Even well-executed techniques can fail when there's a weapon involved.

The light scattering of pebbles at the top of the ridge alerted her of his proximity. The man did not stop, which indicated he did not realize he was making noise. This was a good sign. She heard a snap. Maybe securing his handgun. Perhaps pulling it out.

"Hello? Are you okay?"

She remained silent.

He hesitated a few yards above her, assessing the situation. Maybe wondering why is a young white girl on the top of a mountain in Mexico? She wished she had not showered and changed into clean clothing. A dirty, stinky girl would have made more sense in this situation. She'd been sweating, so perhaps she wasn't as pristine as she envisioned.

She needed him closer, and she needed him to stop analyzing, so she moaned, twisted her head, and grimaced.

Footsteps.

Perfect.

"What are you doing up here?"

A perfectly logical question. Perhaps she'd tell him, but now was not the time for Q and A.

Still on her back, she lifted her hips off the ground, throwing her legs around his neck, and then pulled him over the top of her, using her entire body's strength and gravity, slamming him into the rocks. To ensure he was out, she brought her right leg vertical, then brought it down hard, hitting him in the forehead with her heel. She tried to ease up on the force to not kill him. The initial throw might have broken his neck, or the blow hitting the rocks could have killed him. There were no guarantees.

With the soldier unconscious, Anna zip-tied his hands and legs and taped his mouth. She rolled him onto his side, then sat watching him for a moment. He moaned and tried to move.

"You're tied up. Don't fight it. Don't make any noise." She held a large knife she'd taken from him where he could see it. "I'll cut your throat if you make any noise. Nod if you understand."

The man nodded.

He had already seen her, but she didn't want him to see her now, hoping she'd seem a bit more threatening than he remembered her. "We are here to stop a war. My boss said to take you alive if I could. That wasn't my idea. I won't hesitate to kill you to save millions. Do you understand?"

He nodded again.

"Did you kill the officer out by the highway?"

The man shook his head.

"That's good. I might have killed you for that, regardless of my leader's instructions. I'll be right back."

The soldier had brought his rifle with him. She retrieved it from the top of the ridge and returned. "I need information. If you try to alert the others, I'll cut your throat. Understand?"

The man nodded.

Anna put the knife to his throat and pulled the tape far enough that he could talk. "So far, so good. Did the other sniper kill the officer?"

"Yes. I couldn't even see the guy."

"Did your commander order the officer killed?"

"No. He said to wait, but he shot the guy. He couldn't wait to kill someone. The guy is crazy."

"How old are you?"

"Sixteen."

"They take people at 16?"

"I lied about my age."

"They don't require proof?"

"I told them I lost my ID."

"And they took you? That easy?"

The boy nodded. Suddenly, not killing him made sense, but Derrick had not known there was a 16-year-old kid up here. That part was just luck.

"Do you know what you're doing here?"

"Yes. Mexico is going to invade New America. We are here to bomb Mexico City if they do."

"Where are you?"

"Southern California."

"How many soldiers are here?"

"Five."

"That's a small unit, isn't it?"

"Two snipers, two to operate the launcher, a sergeant as team leader."

"Doesn't it seem odd to need snipers in California?"

"I didn't think about it. A little odd, I guess, now that you mention it."

"Snipers were needed because you are in Mexico. How much do the people launching the missile know about coordinates?"

"Probably not much. They are about my age, right out of basic. They know how to put in the coordinates and launch."

"How about the sergeant?"

"He can do it if they have a problem. He knows the system."

She put the tape back over his mouth. "Just so you know. The weapon is aimed at a town in New America. Justification to start a war. The sergeant probably has orders to kill you once the launch is completed. No witnesses. We are here to stop them. Wish me luck because if I get killed, you'll die up here."

34

SCOTT ATE FRENCH FRIES AND CHICKEN WINGS. His small sample glasses were empty, but the root beer was cold and delicious. John left to take a phone call, then returned with two glasses of beer, both dark as night. John picked the beer Scott liked best, but he had no intention of drinking the entire glass, only a sip or two to ease the fire in his mouth from the spicy chicken, which he liked more than he expected. It puzzled him that out here in the middle of nowhere, in a small commoner town, people enjoyed things the Chosen had never experienced. He understood the Chosen were imprisoned, but he always thought they enjoyed the best of everything, which kept them content. Like many things, it wasn't true. Scott wondered if everything in New America was based on lies.

Despite the deceptions, the Chosen were safe in their prisons. The world out here was dangerous. Not the way Derrick had envisioned it. Derrick's news feed was propaganda like others watched, although his news feed was far worse. His fears were monitored, and the news was further tailored to amplify those fears. That Derrick could function at all was an unexplained phenomenon. That he overcame those fears was a miracle.

Scott didn't believe in miracles and couldn't help Derrick, even if he wanted to. He needed to get to Canada. Knowing that New America would soon be at war with the world reinforced the need to escape.

John pushed the glass of dark liquid in front of Scott. "You liked this one. Am I right?"

Scott nodded. "Yes. How did you know, and what is it called?"

"I could see it in your expression. You don't hide your reactions as well as you might think. It's a porter."

"I should go."

"No rush. Don't get me wrong, I have work to do, but we have time for a pint. There's always time for a pint. Then you should rest. You've had a tough couple of weeks." John took a drink, staring at Scott over his glass. "On the trail."

Scott nodded. "I'm exhausted." Not so exhausted that he couldn't get on the trail again as soon as he got his clothing changed.

"We're still on for dinner tonight, right? My treat. Part of the perks of working here."

"I don't work here. I'm going to Yakima."

"My guess is that you're going to Canada. Not a bad plan, but Derrick and Miriam need you. You don't trust me. I get that. I don't blame you. Maybe I can ease your fears. Just a little. First, if my intention was to turn you in for the reward, you'd already be at one of Prime's Headquarters. Second, you need to have a makeover."

"A makeover?" Scott frowned. "I don't understand."

"You've changed the color of your hair and grown a beard. It makes you harder to spot, that's for sure, except for one thing."

"I am who I am. I've changed nothing."

"See, here's the thing. You look like a guy on the run. Even someone who doesn't know what Lawrence King looks like would guess you're the guy. A guy on the run doesn't have time for grooming."

"You still have the wrong guy." Scott took a drink, mostly to hide as much of his face as possible, hoping his reaction wasn't apparent.

"Right. Well, Scott, my guy will take you to a lady who does hair in town. She'll fix you up. You don't want someone to think you're this Lawrence King guy and turn you in. Trust me, having Prime snooping around here isn't on my wish list."

"Thanks for the offer, but I'm fine."

"Are you, Scott? I think you're not as fine as you want me to believe. I'm being honest with you. See, here's the deal. You must cross that bridge," John motioned over his shoulder, "and it's impossible to get across without being seen. And, if you think you can swim across, forget it. The water's running high and cold this time of year. You'll never make it. So, you get cleaned up, get some rest, and I'll see you tonight. We'll talk further about your employment."

Scott said, "I need to get to…"

John held up his hand. "I know. You need to get to Canada, I mean Yakima, but that's not going to happen, Scott."

A big guy, carrying a large silver cylindrical container, walked up. "I'll take this to the taproom and be right back."

John said, "This is Bob. He'll take you to the hairdresser and then to your room."

Scott tried to think of something to say but failed. John didn't sound threatening, but he'd made his point. Scott's only option was to backtrack and find another way across the river. It would take him miles out of his way, along roads, and through towns. Perhaps if he traveled at night and hid from vehicles. That was his only hope.

If what John said was true, New America would be at war before he got to Canada. He'd never make it to the border, but perhaps he could make it out of town and take his chances of surviving the war in the mountains. His small glimmer of hope faded.

Bob returned, and Scott followed him to a truck parked in the back. Bob drove to a small house with faded white paint and a rickety picket fence of weathered wood. "Sue is expecting you. I'll wait here."

Scott thought about telling Bob he didn't need a ride to the hotel. It wasn't far. From one end of the town to the other was under a mile, but he didn't think Bob would leave, so why bother? Scott was accustomed to having a Barber-Bot™ cut his hair, which he used twice a week until he fled from Pacific Edge a few weeks ago. The machine didn't talk, but Scott assumed that was not the case with Sue.

Before Scott could rap on the door, it opened, and a woman, younger than he expected, with long, braided hair displaying a rainbow of colors, stood inside.

"Welcome. John called. I'm Sue." She extended her hand, which Scott accepted. Then she held his hand with both of hers, longer than seemed typical. Once inside, Sue held him at shoulder length, cocked her head from one side to the other, then spun him around. "I've got some ideas. This looks like about two weeks of growth, and there's not much to work with. The beard is important."

Scott said nothing. John had a point. Changing his look to something different but well-groomed was a good idea. He had not packed a razor, thinking he'd grow a beard, but he had not thought about how predictable that was. Perhaps he could pick one up at a store on his way out of town. Keep the newly styled beard looking fresh.

Smart move.

Another smart move Scott had not considered was clothing for towns, slacks, button-down shirt, tie, and black shoes. Not the sort of clothing one wore when hiking hundreds of miles. But the thought had not crossed his mind. Neither had a guy at a brewery recognizing him in the first town he entered. What were the odds?

Sue motioned him to a chair in the kitchen. Just a plain chair. "You could take your shirt off if you like. It looks clean. I'll put a towel around you, but no use having hair clippings on your shirt. It's a dead giveaway that you just had a haircut. I assume you want to avoid that."

Scott hesitated, then pulled the t-shirt over his head and sat. Sue draped a faded green towel over his shoulders. "You're in good condition."

"Fieldhand."

"Right. John told me. He said you might stay for a while. Working at the brewery."

"I'm thinking about it. I'm headed to Yakima. I heard they needed fieldhands."

"I see. Do you have experience growing potatoes?"

Scott thought for a moment. John had said something about the crops in Yakima, and potatoes didn't sound right, but they probably grew many crops there. "Yes. I have a lot of experience."

"I see." Sue started cutting.

It did not feel as if she were cutting it short and her movements felt much different from the Barber-Bot™ and the sensation was not unpleasant. It had been a long time since he had felt a woman's touch. He did not know how much he missed it until now. "You do this for a living?"

"I wish. Mostly I do it for free. People can't afford to pay. I work at the bridge."

"At the bridge?"

"It's a toll bridge. You didn't know? You must pay to cross."

"Right. I remember someone told me, but I forgot." Scott had not forgotten. He didn't know people had to pay to cross bridges. He hoped it wasn't expensive because he didn't have much money. However, he wouldn't ask the cost. The less he said, the better.

"Are you in the Resistance?" Sue asked.

That question shocked him. Why would she ask a stranger such a thing? "I'm just a fieldhand."

"Right. But laborers can be in the Resistance. This must be your first stop in a town on your way to Yakima."

"What makes you say that?"

Sue moved behind him. "Just a hunch. You got to pass through this town to cross the river. No reason to stop in towns if you're on the run."

"I'm not on the run. Just hoping to find work."

"I see. Then it's lucky you ran into John. He'll put you to work tomorrow, so you don't have to go to Yakima."

"Maybe I want to go to Yakima."

She walked in front of him, bent over, and combed his bangs, snipping here and there. "You don't want to go to Yakima, trust me. Now, let's work on that beard."

She went to a drawer and pulled out electric clippers. "I'll use these first, then a razor. Tilt your head back."

Scott stared at the ceiling, feeling vulnerable, a razor to his throat. "I can shave once you're finished trimming."

"Don't trust me? Why would I hurt a farmer? Makes no sense."

This conversation wasn't going well. Sue knew. John had filled her in. Perhaps he could work the conversation to his advantage. He needed to be asking questions, not answering them. "What's wrong with Yakima?"

"Hold still." Sue started trimming. It didn't take her long. A few swipes on each cheek and a bit on his neck. "Don't move."

In a few moments, she put a warm lather on his face. It was a wonderful feeling.

"Now, hold still. I don't want to cut you. You let me know if the razor hurts."

The blade must have been sharp because it felt like butter on his skin to the extent he wondered if it was cutting any whiskers. While she worked, he considered several questions he needed answers to. After a few minutes, she placed a warm towel on his face. Questions would have to wait.

"You know, this town ain't so bad. I mean, you gotta be somewhere, right? We get rain sometimes. You probably noticed the forest is still alive here. We have fresh fish from the river. Few people travel the highway. We get as many folks off the trail as we do from the road. Often, they are running from something or to something. You know, running from something bad, running to something better. We feed them, give them rest, then they move on. And we've got local crafted beer, wine, and sodas. Most folks don't have that. We have a few regulars who walk many miles on the trail to come here. They come every year, just for a beer or two and a good meal. It's their vacation." Sue pulled the towel from his face and held a mirror for him to see.

He turned his head from side to side. "Nice. Thanks." He hesitated. "Can I ask you something?"

Sue sat on the counter. "Ask away."

"What's wrong with Yakima?"

"Well, it's a bigger town. Harder to control, if you know what I mean. It's not that people are bad: it's just that, well, they don't all see things the same way."

"See things the same way?" Scott asked.

"You know. The divisions. Pretty much the same everywhere, isn't it? Other than places like Cascade Locks. Don't get me wrong, we don't agree on everything, but on the main things, we do. Would you like a cup of coffee?"

He didn't plan on sleeping anytime soon, so he said, "That sounds great. Thank you."

While Sue busied herself making coffee, he said, "Tell me about the divisions."

"Same old, same old. You got your average folks just working to get by. No big hopes or dreams. Just putting food on the table. Then you got your Chosen wannabes. Preaching this and that and always looking for a way to get one up on each other, hoping someone is keeping score and the winners make it to a Chosen Community. Within both groups, there are other divisions like race, religious beliefs, and social/economics—poor and poorer and poorer still. The media keeps them stirred up. Fights among themselves aren't unusual. Mostly fist fights and rocks through windows, but too often blood is spilled, which starts an endless cycle of violence."

Scott took a deep breath, regretting he'd asked, but it set up other questions. "Is there another way to Yakima? Other than crossing the bridge here?"

Sue looked over her shoulder. "Sure. Just follow the highway to Hood River. It's about 20 miles. There's a bridge there. Then northeast toward Yakima. It's about the same distance whether you cross the bridge here or there."

"I see. What if a person wanted to get back to the Pacific Crest Trail?"

"Cream? Sugar?"

"Black is fine."

"Head back west, I suppose. I don't know much about the trail, except that it comes through here. But it doesn't matter because you aren't going to Yakima."

"I don't know what John told you."

"He didn't have to tell me anything to know you're lying."

"I'm just a fieldhand."

Sue smiled. "It's farmhand, and you aren't one. First, not many potato fields around Yakima. Those are further east around Walla Walla or over in Idaho. Yakima is mostly vineyards and hops. Where they still have enough water, that is. Second, your hands are too soft for a farmhand. I'll bet those hands have never done manual labor. Third, you're on the Pacific Crest Trail for a reason."

"I'm on the trail because I don't own a car and I'm trying to get to Yakima."

"Still lying. Perhaps not about the car. That might be true. You're not going to Yakima because you're not looking for work. If it was work you wanted, you just found it. John offered you a job, and a man looking for work would be thrilled—no more walking. You're hiding from something. The trail isn't the fastest way to get anywhere, but it is the best way if you don't want to be found."

Scott drank coffee and said nothing, thoughts spinning in his head. Go east tonight under the cover of darkness. Twenty miles would take him six to seven hours. Take the bridge there across the river, hide, and go back to the trail tomorrow night. Then on to Canada. His plan was still within reach. He could make it happen. Traveling the trail was safer than being in a city. No reason to bomb the mountains. They would bomb the cities.

"Scott, those kids need you."

He set the coffee down, harder than he'd intended. "You said John didn't tell you anything."

"He might have mentioned a few things."

"I'm not who John thinks I am. I keep telling him that."

"Those kids need you. They need the VPN you and Patel developed."

"I don't know Patel. And if this Patel exists, why doesn't he give it to those people, whoever they are?" That was perhaps his best volley. He sounded convincing. At least, he thought he did. Plus, he asked a question that he needed an answer to but had no way of asking until now.

"You know why Patel can't give it to them because you took it. Besides, Patel is hunkered down in Potterville. After getting you out of Pacific Edge, he loaded up his family and went there. He made one last call to John and then tossed his phone out of his car window. Patel can't contact Miriam because no one knows where they are. However, Miriam gave Patel a burner phone and said she'd call at 6 p.m. each night. If we can get a message to Patel, he can tell Miriam your IP address so you can get the VPN to her." She placed her hand on his. "Lawrence or Scott, it makes no matter to me what name you use. Give the kids a chance. You brought them this far. Don't abandon them now."

Scott thought for a moment. This woman knew far more than she had indicated. One thing seemed clear. He wasn't fooling these people. But they didn't know everything. He crashed the VPN, that much was true. And he took codes needed to reactivate it. But he left Patel with a file containing the VPN. Patel must not have found it or doesn't realize he has it.

Not that Scott didn't want to help, but he doubted Miriam and Derrick would trust him. Besides, he knew a few things about Prime. If the world's armies can't destroy Prime, how are three kids going to?

He took a deep breath. "Suppose I was this Lawrence everyone says I am. Why should I stay here instead of moving on?"

"Because here, we all are in the Resistance. The Resistance is your hope, not Canada. You just haven't realized it yet."

35

Friday, April 9, 3:15 p.m.

NYX FELT LIKE HELL WARMED OVER, EMPHASIS, on the warmed-over part. Her skin felt as if it might turn into one large blister, red and burning so badly it brought tears to her eyes. She'd downed one bottle of water and started on the next, sitting with her back against the tire of the machine she'd driven out into the desert, where she found Antonio and Red. L. Linda had managed to get everything into the hangar, where it was much cooler. Nyx didn't know how L. Linda accomplished that. L. Linda alternated between Red and Antonio, letting them sip. Akira sat crying beside Charlie.

Charlie remained lifeless.

Nyx tried to stand but sat back down. Clutching the water bottle in one hand, she crawled to Red. "Where's the plane?"

Red whispered, "Over the ocean by now."

"What's it doing over the ocean?"

"Flying to its death," Red said.

"Where's Derrick?" Nyx asked.

Red swallowed as if his throat hurt. "Mexico."

"Mexico? What in the hell is he doing in Mexico?"

Red said, "Trying to stop a war."

Nyx sat. "Can't he let someone else do that?"

Red didn't answer.

"Nyx, do you know anything about the satellite?" L. Linda asked.

"Akira thinks it's gone."

L. Linda smiled. "I need to get all of you inside. You need rest and hydration. If there's saline, I can probably figure out how to start a drip."

"Probably?" Nyx asked. "No, thanks."

"You'll be okay, but these two," L. Linda indicated Red and Antonio with her head, "need medical attention."

Nyx said, "You have a Prime aircraft, right? You can fly them to Potterville. They've done their part. They don't need to be here."

"The aircraft is gone."

"What happened to it?" Nyx asked.

"Crashed it. Long story. Are there wheelchairs here?"

Nyx tried to stand. "Yes. I'll go."

L. Linda said, "Give me directions. You stay and take care of these two. Keep them drinking and wet. Small sips. Keep them on their sides because they are likely to throw up."

"What good is water if they keep barfing?" Nyx asked.

"Every little bit helps. How does the medical unit work? I mean, who gets them in and such?"

Nyx pointed. "Charlie does it."

"What's wrong with him?" L. Linda asked.

"I don't know. I found him in the desert like that. He was alone. Red and Antonio were farther out. I don't know what happened."

Red whispered, "I kinda bent the plane when we landed to let the people out."

Nyx said, "You got the town's people to safety? All of them?"

"Most of them. I think three of them stayed with Rebekah, Anna, Miriam, and Derrick. We parachuted, but I couldn't get as close to the Base as I wanted."

"Why not?" Nyx asked.

"The military shot up the plane."

"When?"

"As we were leaving."

"Leaving where?" Nyx asked.

"The town."

"You left Derrick surrounded by the military?"

"We just barely got away. I did not know that Derrick wasn't with them until we landed to drop off the people."

"Maybe he's been captured."

"I don't think so. The town blew up right after we were airborne."

Nyx shook her head. "If he's alive, I'm going to kill him."

L. Linda had moved to Akira's side. "What's wrong with Charlie?"

"I don't know. He won't start. Nothing I've done has worked," Akira whimpered.

L. Linda said, "Let me have a look."

"Don't hurt him."

"I'm a bit of a mechanic, you know. I won't hurt him." L. Linda studied the machine. It was face down. She tried to roll it over. "He's heavy." Looking at the robot's back, she said, "This might be it." She pointed. "The battery might have overheated." Many things might have been fried, but she didn't say that. "Are there any more robots like Charlie?"

Akira said, "Yes, in crates at the Administration Entry."

"Great. Can you show me? We can get wheelchairs too." L. Linda knew the crates but needed to get Akira moving.

"I don't want to leave Charlie."

"I understand, but the faster we get his power back on, the better. I need your help, Akira." L. Linda stood and looked at Nyx. "We'll be back. Remember, small sips."

Akira led L. Linda to the crates, not to the wheelchairs. Akira wasn't thinking straight, and her future might be in a place with padded cells. Under different circumstances, L. Linda would have felt despondent about Akira, but the situation didn't allow for that. Instead, a clear head and decisive action were vital. Otherwise, death awaited the three kids in the hangar, and that wouldn't fix Akira. Perhaps nothing could.

L. Linda wasn't concerned about the robot, but she felt sure Akira wouldn't take her to the wheelchairs unless she dealt with Charlie first. The lid on one crate wasn't nailed tight. It looked as though it was removed and then replaced. The nails had been pressed into the wood about a quarter of their length. Sliding her fingers under the lid, she squatted, then straightened, forcing it upward. The top flew off, traveling several feet before landing with a thud.

Inside the crate, surrounded by dense, form-fitted foam, was a robot that looked just like Charlie. A sticker, slightly yellowed and pealing, read: A-Series. Unfortunately, it was facing up, and the battery was on its back. Having tried to roll Charlie over, she knew the machine was too heavy to lift, and the foam would prevent rolling it over.

"We need to lift it to get the battery," L. Linda said.

"Then lift it," Akira said, the panic in her voice evident.

"It's too heavy." L. Linda thought for a moment. "We need Antonio and Red. We must get them to the medical unit so they can help us. Quick, take me to the wheelchairs."

Akira looked furious. "There's no time for that. I'm… I'm… fading. I can feel it."

Akira was serious, and her expression suggested she believed it. Whether or not Akira was correct in self-assessment, L. Linda did not know. She knew that if Red and Antonio didn't get help soon, both would die or suffer severe damage to their internal organs. "If you have a suggestion, I'm listening, but if not, I'm going back to Red and Antonio. If you're fading, arguing isn't helping."

Akira said, "The robots could get them to medical and lift this robot. Charlie activates the medical unit. Red and Antonio need Charlie as much as I do."

"How do we get the robots?"

"I don't know. Most of the time, they ignore us."

"Define most of the time."

"Nyx asked for food once, and they brought it." Akira paused, then looked up at the entrance. "QR-3! Charlie wants you to help us. We need help here, and three patients in the aircraft hangar must be taken to the medical unit. Charlie must be taken to the docking station. Do it now! Quickly!"

L. Linda drawled, "Okay. You think that will work?"

"No idea. We'll find out soon."

"And if it doesn't?" L. Linda asked.

"Then it's your turn to think of something."

36

DERRICK STUDIED THE MOUNTAIN, LISTENING and watching. He estimated Anna had reached the top. They had not discussed how she would signal them when it was time to move. He had not heard gunfire, and with each passing second, his anxiety amplified, but hope remained she was okay. He should have gone with her. It wasn't because she was a girl or because he didn't trust her. Derrick had run that over in his head to ad nauseam. He should have gone because it was his idea, and she shouldn't be taking the risk.

There it was.

It was about not putting Anna at risk.

He didn't want her to kill the soldier. So, another way to say it, he didn't want to put the soldier at risk either.

He wanted to protect Anna, and he wanted to protect the soldier.

However, he could not protect everyone. Still, that he had not protected the police officer haunted him.

They had to prevent a war and then stop Prime. He wanted to do that, putting no one at risk.

Did that include Prime?

If he had a chance, would he hesitate to destroy Prime?

Hesitation gets people killed.

Then there were the kill commands. None of them knew if they could overcome those commands.

And there was the unlabeled door in his memory. He still didn't know what was behind it. The door was locked and might contain the information he needed to control his thinking, but he could not access those hidden memories.

The sound of a rock tumbling down the mountain startled him. *A poor time to be daydreaming.*

Derrick said, "That must be Anna. Time for us to go." He looked at Rebekah. "First, a quick lesson on the machine gun."

"Are you sure about this? Maybe Miriam should handle the machine gun," Rebekah said.

Derrick said, "She could do that, but can you fight a soldier or two and figure out the launcher?"

Rebekah said, "My fighting is probably better than my machine gunning."

Derrick said, "Perhaps. But it's easy to operate, and you don't have to hit the soldiers. You just need to draw their attention and machine gun fire has a unique way of doing that."

Derrick instructed Rebekah on the operation of the big gun. "Aim it into the front of the trucks. The radiator will slow the bullets, and the fenders and such should prevent the bullets from exiting the truck. Ricochets are deadly, so let's avoid having them. If you don't feel confident you can hit the trucks, aim over our heads. Remember, they don't know you can't shoot. The hard part is carrying the weapon and ammo. If you can't carry it, then we have a problem."

Rebekah lifted the gun. "I can carry it. I play soccer, you know."

Derrick said, "I know. I'm going to watch you play when this is over."

"Sure, you are."

Derrick kneaded Rebekah's shoulder. "I promise."

Miriam said, "We need a plan and a signal for Rebekah."

Derrick said, "Stick with our original plan. We're running from drug dealers."

"What about the dead police officer?"

Derrick thought for a moment. "He's why we left the highway and ran into the mountains."

Miriam shrugged. "Good as any, I guess. What about a signal?"

"No signal. Rebekah will stay behind the rocks and watch. She'll have to decide if gunfire is needed depending on how things go. Also, she needs to spot the sniper and try to find a spot where he can't shoot her."

Rebekah said, "I like this assignment less and less."

Derrick said, "If you can't see the sniper, he can't see you. However, don't be a hero. If things go south, just run."

"Go south?"

Derrick said, "I heard it at school. It means when things go wrong."

Rebekah said, "Got it. But I'm not running. Anna is on that mountain. Besides, I like this new Derrick, using folksy sayings and such."

Derrick said, "Thanks, but if things go wrong, someone has to warn the others."

Rebekah said, "By others, do you mean Nyx?"

"Yes. And everyone else."

Miriam said, "Rebekah! Not the time or place."

Rebekah looked down. "Sorry. I'm not even sure where that came from."

Derrick said, "Don't worry about it."

Rebekah looked Derrick in the eyes. "I'm scared."

"You'd be crazy if you were not. I'm scared too, but it's time."

37

Friday, April 9, 3:35 p.m.

AFTER MAKING SEVERAL PASSES THROUGH downtown, Collins parked around the corner from the Bistro. He found it difficult to believe an assassin was walking the streets in Potterville, but one had been here already, and she was dead, along with four of the town's folk. People he was sworn to protect. It could have been five had his deputy not killed the assassin first. Lori would have been dead had it not been for L. Linda Maxton. How L. Linda knew there was an assassin and how to kill her was unclear. In fact, it was murky as a mud puddle. There were things about L. Linda and her father, Jason, that Collins didn't understand, which was an understatement of grand proportions. He was the sheriff, duty-bound to protect the people in Potterville, although that was predominantly just something he believed. Most people saw a sheriff as an obligatory fixture in a community, like a fountain in a park or a statue of some long-forgotten historical figure riding a horse.

Sheriffs like Collins were not real lawmen. Solving crimes and keeping the peace was left to the state police, not that they ventured into small towns like Potterville often, or that they were interested in solving crimes or keeping the peace. Local sheriffs were supposed to drink coffee and show up at high school sporting events. Collins did both. But he had strived to do more.

However, a high school girl had done the protecting. When Collins understood how close the assassin came to killing Lori Martinez—well, he didn't want to think about that, but he owed L. Linda Maxton, and he'd never forget that. That's why Collins was following her father's instructions. Jason seemed to know as much about killing assassins as L. Linda. That Jason showed up with an arsenal of weapons emphasized there was more to the Maxton family than anyone could have predicted.

Two blocks from Donna's, Allen Patel waved for Collins to stop, and they were now walking toward the Bistro, trying to look nonchalant. Browning mirrored them from across the street.

Allen said, "The streets seem empty. I've never seen it this quiet on a Friday afternoon, especially during Spring Break."

Collins said, "It's spooky. I assume are we going to Donna's. Can I ask why?"

"I must check on something, and Donna has a good internet connection."

"Fletcher has internet. Kind of surprising, but he has it."

"Yes, but I set up the router at Donna's." Allen paused. "It has attributes I needed when I was in Potterville."

Collins said nothing for a moment. "How deep are you into this, Allen?"

"Deep into what?"

"Whatever it is you're doing. You know things about Miriam and Derrick. You tried to help Anna Ford. You're on the run. I'm sure there's much more to the story, and I'm just trying to understand the basics."

"I guess there's no hiding it now. Like I said earlier, I'm in the Resistance. I have been for a few years, but my part was small until an acquaintance discovered an old technology called VPN. This acquaintance told me about the Test Subject Program. Things changed after that."

"Changed how?"

"I became more active, took a larger role, learned more secrets, and accepted more risk. All of that made me more valuable and more dangerous. And that made me a bigger target."

"What's a VNP?"

"VPN. It stands for virtual private network. Used with the encoding which I improved, it allowed the Resistance to communicate and share information without being traced."

"But 'they', whoever 'they' are, take down Resistance websites all the time."

"Only the ones we gave them. We are controlling much of the web now. They have no idea."

Collins thought for a moment. "Your involvement doesn't coincide with Derrick and Miriam being here, does it?"

"Oh, yes. Very much so. In fact, I am somewhat responsible for their current situation."

"You were involved in Derrick's exile?"

"Not directly. That was his keeper's doing. Initially, the experiment was putting Derrick in a situation outside a controlled environment to test the controls on his anger, suppress responses."

"Outside the controlled environment means the school in Pacific Edge, which is when that Carver kid threatened to hit Miriam."

"Exactly right. The desired outcome was that Derrick would do nothing and blame Miriam for creating the problem."

"What's a keeper?"

"Scientists in the Test Subject Program who are assigned to monitor and conduct experiments on specific Test Subjects."

A Derrick King Novel, Book 6

"You make it sound as if they are not humans."

"The program doesn't treat them like people. More like test rats."

"I'm feeling less and less sympathetic to the Chosen."

"The Chosen don't know the program exists. The Chosen are another topic for another time."

"Let's see if I have this straight. Derrick's father isn't really his father but a researcher. Right?"

"Correct, except Derrick's keeper wasn't just a researcher. He was a pioneer in the program. Test Subjects do not have parents. Derrick and Miriam were labeled Number Six and Number Seven during the facility testing. Mr. King, Derrick's keeper, convinced the oversight committee to let him continue the tests on three Test Subjects outside the testing facility. The oversight committee got Prime's approval. He and his wife assigned themselves to Number Six and Number Seven and named them Derrick and Miriam."

"This keeper wanted to prove he could control Derrick."

"That part is inconclusive."

Collins paused at the intersection, studying the streets before crossing. "Which part of this situation are you responsible for?"

"Miriam, Anna, and Rebekah's escape from Pacific Edge."

"You planned that?"

"I did not. I opened a door. Miriam did the rest."

"Their father, the keeper, knew about that then?"

"He did not. It wasn't planned. Here's how it started. I saw a request for technical service at the King home. I took the call myself, hoping Mr. King was there alone. As I mentioned, we had to be careful when communicating. I assumed Mr. King had placed the service call for that reason. However, when I arrived, much to my surprise, Miriam was there. I suspect she had feigned illness just to be there when I arrived."

"So, Miriam knew you?"

"She did not. We had never met. I think she was simply curious about how the monitor in her room worked, so she stayed home from school that day. Usually, at least one keeper would be home monitoring Miriam, but they had meetings that day at the test facility. However, I knew a little about Miriam. When Samantha attended school in Pacific Edge, she knew Miriam. I knew Miriam was a Test Subject, so I paid particular attention when Samantha talked about her."

They reached the Bistro and Collins stopped. He spun a seat out and sat. "I'm trying to get my head wrapped around this. I feel like this is a dream, and I'll wake up any minute."

Allen sat. "More like a nightmare. I've felt like something bizarre was going to happen for quite some time, so believing is not difficult."

"What about Anna? Prime came looking for her specifically. Even offered the others their freedom if they gave him Anna. Samantha knew Anna, right? What's so special about her?"

"Samantha and Anna were close friends before we were removed from Pacific Edge. Anna was shy and bullied, which was something she endured even in the testing facility."

"Why was she bullied in the testing facility?"

"That was her purpose. The tenders and keepers tormented her. They meant to see how far they could push her until she broke. She never did. The keepers declared her control protocols a success. However, I have wondered if Anna's self-control was more about her inner strength than it was about the controls they used on her. Derrick protected her sometimes. He hit a tender in the back with a chair, and they adjusted his controls. However, when he hit Marcus Carver, it was proof that his test had failed."

"What was Derrick's test exactly?"

"Several things, but primarily, Derrick wasn't supposed to care about anyone other than himself. He was to be devoid of emotional attachment to any other person. He was to be completely self-absorbed."

"Why on earth would they want that?"

"I don't know the entire answer to that. I assume that Mr. King knows, but we never had time for such discussions. I can speculate on a few reasons they wanted to achieve that. With no emotional attachments, one could do any number of things that normal people wouldn't do. He could lie, cheat, steal, and be completely devoted to Prime. Such traits would be high on Prime's wish list because those traits describe James Carver."

"You think Prime wanted someone like Carver?"

"Yes."

Collins whistled. "How can this be happening? Why Potterville?"

Allen shrugged. "My fault, I'm afraid."

"Explain."

"I had mentioned Potterville to Lawrence King. Told him it was a nice town and safer than most. When Derrick hit Marcus Carver, the Tribunal wanted to terminate the experiment immediately. Things happened fast. Lawrence fought hard to keep Derrick alive and convinced them the data from the fight was vital to dialing in Derrick's protocols, and he was certain they could still control Derrick. He just needed a little more time. He convinced them that exiling Derrick was the perfect solution. It kept Pacific Edge safe and put Derrick in an even more difficult situation. Potterville was the only town outside Pacific Edge that Lawrence knew anything about. That's why Derrick came here. My fault."

Collins said, "Back to Miriam. How did you help her escape? Was that your plan all along?"

"I had no plan. Miriam watched what I did to fix her monitor and remembered everything. Samantha said Miriam was smart, but I had no idea. Miriam talked me into giving her a mouse and keyboard. I stole one from Technical Services and left it for her to pick up. That night when she came to pick it up, she entered my passcode into the locking system and tried the door. I thought she might return, so I left my door unlocked and then left her some instructions."

"She came back and got into the computer system?" Collins asked, then continued, "Sounds high risk. Aren't there security staff there? And doesn't the system require, I don't know, like identification or something?"

Patel nodded. "It does. I might have done a few other things, like set up a fake employee file for her. She was known as Maranda Kingston in Pacific Edge."

"But there must have been other people working."

"She went at night. There were two security staff, but they are not, how do you say it, the sharpest tools in the shed. They even caught Miriam. She had gotten careless. But she convinced them she was an employee, working on a special audit. From what I understand, they became friends."

Collins said, "She is amazing. I'll give her that. I assume her test was about how smart they could make a Test Subject."

Patel said, "It was not. At least, as far as I know. Lawrence told me they didn't understand why she was so smart. Her test was to use the hypnosis protocol to block memories, but not to control her behavior with the 1984 chip. She was out of control by Chosen Standards."

"So, you did not help her escape?"

"I did not. I was going to help her if she got out, but that didn't work out. The entire escape was on her own. She exceeded my expectations."

"Back to Anna. What was so important about her to Prime? I mean, being bullied doesn't seem like a desirable trait. Also, you said Derrick was supposed to be self-centered. We saw that firsthand, although he changed before our very eyes. But becoming a fitness phenomenon and fighting machine must have also been part of the test."

"I don't know why Prime was looking for Anna. I've been puzzling over that. My best guess is Prime hoped they would turn Anna in, then he would capture them all and put an end to this test."

"By end, you mean, kill them."

"Yes. Pacific Edge assumed Miriam, Rebekah, and Anna escaped together, but when Miriam and Rebekah showed up in Potterville without Anna, Anna became a bigger problem, a missing piece. Prime sent the assassin, and the assassin had a spy."

"Jimmy Priest."

"So, it appears. I believe that Prime's offer of freedom to Derrick, Rebekah, and Miriam in exchange for Anna's whereabouts was an attempt to find them all."

"Just a trick. A lie."

"Yes. Lying is what Prime does best." Allen paused. "You're wrong about fitness and fighting skills being part of Derrick's test. It was not. Lawrence started that after the kids were removed from the test facility. As you may have gathered, they hypnotized the kids for several reasons. One was to make them forget about being Test Subjects. Lawrence used hypnosis to set up a training regime. They trained every night, every weekend, and several days a week, but they remembered none of it. Funny thing about that. Anna, the shy, bullied girl while awake, became a fierce competitor during training. She easily bested Miriam in every phase and challenged Derrick in everything. Overall, she was better than Derrick. I learned this from Lawrence. He thinks deep down Anna carries a lot of rage about the way they treated her in the program. He's afraid she could become dangerous."

"But Derrick remembered how to fight."

"Yes. It seems the memories were leaking through. When it was needed, Derrick remembered."

"You said there was more."

"Yes. Unfortunately, before Lawrence had a change of heart, he had kill commands installed in their memories and then had those memories locked away as much as possible. Even if the kids could remember those commands, they might be unable to overcome the command if initiated."

"Does Prime know these commands?"

"Yes. It was Prime's condition to approve continuing the program in Pacific Edge."

"So, whether robots or assassins, anyone Primes sends could speak the kill commands, and the kids would obey?"

"I assume that's correct."

"And their keeper knew that?"

"He did."

"Why would he do any of that? I get the kill commands. Prime required them. But why the training. They would be less dangerous if they were just normal teenagers."

Patel took a deep breath. "Because he believed they would eventually have to fight to survive. Remember, the kill commands were installed before Lawrence changed, before he joined the Resistance."

"It's a lot to take in. Allen, why did you get involved? No offense, but you never impressed me as a risk taker. Now, you've put yourself and your family in grave danger. I don't get it."

"We are all in grave danger. I've been watching this secretly for a while. Because of my position, I can access the internet outside New America. The world has grown tired of New America's arrogance and constant aggression. They have been building up forces, waiting for a reason to attack. They plan to crush us. There is no safe place."

"What made you think three kids could make a difference?"

"I didn't see it that way. I didn't foresee Miriam escaping or any of this happening. Maybe I hoped she could escape, and that outside Pacific Edge, she would have a better chance of survival. However, since they escaped, something unexpected has happened."

"What?"

"Prime sees itself as immortal, invincible, yet those kids scare Prime. Perhaps Prime will make a mistake. Maybe a mistake will make a difference. I'm a realist, not an optimist. We are trapped. I should run, but we have little chance of escaping. Even if I could survive, the entire town can't run. Plus, there's no place safe to run to. I've decided we will live or die with the rest of the people here. I'm fully committed to the Resistance, but to be truthful, when it comes to helping the kids, it's just throwing as many clay balls as possible against the wall, hoping one will stick, and assuming none will."

38

L. LINDA STOOD BY THE OPEN CRATE, waiting, and watching Akira, who fidgeted, staring at the comatose Charlie-lookalike robot. About two minutes had passed when a black robot exited the building and walked straight to the crate. It stood there a moment, silent.

"Stand it up," Akira demanded.

The robot stepped to the end of the box, grabbed the Charlie-like robot by the shoulders, and stood it up.

L. Linda studied the battery for a moment, then pushed a button. The battery popped out half an inch, and she slid it out. Looking up at the robot, she asked, "Where is Charlie?"

The black robot remained motionless, but said, "Dock."

L. Linda said, "You can put this robot back in the crate." She assumed the robots did not have feelings but to be safe, she added, "Thank you." Looking at Akira, she said, "Can you find the docking station?"

Akira ran into the building. L. Linda followed her. She had no difficulty keeping up with Akira, sprinting down the hallways. Akira slid to a stop and jerked open the door. Pointing, Akira said, "There."

Charlie sat in a large white chair, which must be the docking station. His eyes had a dull glow. At least something was happening. L. Linda stepped to a monitor on the station, where a red light appeared under the section that read: CHARGING, and red letters flashed BATTERY FAILURE. L. Linda pulled Charlie's battery out and pushed the new battery in. The lights went out completely.

"What have you done?" Akira screamed.

"You've watched me the entire time. I put in the new battery. That was the plan, wasn't it?"

The lights on the panel flickered, the charging light turned green, then a scale showed a battery charge of 81%. Charlie's eyes lit as did Akira's. "Mr. Red Badowski and Mr. Antonio Morales. Where are they?" Charlie asked.

Akira said, "I hope they are in the medical unit. Nyx too. They all needed help."

Charlie said nothing.

Akira fell against Charlie, sobbing. "Charlie, I need help. Do you still have a part of me? Part of my brain? I feel as if I'm fading away. You must help me. Please?"

After a brief moment of silence, Charlie said, "Ms. Nyx Belos, Mr. Antonio Morales, and Mr. Red Badowski are in the medical unit. I remember when Mr. Red Badowski switched on my power, calculations indicated I could get them to the hangar. Why are they in the medical unit?"

"What about me?" Akira screamed.

"Damn, girl," L. Linda snapped. "Calm your ass down before I do it for you."

Charlie said, "I am not ignoring you, Ms. Akira Nakamura. The treatment unit is processing this issue and looking for a solution. I am not fond of your emotions and will gladly give them back. This experience has caused me to regret wanting to be more human."

Akira walked to a chair and flopped into it, her arms tightly folded.

"Charlie, what do you know about Derrick?" L. Linda asked.

Charlie looked at L. Linda. "You are Ms. L. Linda Maxton. You brought us a message from Mr. Derrick King."

"Correct, but that doesn't answer my question. And why are you doing that?"

"I am charging, Ms. L. Linda Maxton. How did I get here?"

L. Linda said, "Akira ordered the robots to bring you here. The reason the others are in the medical unit, and you are here, is because your battery overheated and failed. I know you are charging. I replaced your battery."

"Thank you for doing that, Ms. L. Linda Maxton."

L. Linda rolled her eyes. "Why are you saying Mr. and Ms. and last names all the time? You didn't do that when I first came here."

Charlie said nothing for a moment. "Charging is at 92%. That is sufficient." Charlie separated from the charging unit. "You are correct. I cannot answer your question. Perhaps the heat damaged more than my battery. Running diagnostics. Modifying greeting protocols. Why is Ms. Nyx ill?"

L. Linda said, "Akira, can you answer Charlie's question?"

"She went out looking for you. Apparently, she found you, Antonio, and Red out in the desert and dragged you all to the hangar. How about gluing my memories and emotions back together?"

"Memories cannot be glued to anything. I shall proceed to the medical unit." And with that, Charlie left. L. Linda and Akira followed.

Inside a treatment chamber, Nyx sat next to Antonio, dabbing his forehead with a damp cloth. Both sipped from a glass using separate straws. Antonio wasn't hooked to machines like Akira had been but had one intravenous line running to his arm. Red was sitting outside the unit, a similar intravenous line running from a bag on a pedestal next to the chair.

L. Linda stared at Nyx and Antonio for a moment, then walked to Red. "Why aren't you in a room like Antonio?"

"I was in the bed next to Antonio. Then Nyx came," Red paused, nodding toward Nyx and Antonio, "and, I left."

Charlie said, "What happened, Mr. Red? I recall that when you activated me, Mr. Antonio was already lying on the parachute. You fell unconscious just as I became operational. I placed you on the parachute and then headed to the hangar."

Red said, "Antonio couldn't go farther. I wasn't sure we were close enough for you to finish the trip, so I went it alone for a while."

"Mr. Red dragged both of us?" Charlie asked.

"Yeah. Not that difficult."

"It would have been extremely difficult. I must have stopped working. Then Ms. Nyx found us? It is extremely hot in the desert and the sun is deadly."

Red looked at his sunburned arm. "Tell me about it."

L. Linda put her hand close to Red's arm. Red jerked away. "Don't touch me."

"I wasn't going to touch you, Mr. Touchy Pants. It must burn like hell. I'll look for something to put on it."

"They already sprayed us with something. It's better than it was, but it still hurts."

Charlie looked at L. Linda. "Why do you get to say it?"

"Say what?"

"Mr. Touchy Pants. Why do you get to say Mr.? And Mr. Red's middle name is unusual, isn't it?"

L. Linda said, "I get to say it because I'm weird. And you can address Red as Mr. Touchy Pants from here forward."

Red said, "Very funny. Don't listen to her, Charlie."

Charlie said, "I'm confused. I don't like to be confused."

Red glanced at Antonio and Nyx. "Me neither. Can we eat?"

Akira eased to Charlie. "I'm sorry about earlier. How's it going?"

Charlie said, "Food and drinks are being served in the break room. You should eat. Red, I can take you in a wheelchair. Oh, look. Protocols are updated."

"Thank God," L. Linda curtsied, then said, "or, thank you, great central computer."

Charlie said, "Weird."

"I can walk." Red stood and grabbed the IV pedestal, which was on rollers. At the door, he stopped. "Do I have to eat alone?"

"I'm starving," L. Linda said.

Red stared at her for a moment. "What happened to your clothes and shoes? It looks like you've been in a fight."

L. Linda looked down. Her white t-shirt was dry and no longer semitransparent. It was no longer white either, but dingy with dirt, a splatter of knife-boy's blood, and a piece of seaweed that had made the journey back to the Base. Her jeans were torn at the knees, although she didn't remember how that happened. She had found shoes, which were necessary to walk in the blazing desert sand, but they were far too large, and she'd kicked them off once everyone was in the hangar. She looked up and stared at Red for a moment. Red wasn't looking at her like knife-boy Tom did. Instead, Red looked concerned, and perhaps a bit embarrassed. L. Linda felt a slight warming deep in her chest that she typically denied herself. With a slight smile, she said, "You should see the other guy."

Red thought for a moment. "Something tells me I don't want to."

L. Linda said, "Good thinking."

"Akira, can you show L. Linda the uniforms?" Red asked. "Then we'll all match like we are in a club or something."

L. Linda rolled her eyes. "We'll be *or something* all right. A quick shower wouldn't hurt if that's possible."

Red said, "I'm glad you mentioned it. I didn't want to, but you're spot on with that observation."

"You're a real gentleman, Red Badowski."

"People do say that about me."

Akira said, "Good grief. How can you joke at a time like this? I'm messed up, and I'm still worried about Rebekah, Miriam, and Derrick."

Red said, "If I thought about them too much, I couldn't function. And something tells me we have a lot of work ahead of us."

L. Linda said, "You're not only a gentleman but also smarter than you look."

"A real catch, I'm told."

"Yeah, well, don't eat all the food before I get there if you know what's good for you."

"Don't take all day then. You ain't getting ready for the prom."

L. Linda smiled. "You asking?"

Red said, "Let's see if we are still alive when the prom rolls around."

39

ROBOTS WERE RARELY SEEN IN PRIME'S Seattle headquarters, but Quigley had seen them occasionally. Prime did not have to see or talk to them in person because he could send messages using his computer-linked brain. Quigley wasn't surprised when one met him outside Prime's office. Quigley regretted not trying to kill Prime. He knew that was impossible without a weapon, and even if he were to be successful, a replacement would be activated within minutes. Still, killing just one of them would have given Quigley a wee bit of satisfaction and a guarantee of a quick death.

Although it didn't feel that way, his time here had been successful. Few make it this far. A total of one, to be precise, but his time had ended. He had relayed valuable information while in this position. Whether it was worth the price he had paid, he'd never know. He was the one who had discovered that Prime existed in six cities, Seattle, New York, Dallas, San Diego, Chicago, and Denver. Quigley didn't know why Prime existed in those six cities. A seventh Prime existed, and it was the central control for the other six. Where that Prime was, he had no idea. He believed destroying the Central Prime was the only way to end Prime's existence. He didn't know if the Central Prime had any humans at that location. He speculated only robots worked there, giving Prime complete control of the facility.

There would be no exit interview, not that Quigley expected one, but it would have been nice to know why his run had ended. There were many plausible reasons. Perhaps Prime discovered he had passed information to the Resistance. Maybe Prime had discovered he had been trying to learn about security protocols and Prime locations. Possibly, Prime had just grown tired of him. The method of death would provide a hint. A slow torturing would indicate Prime suspected betrayal.

The robot held out a black cloth, but the voice was Prime's. "Put this on, Quigley. It is imperative you see nothing."

Quigley hesitated and thought about telling Prime to get…. But that wouldn't accomplish anything. Quigley took a deep breath, having decided to face his death with dignity. He wanted to wax philosophic, say something like, Prime may kill me, but only I can relinquish my dignity. But that was laughable. He had lost his dignity years ago climbing this ladder.

Quigley pulled the hood over his head.

"Good job, Quigley. Now, hold your arms out to your side."

Quigley did as commanded. He wanted to ask where he had failed but knew Prime would not tell him.

He sensed the machine place something around his waist.

"Now, slowly lower your arms."

Bands closed on each wrist, anchoring him to a binding around his waist. He should have fought back when he had the chance. Being killed when helpless appealed less than he had anticipated. The robot's hand closed on his elbow, and he expected the machine would crush his bones. Might as well start with pain. But instead, the grip was firm but comfortable. "Walk with me, my dear, Quigley. Time is of the essence, as I have other tasks for the machines."

They walked toward the elevators, Quigley could sense that much. He heard the elevator doors close. The robot retained its grip on his elbow. As expected, the elevator lurched up.

We are going to the roof.

The elevator stopped. The doors opened, and moist cold air rushed in. "It's raining. Move quickly so you can get this over with," Prime's voice said.

The robot guided him. Rain pelted him, soaking the cloth on his head so fast he thought he might drown on his way to the street. The machine slowed, and he stepped on what felt like a ramp.

Then the rain stopped.

He was inside something. The robot turned him 45 degrees. "Sit."

Quigley sat in a hard-surfaced chair. The machine fastened another restraint, which tightened, snugging him into the chair. He felt the chair rising. Then it turned, g-forces pushing him even tighter into the chair.

I'm in an aircraft.

Prime said, "This won't take long. Less than 20 minutes. I am sorry about the hood, but you'll understand the reason soon."

And with that, the robot put something over his ears, and the world fell silent.

Quigley felt the aircraft slow and descend. It felt more like ten minutes, but he had lost all sense of time and direction in the darkness and silence. The aircraft settled onto the ground. The door slid open. Heat as if from an oven poured into the aircraft. The harness released.

"Stand," Prime's voice commanded.

Quigley stood, but his knees weaker than he expected. Being thrown off a building sounded much better than being cast into a volcano. The robot guided him forward. His feet sunk into sand so hot it burned his feet even through his shoes. The robot stopped and let go of his elbow. He heard sounds of metal on metal and a scraping sound. Then the robot returned and led him forward. The light changed, as did the surface, from soft to hard. The radiant heat and light from the sun disappeared. He heard another sound, which reminded him of a sliding gate. The robot turned him 180 degrees and pushed him back a few steps.

Prime's detached voice said, "Ava Park has not restored communications with the unit in Mexico. I'm sending the robots to give the crew coordinates and launch orders."

Quigley decided things couldn't get much worse, so he asked, "When will the missile launch?"

"As soon as they enter the coordinates. Would you like to know where I've decided to strike?"

Quigley thought he already knew. The only reason Prime would tell him was because he wouldn't be alive much longer, which was also no surprise. "Yes. Where?" he asked.

Prime said, "Potterville, California. They have plagued me long enough. Don't you agree?"

"Yes, sir." Quigley didn't know why he said that. It was simply habit. However, there might have been just the slightest ray of hope that this was not the end, but if that was true, the flicker was so faint, Quigley could not detect it, but before he could retract his statement, the surface on which he stood, fell.

40

WHILE SHERIFF COLLINS CHATTED WITH DONNA, Allen Patel sat in a corner with his back to the wall, staring at his computer. He had already run a series of checks to ensure no one had tracked him here. The network he normally used wasn't up, which was unusual because it was stable. He could not remember the last time it was down. So, he had to set up a path using various servers and find another satellite because the one he always used was offline. In addition, the largest server system in New America, housed in a deserted town in the southern California desert, wasn't responding to pings. These were dependable systems. Having one offline would be troubling. Seeing them down at the same time was downright disturbing. That the desert town housed 80% of the Resistance archives troubled Allen. He feared something bad had happened, but he could do nothing except wait for a reply to a text message he'd sent through a convoluted network, using multiple ghost phone numbers.

The front door opened, ringing the bells above it. Allen jumped, and Collins pivoted with his pistol half drawn. Jason waved to Allen, then walked to the counter.

Securing his pistol, Collins asked, "Anything?"

"No one has seen strangers, if that's what you mean," Jason said.

"That's good news."

"It just means they are staying out of sight, but it doesn't mean they are not here." Jason nodded toward Allen. "Should he be doing that?"

"Be on the computer? Allen says it's safe, but how should I know?"

"Coffee?" Donna asked.

"Yes, please. Black is fine." Jason dug change from his pocket.

"Nonsense. Your money's no good here, Jason. DK Double Honey?"

Jason smiled. "I'd like that. Thanks, Donna." And with that, Jason walked over and sat across from Allen.

Donna said, "Is he carrying a pistol?"

"Probably carrying more than that."

"Our Jason Maxton?"

"Apparently, there's more to Jason than meets the eye."

"Lordy, what is happening to our town?" She moved to the espresso machine and started grinding coffee.

When the grinder stopped, Collins said, "Good question. To be honest, I can't get my head wrapped around it. None of it, really. Jason showed up with cases of weapons and started giving orders. He took over. Everyone fell in line, including me. It seems I don't have much say in my town anymore."

Donna finished steaming milk and started pulling shots of espresso, then said, "This is our town, Bill. Not yours. We're all in this together. It's hard to swallow, I'll give you that, but look at the mess the entire nation is in. Just because we've carved out a bit of functionality here doesn't mean it happens elsewhere. The country is in constant chaos, and it is getting worse. If you think about it from that perspective, it's not hard to believe."

Donna set two mugs on the counter. "That one's yours, and that's Allen's. I'll bring Jason's."

Collins sat next to Jason. He could not see Allen's computer screen, not that he'd understand anything, but he thought Allen would be more comfortable with it this way, although Allen looked anything but comfortable. "Is it okay if we join you?" Collins asked.

Allen nodded as Donna approached. "Thank you, Donna. Could we lock the door and close the blinds? I hate to sound paranoid, but I have a bad feeling."

Donna said, "Sure. It's been dead all day. Sorry, that's a bad way to put it."

"Have you learned anything, Allen?" Jason asked.

"Yes. I had to build a new routing. Two major pieces of our network are missing," Allen said.

"Is that unusual?" Collins asked.

"It's never happened before."

"Do you think it's connected with what's happening here or with the kids?" Collins asked.

Allen shrugged. "My guess is, yes. Directly connected."

"What does it mean?" Collins asked.

"I don't know. I hope to learn something, but my contact hasn't responded."

"Where is your contact?" Jason said.

"I'd rather not say."

"Understood. Sorry I asked."

Allen's computer sounded a light chime. "There he is." Allen read, eyes darting back and forth. "Holy shit," he whispered.

"Care to share?" Collins asked.

Donna returned. "What's happened? Allen, you've turned pale."

Allen nodded. "There's a New America missile in Mexico. Prime will launch it to justify a full invasion."

Collins said, "That makes little sense. How does launching missile into Mexico justify a war?"

"Not launching into Mexico. They are in Mexico. The bomb will hit a target in New America. Prime will claim Mexico bombed us."

Collins said, "That's crazy."

Jason said, "It sounds like Prime. What else?"

Allen said, "The kids went to Mexico to stop them."

Collins said, "That's even crazier. Who do they think they are?"

Allen looked up. "They think they are the only ones who can stop it."

Jason said, "Do you know who went?"

Allen said, "Rebekah, Anna, Miriam, and Derrick."

"When will this happen?" Collins asked.

Allen shrugged. "Don't know. Soon, I think."

"And where will it hit? An unpopulated area, I assume," Collins said.

Jason said, "You assume incorrectly. Potterville is the most likely target."

"Why here?" Collins demanded.

"Because we've made Prime angry, and Prime destroys things that anger it," Jason said.

"We have to evacuate the town," Collins said.

Allen said, "I told you earlier I should have run, but we have no safe place to go, and we can't evacuate the entire town in time even if we tried."

"So, we just sit here and die?"

Jason said, "Derrick and the others might stop the launch."

Collins said, "Sounds like too little too late, but there's a chance. We saw what Derrick did to those soldiers."

Jason said, "If they are successful, it may give us a couple of days."

Collins said, "I'm confused."

Jason said, "Prime will launch a different attack on us and will still invade Mexico."

"He's right," Allen said. "Prime intends to invade Mexico one way or another. Stopping the launch might delay him a few days while he works out a new strategy. I think Jason is also right about Prime attacking Potterville. Prime does not let go of any grievance."

"You're saying we'll go to war with Mexico no matter what?"

"It gets worse," Allen said.

"How could it possibly get worse?" Collins asked.

"Almost every country in the world is moving forces to attack New America if Prime starts a war. The country will be at war with the world," Allen said.

Collins's radio erupted. "Jason! Jason! Are you there?"

Collins keyed his microphone. "I'm here, Jack. Calm down. What is it?"

"A stranger walking toward the bistro. About a block away. Another one in the alley."

Jason said, "There's your answer. Things just got worse."

41

Friday, April 9, 4:45 p.m.

DERRICK PEEKED OVER A BOULDER. HE COULD see the trucks. But these were unlike the trucks he had seen where they fixed the ailing nuclear reactor. Instead of a bank of missiles, one truck carried one huge rocket. The other just carried people, perhaps four. Two soldiers stood at the truck's control panel, and a third walked around, apparently trying to get a signal on a handheld device. He could see one sniper on the ridgeline on the other side of the canyon.

He hoped Anna had spotted the second sniper, whose presence was not unexpected but still complicated the situation. He anticipated Anna had disabled and disarmed the sniper on this side. If not, she didn't have a weapon suitable to shoot the second sniper. Not having a way to communicate was problematic to say the least. He thought back to what he had told Anna: Don't kill anyone unless there are no other options. However, these soldiers were on a suicide mission and may not even know they're in Mexico. They were unlikely to survive regardless of what they did, and he didn't know how to stop that missile without violence.

The weapon was pointed north. Their suspicions were correct. Its destination was New America.

* * *

Anna focused the rifle's scope on the sniper, occasionally sweeping the canyon for Derrick. Something behind a rock looked out of place. Clicking the scope to a higher magnification, she saw Derrick peeking over a rock. She tried to think like Derrick and predict what he'd do. Likely, he'd walk in, hands up, hoping no one would shoot an unarmed kid. But that wouldn't work. The soldiers were too far apart to be taken by one person. That meant he and Miriam would go together. Same reasoning, why shoot unarmed kids? They posed little threat.

However, the sniper had killed the officer for no reason, despite being told not to by his commanding officer. Even if the commanding officer told him to hold fire, he probably wouldn't, and Derrick didn't know that. The sniper was a real problem. She assumed Derrick understood that. If she didn't shoot before Derrick and Miriam appeared, the sniper might shoot before she could. If she shot him now, the soldiers would know they were being attacked, and Derrick and Miriam wouldn't stand a chance.

She could shoot them all, but that might create another problem. Miriam might assume, given proper persuasion, one of them would tell her how to operate the launcher. Miriam was brilliant and could figure it out eventually, but that might take too long. What if the missile was already set to launch? There might not be time to stop it. She didn't know how powerful the bomb was, but felt it was safe to assume it could cause serious damage.

Rebekah could fire on them with the .50 cal., which would send them running, giving Miriam and Derrick a chance to reach the launcher. Derrick would have prepared Rebekah, at least he should have. Anna had to rely on Derrick following his training, but he had deviated on encounters thus far.

The sniper was behind a rock outcropping. Half his rifle and his head were visible. A headshot wouldn't be difficult, assuming the rifle was accurate, which seemed like a reasonable expectation for a military sniper rifle. He had hit the officer a half mile out—an incredible shot. So, yeah, the rifles were accurate. By comparison, Derrick and Miriam would be like shooting ducks in a pond.

Anna had to strike first, and she had to be accurate. Focusing on her target, she moved the crosshairs to the man's head. But she knew what Derrick wanted, and while he had not given specific orders, she considered his wish the same as an order: don't kill anyone if it's unnecessary. Well, it seemed necessary, plus this guy deserved to die. However, she found it hard to ignore Derrick's voice in her head.

Hitting the scope would be a tough shot. An alternative was aiming at the rifle near the trigger. The bullet would travel through the stock, hitting the guy's hand and possibly damaging the rifle, making it inoperable. However, she might not disable him, and the gun might still fire. She'd get one shot, then the guy would turn the gun on her. If he killed her, the others had no defense except Rebekah and that .50 cal. That was a rather good defense, but it wasn't a gun meant for accuracy to shoot at snipers hidden on mountains.

Anna aimed at the sniper's scope. Fire once at the scope. Fire again at the trigger area of the sniper's rifle. Two chances to prevent him from getting off a shot. If a third shot was needed, she would pick a bigger target, and the guy's head was the biggest target. At least, she could truthfully tell Derrick killing had become necessary.

She braced the gun on a sandbag. Nice and steady. Crosshairs on the largest part of the scope.

Breathe in. Breathe out.

Light squeeze against the trigger.

***

Derrick heard an unnatural sound. Ducking behind a rock, he looked toward the noise. A small black dot in the sky was growing at an alarming rate. He scrambled toward Miriam, motioning her to hide, and then doing the same to Rebekah.

A flat-black angular aircraft with a capital P on the side was flying straight at them.

42

QUIGLEY FELT WEIGHTLESS, ALTHOUGH HIS feet were in light contact with the floor. At this speed, when he reached the bottom, it would likely break both of his legs. It seemed as if the fall lasted forever. How far had he traveled? He did not know. Had his descent started at the top of a tall building or was he plummeting into the earth? Why did Prime want to kill him here?

Instead of slamming into the bottom of the pit as he expected, the platform slowed, pressing against his feet, and then decelerated, causing him to tense his leg muscles to prevent going to his knees. The platform stopped. The temperature felt comfortable, and the air fresh, but in an artificial way that he could not describe. He heard the soft hum of machines.

Footsteps.

"Ah, there you are, Quigley! You may remove the hood."

He knew that voice, and it was not coming from a speaker.

Prime.

43

THE PRIME AIRCRAFT SLOWED RAPIDLY AS IT NEARED the military unit, forcing sand into the air. Derrick ducked his head into the crook of his elbow, protecting his face. Before the air cleared, Derrick ran to Rebekah. He grabbed the .50 cal., wrapping the belt of bullets over his shoulders.

Then he heard the distinctive crack of a bullet as it passed by his head, then the pop of a rifle echoed through the canyon. He ducked behind a rock. It was difficult to locate the shooter's position, but he assumed it was the sniper, not Anna.

Derrick heard the swishing sound of the aircraft door, followed by a robotic voice. "Why have you not fired the weapons?"

A man said, "Coms are down. We've been waiting for confirmation."

* * *

The sound of the aircraft had diverted Anna's attention. She had watched the aircraft land but couldn't see Derrick because of the dust cloud it created.

Then a shot rang out.

Anna brought the gun to bear on the sniper. She didn't know if he had hit Derrick, but there was no reason to think he had missed. She aimed at the man's head, then executed her previous plan for reasons she did not understand.

The sniper lay motionless, waiting to see if Derrick moved or if there were others in the canyon. She put the crosshairs on the largest part of the rifle's scope.

Breathe in.

Breathe out.

Hold.

A light, steady pull on the trigger.

It was a slight surprise when the rifle fired. She resisted the urge to see how she'd done and instead chambered another round, put the crosshairs on the trigger, and repeated the process.

This time, she saw the rifle move. A blur of motion made it difficult to see what had happened, given the scope's high magnification and tight field of vision.

She swung the scope back to the aircraft just as a black robot exited.

* * *

Derrick heard two shots. Probably Anna. She was a decent marksman. The sniper was down. Probably. But Derrick remained behind the rock, concealed as best he could because if the sniper was still up there, the top of his head was a viable target.

Lying flat and easing out from behind the rocks, Derrick saw a robot walking toward one soldier. If the robots were here because communications were down, the missile would launch within minutes. If he dove to his left a few feet, he'd have a clear shot at the robot and the sergeant, but not at the soldiers at the controls. If the coordinates were already in the system, it would be as simple as pushing the launch button. The missile would be on its way before he could do anything to stop it.

If the sniper is still alive, I'll be dead before I fire a shot.

Derrick readied the gun's tripod, cycled the bolt, ensuring a round was chambered, and flipped the safety off. He glanced up at the sniper's position but could not see him.

The robot said, "Your assistance is no longer needed."

Derrick heard a crackle of electricity. A blue arc fired from the robot's hand, striking the sergeant. The sergeant stood for a second, his head lolled to one side, smoke drifting from his shoulders, and then he fell face first to the ground. The machine fired two more arcs of electricity and then walked toward the launcher.

Derrick put the gun's sight on the robot and pulled the trigger. The machine gun rocked in a steady motion, matched by the rhythmic crack of the firing sequence. The robot continued a couple of steps before crashing to the ground.

Ceasing fire, Derrick looked up. Smoke drifted from the soldier's body lying next to the launcher, and he felt confident the third soldier had suffered the same fate although he couldn't see the man.

Derrick had just started to stand when a clanking sound came from the aircraft. A second robot appeared, immediately turning toward him, lifting its arm. Derrick flattened himself on the ground and fired the machine gun. The first rounds kicked up dirt in front of the robot, but he quickly raised the muzzle, and the bullets ripping through the robot's metal exterior. He saw the machine's handlike weapon spark, then explode, followed by its arm detaching and falling to the ground.

Derrick stood. Miriam rushed to his side. "I'll take care of the launcher."

Miriam jogged to the control panel, stepping over the dead soldier.

Rebekah put her hand on Derrick's shoulder. "That was intense. Do you think Anna is okay?"

Derrick turned to her. A belt of .50 cal. bullets still draped over her shoulder. "I hope so."

"Then why didn't she shoot the robots?"

Derrick thought for a moment, but nothing came to mind that included Anna being okay, so he said, "She was probably coming down the mountain. Couldn't get a shot off."

"I hope that's true. I don't know if I could handle losing her," Rebekah said, leaning into Derrick.

After a moment, Rebekah and Derrick walked toward Miriam. "Figuring it out?" Derrick asked.

"It's programmed and set to launch. It is aimed at Potterville. Touching the launch button is all it takes, so I don't want to fire it accidentally before I reprogram the coordinates."

"Why not just shut it off?"

"I don't want the missile available to anyone. I'm going to send it into the ocean."

"No. You're not."

Derrick stepped to one side to see a soldier pointing a handgun lefthanded at Miriam's head. The soldier's right hand was wrapped in a white cloth that had turned red. Derrick understood immediately. Anna had shot his hand to stop him. Probably damaged the rifle too. Anna had followed his instruction and not killed the guy. Now, everyone in Potterville might die.

The soldier said, "Step away from the control panel."

Miriam took a step back. She was too far from the man to attack. "Do you know where it is aimed?"

"I don't know, and I don't care. I'm going to launch as ordered."

"It's aimed at New America," Miriam said.

"Did you miss the part where I said, 'I don't care?'"

The soldier took a few steps forward, motioning with the gun for Miriam to step away. He held up his right hand. "Either you did this or my buddy on the other side of the canyon did."

"Why would another soldier shoot you?" Derrick asked, stepping forward.

The soldier pointed the gun at Derrick. "Stop right there." Then he swung the gun back at Miriam again. "Take another step, and I'll kill her first, then you."

"Whoa. No need for any more killing," Derrick said, holding up his hands.

"To answer your question, he got a little pissy when I shot that cop."

"Why? Your sergeant must have ordered it."

"Sarge was a nice guy but lacked balls. Shooting the cop was my decision. Now, with all the witnesses dead, I don't have to explain why I disobeyed orders. I'll get some medals, an honorable discharge, and disability pay. I might even get to live in one of those Chosen Communities. This has worked out nicely. I should thank you."

The soldier stepped to the control panel and studied it. "Did you change these coordinates?"

Miriam hesitated. "I did. I can change them back."

"Is fool written on my forehead? You must think I'm stupid. Trust me, I'm neither a fool nor stupid, and I'm not letting you near this control panel. And don't count on your sniper friend helping you. He must be headed down the backside of the mountain. That's the only way down. This side is a sheer cliff. When he gets here, I'll eliminate the last witness."

Miriam said, "She."

"What?"

"She is headed down the mountain. A girl my age disabled the other soldier. And shot you by the looks of it."

The soldier looked a bit dejected. "Whatever."

Derrick heard panic in Miriam's voice. Things slowed down. He envisioned the best plans of attack for Miriam and himself. Miriam could sprint toward the soldier, drawing his attention. The soldier would fire twice, both bullets ripping through Miriam's chest. He would be running before Miriam's body hit the ground. Then the soldier would fire two rounds into his chest.

He and Miriam would die.

Their story would end here.

44

Friday, April 9, 4:55 p.m.

RED DRAINED A GLASS OF WATER, THEN HEAPED more food on his plate before returning to the table. L. Linda walked in wearing blue scrubs and white sneakers, her hair still wet, creating dark spots on her shoulders. Akira sat across from Red, pushing food around her plate with her fork. Charlie wasn't in the room.

The food's aroma surprised L. Linda. She had anticipated stale noodles in Styrofoam cups. "I wasn't expecting this." She pointed at the warming trays.

With his mouth full, Red said, "It's pretty amazing, isn't it?"

L. Linda placed a spoonful of each item on her plate, but larger portions of veggies than meat. She sat next to Akira. "You should eat, Akira."

"Not hungry."

"It's not about being hungry. You need to keep up your strength."

"You sound like Miriam."

"I do? I'll take that as a compliment. Thanks."

"Whatever," Akira drawled.

L. Linda drained her glass and poured another from the pitcher of iced water. After a few bites, she said, "I thought you liked Miriam."

Akira glared at L. Linda. "What makes you think that, and how is it any of your business?"

"It's not my business, but I'm good at observations. People relax when I'm around. Not because I'm charming, but because they pay little attention to me. I'm sort of invisible to most people, and even if they see me, I'm just the weird girl."

Akira's expression softened. "I didn't mean to be offensive. It's just that, well, my brain isn't right. Not since the incident and the treatment. I'm afraid I might never be the same."

L. Linda said, "Tell me what happened."

"There was a problem with the reactor."

"As in nuclear reactor?"

"Yes. It was critical. I was in the control room."

Red interrupted, "She insisted."

Akira glanced at Red. "A valve needed to be replaced, but there wasn't a replacement. Red made a new one, but it didn't fit."

Red said, "It was my fault."

Akira glared at Red. "It wasn't your fault." She looked back to L. Linda. "Red and Derrick fixed it, but the radiation in the control room was high. I was in there too long. The treatment chamber here does amazing things. Like it completely healed Antonio's knee."

L. Linda said, "That's amazing."

Red said, "It sure is."

"You built a valve? So, you cut and welded it?" L. Linda asked.

Red said, "Yeah, they have a complete machine shop. More stuff than I've ever seen."

"How big a valve?" L. Linda asked.

Red glanced down, then with his hands spread, he said, "About this big. Ten-inch pipe. It wasn't difficult. Fitting the automatically controlled flap was kinda tricky. But the bolt holes didn't align with the bottom pipe."

Akira said, "Red built it to the blueprint specifications. It wasn't his fault the blueprint was wrong."

Red said, "I should have checked it first."

Akira shook her head. "Men. Anyway, the treatment unit couldn't save me."

L. Linda said, "But you're here."

Red said, "Charlie overrode the treatment computer and did something entirely new to Akira. He saved her."

Akira nodded. "But it messed up my head. I don't feel anything. Numb. I remember I liked Miriam, but I don't have any feelings for her. It doesn't make sense, but I can't explain it any better than that."

L. Linda took her hand. "I understand."

Akira said, "But…"

L. Linda held one finger to her lips. "Before you say anything, listen to me. You're the only one who knows what it's like, being you, right now, in this moment. But I've experienced feeling completely numb, shutting out everything and everybody. I—well, there was some trauma in my life, and I didn't speak or go outside for an entire year. I barely ate. My dad saved me. He cared about me, and that's the only thing that got me through it. Many people love you. I can't promise you'll ever be the same girl as before this happened. I'll never be the same, but you'll get through it. You'll be who you decide to be. Give it time."

Red said, "She's right, Akira. And Charlie isn't done with you yet. I think he'll sort you out. I just hope you can forgive me."

"Red, for the last time, it wasn't your fault. You saved us. You saved Potterville." Akira pulled her hand away from L. Linda and went back to pushing food around. "You said something traumatic happened. What was it?"

L. Linda turned back to her food and took a bite. After a few moments, she said, "I can't talk about it."

"Can't or won't."

"Both."

"Too painful?"

"Yes. No. Mostly, it's not safe."

"Not safe for who?" Akira asked.

"Not safe for me. Not safe for you. Back to the reactor. I thought they were banned years ago.

"That's true, but if you haven't figured it out, this place has been abandoned for decades. The reactor has been idling. Only Charlie still functioned here. When we arrived, the reactor increased output, and the old systems started failing. We fixed an entire list of things. The valve was the most critical part."

"Red saved Potterville? I don't understand, but the reactor is a big deal, right?" L. Linda asked.

"Yes. Radioactivity is extremely dangerous."

"When I drove through the cavern where the trucks are parked before you get to the train thing, is that where the reactor is?" L. Linda asked.

Akira nodded. "Yes."

"Yellow lights were flashing there. Does that mean anything?"

"Crap," Red said.

45

Friday, April 9, 5:35 p.m.

THEY SAY LIFE FLASHES BEFORE ONE'S EYES just before death, but Derrick saw nothing except a huge missile aimed at Potterville, a man with a gun, and Miriam. He didn't think not having the flashing life thing meant he would survive. He had processed every possibility, including calculating how long it would take Anna to get off the mountain. The only plausible scenario in which he and Miriam lived was if the man had a sudden change of heart and dropped the gun.

Then he heard a sound.

Apparently, he had not processed every scenario.

The sound was right behind him.

Someone chambered a round in the machine gun.

Then shots rang out so loudly he thought his eardrums would rupture.

A three-round burst ripped through the soldier's chest. His protective vest prevented blood from spilling out, but it did little to slow the metal piercing .50 caliber bullets.

The soldier remained standing for a moment, but he was already dead—an expression of astonishment frozen on his face.

Derrick turned to see Rebekah, flat on the ground, with her hands glued to the machine gun. He went to her, kneeled beside her, and gently removed her hands from the weapon. "You saved us."

"I killed him."

Derrick helped her up and said, "You had to. He gave you no choice. By saving us, you stopped a war. Nothing I say will change the way you feel right now. Only time will help, and even then, you'll never forget. I wish I could fix it, but I can't. All I can say is, thank you."

Derrick heard footsteps. Looking up, he saw Anna running toward them, pulling a soldier in restraints along with her.

"What in the hell happened?" Anna hollered.

Derrick pointed. "Robots came. They killed the soldiers. I destroyed the robots. Then the sniper got the drop on us. Rebekah shot him with the machine gun. She's pretty shaken up."

The other soldier said, "He deserved it."

Derrick stared at the man for a moment. Dried blood below his nose and blood stained his shirt. Derrick said, "He was about to launch the missile. He gave us no choice."

"He killed a police officer. Sarge told him not to fire, but he did it anyway. I know the guy. He couldn't wait to kill people. Trust me, the world is better off without him."

Rebekah said, "What about you? You're in a uniform, in Mexico, about to start a war."

"I didn't know we were in Mexico. They said we were in Southern California. They said Mexico was going to invade New America."

"Mexico wasn't going to invade. New America was." Rebekah pointed behind her. "That thing is aimed at New America. Prime was using that to justify the war."

The man, a kid really, looked down. "Prime. Prime is a myth."

Derrick said, "Prime is real and is behind all of this."

"I didn't know. Honest." Then he looked up and said, "What's she doing then?"

Derrick turned to see Miriam at the launcher's control panel. He walked to her and peered over her shoulder. "Figure it out?"

"Maybe," Miriam said.

Derrick said, "They're all dead. Shut it off, and let's get out of here."

"Prime could send more robots to complete the launch. We need to destroy it."

Derrick turned to the soldier. "What's your name?"

"Kevin."

"Kevin, do you know how to operate the launcher?"

"I had a crash course on the way here in case something happened to the specialists, but to be honest, I didn't understand most of it."

"Fair enough. Can you tell us anything that might be helpful?"

"Not much. The warheads can be altered."

"How so?" Miriam asked.

Kevin said, "They can be set to explode before, at, or after impact."

"That doesn't help," Miriam said, turning back to the panel.

Kevin said, "They can also be deactivated."

Miriam looked at Kevin. "Deactivated? So, they won't explode?"

Kevin said, "Doesn't always work, and it still causes a lot of damage when it hits something."

Derrick said, "Why do they have a setting like that?"

Kevin said, "To damage buildings but kill fewer people."

"Nice of them," Rebekah said. "Why Prime wants to start a war is beyond my comprehension."

Miriam touched the launch screen several times. "Why we have any wars is beyond mine." She paused and stared at the soldier. "Why anyone would join the military makes little sense to me."

"It seemed the best choice at the time."

Miriam said nothing, continuing to focus on the launch screen.

Rebekah stood in front of the soldier. "Explain it to me." She motioned to the dead men. "Does this seem like a good idea to you? Does starting a war seem like a good idea?"

Kevin shook his head. "I didn't expect this. I thought I could get a job like a store clerk or stocking shelves or loading trucks. But everyone who joins now goes to a shortened basic training and then straight to the border. I would have taken Option B had I known, but the New America media said nothing about the possibility of a war with Mexico."

"What was Option B?" Derrick asked.

"Jail or prison. The judge was kind of vague on that."

"What did you do?" Anna asked.

"I skipped school. Three times. My mom was sick. She needed me. But the judge didn't care. He said I could join the military or be locked up." Kevin paused, and a tear rolled down his cheek. "Mom died. She didn't need me anymore. I didn't have any place to go."

"How old are you?" Derrick asked.

"Sixteen."

"No. Seriously, how old are you?"

"I'm not lying. I turned 16 last week."

"How long have you been in the military?"

"Just over three weeks."

"A judge forced you into the military at age 15 for skipping school to care for your dying mother. You expect us to believe that?" Anna asked.

"I'm not lying." Kevin broke into sobs.

Derrick held out his hand to Anna. "I believe you. But I have to say, I don't understand how a judge could do something like that. If we live through this, I'll pay him a visit."

Kevin composed himself. "I think I know why."

"Tell me," Derrick said.

"The soldier who helped me fill out my paperwork said, 'Judge Smith is going to retire early at this rate.' I think someone is paying the judge to get enlistees."

"Despicable," Rebekah said, adding, "Derrick, I'm going with you to visit Judge Smith."

"Okay. I've got it figured out. The warhead is deactivated, and the missile is rerouted to the open sea. It's a big ocean so hitting a ship will be unlikely."

Miriam smiled. "On a positive note, Prime has given us another aircraft. We'll be back before dinner."

"What are we waiting for?" Derrick asked.

"What happens to me?" Kevin asked.

Miriam studied him for a minute. "Fair question. We could leave you here. When the Mexican authorities arrive, you can explain what happened."

"They will put me in prison or kill me."

Miriam said, "Either would be a reasonable expectation."

Kevin hung his head.

"What would you do if we let you go?" Derrick asked.

"If I could make it back to New America, I'll run. I can't go home. The judge would lock me up for sure. I don't have anyone there now. I'd go someplace. Maybe toward the ocean. I've never seen the ocean. Find work. Start over."

"At 16?" Derrick asked.

"I'll lie about my age."

Miriam said, "If the military finds you, you'll be in a military prison, or worse."

"What's worse?" Kevin asked.

"Front line in a war with Mexico," Miriam said.

"I'll take my chances. I'm not going back to the military. Not after seeing this, learning what we were about to do, knowing how they lied to us."

Derrick said, "We could take him to Potterville. Land in the meadow, point him toward town. He can find Donna's and tell her we sent him. Donna will take it from there. Coach Browning and Sheriff Collins will help."

Miriam sighed. "I suppose. If that would make you feel better."

"It would."

"I'll check the aircraft and turn off the tracking device," Miriam said.

"What should we do?" She pointed at the vehicles, robots, and dead soldiers. "About all this?"

"Good question," Derrick said, examining one robot and then walking to the other. "I don't remember seeing these before." Derrick indicated a small round device with a blinking green light.

Rebekah stood beside Derrick. "I don't recall seeing them, although I don't remember things like you guys do. The robots look like the ones at the Base, except the ones there cook dinner and don't kill you."

Miriam stepped out of the aircraft, joining Derrick and Rebekah. "Something isn't right."

Derrick said, "It won't start?"

"Won't activate would be more accurate, but that's not what I mean. The location device I removed from the other aircraft isn't there." She kneeled by the robot, pointing at the round device with the flashing light. "There are two of these attached to the hull. Stuck tight, I can't remove them."

Derrick tried to move the device on the robot. Then gave it a kick. It didn't move. "What do you think they are?"

Kevin said, "They are tracking devices."

Derrick looked up.

Kevin nodded toward the launcher. "They are on the dashboards in the trucks. Same as these. If you don't believe me, look."

Miriam said, "I believe you. That was my guess."

"So, can we shoot them off?" Rebekah asked.

Miriam said, "I don't think so. First, too dangerous, ricochets, and such. Second, Prime will know something's wrong if the devices fail."

"What are we going to do?" Rebekah asked, adding, "Whatever it is, we should be quick about it."

"We'll have to take the old truck the Resistance guys gave us."

Rebekah said, "I was afraid you would say that."

"Kevin, is there a tool kit?" Derrick asked

Kevin said, "I'll show you."

Kevin indicated a panel on the side of a truck. Derrick opened it. Inside, he found a wrench and a pair of cutters.

Miriam said, "What are you doing?"

Derrick said, "We are going to move the vehicles next to the aircraft and drain the fuel tanks. Can you set a delay on the missile?"

Miriam said, "I can, but not long."

"Great. Kevin, does it create fire when launched?" Derrick asked.

"It sure does. It is intense. They warned us to not be close when it launches." Kevin paused. "There are four fuel cans on the launcher. You should empty them under the blast area, and then in and around the trucks and the aircraft. I'm assuming you want to destroy them as best you can."

"You assume right," Derrick said.

"You're being accommodating for the enemy," Rebekah said, her arms folded.

Kevin said nothing for a moment. "I'm wearing restraints somewhere in Mexico, and you guys are my only hope of returning to New America alive. Helping you is the smartest thing I've done lately."

Derrick moved the vehicles and cut the fuel lines, but the stream was too slow, so he removed the threaded piece that attached the line to the tank. More fuel flowed but it was still too slow. Kevin suggested removing the cap from the tank, which helped, but Derrick wanted more, so he put three holes in each tank using a sharp punch and a hammer. Now fuel poured onto the ground, creating small streams that flowed around the trucks and under the aircraft. Next, he emptied the fuel cans, as Kevin had suggested. One in each cab and two in the aircraft. The smell of fuel intensified as the hot sand sent fumes wafting into the air.

When Derrick finished, he looked at Miriam and asked, "Ready?"

"Ready."

"How long is the delay?"

"Thirty seconds."

"That's not long."

"If we run, we'll be about 200 yards out."

"Less than that. The sand will slow us down," Derrick said, then he looked at Anna. "Cut Kevin's restraints."

"Do what?"

"He can't run like that."

"What if he tries something?"

"I don't think that will happen. What would he do while running from an inferno?" Derrick paused, glancing at Kevin. "But if he tries anything stupid, knock him out."

46

JASON STOOD AT THE WINDOW, trying to see through a crack in the blinds. Collins stood at the door. Allen remained at his computer. Donna had gone into the kitchen to lock the back door.

"See anything," Collins whispered.

"No. I can't see much. Just a few feet of sidewalk," Jason replied.

Allen said, "Don't let anyone in."

Collins said, "Not planning to, and this is a little more important than your e-mail."

"It's not an e-mail. It's an upload. This is critical."

"Why is it taking so long?"

"I had to create a network to bounces the message around and encrypt it. The delay was good because I received a message from a friend who has guy at his business. A guy the Resistance wanted to find."

Jason whispered, "Is this important to us? Who is this guy?"

"The man is Lawrence King. Derrick and Miriam's keeper. They called him father."

"How does that affect us?" Collins asked.

"I'll explain soon. This upload is taking too damn long." Allen paused. "The problem is the system. Like I said, it's down."

"Why is it down?" Collins asked.

"I suspect Lawrence King is the cause."

"Trusting him sounds like a bad idea," Collins said.

"We don't have a choice. He has something we need so the Resistance can communicate without Prime tracking them," Allen said, adding, "The kids need it to coordinate their attacks."

Collins's head spun around. "Attack what?"

"Prime, who else?"

"They should leave that to the authorities. I'll take this to the Governor," Collins paused, "clear up to the President if necessary."

Allen said, "Yeah, about that. I just learned something else. Donna, could you turn on the TV? Leave the sound off."

Donna turned on a flat screen on the wall. A breaking news story played, the reporter uncharacteristically pale. They could not hear what he said, but the gist of the news was clear. On the bottom of the screen scrolled this message: "NEW AMERICA PRESIDENT AND VICE PRESIDENT ASSASSINATED. PRIME PROCLAIMS MARTIAL LAW."

Donna gasped.

Collins said, "Holy crap."

"How long on that upload?" Jason asked.

"Ten minutes. Maybe longer, maybe less."

Jason said, "I'll step out. Sheriff, stand over there," he pointed to the left side of the room, "you'll have a split-second advantage if anyone comes through that door. If you don't recognize the person, shoot him."

Collins said, "I can't just shoot someone who isn't a threat."

Jason shook his head. "How about you, Donna? Can you shoot someone?"

"Damn right."

"Then you stand over there and take the shotgun. Bill, have a cup of coffee," Jason said as he pulled an automatic weapon from his jacket.

Jason held the radio close to his mouth and whispered, "Jack, can you see the Bistro?"

Jack responded, "Sure can. No gun that I can see. The guy is about ten yards west of the door. Just standing there. I've got him in my sights."

"If he kills me, shoot him." Jason stepped outside.

On the sidewalk stood a man about Jason's age and size. Jason aimed the weapon at him.

"Whoa!" The man held his hands up. "I was only wanting coffee. I don't want any problems."

"Turn around."

"Now, calm down. I am not doing nothing illegal. Coffee. That's all I want."

"Turn around, or I shoot. I'm not asking again."

The man turned, then held his hand to his ear. "I'm in front of the Bistro. I have a minor problem."

Jason heard a distinctive sound in the distance.

The man said, "Look, pal. I'm in the military. I'm turning around, nice and easy. We have finished our business and are leaving. No need for bloodshed. There's a gunship inbound. They'll cut you to pieces if you're still pointing that gun at me when they arrive."

The helicopter was getting louder quickly.

Jack's voice said, "Helicopter. Just picked up two people. It's headed your way."

Jason said, "What do you mean 'you are finished?'"

"Well, it's not good news. There's a missile headed to Potterville. You can't make it out before it hits."

47

Friday, April 9, 5:45 p.m.

RUNNING AS FAST AS POSSIBLE IN THE LOOSE sand, Derrick heard a tremendous roar. Unable to resist, he glanced over his shoulder. The launch created a blinding flash and a hot-white trail through the clear blue sky. The jet-fuel-soaked sand ignited. But it did not cause the explosion he had envisioned.

Derrick didn't understand the science involved. Until his exile to Potterville, he believed science was the source of evil because that's what he was taught as a Chosen person living in a Chosen Community. He realized now how stupid he had been and recognized how dumb he was for failing to question it. His privileged life was surrounded by technology, all of which were the products of science.

But during his few weeks in Potterville, he had learned some things about earth science and a little about chemistry, but he had not learned the thermodynamics involved here. Something to do with the lack of oxygen, maybe, but the explosion he had expected didn't happen. The rocket streaked into the sky. Flames leaped around the vehicles and aircraft but not as intensely as he had hoped. Then something changed. Whether it was a fuel tank, something in the aircraft, additional bombs on the vehicles, or just the nature of the fire, he did not know, but something exploded, sending a mushroom of fire and smoke into the air. He turned just before a wave of heat knocked him down.

Twisting his head, he saw the others flat on the sand. Derrick shouted, "Stay down!"

Chunks of metal began raining down all around them.

Scrambling to his feet, Derrick yelled, "Forget that! Run!"

48

JASON WATCHED THE HELICOPTER DISAPPEAR into the distance. The kids had failed to stop the launch. He scanned the sky but saw no missile inbound yet. He didn't know how long it would take but knew it wouldn't be long. Should he tell the others or just stand here and watch it come? They wouldn't have time to get to their families. No time for phone calls or hugs. Although L. Linda wasn't his biological daughter, he wished he could say goodbye. But at least she wasn't here. The same could not be said for Coach Browning or Allen Patel.

After a few moments, he eased the bistro door open a crack. "It's Jason. Don't shoot."

Once inside, he glanced at the others. Good people. He wished he'd gotten to know them better. He'd avoided interaction with people since they moved to Potterville. L. Linda became invisible by standing out, while he had simply stayed away from people as much as possible.

"What's happening?" Collins asked.

"They're gone."

Collins said, "We heard a helicopter."

"Yeah. They were military and got evacuated."

"Evacuated?" Collins asked.

Jason hesitated and then said, "The kids failed. The missile is coming. I'm sorry. I'm sure you'd like to be with your families, but there won't be time for that."

Allen didn't look up from his computer. "I need a couple of minutes to finish the upload."

"There's nothing I can do about that," Jason said, adding, "you are all fine people. I wish I'd gotten to know you better. See you on the other side."

And with that, Jason Maxton walked out the door, deciding it was better to stare death in the face than to cower inside.

49

CHUNKS OF STEEL LARGE ENOUGH TO KILL rained down all around. Nothing Derrick could do but run. He was leading, but he could hear the others right behind him. It wasn't a race, yet it was. The prize wasn't a ribbon but getting to live another day. Well, to be fair, a few more minutes because there were no guarantees. The plume of black smoke and the sound of the blast would attract attention. Soon the place would swarm with police. And with a dead officer by the highway, they might skip the asking questions part and go right to the shooting part.

When they rounded the base of the mountain, turning toward where they had left the pickup, Derrick stopped to look at the destruction they had caused. "Well, that didn't go exactly as planned."

Miriam said, "True. But they won't start sifting through the wreckage till it cools and that will take time. Meanwhile, we need to get out of here."

A huge chunk of twisted metal landed 20 yards from where they stood. Miriam turned and ran toward the pickup truck and upon reaching it, climbed into the truck's bed. "Rebekah, you drive. Anna with Rebekah, Derrick and Kevin in the back with me."

Anna was soaking wet. She had grabbed the machine gun and carried it the entire distance. Holding it up, she said, "You'll want this in the back."

Derrick took it. "I'm not sure we want it. Getting caught with a machine gun wouldn't be good."

Anna said, "Don't get caught."

Derrick removed the bolt and threw it into the desert, tossed the bullets behind a rock, and heaved the gun up the hill. "Better that we don't have it."

"We should have voted. Why do you make all the decisions?" Anna climbed into the cab, slamming the door.

"What's with her?" Derrick asked.

"Well, she did carry that thing all the way here," Miriam said. "I'll talk to her. Don't worry about it."

Rebekah stuck her head out the window. "Same way out as in?"

Miriam shrugged. "Maybe. Let me do something first." She pulled the burner phone from her backpack. "I have a signal." She looked at Derrick. "What do you think? Same way out?"

Derrick thought for a moment. He didn't want to decide. Miriam was the smart one. The truck had a window that slid open in the rear glass. He rapped on it with his knuckles.

Scowling, Anna opened it. "What?"

Derrick said, "Should we leave the same way we came?"

"Why are you asking me?"

"Because I'd like to know what you think."

Miriam said, "I need to make a phone call." She entered a number. Anna spun back around.

"Hello? AJ, I mean Allen?—

"We are okay.—

"I sent the missile out into the ocean. Potterville is safe, for now.—

"I had not thought about that. Maybe they can redirect it in flight, but I think it would have hit Potterville by now.—

"Okay. I'm listening.—

"I don't have a pen or paper. I can remember, just tell me.—

"Where?" She held her hand over the phone's microphone. "They found Father. Trying to flee the country."—

Miriam nodded. "Wow. That would be useful. —

"He did what? Why would he do that? —

"Okay. I understand. I guess it makes sense. Is he willing to help?—

"When will you know? —

"We are not coming back. We have a place where we are safe, and we have access to things we'll need, plus food. Yes, they are there and safe.—

"Just tell me the addresses. —

"Okay, 192.578.2.75." Miriam rattled off five more nine-digit numbers.

"Not right now, but we'll have a satellite connection before daybreak, unless something else happens.—

"And if he refuses? —

"Can I get any of the code?—

"I don't know. Maybe I can figure it out.—

"I could come to Potterville.—

"It's all dangerous from this point forward.—

Miriam nodded. "Good luck to you as well."

Derrick held up his hand. "Ask if L. Linda made it back."

Miriam furrowed her brow just a little. "Allen, did L. Linda make it back?

—

"I see.—

"Leave your phone on. In case we need to talk. Bye." —

Miriam said, "Let's go."

Derrick asked, "What about L. Linda?"

Miriam said, "They haven't seen her."

"Where to? Potterville?" Rebekah asked.

"Not Potterville. Johnsondale."

"The place Mr. Jones took us? You want to walk to where we first found Derrick?"

"Yes. But we won't walk this time. We know the road now, so we'll run. It's eight miles. We can run eight miles," Miriam said.

Derrick said, "The place where I found the entrance to the reactor? That's good thinking, but I'm not sure we can run eight miles in this condition. We are dehydrated and hungry."

"We'll eat someplace after we cross the border," Miriam said.

"How long will it take us to get to the Base?" Derrick asked.

"About seven hours, but we can shave some time off if we drive fast," Miriam said.

Rebekah said, "We should leave before someone shows up."

Derrick asked, "Anna, go back the way we came?"

"I think not. I say we stay on the main roads and go straight to the border. People running from a crime would go off-road. Innocent people would stay on the main roads."

Derrick said, "I agree, but how do we cross the border?"

Kevin said, "I know a way. A back road is how we came in. There were no guards at the border, just a warning sign. The road ends before the border and then starts up again, but it is easy terrain."

Derrick said, "We'll get back well after midnight."

Rebekah pulled onto the highway and pointed the truck north.

"Where are you taking me?" Kevin asked.

Miriam said, "We'll drop you in the first town we come to after crossing the border."

Kevin nodded. "Thanks."

Derrick said, "We are not. He needs a change of clothing. Someone will report a guy in uniform wandering the streets. Miriam, do you have money?"

"I can get cash from one of those machines so we can eat," Miriam said, then looked at Derrick. "What are we doing with Kevin?"

"He'll go with us to—where did you say? Johnsondale. Then he can drive the truck to Potterville. I'll explain it to Kevin at dinner."

"I don't understand," Miriam said.

Derrick said, "Fine. I'll explain it now. First, we don't want anyone to find the truck abandoned in Johnsondale. They might link it to us. We don't want them searching for us there. Kevin will drive it to Potterville and go to the Bistro and have Donna call Mr. Fletcher. He'll ask Mr. Fletcher to put the pickup in his salvage yard. No one can find it there. Kevin needs to be in school and spring break ends on Sunday. Monday, he, you, Rebekah, and Anna will register for school. Antonio will show you guys around."

Miriam stared at Derrick for a moment. "We are going to school on Monday?"

"Yes. If we are alive."

"You're saying by Monday either we will be dead or Prime will be?"

"That is precisely what I am saying."

The End

Author's Note:

I hope you have enjoyed the Derrick King series. Please consider write a review. Visit my website daniellcopeland.com to sign up for my newsletter. I want to thank everyone who has read my books. If they gave you a bit of an escape, I'm pleased. You can also purchase my books from Barnes and Noble.

Acknowledgements:

Thanks to the love and support of the love of my life and partner, Liz. She is also a writer and illustrator. Check out her books on Amazon Libby K. Couldn't do any of this without her. She is also my best editor and critic.

Special thanks to those who have provided feedback and guidance: Rod Leonard, Kristy Steen, and Victoria Southwick.

More books from Daniel L. Copeland:

Available at Amazon.com in paperback, eBooks for Kindle, and audiobooks.

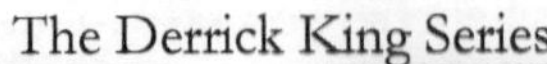

The Derrick King Series

A Derrick King Novel, Book 6

About the Author:

Daniel is a lifelong Idahoan and grew up on a small farm in Southern Idaho. He worked in the criminal justice system for 35 years and is now retired. Daniel has published nine novels. In addition to writing, he and his wife, Liz love to travel on their BMW motorcycle. They have ridden in most of the US, including Alaska, the Great Lakes, and Florida. They have also ridden in Canada, New Zealand, and Australia. Daniel is an award-winning home brewer and a certified beer judge.